small melodies and rewritten conclusions

# marriage, melodies and rewritten conclusions

## V. JOY PALMER

WhiteFire
PUBLISHING

This is a work of fiction. All characters and events portrayed in this novel are either fictitious or used fictitiously.

MARRIAGE, MELODIES, AND REWRITTEN CONCLUSIONS

WhiteFire Publishing
13607 Bedford Rd NE
Cumberland, MD 21502

ISBN:978-1-946531-77-3 (digital)
978-1-946531-76-6 (print)

To everyone who feels like they can never escape
the chains of the past,
the cycle of brokenness,
or attain TRUE love and forgiveness,
this story is for you.
Victory is for you.

## Prologue

When real life starts to mirror the first verse of any number of country breakup songs, you should expect it to get messy.

I didn't. That's my bad.

Mistake Number One: thinking that it was just a coincidence that "What Hurts the Most" by Rascal Flatts was playing on the radio that day. I should have recognized the foreshadowing in the brokenhearted lyrics.

If I had, maybe I could have prevented complete and total devastation, humiliation, and did I mention devastation? The memories of that last day together flood my entire body like a crashing tsunami, from my trembling fingertips to the dumb look of shock that graces my stiff face as I stare...

At *him*!

I beseech thee, learn from my mistakes as I share my tale of woe....

*Everything feels very* Boy Meets World, *but what's wrong with the idea of two eighteen-year-olds running away in the dead of night to a justice of the peace's house to complete the final phase of their elopement? Who cares that my walk down the aisle is essentially a drive down the New Jersey boardwalk?*

*I look out the window and squint.*

*A boardwalk that I can just make out in the distance behind some buildings...*

*A line from* Boy Meets World *about how only creeps and weirdos are out this time of the night flashes through my mind.*

*That's us. A couple of creeps and weirdos. In love. Totally worked out for Cory and Topanga. (Not one word out of you about their multiple breakups! Or the fact that they're, you know, not real!)*

*I glance at Gabe, noting the tense set of his shoulders that scream everything is* not *okay in Whoville.*

*Gulp. (I mean it. Don't say anything!)*

*Everything is quiet. Very quiet. Even the ever-present jukebox of songs in my head are quiet. Nothing is playing. No confirmation. No warning. No feeling. Just the eerie quiet before the internal storm rages.*

*I resist biting my lower lip because if I do, Gabe will know I'm about to freak out. I will remain calm. Wesley calm. Calm like the sea after a storm...*

*Oy. Bad analogy. Who wants to go through the storm to get to the calm?*

*We turn down a long driveway, and a big orange house comes into view. Behind the hideously painted house, the ocean catches bits of moonlight to toss back and forth. The car lurches to a stop next to a blue Sedan.*

*Behold, our future.*

*"You ready?" Gabe askes in a wooden voice.*

*And that's when the conga line of panic starts to dance through my head. Like I can hear the annoying rhythm as each doubt shimmies by. How could I do this? What about my parents? I know that we are not close by any stretch of the imagination, but what if they wanted to be at their only daughter's wedding? My brother is only ten and vehemently believes girls are gross, so they won't get another chance for a long time—or ever, if my brother sticks to the he-man, woman-hater vows, courtesy of* Little Rascals. *And what about Izze? She's the kind of best friend who's closer than a sister. She would be devastated if she missed my wedding. And what about Gabe? He's not exactly in the best place right now...*

*"Gabe," I whisper, "are you sure about this?"*

*"I'm not sure about this necktie you talked me into." He tugs at his collar in an attempt to loosen the offending, paisley-patterned garment. "Paisley, seriously? Do I look like a paisley kind of guy to you?"*

*"That's not what I mean." I shift so I can look at him better, but I can't read his gray eyes thanks to the dark car. "Three days ago, this all seemed so romantic, but you just had a huge emotional bomb dropped on you. And it's like...it's seriously only been three days since everything happened. Maybe this isn't the best time. I mean, you're—"*

*"Has nothing to do with this," Gabe says as he cuts me off and grabs his black suit jacket from the backseat.*

*Cue awkward silence.*

*Gabe lays the suit jacket across his lap and takes my hand in his. "Yes, to answer your question. I love you, and I want to marry you." But that muscle on the left side of his jaw starts to twitch, something that only happens when he's anxious in a bad way.*

*But I choose to ignore it like the dolt I know I will call myself in the future. I coax a tight smile out of my strained facial features. "Okay. Let's do this."*

*He passes me a lemon drop candy. "Eat your nasty version of chocolate, Love." He winks, but even that looks stiff.*

*I unwrap the sour candy and pop it into my mouth, tucking the plastic wrapper into the cupholder in the middle console. Normally, these are like magic to my overwrought nerves.*

*But I'm worried about him.*

*He's shutting me out. He won't talk about his parents' abrupt separation and impending divorce. I can barely wrap my head around the thought of two people who have always struck me as the perfect couple divorcing. And if I can't believe it, then it's a hundred and twelve percent more world-shattering for Gabe. And he refuses to talk about it, changing the subject to our impending marriage whenever I bring it up.*

*Impending sounds bad right there, doesn't it?*

*"Do you think we could use a Taylor Swift song—like "Mary's Song"—for that part where we walk down the aisle afterwards? What is that part called?" Despite the question, he stares out the window as if in a daze.*

*"It's the recessional." I finally succumb to the urge to bite my lower lip. Not that he's even looking at me, so it's not like he'll notice anything is wrong.*

*I love him.*

*This is a good idea.*

*It is.*

*Not. One. Word.*

*We climb out of the car at the same time. All at once, something sweet-smelling yet oddly revolting hits me. Oh, my. You can really feel this stink in the eyes. I think this is the stink that "Weird Al" Yankovic is referring to in "Trash Day."*

*"What is that?" I choke the question out in between gasps of tainted air. It even burns the throat. I yank my dark blue, sparkly sweater off and attempt to wrap it around my head like an air-filtering turban.*

*"The ocean would be my guess," Gabe says between his fingers.*

*Great, so this is my fault thanks to my life-long dream to get married on the beach. I thought the miraculous discovery of a justice of a peace who did weddings in her home on the beach was like God blessing this. But thanks to the acidic feeling that's working to actively liquefy my eyeballs, I'm starting to wonder about this omen business. Does God send bad omens to say,* Stop! You are making the biggest mistake of your life! *these days? Is this co-ma-inducing smell my talking donkey?*

*It would be so much easier if He used that big, booming voice of His. Then the message wouldn't get lost in translation, and I wouldn't be blind by the time I said I do.*

*Gabe winks at me. "Something to tell the grandkids."*

*And just like that, all my doubts and fears melt away. Because I do love this man, and I have no doubt that he's the one God picked for me. My Daddy wouldn't steer me wrong.*

*I grin at him. "Let's do this," I say again, but this time, I mean it.*

*We run to the house, and Gabe knocks on the door. An elderly man in a brown suit opens it and without missing a beat (remember, my sweater is still wrapped around my head) steps to the side. "That algae is pretty sulfurous smelling lately. Come in before your bride faints."*

*My heart skips a beat at being called Gabe's bride, and my feet are more than happy to cross the threshold into what I hope and pray is an odorless home.*

*"My name is Roland, Rolly for short. Delia, the justice of the peace, is my wife. She'll be downstairs in a few minutes." He sticks his hand out for me to shake, then moves to Gabe. The overhead light of the entryway glints off the top of his balding head.*

*When Rolly turns around, Gabe taps the top of his head and mouths,* It's safe to breathe now.

*I smile at him with my eyes and unwind the sweater from around my head. Slipping the light cardigan over my shoulders, I then attempt to smooth down my static-infused red tresses.*

"Do you have the money?"

*I jump, the unexpected mafia-ish question startling me as much as the short, blunt woman in unicorn slippers suddenly standing before me. Where did she come from?*

"Yes." *Gabe passes her an envelope overflowing with cash.*

*Yeah, not helping the mafia image.*

*Delia, I presume, snatches the envelope from Gabe's hand and counts it, occasionally muttering under her breath.* "Okay." *She lifts her head, and her countenance immediately changes.* "Let's make our way to the sunroom where the ceremony will be held." *Her voice drips with a sweetness that comes from being paid.*

*Delia charges ahead, informing us all about what we can expect at the ceremony—our wedding!—as she walks. However, I don't hear any of it. I reach out and grasp Gabe's clammy hand, giving it a gentle squeeze.*

*But he doesn't respond.*

"Here we are." *Delia stops in front of two rather ornate doors and pushes them open.*

*I study the room I will remember for eternity. Three of the four walls are made of floor-to-ceiling glass, providing a stunning view of the moon-lit beach and ocean. The room is set up to look like a chapel, complete with five white-painted wooden chairs on each side of the room to make an aisle, a matching wooden arch, and an old organ centered at the far side of the room. I step into the room to get a better look, and I swear the worn wood of the floor creaks before my navy-blue flats brush the surface. There's some type of fern in a gray ceramic vase in each corner, but the rest of the room isn't decorated.*

*It's beautiful yet simple...but not what I had been imagining for the last three years. I should feel something more about this sacred space, but I don't. And that scares me almost as much as the fact that Gabe hasn't even tried to hide the way he's flinched every eighty-four seconds since we stepped into this house.*

*He flinches like that when he's hiding something.*

*"I'll be right back. You can set the marriage license on top of the organ," Delia instructs.*

*Gabe crosses the room to do as she says, and I attempt to smooth the wrinkles from the ivory lace dress I secretly purchased from a thrift store two days ago. Long car rides and dresses don't mix.*

*"Hey." Gabe shuffles over and takes my left hand. "I want you to have something." He slips something onto my ring finger. I look down to see his class ring, the emerald looking huge on my bony finger. I smile. He always said he picked out the "green stone" because it reminded him of my eyes.*

*I look into his gray eyes. "Thank you."*

*He squeezes my hand. "It can be your something, uh, new? Or old?"*

*"Both. And borrowed."*

*"No, it's not borrowed. It's yours. Forever. No matter what."*

*Cue the pile of ooey-gooey me.*

*With a hint of paranoia over his word choice...*

*A shadow darkens his eyes, but just then, Delia and Rolly reappear.*

*"Okay, love birds, it's time. Rolly, man your station. Gabe and Kaylee, right?" She waits for us to nod before continuing. "Why don't you guys stand at the back of the room and walk down the aisle together, but count to ten before you start." The way Delia says this makes it clear that she's instructing us and not asking us what we'd like to do for our wedding.*

*Gabe and I move to take our places. Delia, who is still wearing her unicorn slippers, stands square under the arch. Rolly starts to play Mendelssohn's "Wedding March." After counting to ten, we start to walk.*

*The strains—cough, cough—of the wedding march fill the small room.*

*This is nothing like how I imagined this day would be. But it doesn't matter.*

*It doesn't.*

*Is Gabe squirming? I glance at him out of the corner of my eye. I must be crazy.*

*I hope... Once again, that sliver of doubt seems very, very possible.*

We stop in front of Delia, her musky perfume settling around us, and Rolly stops playing. "You walked too fast," he mutters.

Delia shoots him a withering look, before smiling at us. "We are gathered here today to join the two of you in marriage. Turn to face each other and join hands."

We do as we are instructed. Apparently, that's the theme of our wedding. Very original. I attempt to smile at Gabe.

He grimaces.

Repeat after me," Delia says, looking at Gabe. "I—"

Gabe drops my hand and takes a step back, casting a look over his shoulder.

The music of my soul Zips! to a stop like it's scratched up vinyl.

"Oh, not again," Delia mutters behind me.

"I'm sorry, Kaylee. I can't do this."

The world slows down. Everything feels surreal. You know when something awful happens and your mind can't process it, so everything starts to feel fuzzy and disoriented? Yeah, that's only a fraction of how I feel right now.

Everyone stands there in painful, frozen silence for approximately six beats.

"I-I can't do this," he says again.

"What? What do you mean you can't do this? You said you loved me. That you wanted to marry me. For crying out loud, you were the one who proposed!" I burst. This can't be happening. I fell asleep on the way here. I'm dreaming. When I wake up, Gabe and I will get married—minus the sulfur smell.

He runs a hand through his wavy black hair. "I know, and I am so sorry. Please, please believe that." His voice breaks, but I refuse to feel an inkling of compassion.

The truth hits me in full force right then, and my knees warble. Even though I'm almost twice her size, Delia reaches out to steady me.

"But you're walking out on me? You don't abandon the people you love." I know that firsthand thanks to my parents.

"I can't hurt you, Kaylee. If I marry you, I'll hurt you."

"As opposed to right now, where you're hurting me?" I spit.

"You won't get your deposit back," Delia chimes into the conversation, as if that will convince him.

But it won't. I know that look. I know how stubborn he is.

*And he's made up his mind.*

*"I'm sorry, Kaylee. I am so sorry." His voice breaks, and he clears his throat before continuing. "But I can't do this to you." With that, Gabe turns around and jogs through the doorway. A moment later the front door slams shut and the sound of the car engine roaring to life fills my ears.*

*"Maybe you're cursed, Delia," Rolly says.*

*"Now is not the time for your dumb jokes, Roland."*

*So much for happily ever after.*

# Chapter One

I grin at one of my best friends as she thrusts the bouquet of wildflowers into the air and lets out a whoop of joy.

Apryl grins at Chance, and they share a quick kiss as everyone claps for them. "Let's get this party started!" she shouts.

That's my cue. I'm in charge of the music, you know. But by "music," I mean the playlist. I go to the little table where an iPod dock is set up, and I start the reception playlist. First up, "Ride of the Valkyries."

Apryl wanted to greet married life with an enthusiastic battle cry.

The small, small wedding took place in the willow grove near the house Apryl and Courtney grew up in, which is also now the headquarters of Willow Grove Weddings, a wedding venue decoration service. So obviously this is a Willow Grove Wedding. It's definitely...eclectic, but that's Apryl. The color—brownish sepia, burnt oranges, deep greens, and touches of sapphire blue—of the pieces created the theme of the wedding, and everything looks lovely amidst the willows. The delicate branches, fully intact thanks to the unusually long summer, sway in the breeze, creating the perfect Kodak moment.

The next song on the playlist starts, and Frank Sinatra croons out "The Way You Look Tonight" over the speakers.

Something moves out of the corner of my eye. A photographer shuffles at the outskirts of the reception area, attempting to capture that Kodak moment. Oh, that's right. Miles thought it'd be cool to post some pictures from Apryl and Chance's wedding on the website.

"Hey!"

I whip my head back and forth, attempting to follow the call of my bestie. Is it possible to give yourself whiplash from turning too fast?

I must be getting old.

Izze—who is apparently standing right next to me—tilts her head, waiting for me to say something.

I blink at her. "What did I miss?"

"Seriously? I've been talking to you for at least three minutes."

"Oh." I give her a sheepish grin and gesture toward the makeshift dance floor where Chance and Apryl are already attempting the Charleston. "Sorry. I was just looking around. It's gorgeous."

"Right? A part of me can't believe they actually got everything done in just a few weeks." Izze shifts to look around at the "intimate gathering of family and friends," as Courtney put it when she declared herself Wedding Planner and Sister of the Bride.

"If anyone can pull off a wedding that quickly, it's Apryl. Besides, she's not the type to go for a long engagement." But to be fair, while none of us expected her to wait as long as Courtney and Dallas (whose wedding isn't for another couple months), we were all a bit thrown when they announced the day after Chance proposed that they would be getting married in three weeks.

Izze snorts. "I can't blame her there. I wasn't a fan of ours."

"You weren't a fan of our what?" Miles asks as he steps behind his wife and wraps his arms around her waist.

"Our long engagement." Izze makes a face.

Miles snickers. "Really. I never knew that. I wish you were more vocal about what you do and don't like. You should really work on that, love of my life."

Izze hasn't finished rolling her eyes before Miles leans in and whispers in her ear. The next second, he's whisking her to the dance floor.

And I'm alone.

Again.

It seems like that melody is the soundtrack of my life.

I walk into Sew Magical still clad in my wedding attire, a simple A-line dress that I had made from some fabric that Ann (my boss) had given me as a birthday present. After Apryl and Chance left for their honeymoon, and the rest of us spent a few hours tearing down Apryl's magical garden party in the willow grove, I went to Sew Magical (the alterations and fabric store where I work) at the request of an urgent voicemail.

And I'm trying not to panic.

Uber urgent voicemails are never good. Especially the ones that insist you, "Please come immediately because it is urgent!"

I make my way to the office and knock on the door.

"Come in."

I open the door and immediately freeze.

What on earth?

Ann flits from one corner of the room to the next, stuffing things in boxes that are scattered everywhere. The Kimono she made out of scrap fabric whirls and twists with each spastic movement like she's performing an interpretive dance. While the forty-seven-year-old wife and mom of two grown children had always been eccentric, this is a new level of intensely weird.

Ann jerks to a stop, having just noticed me. The sheer fabric of her Kimono takes two beats to follow her lead. "Kaylee." She glances around at the chaos and sighs. "I'm so sorry."

That's a bad sign.

"You don't need to be sorry." I offer a comforting smile. I have no idea why she needs to be comforted, but it's obvious that she does. I'm getting the overwhelming urge to make her my famous boxed brownies.

Yes, I said boxed. I can cook all sorts of things, and I have been doing just that since I was old enough to operate the oven un-supervised. Sometimes Izze even gifts me cookbooks and marks the recipes that she wants me to try. I won't be auditioning for *Chopped!* or anything like that, but I can make almost anything.

Except brownies. I undercook them or overcook them when-ever I try to make them from scratch, and the kitchen always looks like Izze tried to make a grilled cheese (don't ask). It is my second biggest secret, and my greatest cooking shame. Only Izze knows, something she takes great pleasure in knowing. The cookbooks that she gives me always have a brownie recipe that's marked with an *LOL!* and a taunting smiley face.

But back to Ann, who's practically leaking saltwater from every pore.

She reigns in her emotions and lets out a heavy sigh. "Take a seat, Kaylee."

A sense of foreboding fills me as I shuffle and sit in the oversized orange chair on the other side of her desk. She takes the purple furry chair across from me.

I start to subtly bite my bottom lip. I can't help it. My spirit knows what she's going to say before she says it. I've been here before. I've been the one who's been *let go* because of budgets and bottom lines and whatever.

*No, no, no! NO, God! I was supposed to have more time. She promised!*

"I'm closing the store," she announces.

Yup. There's my trusty intuition. It never fails me. Well, that one time...but that was more because I ignored it. Looking back, my intuition was screaming at me on The Day That Shall Not Be Named.

I open my mouth to ask why or say that I'm sorry, but Ann doesn't notice and continues to explain. "We are moving to Oregon this weekend. As you know, my father has dementia, and he ended up in the hospital over the weekend due to a bad fall. My mother is overwhelmed by the whole situation. Pete and I have decided to accelerate our timetable, so we're moving. This weekend."

"I'm sorry, Ann," I finally say. What am I supposed to say? *How dare you leave now when you promised it would be six months to a year! There's no way you're leaving!* One of the many lessons *Friends* has taught me is that chaining her to the desk will result in more problems.

She hangs her head. "I'm the one who is sorry. I assured you that it would be months, giving you time to find a new job. I hate to do this to you. I am really so very sorry, but we need to go. I need to be with them."

"It's okay, Ann. I understand. Really," I say because that's what you're supposed to say. And because part of me really does understand. I just wish the other part of me—the part that's convinced I'm going to have to sell a kidney on the black market to make next month's rent—wasn't shrieking so loudly in my inner ear.

Ann sniffles. "Thank you, Kaylee." Her hoarse voice squeezes every ounce of compassion and empathy from my heart.

Ann keeps talking about all the details as my rear end goes numb in the old, uncomfortable chair. Then I offer to help her pack up her office. Because that's what you're supposed to do. A few hours later, I'm handing my key to Sew Magical to Ann and grabbing my small box of belongings. I won't be coming back after this. The radio in my head starts to play "This Is the Stuff" by Francesca Battistelli, a catchy tune about how annoying and frustrating stuff in life points us back to God.

No offense to Francesca, but I'm not feeling it.

I don't think I'm feeling anything.

Shouldn't I be feeling sentimental?

I feel like I should be, but I think a small part of me always knew my time at Sew Magical was temporary. I never felt settled.

However, I'd take anything over the completely-at-the-mercy-of-the-raging-ocean feeling that's threatening to consume me right now. A scratching starts in my chest, the panic dying to get out and unleash havoc on me. Balancing the box of measly belongings on my hip, I yank the car door open, throw the insulting cardboard cube of failure into the passenger seat, and climb into my ancient Subaru.

"Get your act together," I tell myself. "You cannot fall apart here. Ann is under enough pressure as it is."

When my internal radio switches to "Going to the Chapel," I know where I'm going. My secret place. My hideaway. The haven of my soul when I'm falling apart.

My childhood church. Or more specifically, the wedding chapel behind the church.

Gabe took a deep breath and brushed from his clothes the wood shavings from the carving he'd been working on earlier in the day before pushing open the double doors of the small wedding chapel. Thankfully, the pastor still left it unlocked, something that always used to baffle Gabe in his teens. But after each spontaneous trip to the unexpected sanctuary over the years, he was thankful the pastor had deemed the small neighborhood safe.

He glanced around the familiar room. It wasn't like there was anything to steal in this building. Besides the sparse furniture in the bridal room, the only things in the chapel where the pews and the podium, all of which were bolted to the floor in a way that could only be described as the overkill that killed overkill.

Gabe went to the first pew on the left, narrowly dodging an old piece of gum that someone had left in plain view. Reaching into his pocket, he pulled out a receipt from the gas station he'd stopped at on his way here and used that to pull the gum off the seat before some poor woman sat in it at the next wedding. Crinkling the gum-plastered receipt into the palm of his hand, he mentally flipped through his To-Do List.

He had to find an apartment.

He had to convince the remaining members of the band to relocate with him for the time being *and* find a new lead singer.

He had to help his mom—the most frustrating part of all.

Okay. It wasn't like she asked for diabetes. It wasn't like she asked for the reduced blood flow that was making her diabetes difficult to manage, putting her at the brink of an amputation. And it wasn't like she asked Gabe to upheave his entire life and move home to support her.

She hadn't asked, and that's why he was annoyed. If she had at least asked, then he felt like he could justify his annoyance at—hopefully temporarily—moving back to the area. But she hadn't asked, hadn't even hinted, so Gabe couldn't be annoyed about his own stupid decision to return to the place he'd abandoned. But after everything hit the fan, his mom had been a rock. Gloria Sanders was strong. She'd adjusted to a life she never wanted and never could have imagined, but Gabe wanted better for her. She tried to help Gabe the best she could through the aftermath. The least Gabe could do was help her through this.

He leaned back in the pew, soaking in the musty, wooded scent of the tiny chapel. His Bible lay beside him, forgotten. He'd been instructed to read the books of Luke, Acts, and 1 Timothy before his recovery group met later this week. Gabe had figured if he was going "to strengthen his spirit with truth" then he might as well start reading the passages here.

The stale air strengthened Gabe. The hard pews strengthened him. This place strengthened him. Year after year, the tiny wedding chapel grounded Gabe in his promise, his resolve, his purpose because her siren's call to come and find her was too great to ignore with white-knuckling willpower. One note of her loving song would ensure that he never emerged. That note would guarantee devastation he would be powerless to stop, devastation that would destroy that siren herself.

"Siren" wasn't really a fair way to describe her. With the exception of singing, the two had nothing in common. The call to love her was the true siren.

And Gabe couldn't do that again. He wouldn't do that to her again.

Which made what happened next seem like the Heavenly version of the legendary Kobayashi Maru Test from *Star Trek*, designed to make him fail and fail hard.

The double doors where flung open for the second time that day, and Gabe could almost hear them groan from the strain of it. He slouched down in his seat, hoping the intruder would take the hint.

"Oh, sorry. I didn't realize anyone was in here."

Gabe's entire body whirled in the pew to face the back door, fully under the spell of the siren's song he hadn't heard in nine long years.

"Kaylee."

# Chapter Two

I blink and shake my head to clear the memory of The Day That Shall Not Be Named, hoping that it will also clear the image of *him* from my vision. Please, please be a hallucination.

Nope. He's still here.

I'm not sure how I got here...

In an empty wedding chapel.

With...Gabe!

And that's not an exclamation of joy like *I'm so happy to see you, my long-lost love!* Nope. That's a big, ginormous, *No!* It's an exclamation of anger, annoyance, and a smidge of hurt. I can't help the sense of betrayal that fills me.

*Why, God? Why? Haven't I had enough dropped on me today?*

"I Knew You Were Trouble" by Taylor Swift starts to play in my head. This is probably one of the most on-point songs my internal DJ has ever picked.

My ex-boyfriend/fiancé from nine years ago takes a tentative step toward me. My number one biggest secret that not even Izze knows about sweeps his eyes over me, studying me. My only heartbreak offers me an uncomfortable smile.

And I want to slap that small smile off of his face.

I haven't seen or heard from him since That Day, but I've spent so many hours (that probably add up to a shameful number of days) wondering, thinking, and planning what this moment would be like. And so far, it's going nothing like I'd imagined.

I should have slapped him thrice according to my schedule.

He looks different, yet the same. Broad chest and toned arms. Soft middle. The same gray eyes that crinkle at the corner. But instead of the shaven, pubescent face I knew, he's grown a full beard that is neatly trimmed. He may only be twenty-seven, but a few silver hairs are already showing at his temple. Because life is unfair, he'll be a silver fox in another decade or so.

Gabe breaks the silence, an unwise choice if you ask me. "Can you believe someone stuck gum on a seat up here? Not under the seat, but right on top for someone to sit in." He holds up a crinkled receipt. "I, uh, almost sat in it—"

"Why are you here?" I burst, cutting off his rambling diatribe.

The muscle on the left side of his jaw twitches, and I flinch as his face from That Day floods my vision once again. So many warning signs that I ignored...

"I come here sometimes. When I'm in town," he finally says.

A part of me is thankful, saying, *Thank you, God, that we've never run into each other before now!* while the other half says, *And why couldn't we continue the "deliverance from thine enemies" thing?*

A man who leaves a woman at the altar in another state with no transportation home is an enemy of the heart, soul, and body in my book.

He shifts uncomfortably.

Well, he *should* be uncomfortable.

This isn't like me—this bitter attitude. I forgave Gabe a long time ago.

Really, I did...

I think I did...

Maybe I did...

I can hear y'all adding the "n't" to my halfhearted statement.

Here's the thing—to take another cue from TSwift—I never expected to see him again because "We Are Never Ever Getting Back Together." But now he's here. In the wedding chapel where he proposed. With a piece of wadded up gum gripped in his hand like it's his *Get out of Jail* card.

Wait a second.

"You've been back to town before this?"

"I, uh..."

"You are unbelievable." If he was a little closer, I would spit on him. Okay, not really because gross, but I want to do it.

His gray eyes widen in surprise.

Yeah, well, so do mine.

"I'm sorry, Kaylee," he chokes out.

I snort in derision. "You have a lot to be sorry for, Gabe. You shouldn't be here."

Now his eyes narrow. "Why? This is public property. And Chip knows I'm here."

"Chip," I stutter. "Chip knows you're here. Pastor Chip knows you are here. Pastor George G. Chiplain knows you're *here*." My flabbergasted statement stumbles from my mouth like the words themselves are drunk.

"Okay, you're kind of making me doubt it now, but it's true."

"So you've kept in contact with Chip?"

"Yes. I, uh, talk with him regularly. Do you have a problem with Chip?" He raises an expectant eyebrow at me in a pathetic attempt to deflect the focus of the conversation.

"No," I growl, "I have a problem with *you*. You bail on our wedding, leave me stranded in the home of strangers in another state, and I don't hear from you again for nine years. And I probably never would have heard from you again if it wasn't for this twisted fluke that feels like the handiwork of a vengeful screenwriter from a soap opera. But you talk with our old youth pastor regularly. Makes perfect sense. Makes perfect stinking sense."

A burst of rage so intense, so unlike anything I've ever felt before, overcomes me.

I am going to throw something.

Dropping my purse onto the seat of the nearest pew, I start rummaging through it for something to throw.

Wow, I am surprisingly attached to everything in here. Even the purse, a used Coach tote bag that Courtney gave me for Christmas last year, feels too valuable to throw at Gabe.

"What are you doing?"

I ignore him.

"Are you looking for a knife or something?"

"What's it to you?" I shoot back without looking up.

"Because if you took up knife throwing just in case this moment ever came, I think I at least deserve to know before I become your next target."

"You don't get to know those details about my life anymore." I growl again as my rage gives way to frustration with my fruitless search, which drains me of all physical and emotional strength. I shove my purse to the side and drop into the pew before leaning down to undo the straps of my red wedge sandals.

"Woah!" Gabe holds up his hands in surrender. "Are you seriously going to throw your shoes at me?" He takes a step back.

Yeah, like that pathetic step has removed him from my eight-year, state championship winning, softball pitcher's arm.

"You're safe. Not that you deserve it." I kick them off my aching feet and sit up, rubbing my face. I squeeze my eyelids together, as if that will erase, rewind, and rewrite everything.

*Daddy, why? Why today of all days?*

"What's today?" Gabe asks.

And apparently, I said that out loud. Can this day get any more mortifying?

"In addition to being the only single gal under the age of sixty at one of my best friends' weddings—" Why am I actually telling him this? "—I also lost my job today."

His footsteps are silent, but I feel him moving closer. The result of a bond I thought was dead and buried. "Izze's wedding?"

I open my eyes and roll them. "Izze got married a couple years ago."

"Oh, wow. I, um, I hadn't heard." He takes a seat in the pew in front of me, angling himself so that he can see me. The old wood creaks under his shifting weight. "I'm guessing my invitation wasn't lost in the mail."

"If that invitation existed, Izze would have used it as a dart board, cleaned out a bird cage with it, and torn it to shreds before lighting it on fire and spitting on the ashes."

Gabe flinches. "That's extreme."

I smile like I always imagine the Mouse King smiling in the first act of *The Nutcracker*. "That's what she did with your yearbook photo."

"Wow," Gabe says slowly. "I'm really thankful I ran into you and not Izze."

"Funny, but I was thinking the exact opposite."

"What happened to your job?" Gabe asks softly, ignoring my jab.

"My boss had a family emergency and decided to relocate immediately."

"Ouch." There's compassion in his voice, but it only continues to grate on my frayed nerves.

I shake my head in response and stare at the front of the church where a small, hand-carved podium stands all alone. "I knew it was coming, but it wasn't supposed to be for several more months."

This is...familiar. Uncomfortably familiar. Why am I still talking to him? Why does it feel like I'm falling into those old habits and rhythms after ten minutes in his presence? Why do I want to cry into his shoulder and kick him in the crotch at the same time?

Gabe lets out a ragged breath, drawing my eyes back to his face. "Listen," he starts but then stops.

I don't bother to acknowledge his false start. I don't care. I don't care anymore.

"I might be able to help you."

I laugh harshly, but he holds up his right hand to stop my unjoyful mirth.

"I need a singer. For my band."

I blink. I would have expected some vague encouragement or referring me to a friend of a friend. But asking me to sing in his band? I at least expected something legit.

"I'm not in high school anymore, Gabe. I've got nine years of wrinkles around my eyes to prove it. I need a real, grown-up job that can pay the bills and ensure that I don't have to sell vital organs to keep a leaky roof over my head."

"This would pay the bills."

"A band?" I raise my eyebrows. "Do you have a record deal or something?"

"We're a wedding band called All Yours. Trust me, it pays the bills and then some."

"A wedding band?" I scoff. "Do you not see the irony in that?"

"I didn't until you pointed it out right then, no." Gabe at least has the decency to look sheepish.

I hate that his sheepish expression is still cute. It's infuriating!

I stand up, scooping my shoes by the straps and dumping them into my purse. "I wish you a lifetime of Drew Barrymore and Adam Sandler moments with your wedding band and some other gullible sap, someone who still believes in the power of love or recently had a head injury. But that person won't be me. So goodbye, Gabe. I'm sure we'll meet again at the next most inopportune moment of my life."

"Kaylee, wait!" I don't bother to turn around, but I can hear him hurrying to catch up with me. "Don't make me chase you."

"Please," I call over my shoulder with a snarl, "we already know you won't bother to chase after me."

As my hand grasps the brass doorknob and starts to turn it, his hand slams onto the heavy, old door. Gabe steps between me and the door, effectively blocking my escape with a broad chest that has seen the benefits of maturity and consistent workouts. He's...close.

Way, way too close. "Bubble space!"

"Just hear me out," he pleads.

"Get out of my face."

"Okay, okay." He takes three steps to the side, but his foot catches on a warped board in the hardwood floors. Since Gabe has always been top-heavy, his center of gravity is completely thrown off balance. He starts waving his arms in that circular motion that makes it look like he's trying to be a bird.

Well, you're the only bird here, buddy. This chickadee is out.

The overdramatic image gives me a small sense of satisfaction.

Until my foot catches the other end of the warped board as I'm shifting away from his propeller arms.

I am not a bird.

So down I go.

Followed by Gabe's sudden but ultimately inevitable crash landing three feet away.

"And with that graceful turn of events, I'm leaving." A burning pain circulates through my backside and legs as I hoist my bruised body to a semi-correct standing position that I'm going to pretend is an advanced yoga position.

Gabe scrambles to his feet before I can make my escape. "Please. Just hear me out."

"Fine." I take a step back and grab my not-so-smart smartphone out of my purse. "You have five minutes. After that I'm calling the cops." I tap on the nine and a one before holding the screen up for him to see.

"Kaylee, it would be a great opportunity for you," Gabe starts.

"Gag me."

"It would pay your bills."

"So would a job at the local dump, and that would be less disgusting. What else you got?"

"You would love this. You love music, singing, and writing songs. I know you do."

I point a finger at his annoyingly broad chest. "You don't know anything about me anymore. You no longer have the right to make statements about what I do or don't love."

He sighs. "I, I feel bad for you."

The words hang in the air between us.

I had to watch the man I love practically run away from marriage to me. That betrayal stung and ached and destroyed me for a long time. If I'm being completely honest with you (because I know you won't tell), sometimes that devastation still feels fresh.

But that heart-wrenching betrayal feels like a newborn stroking my arm compared to the emotional kidney punch that is Gabe's pity. When the man who dumps you genuinely pities you, you know you've finally busted through that false bottom and landed on those rocky shards of self-loathing.

"Listen to me carefully," I say slowly and with a touch of death to boot, "I do not—I repeat, not—want your pity."

"Kaylee, I want to help." He holds up his hands when he sees me open my mouth to eviscerate him with my wrath. "I do, and I won't apologize for wanting to help you. It would be a chance for me to do something right after what I did to you, but you'd also be helping me."

"Of course." I roll my eyes. "There's the truth, out at last."

"You would be helping me, yes. But that's no less true than the fact that I want to help you."

"But I don't need your help."

Gabe raises his eyebrows in a silent challenge.

I drop my purse and cross my arms across my chest. "You think you're going to out-stubborn me? You should know that in the last nine years, I have won two of those contests where you have to keep one hand on something like a car at all times. My record was fifty hours straight." I was then hospitalized for a week, and Izze made me promise to never—as she puts it—be so flinging stubborn that it borders on suicidal ever again. But Gabe doesn't need to know any of that.

"What did you win?" Gabe asks like we're discussing the weather and not on the cusp of one of Vizzini's famous impasses.

"A Subaru and a boat. The Subaru is parked outside, and I sold the boat."

"Impressive, but I can top that. I've had dinner with my Aunt Ida three times in the last nine years," he says, referring to the aunt that always pinches his cheeks upon arrival and attempts (unsuccessfully) to domesticate skunks.

"In what universe is that more impressive?"

"Three times beats two times."

I stare at him as a house fly chooses that moment to zoom around my head. Please don't make my wide-open mouth your temporary home, Mr. Fly.

Or I suppose I could close my mouth.

Gabe sighs, shuffles his feet, and meets my eyes with that heart-fluttering, stormy gaze of gray. "Here's the truth: I'm moving back to the area. Mom's diabetes is out of control, and while she didn't say it or ask for it, she needs my support or...well, you get the picture. We need to get a handle on her treatment and care, and I need to support her any way I can. I can't do that effectively in Boston. And right after I made the decision to move, my lead singer announced she would be leaving the band."

My breath catches with Gabe's use of a feminine pronoun. A new ex-girlfriend? Unless they're making it work long-distance. My gut twists at the thought.

"She and her boyfriend are eloping and planning to move to Tennessee. She has dreams of being the next Carrie Underwood or something. I'm trying to convince the rest of the band to move here, but some of them are a little worried that there won't be a big market for a wedding band."

Between Izze's position at the Ever After Bridal Salon and Courtney and Apryl's wedding decorating business, I happen to know for a fact that the wedding market in this area is amazing.

But I keep my mouth shut.

"Just think about it. Please. I know I have no right to ask. But please think about it." His plea makes me remorseful and angrier at the same time.

"Fine. I will think about it," I choke out. And with that strangled agreement, I turn around and march toward the other door on the back wall of the chapel.

"Did you just remember about the other door in the bridal room?" Gabe calls.

My growl is the only response he gets.

# Chapter Three

"Are you crazy?" Izze shrieks.

"I must be," I mumble as I walk out of the kitchen balancing a cup of strong coffee with some almond milk in my hand. "Because I'm actually considering it."

"No, no, no. No. Kaylee, no." She follows me with her own cup of coffee that's been sweetened to a candy-like state.

"That puts your total up to four hundred and sixteen since you got here an hour ago." She spent the first twenty minutes repeating the declaration in every language she could Google on her phone.

"How could you consider working with him? It's," Izze flutters her fingers like she's flipping through an invisible dictionary, "disgusting."

"Really? Disgusting is the best you could come up with?" I set my mug on the coffee table and belly flop onto the couch.

*Rip!* Awesome. I tore the patchwork slipcover I made for the old couch. Again. And I don't have any money to buy the supplies to fix it. I literally don't have the money for thread. And sorry, but I literally mean literally.

"Appalling. Disturbing. Shocking. Foul. Shall I continue?" She kicks my legs until I sit up and move over for her to sit. I grab some lemon drops from an Aragorn cookie jar I keep on the coffee table while she does, in fact, continue her impressive list of adjectives.

"Izze," I interrupt, "I need money. It's been two weeks since

I've seen a paycheck, and the measly savings I had ran out eight days ago. I haven't been able to find a job that pays enough. I thought about moving—I even looked at studio apartments in sketchy neighborhoods, and I can barely afford just the rent in those places. And you should go look in my cupboards. I've been living off of Ramen noodles and Spam sandwiches for two weeks. I'm one bite of edible Styrofoam away from needing my stomach pumped."

Apparently, there is no limit of false bottoms that one can hit on their way to rock bottom. "Paycheck" by Family Force Five been my spirit song since being let go again, but I'm not even living paycheck to paycheck at this point.

"Simple solution: come stay with us." She holds up her coffee cup for a toast.

"I can't do that."

"Why not?" she asks. "You would do the same for me, for us."

It's true. I would. Without hesitation, and then I'd be badgering Izze the same way. We are friends like family, and a family makes those sacrifices for each other. But I can't. I won't. Few things would hurt my already bruised pride at the moment; however, having to move in with my married bestie would bruise it more than a peach. Not when I have a viable, if completely undesirable option.

It's temporary. It's temporary. It's temporary.

She sighs. "I understand."

"It won't be so bad," I lie. "Gabe had Chip e-mail their website link to me. They've actually built up quite a reputation in the Northeast. And Gabe via Chip got me in touch with the manager, a guy named Ethan."

"Gabe isn't the manager?" Izze asks after taking a sip of her coffee.

"No. According to Ethan, Gabe does a lot of managerial things, so they more or less share the responsibilities. Ethan handles more of the scheduling, number crunching, contract stuff, and those kinds of details."

Izze's dark eyes search my face, studying me. "Do you want to do this? I know I've given you my opinion loudly and a lot, but is this something you want to do?"

I stare at the wall for a long time before moaning like it's the last dramatic note in an Italian opera. "I don't know. I guess a part of me does. The idealistic part of me says that it would be awesome to have a job that I would love doing. I mean, singing for a living? That's the dream, but what if I can't do it?"

Izze blinks. "Of all the things you could have said, I didn't expect that."

"What?"

"That you can't do it."

I pick at a hole in my leggings. "What if I'm just kidding myself? What if I'm not good enough to sing lead vocals?"

"Kaylee! You've been singing on the worship team at church for years. Like, years!" Izze throws her free hand out like she's pelting a newly married couple with bird seed.

"But I'm just a singer—and a disposable backup singer at that. And then there's the Gabe aspect of it all." I rub my face for the millionth time. Maybe I'll get lucky and rub it right off of my head. I don't know why that would be lucky per se, but anything seems luckier than the strange twist of fate I've been handed.

"Who is positively awful. The only person I hate more than your Gabe is Gabe from *The Office*," Izze grumbles.

"He's not mine." My response carries more bite than I intended.

Her demeanor softens. "I'm sorry, Kaylee. I know the last few weeks haven't been easy on you. I'd like to imagine that if my ex-toad showed up, it wouldn't phase me. But you've actually had to confront that reality. I am so sorry, but I am also so proud of you, dear friend."

"I'm not sure I'm handling it well enough to deserve your accolades, Izze." If anything, Gabe's arrival is shining a light into some dark places I'd rather ignore. "Primarily because I'd like to stab him in the thigh with a spork."

"Seems reasonable to me."

"I just feel so angry about everything," I ramble as I widen the hole to the size of a quarter. "He abandoned me, so why do I have to put up with him? It's not fair. It's like my parents all over again. Parents who can't bother to remember to send a stupid text message to tell me happy birthday, but I'm a terrible daughter if I don't say it to them."

She hugs me, and we sit like that for a few minutes.

"Will you be here?" I ask, making the decision once and for all.

Izze answers with the language of my soul and starts to sing the chorus of the *Gilmore Girls* theme song, "Where You Lead."

Gabe wiped his sweaty palms on his black jeans and leaned back in his car seat. Great. He was the first one here.

A car door slammed to his right. Gabe turned and saw an older but no less loyal Izze glaring at him with unmasked disdain before she stormed into the house.

*Gulp!* There was no way he was going into the lion's den without backup. Kaylee hadn't exaggerated. If anything, Kaylee had played down Izze's opinion of him.

If only God would send an angel to hold Izze's sharp mouth closed. But Gabe knew he couldn't expect any favors from Him. Gabe didn't deserve it, so why bother asking for it?

Another car door slammed to his left. A breath of relief escaped Gabe's lips as he saw Ethan climbing down from his tweaked-out truck.

Maybe God had answered his not-a-prayer prayer.

"Hey, man. You hiding?" Ethan asked.

Gabe didn't bother to answer as he gave his buddy their own version of the man's shake/hug combo. Ethan was somewhat aware of the...circumstances surrounding the unique arrangement Gabe had struck with his ex. Somewhat.

"What should I expect in there?" Ethan asked, nodding toward the house.

"Open hostility."

Ethan raised his eyebrows. "Are you sure that *you* want to do this?"

Gabe huffed. "Yeah, man." Gabe had been shocked when Ethan told him that Kaylee had accepted their offer last week. He hadn't expected Kaylee to agree, so he hadn't spent any time worrying about this moment.

Turns out, he should have.

He would never back out of their agreement. At the very least, he owed Kaylee this. And she made it very clear to them that her involvement would be temporary. Gabe could live with that.

He thought he could live with that, but if he was being honest, he felt like the stakes where higher than what he had to offer.

"Let's get this party started then." Ethan rubbed his hands together with a smug expression on his face.

"Why do I get the impression that you're enjoying this?"

"Ha! Man, you always exude—"

"Exude? Seriously? I don't want to exude anything."

"—confidence. It's a little funny to watch you squirm."

"It's amazing how quickly you can flip from being helpful to being a pain in the backside."

Ethan turned toward the house. "Funny. I wonder if Kaylee would say the same thing about you."

Gabe rolled his eyes. "Stop talking."

Ethan's laughter followed him up the walkway to the modest-sized, albeit dilapidated house. Taking a deep breath, Gabe knocked on the door. It swung open after one knock, putting Gabe face to face with Izze. And she had not calmed down in the last five minutes.

Despite her small stature, Izze was fierce. Like a wolverine someone had caught and starved before releasing it for the fight of its life.

Behind him, Ethan immediately stopped laughing as he felt the full force of Izze's glare. Without a word, she turned and walked away, leaving the door open if they dared to follow her.

Or run away. Which seemed like a legitimate and completely manly option at the moment.

"Woah," Ethan muttered. "That chick would scare a Nazgul."

"That's Izze."

"Your ex?"

"Her best friend."

Ethan laughed as they stepped across the threshold. "Man, you are in deep."

"And there's that support again," Gabe muttered.

No one was in the living room, so they stood by the doorway. Minutes ticked by as they stood there like the awkward intruders that they were. Gabe could hear loud whispers, but he couldn't make out any of the words.

He slipped his phone out of his pocket and texted his mom, asking how today's doctor's appointment went. Anything to make him feel less like a puppy who hadn't been housebroken yet. Or the impure jerk who ruined the life of the only woman he'd ever—

*Nope. Not going there.*

After a few more minutes, Kaylee and Izze walked into the living room. Gabe's pulse leaped at the sight of her like he had just pounded six or seven energy drinks. Was he getting tunnel vision too? Suddenly, all he could see was her.

This was a bad idea. A very bad idea. This would go down as an idiotic idea with a couple capital I's. He was breaking every rule he had made for himself over the last nine years. Rule Number One: *Don't screw up Kaylee's life again!*

Followed by Rule Number Two: *Stay away from Kaylee!*

Gabe opened his mouth to shut down one of the worst plans of his life—and possibly forfeit his life to Izze's revenge—when a knock reverberated throughout the room.

Deep breath. Gabe caught Kaylee's eye, silently asking if he could open the door.

She nodded while biting her lip.

Izze seethed.

Ethan laughed under his breath and covered it with a not-so-subtle cough.

Ignoring all of them, Gabe turned around and opened the front door like he did this all the time.

*You could have*, that familiar voice said, the voice that told him how worthless and terrible and messed up he was. The voice that usually sounded so much louder and closer than God.

And yeah, he could have had this life. But he said no. End of story.

*Not quite*, the familiar voice said.

Summer, Natalya, and Drake stood on the other side of the door. "Hey, guys." Gabe moved to the side.

Natalya offered him a warm smile while Summer and Drake returned his greeting, and he breathed a little easier. They had fought for and with each other about this band. They had written songs together over countless nights of practice and had driven hundreds of miles for a single gig in order to pursue their passion. They were bonded, and he was thankful the group had decided to relocate to the area for the time being until Gabe figured things out with his family.

He turned back to face Kaylee and Izze as the rest of his band—the brothers and sisters that he'd never had—filtered through the doorway. Natalya stopped next to him and bumped his shoulder with her own, offering him another smile when Gabe glanced at her.

Shifting his vision back to Kaylee, Gabe watched as she studied each of his people. Her eyes lingered—and narrowed?—a little as she studied Natalya. If possible, Izze's countenance darkened even more.

Okay, time for introductions. "So, guys. This is Kaylee," Gabe said, while pointing at her. "We, uh, know each other from high school."

Izze snorted.

"The scary chick next to her is Izze," Gabe shot back with a glare of his own.

"Se—" Izze started to say, but Kaylee pinched her and mumbled something Gabe couldn't hear.

Drake raised his eyebrows at Gabe. "Something you want to share with the group, man?" he asked in that direct way of his, something Gabe had admired when he first met the younger man.

Unfortunately, now it looked like they were going to have to kick Drake out of the band for it.

"As Hans Christian Andersen said, 'Where words fail, music speaks.' So speak." Drake offered a goofy grin to cut the scorching tension.

"Drake likes to speak in weird music clichés and quotes," Summer informed Kaylee and Izze, clearing their confused—and possibly alarmed—expressions.

Natalya's gaze darted back and forth from Gabe to Kaylee, assessing the not-so-romantic tension between them that could fuel a dozen or so songs. "You were a couple," she finally stated.

"*Were* being the operative word," Kaylee stated.

Natalya's eyes flickered to Gabe once more in a way that was very telling of how she felt about this newsflash.

Gabe stifled a groan and tried to ignore the beads of nervous sweat forming along his forehead. It would be the worst timing known to man for *their* history to also come to light in this little meet and greet.

Ethan moaned. "You didn't tell them?"

"I was going to get around to it," Gabe muttered.

One... Two... Three beats went by, each one building in crescendo until...

Summer started to laugh. "This is awesome! Finally, some romantic tension." Everyone stared at her, but Summer just shrugged. "Sorry, Gabe, but you had no chemistry with Ari. You were both awesome musicians, but your duets sounded like a couple of robots trying to understand human emotion."

Izze snorted in amusement this time.

Summer grinned at Kaylee. "I like you," she stated in her typical matter-of-fact way.

Kaylee frowned. "Um, thanks?"

"You're welcome. It was a compliment. Any woman who's willing to help out Gabe after whatever happened between the two of you is a cool lady in my book."

"For all you know, it was my fault," Kaylee challenged.

"And for the record, I'm also helping her out," Gabe interjected.

Summer ignored Gabe and answered Kaylee. "Considering what I know of Gabe, you were probably justified if it was your fault."

"Hey!" Gabe said while Ethan laughed once again.

"And I would like to add to the record that it wasn't her fault," Izze interjected. "Her ex-boyfriend over here left town without any explanation."

*Wait...what?*

Gabe's watched as all the color drained from Kaylee's face.

"Woah, man." Drake shook his head. "That's cold."

"I was eighteen," he mumbled, tearing his eyes away from Kaylee's guilty expression.

"And I think we should move on," Kaylee said, jumping into the conversation. "So let's talk about the reason we are all here."

Drake nodded. "I agree."

"Awesome," Ethan said, finally offering something other than laughter at Gabe's poor choices. "So you know the basics—we're predominately a wedding band, but we'll perform at the occasional prom or fundraising event."

"My personal favorite involves events at the zoo," Summer interjected.

"Fundraising galas?" Kaylee asked.

"Penguin wedding," Summer informed her.

"An unfortunate breakdown in communication." Ethan rolled his eyes. "If you got a chance to look at the website, you saw that we have a number of packages for our clients, like building their own playlist or having us select most of the music. We don't play explicit songs or anything with graphic language. We have a catalog of songs available, and we're willing to learn new songs for a wedding, provided those songs meet the guidelines and they're requested by the deadline."

"So the band plays a lot of covers? Does that mean I need to get a special license or something?" Kaylee asked.

"The venue is actually responsible for paying the licensing fee to a licensing agency, not the band," Gabe said. *That's right, you dolt. Throw yourself into the conversation like all your past failures aren't in a room and potentially about to duke it out like Captain America and Iron Man in our own twisted civil war.*

"So if everyone is game, I think the next step would be to start regular rehearsals up next week. That way Kaylee can learn your rhythm and sound," Ethan said, glancing around the room. "Next week, we can work on getting some videos of all of you playing together and some solo audio samples should a client want you to sing a solo or something like that."

"When are your, uh, our regular rehearsals?" Kaylee asked.

"They're usually late afternoon on Monday, Wednesday, and Thursday. Unless there's a gig or you're traveling to or from a gig. Is there any conflict with your current schedule?"

Kaylee shook her head. "No. I'm on the worship team at my church, but it's a rotating thing now, so I don't sing every week anymore. Practice for that is on Sunday mornings, but they'll understand if I'm out of town some weeks."

"Great. So our first rehearsal together would be next Wednesday because Drake and I need to make another trip to Boston with a U-Haul." Ethan grabbed his iPad from the messenger bag he'd slung across the couch and started entering details into the band's calendar.

"There's just one problem," Drake said in a *Duh!* tone of voice, "we don't have a rehearsal space."

Summer eyed the living room they occupied like a can of sardines. "Maybe we could do it here? Just until we find a place."

Natalya, Drake, and Ethan scanned the room while Kaylee stood there looking like she wanted to scream at them to get out before she sent Izze after them.

"Yeah, this could work." Ethan raised an eyebrow at him, waiting for his opinion on the proposed, uh, *suggested* arrangement.

Gabe rubbed the back of his neck and dared to meet Kaylee's horrified gaze. "I mean, yeah. This could work. I know it would be a big inconvenience, but it wouldn't have to be forever."

He could literally feel Izze's glare. It burned like Nebuchadnezzar's fiery furnace.

"Okay," Kaylee choked out. Izze shot her a look, but Kaylee shook her head in response.

"When is our next show?" Natalya asked woodenly, changing the subject since apparently their rehearsal space was all figured out now.

"In seven weeks. I know that's not a lot of time, but it will have to work," Ethan answered.

Or it would be enough time for Kaylee to decide this was a huge mistake. Or for Gabe to screw everything up again. Or for Natalya to spill the details of Gabe's sordid past.

The group continued to talk logistics, but Gabe watched for an opening to talk with Kaylee alone. Once he saw Izze leave the room, heading in the general direction of the restroom Kaylee had pointed out earlier to Summer, it was time to make his move. Gabe subtly maneuvered through the room to stand next to Kaylee.

She stiffened at his presence just like she had in the chapel, but she didn't acknowledge him.

Fine. She could ignore him all she wanted, but Gabe had a burning question that needed an answer. "What was that?"

"I believe it's called a snub."

"Not that." Gabe turned his back to the doorway Izze had disappeared through—a dangerous move—so that the delicate conversation would stay between them. "Izze doesn't know, does she?"

Kaylee pursed her lips. "No, she doesn't know...that part."

Gabe let out a breath. "You seriously didn't tell her?"

"If you'll stop being all egotistical, you'll recall that no one—not even Izze—knew about The Day That Shall Not Be Named."

"Are you comparing me to Voldemort?"

She gave him a scorching look. "If the shoe fits."

"Why did you lie to her?" he shot back.

She glared at him. "It was a lie of omission. And that's none of your business."

"It directly involves me."

"Do you think the truth makes you look any better?"

He winced. "No, but..."

"No." Kaylee lasered him with a cold glare. "It's over. I don't want to talk about it with you ever again. The past is dead to me." To emphasize her point, she walked away.

When Gabe was a little kid, he wondered what it would be like to be invisible.

As he watched Kaylee seek refuge by Izze's side, he had a feeling he was going to find out.

# Chapter Four

I stare at the verse of the day on my phone's Bible app.

"Therefore lift your drooping hands and strengthen your weak knees."

Seriously? How is that a verse in the Bible? And why did someone feel like that should be highlighted as the verse of the day?

Unless that's the plan. Get a person all confused about the bizarreness that is the twelfth verse in Hebrews chapter twelve, and then they'll be so curious that they'll have to read the rest of the chapter.

A plan that is apparently working on me. God's crafty like that.

I click on the Read Full Chapter option to keep reading. My breath catches as I read.

Here, let me share verses twelve through fifteen with you:

"Therefore lift your drooping hands and strengthen your weak knees, and make straight paths for your feet, so that what is lame may not be put out of joint but rather be healed. Strive for peace with everyone, and for the holiness without which no one will see the Lord. See to it that no one fails to obtain the grace of God; that no 'root of bitterness' springs up and causes trouble, and by it become defiled."

Suddenly that Bible verse feels way more applicable.

I don't know how to process this right now. So I'm not going to deal with it. I close the Bible app and toss my phone onto the counter.

I feel kind of like I just got spiritually slapped with truth.

It's an uncomfortable feeling.

All I wanted was something that would uplift and encourage me before I had to deal with Gabe and his musical posse. But no. I get possibly the weirdest verse in the entire Bible, and that verse leads to some other verses that make me feel very, very uncomfortable.

They make me think. About Gabe. And to make matters even worse, about my parents.

I've never been close to them, and to be honest, I'm not sure there was ever a time we could have been considered a happy family. My parents fought all the time, and when they weren't fighting, they weren't talking. They were divorced before my eighth birthday because they'd "grown apart" and "had fallen out of love." My brother and I were shipped back and forth between them in some twisted version of custody ping-pong until we were considered old enough to tell the courts what we wanted.

Yeah. It's as awful as it sounds. For those of you who've been in similar situations, my heart breaks for you.

I never knew how close a family could be until I met Izze's family. I vowed that I would have that one day. And, okay, I may have also vowed I'd never forgive my parents. Obviously, I knew I couldn't continue with that mantra once I became a Christian. It took a while, but I managed to push that anger toward them into a box. That box sits in the attic of my heart where it won't bother anyone again.

At least, that's what I thought.

Seeing Gabe again is like being slapped in the face with all my false hopes for the future and my future family. And all the volatile emotions are bringing my long-buried anger toward Gabe and my parents to a simmer.

A part of the verse whispers through my head and my heart again, "that no 'root of bitterness' springs up and causes trouble."

I'm not in a place to handle this. I don't want to handle this.

My phone starts to play "Shackles" by Mary Mary. The ringtone I gave to Gabe when Ethan insisted that I needed to have his number. I think a song about God delivering you from the shackles that are holding you is appropriate. As in *Hint, Hint!* to a certain Someone.

My thumb hovers over the *Ignore* button.

Don't give me that look!

I. Have. Forgiven. Him.

Swiping my finger to the right, I answer his call. "Hello," I growl.

"Hey. Are we still on for today?" Static interferes, adding a Mr. Talkbox (a friend of TobyMac, guys) quality to his voice.

Let me think about it. Oh, wait. If I had actually been thinking, I wouldn't have agreed to any of this.

"Yes," I say. Because I am a nice person. I won't say what I'm actually thinking and feeling. Not unless poked with a stick.

Unfortunately, Gabe's very essence seems to be that stick. If only I could change what I was thinking and feeling before I get all Meg Ryan to his Tom Hanks like in *You've Got Mail*.

"Okay," Gabe says slowly, like he can still read my mind. "Well, Summer and Natalya should be there any minute."

"Fantastic," I say dryly.

"Tone down the enthusiasm, please."

"Is there anything else?"

"Nope."

"Bye." I hang up without waiting for a reply.

Walking into the living room, I feel that pang of loneliness hit me all over again as I look around the empty room. The discolored spots on the walls, floor, and furniture where my friends' belongings used to be is just a stark reminder that their lives have moved forward.

While mine seems to be continually regressing.

And I'm happy for them and for all the awesome things that have happened to them. Husbands, new jobs, new homes, new lives. I'm expecting a pregnancy announcement from Izze and Miles any day now.

But despite all that happiness, sometimes I feel like I've been left behind.

My grandfather used to tell me that when life gives you lemons, make lemonade. I'm sure you know the expression by heart and were cringing before I even said two words. Sorry, but here's my problem: I like lemons. Love them, actually. Plain old lemons. So I've never related to this theoretically "wise" advice because I feel like I've been given a life full of lima beans.

Gag with me, won't you?

Now despite the amusing pun, limeade is not made with lima beans. There's no way to make those fowl green things taste any better. All the lima beans of my circumstances and the happiness for everyone else are adding up to equal a psychotic break that will result in me purchasing lima beans to throw at people. I'll be that crazy house (assuming I don't get evicted) that every kid in the neighborhood will want to avoid. Children won't walk past lest they be pelted with a lima bean soaked in lemon water. I can almost hear the screams now... *Run, children! Run!*

I squeeze the bridge of my nose. Maybe the psychotic break has already begun.

Grabbing the *Lord of the Rings* cloth mug rug that I made from the coffee table, I scan the room for any more paraphernalia. Ah, yes, my Samwise Gamgee bookends. Got to hide those.

Normally, I don't hide my love of Middle Earth. It's part of who I am. I'm not the book nerd that Izze is. (Fun Fact: a scholastic book fair in third grade is how we met. And yes, I was looking for more Tolkien books, but I didn't know then that *Lord of the Rings* isn't the average reading material of most nine-year-olds.) However, I read, collect, and watch anything relating to Tolkien's beloved world.

Except for today, that is, because I am not in the mood for mockery from strangers. I must protect what's precious to me.

Ha! The precious...

I am depositing the nerd contraband into my room when I hear a loud knock.

Time to make some beautiful music.

Gag with me again, won't you?

I'd slap on a *Happy* face, but who am I kidding? The best I can do is an *Uncomfortably Polite* face under these circumstances.

I open the door. Natalya mirrors the same expression as me, while Summer gives me a genuine smile. They're each holding cases of equipment, and Summer has a small amp crammed under her arm. Guess who got suckered into hosting band rehearsal for the time being? Oh, wait—you were there for that little manipulation.

Okay, *now* I can see how that "root of bitterness" thing factors into this.

"Hi, um, guys." I'm the epitome of awkward in new situations, the introverted personality that I hide so well when my people—also known as the dear friends who've left me behind in life—are not there to put me at ease.

"Hey, Kaylee," Summer says brightly.

"Hi." I will be evaluating that single word and the corresponding smile for the next twenty years.

Natalya gives me a closed mouth smile and a little nod that says she's not so sure about me.

It's okay. I'm not so sure about her yet after watching her around Gabe. There's a story there. She obviously likes him, but I can't tell if he likes her. Maybe they already have a history.

Not that I care.

A lot.

I wish I cared less, like not at all.

I move back so that they can come inside while we wait for the guys.

*Tick. Tick. Tick.*

Oh, right! Try to make conversation. "So where are you guys staying?"

"In a motel about twenty minutes outside of Keene," Natalya says without any emotion.

My eyes widen. "That stinks."

"Yeah." Summer flippantly waves her hand. "But it could be worse."

"You're not the one who found hair on your pillow," Natalya mumbles.

"Gross!"

She gives me the first smile I've seen from her. It transforms her whole face, adding a beautiful glow to her already lovely heart-shaped face.

Thoughts of inferiority flutter through my mind with an annoying melody as I flash back to the brief moment I witnessed between her and Gabe the last time this group invaded my home.

"Right. Yeah, that's gross. I understand about housing issues."

"You do?" Natalya raises an eyebrow at me before flicking open the latches of a smaller case and pulling out a violin.

"I lost all my roommates. I used to live here with my best friends, but they all moved out over the last couple of years."

"Hey, are you struggling with rent?" Summer asks from where she stands by the fireplace with the amplifier.

Uh oh. I've got a bad feeling about this. The melody from "Gaston" from *Beauty and the Beast* starts to play in my head, and I can hear Gaston and Lefou plotting in the background.

"Um—"

"If you are, maybe we could be your new roommates," she continues enthusiastically.

"I—"

"It would be perfect. We could practice here and live here, which would take care of our problems. And of course, we would pay rent, which would take care of your problems."

I think the air just turned to burning acid. My throat burns. Can't. Breathe.

Natalya studies me for a moment. "I'm not sure that would work long-term," she says slowly.

Saved!

By the girl who probably hates me for my past with Gabe.

The door opens, preventing me from having to close my gaping mouth and respond to Summer. I declare this person is my hero.

And it's Gabe, but you probably saw that coming. "Sorry, I knocked a few times, but then I saw the door was unlocked."

I quit adulting today.

"Gabe, look at Kaylee while you're singing."

Gabe shot Ethan a glare that would incinerate a zombie.

Ethan responded with one of his own that effectively communicated what he thought of Gabe's pathetic attempt of music: *Get it together, man! You got yourself into this mess. You said everything would be fine. If it's so fine, sing the stinking love song!*

Basically, a repeat of everything Ethan had already said to him in private.

They'd been practicing for half an hour, and it had been okay. Until they got to one of the dreaded, romantic duets that had made the band so popular. There was nothing more awkward than making eye contact with your ex-girlfriend/almost wife while you sang a love song to each other. Except when this occurred in front of a bunch of people. That detail made it so much worse.

The music around them faded to an off-key halt as Gabe and Ethan silently argued.

Ethan won, raising his eyebrows and crossing his arms in a challenge.

Kaylee—because she'd always been intuitive beyond what a single human should possess in this area—caught Gabe's eyes with her own. She raised both of her eyebrows in an old, familiar challenge that Gabe would never forget. The one that said, *I know how to push you.*

Uh oh.

She turned to catch Ethan's eye. "Maybe we should try a different song?"

"As Arthur Schopenhauer said, 'Music is the answer.' A new song sounds like a good idea to me." Drake gave a snort of laughter at his thirtieth corny music joke of the day. "Though I did shorten his original thought to make my point."

"I've got a good idea for you," Summer mumbled. "Stop with the quotes and then you don't have to worry about properly citing the source."

Ethan, the traitor, seemed to catch the fact that Kaylee had something on him. "Yeah, I agree. Got any suggestions?"

Did they plan this? Gabe narrowed his eyes, but they both ignored him.

"So," Kaylee started and paused, gathering her nerves in front of a group of people she didn't know very well. "I know it's a little old, but what about 'Mary's Song' by Taylor Swift?"

"Really?" Drake asked, wrinkling his nose from where he stood behind Kaylee with his red bass guitar. "I don't know. That seems weird."

And uncomfortable. Gabe had the distinct memory of suggesting that song when they ran off to elope.

"Plus, didn't she, like, bury her Nashville twang and burn her cowgirl boots or something?" Summer asked.

"I understand what you mean, but Taylor Swift has managed to continue selling her country albums even after transitioning to pop. I'd be willing to bet that a lot of brides are going to want to use her songs—new and old," Kaylee said. "I'm not a super big fan, but she's popular. This could help us appeal to potential clients."

Gabe guffawed and frowned, more than a little disturbed at the weird noise that had escaped his lips. Judging by the look Natalya was giving him, he'd weirded out the others as well. He didn't know a guy could do that...guffaw. Maybe he was the first.

But he couldn't help it.

Gabe couldn't believe the way Kaylee was goading him right now. They had gone to a half dozen Taylor Swift concerts while they were dating. He'd be willing to wager his next payday that she had an "I Heart TSwift" shirt in her closet that would disprove her claim. Of all the rotten tricks.

Ethan clapped his hands. "I love it! Good suggestion, Kaylee. Let's try it, guys."

"Fine," Drake grumbled, "but nothing weird."

"Weird?" Natalya asked.

"You know what I mean," Drake exclaimed. "Songs appropriate for weddings, not a hot date. That would be weird."

"Agreed," they all said.

"'Forever and Always,'" Kaylee added.

She and Ethan had to have planned this.

"So we should 'Begin Again' with this new song," Kaylee said with a straight face.

Ethan's "manager" composure slipped a little with Kaylee's subtle mocking of Gabe's secret guilty pleasure with that musician's song titles. While there were plenty of things Gabe didn't appreciate regarding that particular music artist, he could respect how she made herself vulnerable in her music. That—and only that—was the reason he liked her music.

Okay, and some of the songs were catchy.

But that didn't mean he was ready to open himself up to the mockery that would undoubtedly ensue if the others knew he had a matching "I Heart TSwift" shirt in his closet.

The rest of the group gave halfhearted murmurs of agreement as they started to search for lyrics and sheet music on their phones. Gabe shot Kaylee a glare before he pretended to look up the music he knew by heart.

She didn't meet his eyes, but her triumphant smirk said it all.

Ethan snorted.

After looking everything over, they started to play the sweet melody. One... Two... Three times and then Natalya jumped in with her violin, adding another layer of strings to their rhythm as Summer started to add drumbeats.

After the fourth time, Kaylee started to sing.

And this moment was the moment Gabe had been dreading ever since Kaylee had accepted his impulsive offer because he knew it would be his undoing.

His siren song.

Because Gabe always knew that if he heard her sing again, he'd be sunk. It was the reason he had never sought her out after abandoning her, not even to beg for her forgiveness. It was the reason he always went to the wedding chapel when he returned to the area. The little chapel where he'd originally proposed to Kaylee fortified his resolved to never go back, because then he'd want to be a better man, a man who could love her the way she deserved to be loved.

And Gabe couldn't love her that way. He was too far gone.

Gabe tried to resist watching her sing, but her song called to him. With eyes closed, hands reaching like they were trying to grasp the soul of the lyrics, heartbreak etched across her face and longing bursting from her lungs, Kaylee sang the first verse. Her sweet soprano was just as mesmerizing as it had been the last time Gabe had heard her sing.

And he was sunk.

Missing his cue, Gabe tried to jump into the third line of the chorus. His hoarse voice earned him a few looks from the others. He ignored them, letting his eyes close for a brief moment before he started to sing the second verse. When he opened them, he focused on Kaylee like Ethan had instructed.

Liar. Like that was the reason. Gabe couldn't have picked Ethan out of a lineup of women in that moment because all he saw was Kaylee.

Eyes on her, he sang. The memory of their first kiss flooding him as the lyrics wrapped around them, sealing them in a bubble that was just them.

Them and the past. Memories that would never be recreated.

Ethan clapped again, unintentionally allowing Gabe to resurface from the musical trance in which he'd been drowning. The rest joined into Ethan's clap while Drake let out a whistle of approval.

"Now that is what I'm talking about!" Summer exclaimed.

"And *that* is why Leo Tolstoy said, 'Music is the shorthand of emotion.'" Drake grinned, and Ethan rolled his eyes. "True story, man."

Kaylee's face turned a charming shade of red that matched her hair. Her "tomato face" he used to say when he teased her.

"Man," Drake said, shaking his head. "You've been holding out on us."

Ethan nodded. "If you're going to sing like that, maybe you guys should be a Swiftie cover band."

Drake moaned. "Oh, please no."

"You guys were amazing," Summer said. "There's that heat we've been needing."

Natalya scowled.

Oy, great. The potential problems behind that scowl and the ramifications were worrisome. He knew Natalya hadn't moved on—he wasn't a clueless jerk even if he was, in fact, a jerk. However, he was more worried about Natalya sharing their past with Kaylee.

Summer glanced at her phone. "Guys, I'm sorry, but Natalya and I have to run. Some of our stuff is supposed to be dropped off at the motel by four, and we've got to be there to sign for it."

"Hey, can I get a ride with you guys?" Drake asked.

Summer raised a pierced eyebrow. "I don't know. Can you ride without spouting off cheesy music quotes? If so, then yes."

Drake rolled his eyes.

"But what about all of our equipment?" Natalya pointed at the instruments, microphones, amps, and other musical equipment that was scattered around Kaylee's living room.

"Aren't we using this as a temporary rehearsal space?" Drake said.

"Oh, yeah. Right," Natalya mumbled.

"All right. So rehearsals will be every Monday, Wednesday, and Thursday at this time for the time being," Ethan said, and everyone voiced their understanding as they quickly broke down the rehearsal space, transforming it into Kaylee's living room once again.

Summer gave Kaylee a sly grin as she headed out the door a few minutes later. "Think about what I said, okay?"

"Uh, yeah. I will." Kaylee offered a tight smile.

Gabe shot Summer a questioning look.

She jerked her head toward the front door, gesturing for him to follow her.

"I'll be right back," Gabe said as he brushed by Ethan.

He pulled the screechy door shut as he stepped outside, near-ly bumping into Summer, who had waited for him right outside the front door while Drake and Natalya climbed into Summer's beaten up VW van. Natalya pretended not to stare at them from the passenger seat.

"Kaylee's going to solve all of our problems," Summer said in a cross between a whisper and a squeal.

Gabe muffled a groan. "Yeah, she's the bomb. What did you need to talk about with me?"

"Kaylee!"

"Yeah, that's not going to happen." Gabe turned to go back inside the house.

"No, not about that." Summer grabbed his arm. "She's living alone."

"Creepy much?"

"Would you just let me talk?" Summer sigh of frustration.

"Fine." Gabe gave a huff of his own.

"Okay, so she's living alone. She told us that her roommates all moved out over the last few years."

Gabe knew that much from his own conversations with Kaylee. "Yeah, and?"

"I asked her if Natalya and I could move in and be her new roommates."

Gabe blinked. What?

"It would be perfect," Summer continued, ignoring Gabe's non-reaction. "We could live here and use one of the bedrooms for a rehearsal space. Or at least to store the equipment when we're not rehearsing."

Oh, man. Summer had already sunk her teeth into this idea. How was he going to discourage this?

"I doubt Kaylee is looking for roommates," he tried.

She raised an eyebrow. "I got the impression that she was having a hard time with rent."

"But we don't know if we're going to stay in the area. Kaylee is probably looking for long-term renters, or maybe she'll decide to sell the house."

"Does she own it?"

"Maybe she rents it, but that just proves my point. It's not up to her."

"Even still, the money would probably help her a lot. I think you should talk to her, try to nudge her in the right direction," Summer said.

That did it. "Summer. You need to back off."

But Summer had never been one to back down.

"Gabe, we are living out of a motel. Temporary or not, we don't have the money to live there much longer." She paused, letting the truth of their current reality sink into his thick skull. "I know you, Drake, and Ethan are trying to find a place, but Natalya and I still need a place to pass out every night. And we need a rehearsal space. This," she said, motioning toward the front door, "could be it."

He was such an idiot. And she was right. They had moved to another state for him. They had uprooted their lives for him and their music. He needed to help them any way he could.

But did it have to be this way? Never mind the pretty much guaranteed destruction that *would* rattle the band if they lived under the same roof, he had a good idea of how that conversation would go with Kaylee.

Badly.

"I'll try," Gabe finally said as he flicked a stray wood shaving off his elbow. "But I can't promise anything."

Summer's grin looked like it might permanently distort her face. "That's all I ask."

He rolled his eyes. "You're asking a lot more than that, but I'll try to talk to her."

"Thank you!" She bounced down the steps and ran to her van.

What had he gotten himself into now?

Sighing, Gabe walked back inside the house. The old door

screeched behind him like it was disgruntled by his audacity to open and close it when it had better things to do.

He stepped beside Ethan, preparing to bug Kaylee about Summer's request when Ethan slapped him on the back. "That was amazing, man."

Amazingly idiotic? Yeah, no doubt about that. Those two words could describe every one of Gabe's actions, decisions, and stupid thoughts over the last month, ever since he saw Kaylee standing in the chapel. "Thanks," Gabe muttered instead.

Kaylee cleared her throat. "You did a good job."

Gabe searched her expression, looking for all the cues he used to know better than the strings of his guitar. She was forcing herself to maintain eye contact, that much he could tell. But was the compliment genuine? Hard to say.

The fact that her opinion mattered so much to him was the bigger problem.

"So," Ethan said, drawing the word out.

"Just spit it out," Gabe griped.

Ethan held up his hands. "I thought maybe you and Kaylee could work on some original songs together."

"What?" Kaylee squeaked.

"I'm not sure that's a good idea," Gabe said at the same time.

"Look," Ethan said in that *Who's the boss?* tone of his, "the way I see it, this is business. It's about your careers. You write. Kaylee writes. So why not write together?"

For the second time that day, Gabe felt cornered with some pretty sound logic. Logic that made him angry and uncomfortable and a whole lot of other things that Gabe didn't want to feel right now. Fortunately for him, Kaylee's emotions exploded first.

"Because!" Kaylee thrust her hands back and forth between her and Gabe.

"You know why," Gabe added. "There's too much history." And some not-so-history stuff.

"Which I was assured would not be a problem." Ethan swung his piercing gaze from Gabe to Kaylee.

When did his best friend become such a donkey's butt? Well, Gabe could be just as stubborn as the mule in the sports coat standing next to him. He gave Ethan an unwavering glare of his own.

Ethan sighed. "Look, I can't make you guys do anything, but you seem to have real chemistry that would translate into some pretty awesome music."

Yeah, there was a reason for that chemistry...

"Just think about it," Ethan insisted.

"Sure," Kaylee finally said after several heavy minutes of silence.

But Gabe still knew her well enough to read that cue, and she'd reached her max for helping Gabe or anyone associated with him.

It wasn't going to happen.

# Chapter Five

It wasn't going to happen.

"I can't believe you," I say unevenly, thanks to the teeth I'm clenching so that I don't scream like a feral hyena.

"Kaylee, it would be a big help."

"Gabe, I would rather give you my left kidney."

"You're B positive, so you know that's not going to help me when I'm A negative."

"Exactly! That should tell you how much I don't want to rent my home to all of you. I would rather undergo surgery to have my kidney removed for no good reason." Oy, there goes what remained of my composure.

Who am I kidding? My composure died a very graphic death the day Gabe waltzed back into my life.

Gabe leans against my kitchen counter, and my chest constricts at how natural—how right—the action appears even though today only marks our second practice. His scruffy face wrinkles in confusion. "Why the left kidney?"

"What?"

"You said the left kidney. Why the left kidney?"

"Because I am always right, so I'm not going to give you my right kidney."

Gabe snorts. "That was terrible."

I open my mouth to respond with, *Well, so are you!* but I bite my tongue instead to keep the comment to myself. I can think it, but I won't say it.

Usually.

And ouch!

My tongue starts to throb. In order to hide the tears filling my eyes, I turn away from Gabe to rinse the coffee mug of pumpkin spice deliciousness that I had been blissfully sipping from before I opened the door to find Gabe on the other side. When was the last time Gabe *wasn't* on the other side of the door? Oh, days of bliss, how I miss you.

I can feel Gabe studying me like he's aware I was about to *Zing!* him. He wisely doesn't comment.

Oh, my tongue hurts so much. I blink like a cartoon character who's fluttering their eyelashes in order to seduce some fool.

"I know it's a lot to ask," Gabe starts.

"Yo sink?" I say with my deformed tongue that still feels too large for my mouth.

"But it would help Summer and Natalya a lot. They uprooted their entire lives for this band." He speaks over the sound of running water that I may be leaving on longer than necessary.

"Then you do something." I don't even look at him as I rinse the mug for the twelfth time. Why did I open the door? The first rule in *The Handbook for Single Ladies Living Alone* is don't open the door.

By the way, not a real book. At least I don't think it is. But don't you think it should be?

"I would if I could, Kaylee."

I grind my teeth together and turn the faucet off.

"It would mean a lot to me," he says softly.

Tears fill my eyes again, but it's not from my self-inflicted tongue injury. I turn on him in a red-colored rage. No lyrics accompany the fight song filling my head, but the harsh, angry notes all but consume me. "Seriously? That's what you're going to say to me? After everything that's happened between us, why am I doing you all the favors?"

"You're right. I'm sorry. I shouldn't have said that." He starts walking backward. "My guitar is still in my car, so I'll be right back."

"Dude, I am not finished, so stop right there."

Gabe halts his backward retreat.

"At the risk of sounding like I think everything is about me, this *was* supposed to be about me. It was supposed to help *me*. Not you. Me! Your original offer to join the band was because you wanted to help me. But then in less time than Taylor Swift claimed it took to be dumped in a phone call, it went to being about *you* and helping *you* out. Then I get suckered into letting the band practice here until a rehearsal space can be found. Now you not only want me to let Natalya and Summer move into my home but also consider my home our permanent rehearsal space? What's next? Do you want me to become a Justice of the Peace and marry you to your new girlfriend?"

Gabe flinches, and panic flashes through his eyes. If The Day That Shall Not Be Named taught me anything, it was to recognize Gabe's Warning Signs without any shadow of a doubt.

He's hiding something.

But whatever he's hiding flashes in and out of his eyes in seventeen seconds (Taylor Swift taught me to count these things) before a dark look crosses his face. He opens his mouth.

"Hey! I wanted to see if I could borrow that cookbook with the good cauliflower pizza recipe. I want to convince Miles to make it—" Izze says as she walks into the kitchen. Upon sighting Gabe and me fully prepared to go ten rounds in a boxing ring, she stomps right up to him. "What's going on?"

Gabe glares at me over Izze's head. "Can you call off your watchdog?"

"What did you just say to me?" Izze questions with a growl. I know this sounds crazy, but I think she's taller. Like rage has made her taller.

It's unnerving.

"I didn't say it to you, Izze. Can you back off and let us handle this?"

I jump between them, clamping a hand on each of their shoulders to keep them apart. "Guys, take a breath."

Izze's eyes slide shut, and I can see her lips moving as she counts to ten an indefinite number of times. Releasing a deep breath, she looks at me. "What would you like me to do?"

"Do you want to hang out for our practice?" I suggest because I don't want to deal with Gabe's mouth any more than I want to clean up the blood if I let Izze kill him. She would tear him to pieces, and then I'd have to deal with my best friend being brought up on homicide charges.

She takes a deep breath and nods. "Sure," she says through gritted teeth.

"Okay. Why don't you go into the living room? After practice I'll help you find that recipe."

"Awesome. Thank you." She gives Gabe another withering stare and then walks through the arched doorway that leads to the living room.

Gabe tries again. "Kaylee—"

I hold up my other hand, trying not to think about the fact that my left hand is still clutching his muscular shoulder—another thing that feels way too familiar. "No," I say before dropping both of my hands and joining Izze in the living room.

"So, Summer told me about her request," Izze says from where she sits on the couch, covered in a dozen or so cookbooks an hour after practice has ended.

"Oh, yeah?" I grab one more cookbook from the bookshelf behind the couch to add to the pile of ten that I have going on the floor next to my feet. "I think it's in one of these."

"I need to stop buying you cookbooks." Izze studies a picture of homemade ravioli. "Why is the filling green?"

I glance at the open cookbook she's holding up for me to see over the back of the couch. "It's kale."

She wrinkles her nose. "Ravioli should be stuffed with cheese. Or cheese and spinach. Kale is too bitter for ravioli."

"I actually agree with you on that point." I load my pile of books into my arms.

"So what do you think about it?" She takes a sip of the iced coffee she had brought with her.

"About what?" I ask, pretending I don't know.

"Yeah, I know you know what I'm talking about, so out with it."

"There's nothing to think. I told Gabe no." I sit on the couch next to her, balancing the pile of cookbooks in my lap.

"Ah. That's what you were arguing about earlier."

"Yup." I sip the iced coffee she picked up for me.

"I'm going to say something that may shock you."

"You're giving up coffee after today?"

"As long as there's breath in my lungs, I will never give up coffee," Izze says, lightly shaking the plastic cup in her hand. "I think you might want to reconsider Summer's idea."

I stare at her. "Who are you and what have you done with my best friend?"

Izze leans back, disrupting the precarious balance of cookbooks scattered on top of her. One crashes to the floor, but Izze holds my gaze.

My eyes narrow. "Did he get to you?"

"No!" She rolls her eyes. "Gabe's less-than-stellar persona has nothing to do with my opinion. But Kaylee, I hate that you're here alone. I hate it! I'm seriously only thinking about you."

"I'm fine," I say defensively.

"I know. That's what you keep saying, but first I moved out, then Apryl and Courtney moved out. We all still see each other, but we have to be more purposeful about our hanging out time."

"Yeah, but that's life." I shrug even though I've been wallowing in these exact feelings for a long time. But I will not make my friends feel bad about embracing the new seasons of life that God has given them. Nope. Not happening.

"But that doesn't mean it's not lonely. I know that you have a hard time making friends, Kaylee. I know it's like your brain freezes and every interaction feels awkward until you're finally comfortable around that person. I know that shy side of you comes out with a vengeance, and by vengeance, I mean that side makes you want to run and hide or stay in your room for days at a time so you don't have to deal with the emotionally exhausting task of actually talking to someone new." She puts her arm around me in a sideways hug. "I know how hard it is for you, but you are amazing. You are worth getting to know."

Unexpected tears fill my eyes. Izze, Apryl, and Courtney are my people. Around them, I could be the most extroverted person in the world. But without them...that's when I feel like an incoherent fool who can barely string together a sentence. They're some of the few people who see and understand my social anxiety. And in this moment, it's nice to know that I'm not as forgotten as I thought I was.

Izze squeezes my shoulder. "I just don't want you to feel like you're alone. And I don't want you to be alone, literally. But I really, really don't want you to feel like you're forgotten. I know that feeling. It's not a good feeling. Maybe Natalya and Summer will become good friends. Maybe they won't—in which case I give you full permission to say, 'I told you thusly.'"

I laugh. "I'll think about it."

"And pray about it," Izze encourages.

"Yeah." Condemning guilt grips me. Several faces flash before my mind's eye, but instead of causing my blood to boil, I feel ashamed. Some Christian I've been. "I guess I haven't been good about giving these things to God the way that I should have been."

She shrugs. "Isn't that something we all struggle with? You know I've had my own difficulties in this area, but He's always patiently waiting for us, and then He lovingly guides us. That voice that tells you how much you suck as a Christian isn't from Him. Your position with Him hasn't changed. I know that when I believe that lie, it makes it hard for me to approach Him."

"It does," I say, laying my head back against the couch cushion as the words of truth roll over me, soothing a place in my soul that I hadn't realized was hurting. "Your age has made you wise."

"Girl, you're two weeks older than me."

"Shush. Just take the hit."

It's moving day.

Yeah, I decided to listen to Izze's advice last week. Miles helped me get a specialized six-month rental agreement set up for Summer and Natalya and a separate rental agreement for the rehearsal space. Now my house is a beehive of activity as Gabe, Ethan, Drake, and Miles move the heavy stuff while Izze and I help Natalya and Summer with the lighter stuff.

Despite the nudge I got as I prayed, I'm all sorts of conflicted about this day. Unfortunately, it's too late to follow through with my cowardly feelings at this point.

Which is why I spent last night hyperventilating into a paper bag to the beat of "Staying Alive."

Summer—who I've learned is as extroverted as God makes a

person—nudges me in the shoulder with her own. "Thanks again, Kaylee. I know this was a lot to ask."

Girl, you have no idea.

I meet Gabe's eyes for a brief second as he helps carry a six-drawer dresser up the stairs.

No idea at all.

"You're welcome," I respond with a rasp in my voice that they all ignore with the kind of mercy that comes from pretend distraction.

Natalya sets a large box down on the coffee table and grabs her water bottle. "Yes, thank you." She offers me one of her rare, genuine smiles.

I respond with one of my own. Maybe this will work out. Maybe we will become friends. Maybe I heard God correctly this time.

Gabe comes back down the stairs, laughing at something Miles is saying.

And maybe I'll wake up tomorrow with no lingering feelings for Gabe. Better yet, maybe those memories will be gone.

Or maybe I'm setting myself up for another emotional smackdown of betrayal.

Is it bad to pray for a head injury that results in memory loss? Tell me I'm not the only one who has done that.

Natalya frowns as she looks at something on the mantel over the fireplace. "What's that?"

Summer squints. "Is that...a dragon?"

Heat singes my cheeks. Man, I thought I had gotten all Tolkien objects safely behind my bedroom door. So much for making new friends. "Um, yeah. Smaug. He's actually the oldest firedrake—"

"I read the books once," Izze interjects. "While they're good, I'm not reading them again any time soon, so stop trying to convince me."

"You watched the movies with Miles," I rush forward and grab Smaug from the mantel. I should have known he'd try to ruin me. It's in his nature.

"And he would tell you that he won't watch them with me again because I went to *great* lengths to name each weird creature, elf, and orc. And there was dialogue. Oh, there was dialogue."

"There's already dialogue in the movie," I point out.

Izze crosses her arms, looking smug. "Not my dialogue."

"What about *Beren and Luthien?*" I suggest. "It's a love story."

Izze lets out an exasperated sigh. "I will think about it."

"Wow," Summer says with a grin. "Someone is a little obsessed with Tolkien."

I shrug. "What can I say? I'm weird."

Summer grins. "It's okay. I like weird. I come from a long line of weird people."

Izze swipes Smaug from me and studies it. "I don't remember this one. Is it new?"

"No. I don't remember buying another one." I study the wooden figure. This wasn't part of my collection. The dragon gives the appearance of being rough because of the many facets from a carving knife, but it's been lightly sanded and painted. "It looks like someone carved it by hand."

"Buying stuff in your sleep from the Home Shopping Network again?" Izze jokes.

"That was you, Izze."

"I hardly think ordering my morning usual through an app counts as sleep shopping—a dangerous and expensive condition."

"I'm sure Miles would agree with that last part," I shoot back as I continue to study the mystery present.

Summer snorts. "Oh, snap!"

Natalya steps beside me and studies the wooden figure. "Whoever made this piece cares a great deal," she says, her lyrical tone dipping into a near-whisper.

I frown in confusion. "I suppose most craftsmen care about their pieces."

She runs her thumb over Smaug's eyes. "I'm told they care more for the meaning behind the piece."

Natalya's words pierce my heart. "Like a song," I mutter.

She meets my eyes, and a bizarre understanding passes between us. "Yes, like a song," she finally says.

# Chapter Six

Ithink Summer's getting ready to smoke me out of my foxhole, also known as my bedroom.

It's been a week since they moved into my house.

Yes, my house. Back off. Saying "our house" feels weird, so I'm retaining emotional ownership of the estate. Besides, I barely know these freaks. For all I know, they'll turn out to be like Eddie from *Friends*. One day, I'll wake up to find them watching me while I sleep and jars of what I hope are dehydrated fruits will fill my cupboards.

Is it excessive to get a deadbolt and a security system for a bedroom?

Thus far, I've managed to achieve only minimal contact with Natalya and Summer. Yeah, yeah. Don't say it. I know I agreed to letting them move in because I was lonely and thought we could be friends. Again, and I say this with love, back off. I'm an introvert through and through. My people are walking—not talking, if you catch my drift—contradictions when it comes to interacting with other people.

I'm curled into a ball on my daybed in the furthest corner of my room, reading my favorite, leather-bound copy of *The Hobbit* for the sixty-fourth time (and yes, I count). I'm even reading with a flashlight so that maybe they'll see the lack of light under my bedroom door and assume I'm asleep. The actual time of the day (ahem, two o'clock in the afternoon) is irrelevant.

Someone stops outside my door.

I tense, expecting a knock and Summer's bright voice asking

if I'd like to watch a movie or work on a song or show her where the laundry detergent is.

But only silence greets me. This makes me both happy and sad. Like I said, I'm a walking contradiction.

The song "Happy When I'm Sad" from the Jonas Brothers' comeback album fills my senses, and Gabe's face flashes before my mind's eye. Another reason why I feel happy and sad all the time.

I stifle a growl. If only one could gorge out their mind's eye. Sorry for the graphic imagery, but I'm sick of thinking, seeing, or hearing about *anything* pertaining to Gabe Sanders.

A smell wafts past the fuzzy blanket that's wrapped around my head and shoulders. What is that? It reminds me of Izze's attempt at pancakes a couple months ago.

I sniff again. Close... It smells like a burning toaster. The kind for bread, not the Cylon kind in that *Battlestar Galactica* show (and this is the part where Miles interjects that it's the original series, because that somehow makes a difference) that Miles makes Izze and me watch whenever I go to their house. Miles seems to think that I'm his ally when it comes to introducing Izze to the nerdier things in life because I have an excessive crush on Samwise Gamgee.

Unfortunately for Miles, my nerdiness starts and ends with Tolkien.

So I started inviting them over here so that I have control of the remote. But now I'm starting to wonder if the mandatory *Battlestar Galactica* viewing was a ploy concocted by my dear friends. Miles gets a night off from cooking, and Izze...well, Izze doesn't melt any more kitchen appliances.

The smell gets stronger, and I finally notice the discolored haze coming through the bottom of my door.

Throwing the book and blankets onto my bed, I drop to the floor and army crawl to the door. My heart pounds frantically, and I'm trying to remember all the instructions the visiting firemen told my third-grade glass to do in the event of a fire.

I'm almost to the door when I see it: a small hose that's been jammed under the door.

She is literally smoking me out of my room! Who on earth does that? Not even Izze is that crazy.

I stand up as quietly as possible and tiptoe to the door before I whip it open. "Are you insane?"

Summer looks at me from where she's lying on her stomach next to plates, pans, and pots filled with...something. I'm not sure what it is. It's all burnt beyond a crisp. Most of the unidentified food (please only be food!) has crumbled into piles of ash with some lumps. An empty toaster—unplugged and smoking—sits behind her.

Appetizing, yes?

The smell hits me full force, and I start to violently gag. Time to resort to pulling the neck of my shirt over my nose, not that it will help much against a smell you can feel in the back of your eyes.

You know, because of the smoke.

"For crying out loud! What is that?" I yell.

With her right hand, Summer turns off the small fan positioned behind the World's Worst Banquet that had been blowing the smell toward my bedroom door. With the other hand, she drops the aforementioned hose that she had been holding against a small machine.

Summer swings her legs around and sits up, grinning wickedly. "It worked!"

"Is that a fog machine?" I ask incredulously.

"Yup. We use some of these smaller machines for gigs occasionally."

"What? Seriously? This is...this is unbelievable," I shout.

"Oh, I assure you it's not. I've done much weirder things." Summer maintains that eerie calm that comes from being an undiagnosed, pathological killer.

I'm beginning to genuinely fear for my life. And yet I've got to know...

"What is that?" I ask, gesturing to the piles of ash.

"Oh, that? Toast."

"Toast?" That does not smell like any toast I've burned.

"Different kinds of bread." She points to the remains of each bread as she names them. "Pumpernickel. Rye. Sourdough. Wheat. Amish Friendship Bread. My mom will not be happy about that one going to waste, so don't rat me out if you ever meet her. And I'm actually not sure what this one is...maybe Whole Grain?"

"You're worse than Eddie," I mutter.

"Nah, I would never use a mannequin head as a centerpiece. I have made dozens of paper mâché faces to use as centerpieces, but I don't consider that to be the same thing," Summer states matter-of-factly.

"I...What...How..." I'm struck by the absurdity of this ridiculous moment, and I start to giggle. Summer wiggles her eyebrows and starts to laugh as well. Before I know it, I am on my knees and smacking the floor like it's responsible for the lack of breath that laughter has stolen from me.

I hear thumping behind me and look up to see Natalya's eyes widen.

"Whoa, where's the fire?" Summer says with a straight face, causing me to collapse into hysterics all over again.

Natalya shakes her head, causing her brownish-black hair to swish like a shampoo commercial. "I don't understand what's happening here."

"That's probably for the best," I say in between more giggles.

"Okay," Natalya says slowly. "I was about to get something to eat. Do you guys want anything?"

"How about toast?" I quip, and Summer snorts.

Natalya finally notices the burnt remains on the floor and smiles in understanding. "Ah, she finally resorted to that trick. She did the same thing to me when we became roommates in Boston."

"So this psychotic behavior is normal for her?" I ask while Summer just laughs.

"Oh, definitely. Remind me to tell you about the time she took a page out of Dwight Schrute's playbook and staged an apartment fire."

"I told you," Summer says, verifying Natalya's story with a grin. "This is nothing on the weirdness scale."

"Yeah, but the Ursula laugh isn't helping your case," I say.

"Ursula? Finally! I've been trying to nail her laugh for almost a year." Summer does a vigorous fist pump of victory.

A happy feeling warms my heart as Natalya helps me stand up.

Weird? Yes.

A little bit of Eddie crazy? Affirmative!

But I like them. I genuinely like them, and I want them to like me. And it's going to be a lot harder to keep an emotional distance from them because of their association with a certain individual now that I know I like them, questionable associations aside.

Despite the warnings that only I can hear, my heart opens a little more to these new friends as we clean up the toast ashes and make memories together.

But the pessimistic side of me shakes her head, leans back, and waits for the other shoe to drop.

Gabe studied the three women at the end of band practice with a frown. They seemed to have turned into laughing, loving, long-term friends overnight. It should be a good thing. They were all getting along now.

But it was...

Confusing. Disconcerting. Alarming. Strange. Look it up in a thesaurus, and Gabe was probably feeling it.

Two very different worlds had merged into one, and Gabe wasn't sure how he felt about it. He guessed that was probably something he should have figured out before he set all of them on this course, but Gabe wasn't that emotionally responsible.

"Looks like we're all finally getting along, right?" Ethan said beside him.

"Why did you say it like a question?"

Ethan raised his eyebrows at Gabe. "Why don't you tell me?"

"Be quiet, man."

"I'm just saying—"

"I really don't want to hear it again, Ethan." Gabe slipped out of his guitar strap and deposited the instrument in its case. "We're fine," he added as he closed the case and secured the clasps.

Ethan gave him a look that Gabe interpreted all too well before moving past Gabe and his brooding attitude.

"Awesome job," Ethan proclaimed to the group. "You guys sound like you've been together for years, not a few measly weeks. I'm very impressed. And Kaylee, you are incredibly talented."

Gabe tried not to notice the way Kaylee beamed from Ethan's praise. His hand tightened into a fist. Wonderful. Now he was acting like a jealous idiot, and he had no right to act like that. Well, maybe the idiot part.

"Is that it for today?" Summer asked. "Because Natalya and I need to go to the store."

"We can go some other time if we're not done. It doesn't need to be right now," Natalya said as she glanced at Gabe.

"No, we're done for today," Gabe said with only a little bit of an attitude. Really. Barely measurable on an Attitude Scale, not to be confused with a scale that measures altitude because why would he be measuring altitude at this moment?

Gabe rubbed the back of his neck. Maybe some water would clear his rambling thoughts.

Drake gave him a weird look, but Gabe ignored him and ducked into the kitchen for that water. He grabbed a cup from the drying rack by the sink, filled it with tap water, and took a big gulp.

He heard the door close, presumably from Summer and Natalya's departure, but he could still hear Drake and Ethan yammering with Kaylee. On and on and on.

*Take the hint, fellas.*

The water wasn't working. He refilled his glass and guzzled some more.

Kaylee laughed, and the sound made him want to punch the wall.

*Snap out of it!* Gabe set the glass down and gripped the counter. Then he turned the faucet on again and stuck his face under the icy cold spray. One. Two. Three. He turned the stream of water off and wiped the moisture from his face. Grabbing the blue owl cloth hanging from the knob of the cupboard under the sink, he patted his face dry.

Kaylee's lilting laughter floated to his ears once again.

And something inside of Gabe snapped.

Rolling up the damp sleeves of his long-sleeve button down shirt, Gabe walked back into the living room. "What's up, guys?"

Kaylee stopped laughing, sensing the change in Gabe before

the guys. Drake continued to laugh at whatever had been said before Gabe walked into the room. Ethan launched a backhanded whack into Drake's gut.

Ethan and Drake eyed him. Kaylee started to chew on her lip, the nervous habit she'd developed after years of familial confrontation. The underlying shift in the tempo grew in anticipation of a dramatic climax even though they waited in eerie silence.

"What's going on, man?" Drake asked. Probably thought he was being kind and helpful. In reality, he was just being annoying.

"Would you guys mind leaving now? I need to talk to Kaylee. Privately," he added for good measure.

Drake looked at Kaylee, silently asking with his stupid eyes if she wanted them to go.

He wouldn't punch Drake. He wouldn't punch Drake. He wouldn't punch Drake.

Gabe's fist tightened, and his right arm burned from the tension.

His reflexes were about to make him a liar.

Kaylee gave a single nod in response to Drake's question.

Drake shot daggers with his eyes as he stalked out of the room. Ethan paused next to him. "This wasn't what I had in mind, Gabe. I know you need to talk, but you should take a breath. Cool down."

Gabe kept his eyes on Kaylee, refusing to even acknowledge Ethan's well-meaning advice with anything more than a flick of his eyes, telling him to get lost.

Kaylee waited with pursed lips, arms crossed over her torso, nostrils flaring in a rage he'd only experienced a handful of times in his life.

The engine of Ethan's truck roared to life, like an announcer yelling, "And they're off!"

"What is wrong with you?" Gabe growled.

"You've got to be kidding me," Kaylee said at the same time.

"No, I'm really not. Do you think it's at all professional to be flirting with every guy in the band?"

Her eyes flashed. "Not every guy."

Oh, good sucker punch. "Nice, Kaylee. Real nice."

"About as nice as you accusing me of flirting with your friends when I wasn't. And even if I was, what's it to you?"

"I don't want to see the band that I've thrown everything into for years break apart because of a fling." That almost happened once, and once was enough.

"A fling? A fling!" Kaylee stomped her foot in rage. "I don't know how to fling anything except pizza dough. I can't believe you would insinuate something so vile about me, you...you... I can't think of an insult that conveys just how disgusted I am with you!"

Gabe let out a shaky breath and ran his hands through his hair, gripping the damp, short ends and pulling them—hard. This conversation had turned into an out-of-control wildfire. "I'm sorry. That was...that was inappropriate."

"Inappropriate doesn't even begin to describe it, you deranged clod."

Time to diffuse the situation with some poorly timed humor. "Deranged clod. I like it."

"Shut up, Gabe. Don't try to crack a joke and pretend that you didn't just call me a harlot."

"I can promise that I have never used that word in my life."

"Just because you may choose that lifestyle—"

"Whoa, whoa, whoa!" Gabe interjected, staring at Kaylee with a mouth that hung open wider than one of those singing bass fish. That old, not-so-buried shame awakened within him. "What makes you think I would do that?"

"You were clearly surrounded by beautiful women in Boston, and you immediately accused me of that. Must mean you have some experience in the area."

"No!" Gabe yelled.

*I think you're forgetting to add something*, that nefarious voice in his head whispered.

"No," Gabe growled in a desperate attempt to shut up both voices. "I don't. What kind of backward logic is that?"

"It's really good logic despite the fact that nothing about this conversation has been logical." Then Kaylee covered her face with her hands, and her muffled sobs tore through him.

He squeezed his eyes shut. What had he done? What did he do now?

Kaylee had always been able to calm him down, talk sense into him, support him, and encourage him. Instead of acting like a complete moron in these situations when he would often say something he would regret, Gabe had cherished the way Kaylee used to nudge him toward God.

Before...

Before Gabe had made irreversible choices.

Before Gabe abandoned Kaylee.

Before Gabe had given up on love.

Before Gabe discovered that God's love—and the way He wanted people to love each other—was a joke.

And before Gabe had disqualified himself from any type of help or grace from a holy God.

That was before. This was now. And Gabe didn't have any of those things now. Not God. Not Kaylee. Not love.

But when Kaylee cried, he still needed to do something. It might as well be programmed into his DNA.

Crossing the room in four long strides that almost resulted in him tripping over forgotten cables and amps, Gabe stopped in front of Kaylee. Without stopping to think about it, he took her in his arms, wrapping them around her, enfolding her into his embrace. She stiffened but didn't resist the paltry comfort he offered after being a terrific jerk.

He didn't know how long he held her. Her sobs ebbed and flowed. At one point, she pounded her fist into his chest, but she didn't push him away. But now they were standing there in silence. Kaylee breathed normally, and Gabe had rested his chin against the top of her head.

"I'm sorry," he murmured near her ear, gently stroking her upper arms with his thumbs as the intoxicating scent of her fruity shampoo wafted through his senses, drawing him back to the past.

Kaylee pushed away from him, jarring him from the familiar feeling of holding her in his arms again.

Oh, man. He really was playing a dangerous game. Gabe let out a ragged breath.

"I'm sorry," Gabe said again. "My first instinct is to hold you when you're hurting."

Kaylee studied him with watery, emerald eyes. She shoved a

lock of red hair behind her left ear. "What about when you're the one who hurt me?"

Gulp. "Unfortunately, even then."

She snickered sadly. "Yeah, that is unfortunate."

If only it had felt unfortunate. Honestly, it felt wonderful, and that was a problem.

"Gabe, look. Your personal life is your business. I'm sorry for being all accusatory. But my personal life is also my business. So I'll date who I want to date."

Gabe ground his teeth together and nodded.

"But for the record, I don't have any interest in Drake or Ethan. They're good guys, and I enjoy joking around with them and working with them, but that's it. It's kind of like having two new brothers, which is nice since I'm not close to Jake."

Gabe wished the earth would swallow him whole right now. He deserved it. "Yeah, I bet. I'm also sorry for what I said—"

"And," Kaylee interjected before he could finish, "Drake was talking you up. He told me that story about the bunny song."

Gabe's face heated. Oh, *that*. "I wish he wouldn't make a big deal out of it."

"It was a big deal to the bride's daughter. You wrote and sang a song specifically for her favorite bunny." Kaylee gave him a small smile and shrugged. "It was sweet."

Gabe might as well be buried under six feet of guilt thanks to this unexpected turn in the conversation. He sighed. "I'm sorry, Kaylee. I shouldn't have started this whole ridiculous argument."

"Yeah, I agree with you," Kaylee said with a wry smile.

Gabe let out an unamused chuckle. "I'll apologize to Drake as well."

"That would probably be in your best interest."

Gabe winced. "He'll probably put me in a headlock."

"You would deserve it." Kaylee shifted, causing the floorboards to creak underneath her.

"Yeah...yeah." Gabe needed to wrap up this conversation before he put his big foot in his foolish mouth again. "I'll see you tomorrow."

"I'll see you guys tomorrow," Kaylee echoed and turned to escape into the kitchen much like Gabe had earlier.

"Kaylee," Gabe called.

She turned and raised her eyebrows.

"I'm really sorry, but I also need you to know that my life hasn't been a string of one-night stands since we broke up."

She took a step back. "It's none of my business, Gabe."

"Maybe not, but I need you to know. That's not me."

Anymore...

*You're leaving out some details there, Romeo,* the villainous voice said.

Kaylee stared at him. "Gabe, you don't need to lie to spare my feelings. I'm a big girl. I can take it. Even I've had a few blind dates."

Gabe winced again. That previously unknown detail felt like a knife to the gut.

She studied him when he didn't say anything else.

"I'm not lying, Kaylee," Gabe said, keeping his voice even. The last thing they needed was for this conversation to blow up again. "I've dated one woman since we broke up. I...we...It was a mistake, and I regret it."

*I love how everything you're saying is technically true,* Evil Voice said. *Just with massive amounts of redacted details so that it paints you in the best possible light. Bravo! We wouldn't want someone so pure to know of your sinful past.*

"I don't understand. What are you saying?"

Gabe's pulse leaped. He'd said too much. To avoid answering her, he looked at the ceiling that had seen more than its fair share of water damage, judging by all the stains.

"Are you saying that you...?" Her question trailed off, but Gabe knew what she was asking—did he and this mystery woman go too far?

They did. Once. And it was one of the mistakes he'd regretted most. Especially because if he hadn't run away from his problems, too ashamed and afraid to ask for help, then the mistake never would have happened. But it did, and Gabe had to live with that additional knowledge for the rest of his life.

"It was a mistake," he finally choked out. "It was a relationship I never should have been in, and I regret it every single day." Gabe couldn't bear to look at Kaylee, to see the disgust written on her face. "But this isn't the point I was trying to make."

"Wow. Okay, then what?" Her strangled tone brought his eyes

to hers. "Why is it so important for me to know these delight-ful details if this isn't related to whatever point you're trying to make? Just spit it out already." Frustration reddened her cheeks.

"I don't believe in love. It's...it's actually the reason I couldn't go through with marrying you," Gabe blurted out.

His confession—a confession that wasn't even close to the full story—hung in the air between them. Clearly stunned and confused, Kaylee threw her hand against the arched doorway to steady herself as she rapidly blinked back tears.

He could *not* hug her again. He couldn't. He'd do something stupid. Again.

Which left only one thing for Gabe to do: walk away.

At least he was consistent.

# Chapter Seven

Courtney stands on the other side of my front door. "I have been knocking for fifteen minutes."

"It's been five."

She leans back into her "lawyer" pose. "So you did hear me."

Drat. I step to the side so she can come through the doorway. "Why did you even bother knocking? You have a key."

"Other people live here now. I thought it might be weird if I just barged through the front door," she says while drawing a large rectangle with her index finger before stepping across the threshold.

"No, what's weird is you knocking. That's weird."

Courtney shrugs. "It's all weird and different, but that's what happens when stuff changes."

"And whose fault is that?"

"God's?"

I sigh. "I don't remember being this annoying when *you* were the one going through stuff."

Courtney laughs. "So why didn't you open the door?"

"I thought it might be Gabe, and I didn't want to deal with him at the moment," I say without thinking.

"Why?" Courtney asks as she sits on the couch that's been pushed to the side in preparation for band practice later today.

Remember that non-existent handbook, *The Handbook for Single Ladies Living Alone*? I need to heed its imaginary wisdom.

It's not that I don't love my besties, but I don't want to talk to them about Gabe's latest emotional air raid on my fragile existence. I haven't even begun to process how I feel about it, so forget trying to translate what I'm feeling into actual words for other people to understand.

"Why are you here?" I shoot back at her.

She raises an eyebrow and purses her lips. "Changing the subject, eh? I'll allow it."

"There's no subject to change, Court. We used to be a couple; we aren't anymore. End of story." I bite my lower lip as I sit beside her. And I so don't want to rehash this topic—again.

"I think there's more to the story behind why you want to rip his face off." She leans back on the couch.

"I don't want to rip his face off." I want to punch it. There's a difference.

"That's not what Izze says."

I throw my hands up. "Izze isn't one to talk."

"Which means she knows what she's talking about," Courtney points out.

"I ask again, why are you here?"

"Okay, all kidding aside, you know I'm here for you, right?" She scoots closer to me and gives me a brief, meaningful hug. "We are all here for you whenever this feels too hard or painful."

My eyelids slide closed, and I slowly exhale before opening them again. "I know. Thank you," I say, trying to infuse more thankfulness into my tone than I feel at the moment. Because I am thankful. I just don't want to talk about it anymore.

She smiles in a weird, hesitant way that is very unlike her. It's actually a little creepy. "That is first and foremost what I came to say."

"And the next part is?"

"Izze told me how good you guys are."

"Izze's been talking an awful lot," I mumble.

Courtney flicks my comment away with a wave of her hand. "No more than usual. So in light of this information, I've got a huge favor to ask of you. And I'm prepared to grovel if necessary."

"No. No, no, no." I jump up from the couch and spin to face her. "It's not happening."

She doesn't even bother to stand up. Her confidence in her ability to sway me with undeniable logic both annoys and fascinates me. "Please! It would be awesome."

"I've got a soundtrack ready for you. That's good enough," I retort. The singer in me howls in rage, but I keep my mouth clamped shut.

"Yes, it is. I'm not being snobby. But." She holds up one ruby-red, perfectly manicured finger when I open my mouth for further protest. "It would help you guys even more than it would help me."

"But I'm already writing you a song," I remind her. Okay, so I'm only writing song lyrics, but I'll still sing this song acapella. That's enough. "Remember? You begged and begged me to write a song and sing it at your wedding reception when you got engaged. This has been the plan for over a year."

"I know. I still want you to sing the song...I just—" She presses her lips together.

"You what?" I ask, barely holding my growl in check.

"I just remember how uncomfortable you were with the idea of singing with zero musical accompaniment. I thought you might find singing with *your*"—Oh, I *so* love her emphasis!—"bandmates to be more preferable," she explains.

I glare at her, letting the controlled rage play on my face so she can see exactly what I think of her logic.

"Please?" she squeaks.

"Courtney, your wedding is in less than two weeks. For all I know, we're already booked. In which case, I would still be performing without them."

"Then it's no harm, no foul. But can you ask—"

I cut her off with the slice of my hand through the air, just like butter. "No."

Now Courtney stands up, seeing she might have her work cut out for her. "I know it's a lot to ask, but it would give you guys a low-pressure gig. No stress."

I snort in derision. "You've obviously never borne your soul in front of an audience for the sake of performance if you think there's no stress involved."

Courtney holds up both hands in surrender. "Okay, ouch."

"Sorry," I sigh.

"No, I've never done what you're doing, but I bet it's less stress than if you were performing in front of strangers that don't care about you and wouldn't hesitate to scream 'Boo!' while throwing rotten veggies at you."

"Oh, well, when you put it like that," I say sarcastically.

"Please, Kaylee." She drops to her knees and clasps both hands in front of her face. "I told you I was prepared to beg."

"So I see." I frown. "Are you whimpering?"

"Too much?"

"You sound like a possessed squeaky toy."

Courtney's eyebrows shoot up. "Tell me how you really feel."

"I've never watched those *Chucky* horror movies—for obvious reasons—but I feel like I have now." Hey, she asked for it.

"Okay," she draws out the word while she stands up and absent-mindedly brushes the non-existent dirt from her knees. "Please, Kaylee. I'm asking you as a friend."

"Oh, don't use *Friends* stuff on me," I growl with a smile.

"Could you *be* any more of a friend?" She says with that special emphasis.

I roll my eyes. "Fine—"

"Yay!"

"—but I'm making no promises. Stay and watch, and you can bring it up to everyone after practice. But you may even decide that you don't like our style." That's what I'm praying for. *Please, God! Just this once...*

"In that case, I had better go see if you have anything rotten in your fridge," Courtney calls over her shoulder as she runs into the kitchen.

The final strains of "God Gave Me You" linger thanks to Natalya's violin. Courtney wipes at the corners of her eyes, and I know all hope is lost. We will be playing at her wedding.

"That was amazing!" Courtney exclaims to the room at large. "Gabe and Kaylee sing so beautifully together. And...Natalya, right? You are so talented! The raw emotion you put into the violin is amazing."

I study the floor as Courtney continues to praise Natalya. I'm trying not to feel too intimidated, but Natalya is beautiful, sings beautifully, and plays the violin beautifully. Basically, "beautiful" can be used to describe everything pertaining to her.

There comes that lip chew toy again. Maybe I should invest in an adult binky if I'm going to be this much of a baby.

Natalya and I are finally starting to make real strides in the friendship department. Yesterday, we watched three episodes of *The Office* together, and she shared her almond milk ice cream with me. Do you know how big of a deal that is in girl world? You only share yummy, but relatively healthy treats with people you care about. Getting all bitter and overemotional won't help me get more friendship deliciousness. Metaphorically speaking, of course.

Though, I wouldn't turn down more of that cinnamon bun ice cream if she offers.

I just wish that logic was enough to actually beat that ugly green beast of jealousy into loyal submission, the kind where it fetches your slippers for you on a negative-thirty-degree morning.

Maybe I should invest in some slippers. My feet are always cold regardless of the temperature.

Courtney continues talking. "I know I've said this a bunch of times, but that was amazing."

Ethan smiles at her, and his eyes flicker to her left hand. Upon registering the giant ruby engagement ring, he schools his obvious disappointment into something more professional. "I agree. They are all incredibly talented. And I'm so thankful Kaylee is willing to put up with Gabe—"

"Come on, man," Gabe gripes as he locks his guitar case.

"—because she has really helped to define AY's sound."

"There goes Ethan getting all pretentious again," Drake jokes.

"Is that the band's name? Aye?" Courtney asks, looking around like she's hoping that's not true. "Like pirates?"

Summer nods with her signature wicked grin and mouths, *Oh, yeah!*

Gabe rolls his eyes. "All Yours."

Courtney rears back in her seat on the couch, coiled and ready to strike. "Excuse me?"

"The *name*," he sighs in irritation. "It's All Yours."

"Oh. That's, uh, pretty." A blush of ruby red blooms on Courtney's face. I try to cover my bark of laughter with a cough.

Courtney glares at me.

Okay, so I didn't try very hard.

"Who came up with that?" Courtney asks, trying to take the attention off of her blunder.

"Gabe." Natalya shoots Gabe a sweet smile.

The beast in my spirit roars. At this rate, I should just name the stinking thing. Fluffy, perhaps?

But Gabe doesn't acknowledge Natalya's adoring gaze. In fact, he's not acknowledging anyone.

He swallows, and normally this wouldn't be anything to write home about, but it's the *way* he swallows.

I realize that it's probably a little Jack the Ripper to study the way someone swallows. Oh, well.

Only someone who knows him well would notice the signs. Unfortunately, I know him really well. The deep inhale, the bobbing Adam's apple, and the muscle on the left side of his jaw that's twitching like it's attempting the Macarena give away his secret. Goodness, it's twitching almost as much as it did on The Day That Shall Not Be Named.

He's anxious.

Because he's got a secret.

"Wouldn't it be cool if you guys had a signature song by that name?" Courtney says. "I think I already know a song with that as a title."

My eyes narrow at Gabe as he intently gathers the sheet music from everyone. When he stops next to my music stand to collect my lyrics sheets, I snatch the papers before he can grab them. He holds out his hand for the papers, but I ignore him. Hey, if he can do it, then I can too.

I pretend to absentmindedly tap the papers against my open right hand. "Yeah, that's a cool idea. Why haven't you guys written a song like that before now?"

Summer shrugs and points with her drumstick. "Gabe said he's working on a song."

"Nice," Courtney says.

"It'd be nicer if he'd finish it," Ethan jabs good-naturedly.

I twist my head to look at Gabe, feigning ignorance. But I know. After his truth bomb the other night, this revelation is only ticking me off more. I can't believe I didn't figure it out before now.

That's our song. Our unfinished song. The one we started writing when he proposed.

My stupid, foolish stomach flutters like it thinks I should be flattered by this, not incensed.

"Really, Gabe? Really?" My words sound casual enough (although, there might be a bit of a bite to that second *really*), but Gabe hears the angry loud and clear. My death grip crinkles the sheets of music still clutched in my left hand.

"Kaylee," Gabe murmurs in a low voice, "not here."

"Maybe Kaylee could help you. She's already working on a song for my wedding. Maybe you guys could help each other?" Courtney suggests, but she pales when I swing my angry gaze her way. "Or not," she says quickly.

"I've already tried that," Ethan mumbles to her.

The others study everything but us, clearly not wanting to get involved in yet another round of drama between us.

This isn't going to work.

Relax, I'm not quitting. At least not yet. But this isn't working. I'm not a bickering, angry person by nature. Sarcastic and introverted? Obviously. But the overwhelming desire to start a brawl like I'm starring in a John Wayne film isn't one I'm accustomed to feeling, and frankly, I'm sick of it.

Especially because I hate Westerns.

For the thousandth time, I've forgiven him!

I really, really think that.

But that doesn't mean everything is resolved. Or better. Or anywhere remotely near good. So for the time being, I need to find a way to coexist with Gabe. I've only been with the band for a few weeks, but my heart is entangled with the idea of pursuing this forgotten dream of mine.

The fact that it's keeping me from having to sell vital organs only factors in a little.

Gabe may have delivered my dream courtesy of a fiery reunion that could make the Hallmark Channel close its doors in shame, but he won't be the one who destroys that dream. I will persist.

I meet Gabe's eyes, mash my lips closed, and nod. I won't push for answers.

For now.

"Well, moving past whatever awkward moment that was," Summer says. "What's next on the agenda?"

"Um, I have a favor to ask of you guys." Courtney glances at me, silently asking if this favor is still okay after my silent meltdown.

I nod my consent, then I unclench the teeth I'd been grinding in my fury, and my jaw screams in agony. Ow! Anger bubbles inside of me again.

I should get a snack. I probably have low blood sugar or something if I'm feeling this irrationally angry.

The group looks to Gabe who feigns enthusiasm as he agrees to Courtney's request on behalf of the band. I continue to stand there in my uncomfortable bubble. Jealous? I bet you're jealous. It's so much fun in here. Not at all suffocating. The sheet music that I'm still clutching wrinkles in my hand. I thrust it toward Gabe.

"Okay," Ethan says enthusiastically after checking the band's schedule on his iPad. "It's settled. We are officially booked for your wedding."

"Yay!" Courtney exclaims.

Gabe notices the papers and grabs them from my hand. They slice the tip of my ring finger, but Gabe has already turned his back on me.

"It's a week from Sunday. Will we be ready in less than two weeks?" Natalya asks and glances pointedly at Courtney. "We've normally finalized the set list by three weeks. We won't have enough time to practice."

"Oh," Courtney says, deflating at Natalya's less than tactful approach to the situation.

Summer shoots Natalya a dirty look. "We can start practicing as soon as Courtney gets that info to us. Relax."

"I'll email a list with everything you need to know or do," Ethan says to Courtney.

"I'll get everything to you guys by tomorrow," Courtney promises.

I nod along absentmindedly while discreetly squeezing my throbbing finger. Opening my grip, I look down to see a drop of blood rolling off my fingertip and landing on the floor.

I glance at the back of Gabe's head, and my mind starts to play Jon Bon Jovi's "You Give Love a Bad Name."

I sway to the haunting melody in the empty chapel. Ella Fitzgerald croons "I Can't Get Started" from my phone. Twirling, I throw my arms out wide like I'm dancing on Broadway instead of down the aisle of an empty wedding chapel.

The similarities between the mournful lyrics about a woman who can't find love and my life are, well, all too real. Not a perfect match, but I've learned that few songs fit perfectly with your life.

But the emotion... The emotion reaches out through the lyrics and melody of a song and connects with an individual's spirit in a profound—sometimes alarming—way. So I croon with Ella, my bosom buddy of sorrow and lost love.

I tap my feet (I am not a tap dancer in case you were wondering, so this looks akin to a child shuffling his feet because he needs a bathroom.) in time with the tempo, then I take a leap that in my head looks like what the little ballerina from *Leap!* does, but in reality probably looks like an awkward woman making a isosceles triangle with her stiff legs and the floor.

Wobbling after I land from the mighty jump—if you can call four inches from the floor a "mighty jump"—I raise my arms like I stuck the landing dismount from the balance beam. But I didn't fall, and that's what is important, as I'm sure you know.

Falling is the bane of my existence.

And that's probably the reason I fall on my face—metaphorically and literally—so much. Got to love God's warped sense of humor.

Heavenly chuckles fill my heart with a foreboding, *You haven't seen anything yet!*

A slow clap catches my attention over the music. Turning toward the front door at the back of the chapel (seriously, it's no wonder I get lost whenever I go somewhere new with vernacular like that guiding me!), I see Gabe clapping from where he leans against the doorjamb. His clap tapers off, and he steps away from the doorjamb to close the open door.

My breath feels like it got caught in a wind tunnel as we study each other with Ella's melodramatic serenade in the background.

Maybe it's the moonlight, but I swear he's never looked more handsome than he does right now. A window in the back of the chapel acts like a spotlight, soaking Gabe in the moon's golden light. His black hair has a Cary Grant, swished back look to it, and his long-sleeved flannel makes him look warm and inviting.

Slap me. Please. Right in the face.

"I thought you might be here," Gabe says softly, breaking the moonlight's spell.

I struggle to find my voice. "Why?"

His shrug says, *Because I know you.*

What do I say to that?

He takes a tentative step toward me. "I think we should talk."

"Talking hasn't done us any favors so far."

A genuine, heartwarming, yet heartbreaking laugh spills from him. "That's true. But I still think we need to talk. Really talk. Not yell at each other. We need to figure out a way to..."

"Coexist," I supply.

"Right. Coexist. So we need to talk."

I shake my head, causing the staticky flyways from my bun to accost my face. "I don't want to talk right now."

He raises an eyebrow, silently asking me, *Then what?*

*I want to kiss you, you fool!*

The unbidden thought from my heart doesn't even surprise me, and *that* surprises me. I have been incensed with the man for days. From finding out he'd slept with someone after we broke up (and channeling all my inner Rachel Green from *Friends*), to accepting that we were broken up and it seemed like he genuinely regretted his actions, to discovering the inspiration behind the band's name, I have been ready to start fighting like this is the Seventy-Fifth Hunger Games.

However, I'm not an idiot, despite how I've tried to ignore it. I loved this man, and a part of me still does. Maybe it always will. And I want to kiss him. I want to throw my arms around him and kiss him like you see in every glorious Happily Ever After movie known by mankind.

And for one glorious, achingly short moment, I can see it. Us, tossing all the past and the pain and the questions aside and kissing...and living the life God intended. I see the future as it could be, if we could lay all those burdens down. I see the brightly burning love we would share. I see the joy and laughter and love, a melody sweeter than anything I could imagine.

I see what could be...

But what will never be.

"Then what, Kaylee?" he asks out loud this time.

"Sing with me?"

This one does surprise me, and judging by Gabe's rounded, cartoon eyes, it surprised him as well. But if I can't kiss him—and I can't!—then this is the next best thing. For a few minutes, I can share my heart with his.

Or maybe it's another brilliant move brought to you by the people of Unrequited Love Incorporated, but whatever.

"Wh-what?" he stutters.

"I'm serious." I look down at my bare feet rather than into those shining gray eyes. "I want to sing first. I need to feel free."

"Okay," he says in a voice that sounds far deeper and huskier than it did a moment ago. "What?"

"You pick."

"Anything?" Gabe asks with a mischievous gleam in his eye.

"Nothing by the Jonas Brothers." I chance a look into his eyes before glancing away to study the nearest weathered pew.

"You said anything," he shoots back. "Come on, their new stuff is pretty good."

I point to the door behind him while fighting a smile. "Get out."

He laughs before he crosses his toned arms across his chest, his traditional "I'm thinking" pose. Then his left eye narrows like it always does when he has an idea. "Do you know 'Let Your Heart Hold Fast' by Fort Atlantic?"

I feel like my inner Tinker Bell just ran out of pixie dust. Not a love song, but what did I expect?

Nothing. I should expect nothing.

But on the other hand, Gabe knows me. He knows how I pick apart a song, analyze the lyrics, and latch onto hidden meaning. At its core, the song reinforces the message that you are not alone. And at least there's that. We are not alone. I look into his eyes again, and I see that there.

We have each other, even if we don't actually *have* each other. This is Gabe's peace offering, his first step toward coexisting.

After nodding my agreement, Gabe begins to hum the harmony. He raises his deep baritone an octave higher than he normally sings in, resulting in a tone that sounds emotionally raw as Gabe—for the first time since that ugly reunion—lays his heart bare via the music.

I join him on the second verse, trying to look anywhere but into his eyes. However, those gray beacons pull mine to his like they're magnetized. He's the One Ring to my Bilbo Baggins.

The strains of our broken song echoes throughout the empty chapel. My voice breaks on the bridge, while Gabe's remains strong and steadfast. The version of steadfast friendship he's offering me is...beautiful and wrecking at the same time. And however brief it may be, I want to take it.

I can do this.

I can be his friend.

He can be my friend.

We can move on.

Or crumble to pieces trying.

We release the final strains of the melody, humming the final notes together. And for now, that's enough. Which is why I can extend my own olive branch.

"Gabe," I say after a few moments of silence, moments that allow me to build up the nerve to make my request.

"Yeah?"

"I know it may be a little weird, but..." I cough out of nervousness. "I have this song—well, part of a song—that I want to use for Courtney's wedding. But I need a little help finishing it. And you're a decent songwriter."

His eyes light up. "Really?"

Deep breath. "Yes."

He smiles, seeing the offer for what it is. "I'd love to help you."

His warm, *I'd love to help you,* repeats in my head a dozen times before I remember that social protocol frowns upon my middle school crushing. Time for a plan. Preferably (but not really), a plan that doesn't involve any more daydreaming about kissing him again.

That option is so far out of the question!

"So maybe we should meet next week to work on the song."
Do I look awkward? I feel awkward. This *is* awkward. It's like I
asked my ex on a not-a-date date.

"Should we celebrate with some Jonas Brothers' tunes?"

"I've changed my mind again."

"Relax. I'm kidding." Gabe aims the charming smile I fell in
love with at me, wattage turned up to full-force, hunky cuteness.

I roll my eyes and attempt to ignore the way my stomach
backflips. "Don't make me regret this."

"Sorry." But his grin conveys no regret. "Where should we
meet to work?"

"I don't know. I don't like having people around when I'm
working on a song." Far too many weird, high-pitched and off-
key noises escape my throat in this process.

"I remember," Gabe replies, and I try not to squirm under his
gaze. This conversation feels both familiar and surreal at the
same time.

"What about here? We would need to clear it with Chip, but
I'm sure you can take care of that," I say dryly.

"Ah, there's that wit." Gabe looks around the empty chapel.
"Yeah, I think this would be perfect."

I clear my throat. Time for the second olive branch. "And
since I know it would make Ethan happy, we can work on some
songs for the band. For Ethan's sake."

"Rea—"

I cut him off and hold up my hand. "Stop saying really."

He rubs the back of his neck. "Thank you."

I look away. "It's not a big deal."

"It is. I know it wasn't easy to offer any of that. I want you to
know I'm grateful." His voice takes that husky quality that makes
me feel like I've lost all the strength in my legs.

Wonderful.

Taking a deep breath, I shove all the emotion and longing
from the last few minutes, weeks, and years back into the box
reserved for Gabe—and shove it into a dusty corner in my heart.
"You're welcome," I finally say once the task is complete.

I can do this.

Or crumble trying.

# Chapter Eight

"**R**emind me again why we have to wear red to this wedding," Summer gripes from where she sits behind the driver's wheel of her VW van. We're on our way to our very first gig together.

"Because it's a themed wedding," Natalya says from where she sits behind me.

And perhaps you could remind me why I agreed to ride with them? I could have driven myself. But no, Summer had to go on and on in front of the entire band at our last rehearsal that we live together, so we can ride together, and why would I want to waste the gas?

I have an answer for you: I want to live, and Summer's aggressive driving is testing the boundaries of that desire. After riding with her to the grocery store this week, one of my new missions in life is to not die in a fiery crash with her at the wheel.

"Red is not my color." Summer swerves through traffic, fearless city driver that she is. Perhaps I should remind her we're on the highway heading toward Lebanon, New Hampshire. A highway where each car is spread apart by a couple miles.

Instead, I pop another lemon drop in my mouth. I've needed the constant emotional therapy they provide after making what feels like a deal with the devil.

Not that Gabe is the devil.

But I do feel doomed.

Summer looks over at me, gesturing to my simple sheath dress. "I wish I had your complexion. Red doesn't make you look washed out, and that dress is amazing."

I resist rolling my eyes because, girl, I am paler than pale. But the grass is always greener, isn't it? I smooth the unwrinkled red lace of my dress. "Thank you. You both look beautiful."

No giant eagles show up to deliver me to safety (Yes, another nerdy reference. This one is from *The Hobbit*), but we eventually arrive at our destination in one piece. I was starting to doubt that would be the case based on Summer's driving skills. There's a choice word for Massachusetts drivers—and to be clear, I don't use it!—but I can understand the etymology of this word after spending the entire ride pretending not to notice the angry hand gestures the other drivers waved to our vehicle whenever Summer cut them off.

Summer swings into the wide parking lot and jerks to a stop. I peer out my passenger window to study the local theater/opera house where the *Phantom of the Opera* themed wedding and reception is being held. From the outside, the building looks completely normal. Tall and stately, it could pass for an ornate government building.

I don't know what to expect on the inside.

Personally, I'm not sure how I feel about a couple that wants to play up the "haunted by a crazy man" image with their wedding venue and décor so much so that they're wanting it to be a "production."

To be completely honest, I'm a little scared. I saw *Phantom of the Opera* in New York when I was eighteen. It was supposed to be an early graduation present, but neither of my parents wanted-ed to go. And Gabe had already split by then. Thankfully, Izze's family took mercy on me, bought her a ticket, and drove us down there. All I can say is if this couple is planning any dramatic chandelier plummets, I'm out.

I still have nightmares about being crushed by a chandelier, but it's a fear I've worked long and hard to conceal. It's probably my fourth biggest secret.

Seems my list of secrets is longer than I realized.

But before you say anything, I had to keep it from my friends—especially Courtney and Apryl. I mean, they work with antiques. Chandeliers come with the job, and I wasn't going to be the one cowering outside the front door because chandeliers hung from every available inch of the ceiling of their storefront. Confront fear, and all that jazz.

While silently whimpering.

We climb out of the van, each of us taking a moment to welcome the feel and smell of fresh, non-vehicular air. Ethan's monster truck crunches to a stop on the driver's side of Summer's VW van, and I can feel Gabe's eyes on me now.

Hmmm, maybe I've developed some LOTR powers. That would be cool, wouldn't it? Should I use my newfound powers for good or for evil?

I can feel Gabe's presence moving closer and closer, so I make a beeline to the back of the van, throwing the double doors open and grabbing my equipment as fast as I can. I situate the load in my arms, but it's too late—he's directly behind me.

Maybe I should use my powers to disappear, hmmm?

After the other night, I know I need to keep a distance. A big distance. Like fifteen basketball players between us kind of distance. Otherwise, the carefully constructed fortress around my heart will collapse into a pile of melted Silly Putty.

"How are you doing?" he asks in a low voice.

Natalya's standing on the other side of the van, and the glare she isn't quite quick enough to hide promises a painful, tortuous death at her hands if I don't get away from Gabe *NOW!*

Part of me wants to raise my head and give her an *Excuse me?* look.

But instead, I swallow my natural response. Natalya is a new friend who I actually like. I do not want Gabe to be an issue between us, so I send her a hesitant smile. She returns my smile, silently agreeing to Article Number One of the Girl Code: friendship over thick-headed dudes.

Gabe moves and stands right in front of me, thankfully putting his back to Natalya. "Excited? Nervous?"

I blink.

What kind of idiotic question is that? Sure, I've been singing and songwriting for years, but I've always been "just a singer." I'm disposable. Meaningless. Now I've been shanghaied into singing in a wedding band with my ex-boyfriend/fiancé, and then during my first performance with this group, I have to do a solo.

I. Am. Freaking. Out.

Like I think I'm going to vomit.

And Gabe is the last person I want to be vulnerable with when it comes to this. It hurts too much.

"Yeah, sure," I mumble before running after Ethan, who's carrying one of those manly messenger bags filled with our sheet music and a copy of the contract in case a discrepancy arises. The others are trying to wrestle their instruments out of the van. This is the good part about being "just a singer." My equipment consists of a music stand, amp, and a mic and axillary cord tucked into their own case.

Makes it much easier to run away.

Ethan stops at the front door, studying his phone.

But since I was running after him, I slam into his back. My music stand *Thwacks!* him in the back of his head like it was my lance of choice for this jousting match.

"Ow!" He shoots me an annoyed look over his shoulder while he rubs the back of his head.

"Sorry," I squeak in a way that sounds like I've swallowed a canister of helium.

He raises an eyebrow at me, looks past me, shakes his head, and sighs. "You all right?"

"I'm fine." Add compulsively lying about my mental/emotional state to my current list of sins.

"Right," he says with a sigh before turning around and muttering a string of unintelligible words under his breath.

It's probably a good thing I can't hear him.

"Okay, guys," Ethan then says in a booming voice, "we're going to go in through the vendor entrance around the side. Follow me." He starts walking at a steady clip to the left of the building. I take great care not to run into him when he stops again. He glances over his shoulder in relief before tapping out a weird pattern on the metal door with the word "Vendor" painted on it in chipped, white paint.

Ummm, what sort of secret facility are we walking into? Am I the only one who wants to go home and rethink their life right about now?

Gabe's spicy body spray wafts around me as I wait. Great, he caught up to me.

Natalya materializes beside me. Swell.

The door swings open to reveal a burly looking man with the kind of scowl that consists of miniature ravines of displeasure on his face. "You missed a knock," he says to Ethan in a low voice.

I angle my right foot so that I can pivot and sprint for my life on a moment's notice.

"Good morrow," Burly says to the rest of us with a big, toothy grin on his face. His fake English accent makes Natalya flinch.

I've never cared for the particular taste of dirt. Too gross. Unfortunately, I might as well be licking the ground thanks to my slack mouth and dropped jaw.

Talk about a production...

Burly's grin widens when he looks at me, and my tomato face no doubt makes an appearance. He steps to the side, pressing his back to the metal door, and sweeps his hand to the left with a flourish. "Right this way, lads and lassies."

And now we're Scottish?

Burly—who introduced himself as Lawrence—leads us down a dark, dank hallway. Lightbulbs hanging from swaying cords illuminate—and I use that word loosely—the hallway every six or so feet. Despite the fact that everyone else has been deluded into thinking we're fine, I continue to hold my music stand like a lance.

Because everyone knows that a paranoid chick with a music stand as her weapon is the equivalent of Mel Gibson in *The Patriot*.

Burly stops in front of another metal door with the words "Orchestra Pit" painted on it. "And we've arrived," he says in a southern accent.

Is this a medical condition? Should I be calling an ambulance?

Lawrence the Burly smiles at me as I pass him. He leans toward me and whispers, "I was born to perform." A French lilt colors his words.

Oh-kay then...

I step into the pit and look up, taking in the grandeur of the room above me. Though the room doesn't look to be any bigger than the average high school auditorium—it's small enough that there's no balcony seating—the eloquence and classic décor could rival the theater I visited in New York. The top of my head is even with the black-painted stage floor. Red and gold brocade fabric make up the stage curtains and most of the other fabric features in the space. The sea of fancy theater seats is covered in black (and I'm guessing waterproof) fabric. A thousand (I'm guessing again) red roses (though I'd prefer Lorelai Gilmore's thousand yellow daisies) decorate the stage, ornate shelves, and the aisles. The walls are gold, with elaborate golden wainscoting.

And directly above me, there is a gold, sparkly chandelier that could crush an armored military vehicle.

"Don't hyperventilate. Don't hyperventilate," I mutter as I turn my attention to the orchestra pit itself.

It's dark. The carpet is black industrial carpeting. The walls are gray. And the room is empty except for a dozen metal folding chairs lying against the far wall. Compared to the splendor of the theater above us, the space is a letdown. Another reason why "pit" is so fitting.

Ethan, who'd been talking with Lawrence the Burly, whistles to get our attention. "Okay, guys. So obviously, we'll be down here for the ceremony and reception, with the exception of Kaylee and her solo during the reception." Ethan looks at me, as if that will add clarity to his instructions. "When it's time, you'll want to go out this door, turn right, and re-enter through the door that says, 'Stage Left.' After that, you'll walk—"

"Center stage for the performance," I finish for him. "I remember." Thankfully it's not a creepy song. In fact, we're only playing a few of Andrew Lloyd Weber's famous pieces from the musical: the "Overture" while the guests find their seats and again during cocktail/picture hour and the classic "The Phantom of the Opera" during the recessional. I should also note that when I say we're playing these pieces, I mean that the band is doing the instrumental accompaniment to a snazzy recording.

Sorry, but there's no fancy way to say that. Sometimes it's best to call it what it is, and it's a high-tech recording of the instrumental, full-orchestra performances of the "Overture" and "The Phantom of the Opera." We're adding some in-house instrumental accompaniment and vocals.

On the flip side of this fried egg, the band will play the music for my solo, "Think of Me," while I sing. The bride and groom opted to use this in lieu of any of the traditional dances, so, you know, no pressure.

Not.

"All right, already," Natalya mutters behind me, reminding me of yet another reason why I think she's upset with me. Based on her disgruntled growl when Ethan said the bride had picked me for the solo (based on some sample video and audio recordings that Ethan had uploaded onto the band's website), Natalya really wanted this solo.

"Are the acoustics really good enough for us to be heard down here?" Summer asks. "And why did we have to dress up to be shoved into the Pit of Despair?"

"Lawrence said that instead of using our amps, we could plug into the surround sound system right from here." Ethan points to a small control panel I hadn't noticed as its gray door caused it to blend in with the drab gray of the walls. "And Summer, I could remind you that this is a fancy wedding in a fancy place, and the couple has the right to request that we—"

"Not you, man," Drake interjects while tugging at his neckline to loosen his red, silk tie.

Ethan doesn't acknowledge him. "Wear appropriate attire. Or—as long as it's within reason—even wear something appropriate to the theme of the wedding. Additionally, you're being paid for this. However, I'm just going to take pleasure in your discomfort and channel my inner Phantom vibes with a sinister smile." And as promised, Ethan smiles in a sinister way.

I laugh. He's twisted his eyebrows into a deep V and is baring his teeth in a way that says, *I eat unicorns for breakfast!* "Nicely done."

"I will throw my drumsticks at you," Summer threatens. We all know that she wouldn't dare throw her monogramed drumsticks, but it's the threat that's important.

"Ignore him," I say. "You look beautiful."

Summer glances down at her blood-red dress. The high, cowl neckline and fluttery, jagged hemline make her look like a pixie. "Maybe I'll meet my Erik tonight," she says with a gleam in her heather-colored eyes.

I frown. "Don't you mean Raoul? He's the hero."

"Nah. I love me a complicated anti-hero." Summer's grin grows.

"I'm not sure Erik could be considered an anti-hero," Natalya says slowly.

Drake frowns in confusion. "Who is Erik?"

"Ant Hero? Wait, do you mean Ant Man? I think his name was Scott Lang," Ethan interjects.

"The Phantom of the Opera," Summer, Natalya, and I say at once in booming voice that not only conveys our annoyance but also the acoustic capabilities of the space with its mighty echo. Drake stares at us with wide eyes as the echo reverberates throughout the theater.

Gabe snorts. "That will teach you for asking."

"Who are you talking about?" Ethan asks, slow and careful.

Summer huffs and rolls her eyes. "Erik is the Phantom of the Opera."

"Well, Drake would like to be done with this conversation." An impish grin tugs at Drake's lips.

"Don't talk in third person." Summer growls. "That is my biggest pet peeve, and you know it."

Gabe snickers. "Gabe would like to second that."

"Ethan would like to know what part Gabe is referring to." Ethan manages to keep a straight face despite his taunting tone.

"Gabe was referring to—"

"Stop! Please! Just stop!" Summer yells. "I need to start carrying spare drumsticks to throw at people." She rolls her eyes as the guys ignore her and continue their silly conversation in third person.

We finish hauling everything and set up the area. I organize the music on my stand the way I like it. Everyone else in the band turns their sheet music like the pages of a book, but I like the song I'm singing to be on the left. Out of the corner of my eye, I watch Gabe tune his electric guitar. He tightens the top right tuning peg before flicking his pick between the pickups faster than I have ever seen him play before. He hits each cord, over and over and over.

"Show-off," Drake muttered.

Huh? I raise a single eyebrow.

Summer answers my silent question. "Gabe likes to do this little pre-show warmup where he plays all the chords a hundred times before he actually plays a song."

I look at Gabe. "You play *each* chord a hundred times?"

He just smiles and winks at me without skipping a beat—uh, chord.

My stomach flutters, and I know I'm blushing. Why is he being all flirty? And in front of everyone to boot?

"Ignore him," Ethan says sarcastically. "He thinks he's James Dean or something when he's doing this."

"Like I said, he's a show-off." Drake starts picking through the chords on his bass guitar. He's fast, but not as fast as Gabe.

Gabe catches Ethan's eye and nods.

Ethan holds up his index finger while studying his watch.

Natalya tucks her violin under her chin and looks at Ethan.

Summer impatiently clicks her drumsticks together.

"Fifteen seconds," Ethan says without taking his eyes off his watch.

I wish I knew what we were counting down to... And it feels weird to ask.

Gabe and Drake both stop playing. Gabe doesn't even attempt to wipe the smug grin off his face.

"I'm not racing you, man," Drake growls. However, there's a smile in his eyes.

"Then you won't care when I win again," Gabe taunts.

"Five, four, three, two." Ethan curls his index finger into his palm and drops his hand like he's waving the starting flag. "And go!"

Gabe, Drake, and Natalya start going through all their chords, seemingly as fast as they can. Summer wails on her drums with a blurry, precise speed. I assume she's doing the drummer version of this, but my only knowledge of a drum set consists of naming the cymbals and drumsticks.

Party of one, under Kaylee Clueless.

I stand there feeling really, really awkward and useless. I have never felt more like "just a singer" than I do in this moment.

Ethan takes pity on me, or at least he tries to. "It's their pre-show competition. They go through all their chords—or in Summer's case, tablatures—as many times as they can in two minutes. Whoever wins gets bragging rights until the next gig." He yells to be heard over the loud ramble of incoherent music.

"Ah! I see!" I yell back.

Yup, definitely just a singer.

A very alone singer who's been reminded all over again that I'm not really a part of this group of friends, musicians, performers, confidants...

Partners.

I don't belong.

I never did. I never will.

I cover my feelings of awkward rejection with a cough. "I'm going to get the lay of the land," I announce.

Not that I'm expecting anyone to notice.

Without waiting for anyone to acknowledge me, I take off through the doorway, shutting the door behind me and taking off down the hallway like I'm being chased. And my internal radio playing "Phantom of the Opera" isn't helping with that feeling.

It's too dark.

I find the door marked "Stage Left" and open it. I look for something to hold the door open, but I don't see anything backstage that would be appropriate to use as a doorstop.

Logically, I know it's not a big deal, but...

Gulp!

Time to take a cue from Dory and just keep walking. Navigating the backstage is easy enough, and I'm standing center stage in a matter of seconds, next to (not under, that would be weird) a rose-covered arch. Though I'm supposed to sing downstage, I stay upstage and enjoy the aloneness for a few minutes. A momentary recharge from all the people, though I can see a couple of them from my perch as the gang continues their warm-up in the orchestra pit.

Including Gabe.

Oh, my.

The memories flood me as I study his handsome profile. The slight wave in his black hair rebels against the styling gel I'm sure he used this morning. His suit emphasizes his broad shoulders. Even though I can't look into his eyes from here, I'm positive the smoky, gray smolder in them would be my undoing. In fact, I'm already feeling woozy.

Please catch me if I fall.

I jerk my right foot up and stomp on my left foot, biting my lip to keep from yelping in pain.

Talk about a rude awakening, but I need to keep my wits about me, my guard up, and my heart closed. If I need to harden my heart, then I will. I refuse to fall prey to his magnetic charm.

Never again.

Turning, I limp back to the exit.

I'm so glad I didn't wear heels today.

"I feel like a monkey in a zoo," Drake mutters.

"As long as you don't act like a monkey in a zoo, then we're good," Ethan quips quietly.

"No promises," Drake shoots back as yet another person leans against the golden, waist-high railing to look and point at us in our pit.

Drake's not wrong. As a performer, you're used to people watching you, but this is still different. Being below everyone else is strange. It wasn't so weird during the ceremony when all the guests were sitting, but now they're up and mingling. Some of the guests have even started dancing on the stage, the dance floor for the evening.

I positioned myself with my back to the pit's door, so I can see the theater side and the stage side. Some people laugh and chat on the theater side, hanging out by the golden railing. Every so often, the hem of a dramatic gown flutters into my line of vision as the couples dance. This whole experience has added new perspective to the whole upstairs/downstairs world of *Downton Abbey.*

It's still cocktail hour, so the others are playing and talking in muted tones while I stand here looking very important. Not. I'm standing next to Summer as she plays, swaying, tapping my feet, and bobbing my head so I don't look completely useless to the spectators above us.

Up next is my solo performance of "Think of Me." Those familiar caterpillars are wiggling in my stomach, trying to burst from their cocoon like some horrific Syfy movie.

Ethan, who's standing by the control panel, holds up his right hand to signal that we (and by we, I mean the people who aren't useless singers) should wrap up while using his other hand to cover the Bluetooth in his left ear. "Okay. Got it," he says into his Bluetooth and taps it.

They finish playing, and Ethan steps into the musician version of a football huddle. "Kaylee, via the theater event coordinator, you are due on stage for your solo in twelve minutes."

Summer frowns. "Why twelve minutes? Why not ten or fifteen?"

"I don't know, Summer," Ethan murmurs through his clenched teeth. "That's what the piece of work on the other end of this connection told me."

"I hate odd numbers," she grumbles.

"Technically, twelve is an even number," Drake jokes.

"Divisible by five. I like numbers divisible by five," Summer clarifies.

Ethan taps his Bluetooth again and rolls his eyes. "Got it," he says in a terse voice before he smashes the Bluetooth again.

Probably not wise considering that's on his head.

Gabe snorts.

"He has been micromanaging me all night," Ethan gripes.

Natalya shrugs. "He's just doing his job."

Ethan opens his mouth and then points to his ear again. "Nine minutes. Got it. She's on the way," Ethan mutters through gritted teeth while looking at me, and I nod.

"Good luck!" Natalya exclaims brightly.

I blanch.

Summer glares at her. "Why would you say that? You know that's bad luck before a performance," she hisses at Natalya from her perch on her stool.

"Oh, you're not really superstitious like that, are you?" Natalya asks with an awkward chuckle.

Summer thrusts a drumstick at her. "Of course not, but wishing someone good luck is the equivalent of saying you hope they fail."

"Well, I obviously didn't mean it like that," Natalya reiterates, a bright smile gracing her lips.

Ri-tight. And Elvis Presley is my great granddaddy.

I refrain from rolling my eyes at her Emily Gilmore levels of passive aggressiveness and adjust my wireless microphone. I've never used one this nice before, and I honestly prefer the feel of the microphone in my hand. But esthetics and all that rule the day.

Deep breaths.

Readjust the microphone again.

Tug the wrist-length lace sleeves of my gown. (Look at that, they haven't moved.)

Time to face the music. And use my diaphragm because if I rely on my throat for this song, I will strain my vocal cords.

*God, please don't let me squeak.*

Marching to the door, Gabe whispers to me from where he leans against the wall next to it, water bottle in hand. "Break a leg, and I'll catch you when you fall."

I stop and offer him a small smile. "Thanks." Despite the wall around my heart when it comes to Gabe, the familiar words are comforting to hear. It's what he used to say to me, before. Like when I was performing at school or when I first joined the worship team. Or when I randomly broke into song in the middle of the mall like I was Gisele from *Enchanted.*

Yeah, I was *that* person. Perhaps you wanted to throw a bottle of ketchup at me or my kindred spirits once or twice.

Gabe's head dips in acknowledgement before he turns his attention to studying the label of his water bottle.

Here I go.

"Yes, she's on the way. Yes, I know it's six minutes now," Ethan growls quietly behind me.

Walking out of the Orchestra Pit, I hold my head high. (I mean, I have to in order to see. It was dim in that pit.) Taking the path I traveled earlier, I'm backstage a few minutes later. The theater event coordinator is waiting for me by the curtain.

"Know what you're doing?" he asks me while he studies a clipboard in his hand.

I want to say, *Of course! I'm a graduate of Chuckles University, the university that boasts famous alumni's like Chandler Bing!* However, I decide—begrudgingly—to answer like a professional. "Yes, I'm ready. Center. Downstage."

"Mm-hmm." He glances in my general direction—if I was standing three feet to the left—and flicks his wrist. "Go ahead."

Pasting a smile I *so* don't feel on my lips, I step onto the stage. A spotlight blinds me for a moment, until my high school theater training emerges. There's a small, beautiful table and two chairs under the floral arch I passed earlier. The bride and groom sit there, smiling and holding hands across the table. Most of the guests have returned to their seats and watch me with eagerness. At the back of the theater, I can see the doors are open to the lobby, where we were told the appetizer-style buffet was served. I see waiters and a few guests still mingling, passing in front of the open doors.

Thankfully, I don't trip as I make my way to my mark down-stage. Smiling, I wait for the first strains of "Think of Me" to start. The moment before I start to perform is always the worst. A time-warping blackhole twists this moment into a thousand years while the second hand on the clock across the room moves four paces. In that thousand-year interlude, I doubt everything about who I am and what I'm doing. And my tongue grows three sizes too large for my mouth.

"You Know It's About You" by Magical Thinker blasts in my head.

*Message received, God.*

I've got this. *We've* got this. The lyrics, the ability, everything is all there, so there's no room for those doubts. And as the sweet melody to "Think of Me" begins, it sweeps me into a lyrical world that consists of me and God. My eyelids meet, blocking out the rest of the world. I probably should open my eyes and maintain eye contact (but really, who chooses creepy eye contact over witnessing true passion in a musician?), I should sing to the audience, but...I can't help it.

I am lost in the lyrics.

Like when Lorelai Gilmore serenades Luke at karaoke night, I know I'm singing to Gabe. I don't want to be. My logical self with all its self-preservation instincts will be ready and waiting with a lambasting worthy of the name when this is over. But I can't keep my heart locked away when the music starts.

Music frees the deepest parts of me.

And it's in the freedom that I'm really able to think, feel, and hear God with a clarity that I can't in the everyday jumble of life.

And I want to think "fondly" of Gabe. I don't want to be consumed with hate or anger. Unforgiveness.

Fear.

I refuse to let my heart fully fall in love with him again.

But I can try to open my heart to a friendship. A real one. Not just coexisting.

It's all part of moving on, right?

Remember what I said about moving on while also guarding my heart? It's good in theory.

Not in execution.

Not when your gorgeous ex is singing one of your favorite romantic songs—"You and Me" by Lifehouse—across from you.

He's looking into my eyes as he sings.

Oh, those smoky gray eyes. They would probably be classified as blue eyes, but they are not blue. Far from it. They are gray. The shade of gray depends on his mood. Light gray when he's going about his day. Ash gray when he's angry. Reflective gray when he's sleepy or sick. Smoky gray when he was about to kiss me.

He's faking it. He's faking it. He's faking it.

It's just the song. It is just the passion he's putting into the song.

However, I fear that my gut might as well be purring in response to his catnip voice. Once again, it is just Gabe and me in this musical bubble. Once again, I see the future I want, not the reality I'm stuck with. Once again, I've gotten the short end of the stick.

Seriously, why did they have to choose this song?

But perhaps I should be asking a different question, like why did I think I could do this? Why did I think I'd be fine baring my soul *with* Gabe only to be rejected all over again every time the music stops? There is something seriously wrong with me, and it's an extreme case of delusion.

We're singing the final verse when a crazy laugh cuts through the surround sound. The room is filled with gasps and laughs, and the lights dim. A loud shriek that sounds like metal grinding and breaking cackles like a fairy-tale witch. The sound reverberates throughout the theater.

Then...

The grand chandelier starts to fall.

And it's coming straight for us!

I stare in horror as it plummets toward us. This is it. This is the end.

I knew I should have eaten that Three Musketeers bar for breakfast.

Beside me, Summer laughs in delight, face upturned to greet the chandelier with a deathly kiss. I told y'all she was Eddie crazy.

I scream, drop to the ground, and cover my head and neck. That's what they did for those drills during World War Two, right? Doesn't hurt to try it.

Well, it *will* hurt.

Wait...

I should have been crushed already.

Taking great care, I tilt my head up to see the band and some of the people who'd been right next to the pit watching me. The chandelier sways on a chain as it's cranked back to the ceiling.

Suddenly, I'm wishing the chandelier had crushed me. At least I wouldn't have to endure what comes next.

"Don't worry, dear," an older woman on the theater side waves and calls to me. "It's all part of the act."

From my position, I have a great view of Natalya smirking while Gabe grimaces. "I thought you'd seen the play?" she asks in a way that is probably meant to be gentle but feels haughty to my delicate emotions.

I don't bother to defend myself. My face turns a shade of red that's indigenous to the tomatoes found on Mars. It's fitting as my embarrassment is out of this world.

"Brava! Encore!" someone yells.

"Thank you," the bride coos from where she and her new husband stand downstage. The feathers on her wedding gown flutter as she dramatically throws her right hand into the air and takes a bow while holding her husband's hand.

Standing up, I brush my dress off. Maybe that will remove my awkwardness.

I glance up again.

Nope. Everyone continues to stare at me with varying degrees of pity and amusement.

I jerk my thumb toward the door. "I'm going to get some air. I'll be right back." And I run.

Fast.

But not far. We're in the middle of town. Albeit a small town, but a town all the same.

Bursting outside, I glance around before running to Summer's van. She doesn't keep the doors locked, and the temperature has dropped. I yank the back door open and climb onto the bench seat. Curling into a ball, I bury my face into my arms and try not to cry.

I will not cry. I will not give them the satisfaction.

Plus, I didn't wear waterproof mascara or eyeliner. I don't need to add Racoon Zombie to my growing list of befuddles.

I can't believe I was so stupid.

I know the chandelier falling is an iconic part of the play. I know this! But the deer-in-the-headlights instinct flash froze all logic as the chandelier hurtled toward me.

And now I'm a hilarious joke. Something to be mocked for decades to come. The guests will pass on the story of the ignorant singer down to their great-great-grandchildren. And the haughty Natalya I saw inside will have a field day with this. It won't resemble the good-natured joking I could expect from Izze, Courtney, and Apryl. No, this will be designed to tear my self-esteem to shreds, later to be used as lining for the floor of a rodent's cage.

It hasn't escaped my notice that none of my band "friends" are out here. Probably too busy laughing.

There's a tap on the window.

"Go away," I yell and hiccup.

The door opens. "Not a chance." Gabe's deep voice frees the tears I'd managed to hold back.

"Why are you out here? Have some fantastic joke that couldn't wait until later?"

"Why would I joke about that? Why would *anyone* joke about that?" Gabe exclaims, a fierce, protective growl coloring his words. His eyes would be ash gray right now. "You were obviously scared, and I know you're embarrassed. I'm not a monster."

"Are the others laughing?" A gust of cold wind manages to maneuver itself past Gabe and assault me with its bitterness.

"No, they were worried about you. Your *friends*," Gabe says, emphasizing the word, "wanted to make sure you were okay. But I was adamant that I would be the one to come out here."

I. Will. Not. Loose. Control.

I will not be puffy.

He climbs into the van and sits on the floor. I turn away from him and wipe my cheeks. Exhale. Release. Let it out. I take seven deep breaths and manage to regain some composure.

Gabe sits, waiting. Oddly, his presence gives me comfort instead of adding to my embarrassment.

"I've seen the play," I finally say. "It was a...reaction. I just reacted."

"I know. Don't worry about it." He takes my hands in his. "It doesn't have to be a big deal."

I guffaw. "I made a fool of myself."

"So?"

"Thanks for denying it." I backhand my eyes, which results in a lovely streak of mascara across the back. "What are you doing out here again?"

"I wanted to make sure you were okay."

"But why did you say that you were 'adamant' that you were going to be the one to come out?"

He blinks at me as if the answer should be obvious. "I'm not a monster, Kaylee."

"Why do you keep saying that?"

"I wanted to make sure you were okay."

"Why do you keep saying that, too?" I exclaim in frustration.

"I don't know," Gabe says. "I just...I care, okay? I care." His smoky gray eyes add an emphasis his words do not.

And after the duet we just sang...that combo scares me even more than the chandelier did.

# Chapter Nine

Gabe jiggled the pencil with his thumb and index finger, smacking it against his middle finger over and over as he studied the lyrics.

*Tap. Tap. Tap. Tap.*

"The chorus doesn't sound right," Kaylee said while she paced up and down the aisle.

*Tap. Tap. Tap. Tap.*

"It's missing something."

Gabe looked up and nodded, but Kaylee's back was to him right then. He looked back at the lyrics scrawled into Kaylee's notebook.

"I keep hitting those drawn-out notes and then the ending fizzles like it fell into a pot of water. It's too abrupt." She spun and marched back down the aisle. Her fingers brushed the sides of the pews as she passed them. Except the one he occupied. Then she turned around and did it again. And again.

And again.

*Tap. Tap. Tap. Tap.*

Kaylee snatched the pencil out of his hand, startling Gabe enough that he jumped in his seat. "You are driving me crazy with this tapping."

Gabe rubbed the back of his neck with his left hand while holding out his right hand. "Sorry. Can I have it back?"

"No." She tucked it behind her left ear.

"I need it." To distract himself from staring at her.

"When there's something to write, I'll give it back."

"You're power-tripping," he grumbled loudly enough for her to hear.

"You're annoying," she shot back and resumed her pacing.

Gabe went back to studying the lyrics. Well, trying to study the lyrics. "What's the melody sound like again?"

Kaylee hummed a string of notes that didn't sound anything like a melody, but it did sound remarkably like a Sims character being punched in the stomach.

"Huh?"

She let out an exasperated huff and hummed it again, this time in a way that was somewhat coherent.

"That was...What key are you trying to sing in?"

"Oh, I don't even know anymore." She let out a huff of frustration. A short, fluffy tendril of red hair lay across her temple, having escaped the messy bun on top of her head. "The wedding is in two days, and the song is a mess. I'm crossing over into panic now."

"You're humming it too fast. You need to sing it. I need to hear it again."

She growled. "I don't want to sing it again."

He raised an eyebrow. "Why?"

She stopped pacing and spun around to face him, throwing her arms out wide but with a not-so-welcoming attitude. "Because it's weird to sing a love song over and over to your ex."

"Ah." Well, she had a point.

Kaylee shook her head, causing the bun of red hair to flop this way and that. She started pacing again. "Maybe this was a bad idea. Maybe this won't work."

Something that felt an awful lot like panic gripped his lungs with a vise-like strength. "We can make it work," he said with more calmness than he felt.

She stopped in front of him and jerked her hands back and forth between them. Her violent movements caused the bun to bounce like one of those punching balloons he'd liked as a kid. "There's too much history. It's too weird."

Gabe stood up. Whoa, he did not realize how close that would put him to her lips. "You—we—need to stop thinking of it that way."

She raised her delicate eyebrows. "What? It's the truth. It's

what happened. How am I supposed to think of it any differently?"

"Think of it like a…" Why couldn't words appear in thin air
for him? "A partnership."

"A partnership?" Her tone dripped with skepticism.

"Yes. A partnership."

"With you."

"Yes."

Kaylee rolled her eyes. "You realize one of the many facets of
marriage is partnership."

This would ring in as another one of Gabe's top idiotic comments for the memoir he would never write. "You know what I
mean, Kaylee."

"A partnership," she mumbled, mulling the word over with
her lips.

He really needed to stop looking at her lips. A partner didn't
look at another partner's lips.

Not even pale pink, perfect lips.

Gabe wished he had one of those buckets of freezing ice water for the Ice Water Challenge that took over the internet a few
years ago. Thirty seconds of hypothermia might reset his focus
on something other than Kaylee's lips. Lips were not part of the
plan.

Who was he kidding? The plan went belly-up like every fish
he'd ever owned in his childhood.

But at least they seemed to enjoy the M&Ms he'd fed them.

"Fine," Kaylee said with a nod, interrupting his inappropriate
thoughts about her lips. "We can be partners. But the first time
you say the word with a Western accent, I will kick you in the
shins. Both shins."

"Thanks for the warning."

"I thought it only fair."

Gabe snorted. "I'm sure you did. So. The song. Sing it."

Kaylee rolled her eyes and turned her back to him. Her sweet
soprano flooded the empty chapel like a breaking dam, filling
every space. He couldn't see her face, but he knew her eyes were
closed. When she surrendered to the music, it swallowed her and
everyone in her vicinity. She swayed, moving her hands in a way

that invited the butterfly of emotions the song evoked to land in her outstretched hand.

And he had it!

"Wait!" Gabe shouted.

Kaylee jumped and spun to face him. "Are you trying to give me a heart attack?"

"Please. You're practically a horse."

Kaylee rolled her eyes. "What every woman loves to hear."

"I'm sorry, but I have an idea," he said in excitement. "Add 'My love, for the rest of my life' to the end, but when you get to this line, sing it softly. Like it's fading into silence. Keep hitting the earlier lines with the same passion as before, but when the singer gets to this point of the song, it's comfortable and happy and gentle. It's the beauty of love. Make the audience feel that."

Her eyes lit up and a slow grin stretched across her face. "I like it. I like it a lot."

She resumed her traditional songwriting stance and dove into the song again, but this time, the lyrics found a life of their own, outside of Kaylee's voice.

> *"Hello life, hello love.*
> *All my life,*
> *Baby, you're the one.*
> *Through good times and bad,*
> *I'm happy and I'm glad,*
> *That I'll call you love,*
> *My love, for the rest of my life."*

Next thing he knew, Kaylee's arms were around his neck, gripping it tightly in a hug that didn't evoke strictly friendship feelings of partnership in his heart.

This had to be bad for his health. Hugging an ex when you were still very much attracted to them had to lead to aneurisms or heart attacks or something. There had to be scientific evidence of this somewhere. He'd find it, and then he would never have to hug Kaylee again.

Except he'd rather hack off his left arm with a rusty chainsaw and never again play the guitar he'd spent years wiping tables for if it meant he could feel her head lying against his chest one more time.

Kaylee stepped back. "Sorry, partner," she said with a southern drawl.

He cleared his throat. "No problem, partner." Thankfully, his terrible drawl helped to cover up the way he could barely speak.

Kaylee slid the pencil from behind her ear and handed it to him. "Here. Write it down before we forget."

"Yeah, we'll forget one line," he joked, wishing it wasn't partly true. Far too many perfect lines had been forgotten because someone—himself included—hadn't written them down.

Kaylee watched as he scribbled the words on the piece of paper. "Your handwriting is still terrible. It's like a chicken wrote it with his foot. And his foot is on fire. And the paper is on fire. Basically, everything is on fire."

"Can you read it?"

"Barely."

"But you can read it, so it's good enough."

"So you claim."

"And so I say."

She snatched the notebook out of his hand. "You need to go back to school and learn how to write a proper 'M.' It looks like a 'W.' Do you want a repeat of the Wine Disaster?"

"Oh, will you get off that already? You know there was no wine involved in the incorrectly named Wine Disaster. The note said, 'This is mine.'" Gabe shook his head, pretending to be annoyed. But they both knew this old argument, this old memory, was familiar and comforting. Even a little fun.

And she responded the same way, every single time.

"Your mom and I both looked at the note. It said, 'This is wine.'"

"Explain to me how leftover turkey could be wine?"

"Wine could have been in it. Cooking wine is used all the time in fancy meals," Kaylee said smugly.

"It was turkey that I was going to use for my favorite Thanksgiving leftover sandwich, and I didn't get one that year because Dad threw the remaining leftovers into the fireplace. Then he proceeded to ground me for a month."

Kaylee shrugged and grinned. "That's what you get when you're greedy with the leftovers and can't write."

"You were a big help then, too," Gabe said dryly.

"Hey!" Kaylee said in mock rage. "I told your parents that there was no way you snuck any wine into the food. I would have known."

"Ah, it's all right," Gabe confessed. "Totaling Dad's car the week before probably had more to do with that particular sentencing."

Kaylee's eyes widened in shock. "You totaled your dad's car? How did I never know this?"

Gabe rubbed the back of his neck. What had he just done? "I, uh, didn't...tell you. I didn't want you to know." What were the chances that pathetic explanation would be the end of it?

Kaylee clamped her lips together. "Oh."

That single word said an awful lot, like a foghorn pressed against the ear. "What?"

She marched to the second to last pew, grabbed her purse, and shoved the notebook into it. "Nothing."

He sprinted over to her. "Kaylee, come on. What's wrong? What did I do?"

"Nothing, partner." No joking accent this time. Unless disdain could be an accent. In which case, she had nailed this particular dialect.

"Kaylee," he pleaded.

She spun back around, rage on her face. "So when we were dating, exactly how many secrets did you keep from me?"

Gabe took a step back, but his heart sped up, straining from the weight of that particular secret. He could feel the beads of panic sweat starting to form.

Did she know?

No, no. There was no way she knew, and she would never know as long as Gabe didn't do something stupid. Like tell her.

"I didn't tell you about the car because I felt like an idiot and was ashamed of myself." Gabe ran a shaking hand threw his hair. How could he explain that sequence of events to her? The way his father had exploded in cold rage when he'd discovered Gabe's struggle, then overhearing his mother confronting his father about "the blonde" she'd caught him with...and how in a flurry of emotions Gabe didn't stop to process, he left their screaming match behind...and totaled the car.

He couldn't explain without telling her *everything*, and he could *not* tell her everything.

"I guess I didn't want you to think badly of me," he finally choked out.

"I'm so glad you're over that particular hang-up now." Kaylee's bitterness laced each word. She pushed past him and stormed toward the exit. "I'll see you at rehearsal, *partner*."

"Partner" could have been a four-letter word that time.

Gabe sat in the empty wedding chapel for a couple hours.

He sat in silence.

Didn't help. So he tried playing his guitar.

Also didn't help. So he tried reading his Bible, continuing to study what they'd been talking about in his recovery group yesterday.

That *really* didn't help.

That sounded bad, but...it just didn't help. And there you have it.

It didn't help because he'd been reading in I Timothy, verses twelve through sixteen where Paul was talking about how he'd been a hypocritical, murdering, judgmental psychopath, but then he was shown grace and mercy by God.

That Jesus came into the world to save sinners—of whom he was the worst.

It didn't help, because Gabe doubted Paul was the worst sinner.

Because Gabe thought *he* ranked pretty high on that particular Naughty List.

How could he not think that after all the mistakes he'd made, the different ways he'd given in to lustful temptations just to soothe his own pain, self-image, and bad days? As a Christian, he had known better, and he should have been better.

He hadn't chosen the better then. He hadn't been better then. And he couldn't get past that awful burden of shame.

Paul, worst of sinners? What a joke! Puh, who did that guy

think he was? He was a flipping saint, an idol in the church. Argh!

Which was how Gabe had ended up getting into his car and driving over to "check on his mom." Which really meant that he needed his mom's support, even though he'd been sitting in the parking lot of her apartment complex for twenty minutes.

In more silence riddled with condemnation and shame.

Which led to Gabe doing one of the worst things a person could do in this situation. He opened Facebook, and typed *Mitchem Sanders* into the search bar.

His father's Facebook page loaded, and with it, a string of pictures of Mitchem with his arm wrapped around this year's model. Mitchem and this year's model hiking. Mitchem and this year's model celebrating some event (perhaps lasting two months?) at a fancy restaurant. Mitchem and this year's model laughing, flawless brown hair swishing like it belonged in a shampoo commercial.

Why did Gabe do this? It only made him angry all over again.

Which, now that he thought about it, was probably why he did it. He could channel his anger at himself into the one person Gabe considered to be a bigger hypocritical scumbag than him.

His nostrils flared in rage. His heartrate continued to accelerate in anger. He clutched the phone so tightly, Gabe swore that he heard the outside shell groan in agony.

He needed to calm down if he didn't want to punch something. He swiped the app closed, took a deep breath, and held it.

One...

Two...

Three...

He exhaled slowly.

Didn't work. Maybe he should carry a punching bag in his car. It might be more cathartic than pretending to change his breathing pattern.

After five more attempts at the deep breaths, Gabe got out of his car and slammed the door.

*Thwack!*

See! That right there was a satisfying sound effect. Maybe he could partner with somebody to make an app for that. They'd be rich if they didn't get sued for hearing loss.

After unlocking the front door, Gabe tapped on his mother's door with his knuckles, pushed it open, and pocketed the brass key.

He hated that stupid key. Maybe he should make one of those special keys that had a fandom or funky pattern painted on it. Anything would be better than looking at the same brass key his mother had handed to Gabe on that terrible day.

Check that. Almost anything would be better, but he didn't want Hello Kitty hanging out on his keychain.

"Hi, honey." His mother looked up in surprise from where she sat at the small table, her Bible open in front of her. "I didn't think you were coming by this week because of that unexpected 'gig' this weekend." She used air quotes as she said gig. She claimed that she hated the word and the only way she would say it was with air quotes.

Mothers.

Gabe may not be on great terms with God—being tainted tended to affect relationships like that—but he thanked God every day for his mother.

Gabe shrugged and grinned at his mom. "I decided I needed a Mom Fix."

She pretended to groan. "I'm not doing your laundry, Gabe."

"You can say that again," he said with a disgusted face. He never wanted his mom to touch his dirty underwear ever again.

"I'm not doing your laundry, Gabe." She stood up and maneuvered the chair so that the seat went under the table. Gabe didn't miss the flicker of pain that flashed across her face.

"Funny, funny woman." He wrapped his arms around his mother and kissed the top of her head. At five feet—and a quarter, as she would claim—she didn't even come up to his shoulders.

She pulled away and patted him on the back before taking a seat on her corduroy sofa that had seen better decades. "You know I'm always happy to see you."

He sat down beside her. "There's no agenda, Mom. I just wanted to see you."

"Mm-hmm. Checking up on me?"

"No, but now that you mention it. How are you feeling? How were your numbers today? Any changes since we last talked? When is your next doctor appointment?"

"Everything's fine, Gabe. I'm fine. There's been no changes. Next week." But she winced again.

Gabe looked pointedly at her feet. "Any changes?"

"I believe that's included in 'everything.'"

"Have you been taking your medications and antibiotics?"

"No."

"What?" Gabe yelled.

She swatted his arm. "Of course, I'm taking them. And before you ask, I am following my diet and exercise plan. Stop picturing the worst, Gabe. God's got this."

Right. He let out another agitated breath.

"You're upset about something," she said after studying his face for a couple moments with her all-seeing gaze.

"No, I'm not—"

She held up her hand. "I know you are. I can tell by the way you're sitting, staring, and even breathing. You have the same mannerisms as your father."

He flinched and manually unclenched his jaw. "Please don't compare me to him. You know I hate that."

"Gabe." She shook her head and sighed. "Having pieces of your father's personality doesn't make you him."

Gabe shifted. His spot on this couch was very uncomfortable now. "Could be." A pacifying response he knew she'd see through. "But I didn't come to talk about him; I came to see you."

"I don't doubt that you came to see me."

"Okay, let's move on then." Gabe leaned back against a throw pillow with a crocheted, froufrou pillowcase.

"How's Kaylee?"

Gabe bolted upright and turned to face his mom. "How do you know about Kaylee?"

"Ethan told me," she replied smugly.

"Remind me to fire him when I get home."

"Why didn't *you* tell me about Kaylee?" she asked gently.

Gabe opened and closed his mouth four times before he managed a strangled grunt in response.

She rolled her eyes but smiled. "Oh, yes. That clears things up."

"I just...I didn't know how to tell you." Gabe flopped back against the couch. He gripped the back of his neck with both hands and squeezed his eyes closed, trying—and failing—not to picture Kaylee storming out of the chapel a couple hours earlier. "It all happened so fast, and it's...weird."

"Not for me. I always liked Kaylee," his *dear* (yes, a minorly sarcastic endearment) mother said. "I never understood why you broke up with her."

And it would remain that way if Gabe had anything to say about it.

"Well, this sure was helpful, but I think I've gotten my Mom Fix. See you in one to two months." But Gabe didn't make a move to leave. Plus, it wasn't like she would drop this in one to two months. She'd probably pick up where they'd left off.

"You can run away, but it doesn't mean I won't ask you."

"Yeah," Gabe huffed while pinching the bridge of his nose, "I know."

"So. How's she doing?"

"Considering that I saw her for the first time in nine years when she'd just lost her job, she's probably been better."

"I'm proud of you."

Gabe swiveled to face her again. "What?"

"I'm proud of you," she said again.

Gabe stared at her dumbly. "Wh-what? Why?"

She tapped him on the leg before reaching for his hand and giving it a gentle squeeze. "Because you didn't run away. It would have been so much easier to run away from her, from your past, from your mistakes. You didn't. And because you didn't, God used you to help someone you care about."

Gabe deflated at the mention of God. He wouldn't, couldn't, use a guy like Gabe. "Mom, I don't think I'm the person He'd use to make a difference in anyone's life, much less Kaylee's life."

"God is bigger than your anger at Him and bigger still than any of your past mistakes." Gabe squirmed under her penetrating gaze. "And because He's so much bigger, He can still use you."

Logically, Gabe knew this. He was a Christian. He went to church. He read his Bible. But even as a Christian, Gabe had made mistakes. Big mistakes that had affected how he viewed and communicated with God. So Gabe didn't know how to process his mother's comment. Honestly, it made him uncomfortable, like God had broken the rules of Gabe's standoff. And if that was the case, what would He do next?

Gulp.

"I don't care about Kaylee. Not like that." *Liar!* his conscious chided him. "And she only tolerates me. She has every right to hate my guts, to be honest."

"I know."

"You never took sides. I respect that," Gabe grumbled.

She laughed. "Whatever the story was and is, God still has big things planned—for both of you."

He doubted that, but he didn't say so.

Unfortunately, his face did.

"Give me that look all you want, Gabriel Sanders, but I know. He's got big plans. You wait and see."

Time for a change of subject. "So..."

She rolled her eyes. "Message received. Staying for dinner?"

Gabe nodded. "I can stay for a while, but why don't I make dinner?"

"Why don't you help me since I know the only thing you can make is a tuna melt."

"That's because I don't have time to cook. I spend most of my time working or traveling." He stood up and offered his hand to help her stand. "And I always put tomatoes on my tuna melts to fulfill my fruits and vegetables requirements."

"Excuses, excuses." She took his hand and stood up. "You can help me make some veggie chili."

Gabe followed her to the kitchen, trying to fight the effect their conversation had had on him. His mother's faith and en-couragement had buoyed his spirits. That God hadn't given up on him even though Gabe had gone and believed exactly that... It seemed too good to be true. He wanted to believe it—in a des-perate way he couldn't begin to put into words.

And maybe a small, *small* part of him had started to believe it *might* be possible.

# Chapter Ten

I am more confused than Confucius.

Seriously, who could not be confused by that name? And his parents didn't do him any favors naming him that, unless the goal was to set their son up for generation after generation of corny jokes, so much so that it's not in any baby name book I've ever read.

But back to why I'm currently confused: I'm holding a wooden coaster with Arwen's Evenstar pendent hand carved into its smooth surface. The coaster is covered in lacquer, protecting the design and the thin ring of bark on the outside edges.

I set the random present on the kitchen counter and search the small box it arrived in for a card. Nothing. Nothing but packing material and stray wood shavings.

Don't serial killers send presents like this? Maybe a home security system isn't such a crazy idea.

But don't artists (going with "artist" instead of "sociopath" for a moment) sign their pieces? Maybe whoever made it carved their signature into the back. I pick up the coaster again and flip it over in my hand. Another dead end.

"Hey, Kaylee!" Natalya strolls into the room, heading straight for the refrigerator. Her shiny black hair swishes back and forth as she walks. "How are you doing?"

"I'm good," I tell her, still distracted by the mystery gift. "I'm trying to figure out who sent this to me." I hold the coaster up for her to see.

We've been...cordial? Yeah, cordial ever since the *Phantom of the Opera* wedding.

Polite and completely impersonal.

Natalya steps beside me holding a water bottle and looks at the coaster. A weird expression crosses her face as she studies it. "Um, what is the picture supposed to be?"

"It's from *The Lord of the Rings* movies," I explain. "In the movies, Arwen gave it to Aragorn as a symbol of their love. Their story was so romantic. She was half-elven, but she gave up her immortality to be a mortal with Aragorn." I clamp my mouth shut, trying to keep more details about their love story from spilling out because of the glazed-over sheen that's appeared in Natalya's golden eyes.

Harrumph! Some people don't appreciate an epic story filled with the dark questions of life that are vanquished by victorious love and light, so I'll dreamily sigh to myself.

Woah, I got a little indignant there. Deep breath. That's what I need. I breathe until I feel my ribs pinch my lungs, then slowly let it out. Good, it's working. I don't know why I took that so personally. Natalya's not the first person who doesn't understand my obsession with *The Lord of the Rings*. She won't be the last. After all, Izze doesn't understand it, and she's my best friend.

But Izze doesn't make me feel small and inferior...

"I see." Natalya takes a sip from her water bottle, but she's probably thinking, *That's way more information than I needed or wanted to know about a make-believe world.*

There I go again. Time for another deep breath.

"Yeah, so I was looking for a signature or a card in the box, but I can't find anything." I let out an awkward cough—one of those little coughs that you do when you're embarrassed and offering the person stuck with you an opportunity to run like the wind on an animated Pixar horse to less nerdy ground.

My hidden nerdiness always comes out at the most inopportune times.

"That's surprising," Natalya says, but the flat tone to her songbird voice suggest that it's not surprising at all.

Okay.

I stand there for a moment more, the awkwardness between us growing thicker by the millisecond.

"Um, Kaylee, could we talk for a few minutes?" Natalya suddenly says.

I blink. Weren't we already talking before I brought the conversation to a crashing halt with a mini LOTR lesson? Or perhaps I've developed mind speaking abilities, and we didn't say a single word out loud.

Yeah, not likely, but it would be pretty cool. Except the hero/heroine in this cliché always learns something terrible about someone they love, so maybe it wouldn't be cool.

Oh, right. I should answer her. "Yeah, of course."

She glances around the kitchen. "Not here. Uh, let's go to my room."

Getting weirder. "Sure."

Maybe she's the killer. One of those *The killer is inside your house!* situations.

I follow Natalya to Apryl's old bedroom. I haven't so much as looked upstairs since Summer and Natalya moved into the house—it's too strange for me. Looking around the room now, an invisible vice grips my heart, causing a fresh wave of homesickness for my friends and all those good times to hit me.

It's so different. Apryl's Batman posters and stacks of comics are long gone, and her seasons of *NCIS*, *Bones*, and *Psych* aren't scattered around the room. Her essence has been replaced with framed sheet music and books of poetry. And coral. No, not coral from the ocean. I mean the color. The curtains, bedspread, pillows, and *everything* is done in shades of coral-ish colors.

"You can sit in the desk chair," Natalya says as she lowers her tall frame to sit on the edge of her bed. She draws her legs into a crisscross position.

"I'm going to take a wild leap here and guess that your favorite color is lime green," I jokingly say while sitting in the desk chair, which is white with a coral cushion.

She blushes. "Yeah. I think it's because my favorite movie is still *The Little Mermaid*. I'm obsessed with anything that reminds me of Ariel without screaming, 'I still believe in mermaids!' to everyone." She shrugs. "I know it's odd."

"Oh, I can relate to fandom obsessions. No judgment here." I grin and hold up my pinky finger. "Promise."

She laughs. "Thanks."

And she's silent again, staring at a spot on the wall to my left. *Tick, tock. Tick, tock. Tick, tock.*

I can't find the source with my twitching eye, but I hear the seconds ticking by like someone is holding a clock that's been plugged into a giant amplifier against my ear.

*Tick, tock. Tick, tock. Tick, tock.*

I don't want to pressure her, but this is a little uncomfortable for me. There's only so many times I can shift in this chair before it looks like I'm the poster child for a hemorrhoid commercial, and I'm approaching that maximum number.

*Tick, tock. Tick, tock. Tick, tock.*

Oh, please! Say anything at this point! Ahhh!

Natalya snaps her attention back to me and takes a deep breath. "I need to talk to you about something, uh, delicate."

"Like fine china? Because I'm afraid I'm not the person to ask about that." My joke falls flat as my trusty intuition performs an interpretive dance with a couple red flags. Unfortunately, the interpretation is crystal clear: I'm about to get blindsided.

"Gabe," she says in a breathy rush. "I like him. I like him a lot."

And *Ka-Boom!*

*Oh, please tell me I'm getting punked! Puh-lease, God!*

But Natalya's expression doesn't change as her golden eyes search my face for any clue as to how I feel about this "delicate" revelation.

Like I hadn't already guessed. And from one girl to another, she obviously knows how I feel about this.

Not. Good.

Honestly, the last time this weird, out-of-body feeling of horror occurred was when I watched Gabe leave me at the altar. That's how not good this makes me feel. And what now? I'm supposed to smile and be okay with it? Give her my blessing?

Can a blessing be a clump of her hair dangling from my fist?

"I know it's weird," Natalya says quickly, possibly reading the desire to spring from my seat in my narrowed eyes. "I know you guys also have a history."

"Um, yeah. Yeah, we do." In my head, my words sound aggressive. Very, *Back off, lady!* But it comes out in a squeaky voice that sounds like that short blonde in that nerdy sitcom with all the scientists. And not the parts where this chick sounds scary.

Natalya holds her clasped hands against her heart. "And I

don't want to hurt you, Kaylee. I really feel like we've become friends."

Ah, yes, and I will curse your inevitable betrayal until my dying breath.

"And I know you don't want to get involved with Gabe again."

I'm amazed by how much this chick thinks she knows me and my feelings.

"Do you?"

I blink. Come again?

"Do you want to get involved with Gabe? Do you still have feelings for him?" Natalya asks. "Because I still have feelings for him, but I will back off if it's too weird for you."

Which is what I just said I wanted.

But...

Trust Gabe with my heart again?

Even if I thought Gabe wanted to be in a relationship with me again, I'm not sure I could. Forgiveness doesn't equal trust, and I'm not sure I've even got the forgiveness part down yet. But it doesn't matter because Gabe doesn't want a relationship. He said as much.

Why do I feel like I'm trying to convince myself? Protect myself?

Well, who cares if I am? After everything he's done, I need to protect myself.

Feeling resolved, I look Natalya in the eye. "No, I don't want a relationship like that with Gabe ever again. He's a good guy, and I'm thankful for what he's done to help me, but..." Time for another deep breath. "No."

Natalya shifts like a burden has been lifted from her shoulders and drops both feet to the floor with a soft thud. "I'm so glad." The relief in her voice is clear.

The cause of the rolling sensation in my gut is not.

"I mean, he is such a great guy," she says in a gushing voice that makes me want to throw up in my mouth. "He's so kind and caring and thoughtful. And he's so cute. And—"

Yeah, I can't handle this.

"So if that's all, I'll get out of your hair," I say, cutting her off with no shame whatsoever. I stand up without waiting for a response.

"Actually," Natalya jumps up, blocking my retreat with her waifish barricade, "would you talk to him for me?"

Insert silent screams of insanity here.

"You're kidding, right?" I can't help the tone this time. "Natalya, no. Just no! We're not in fifth grade. Talk to him yourself or wait for him to make the first move. Whatever you do, leave me out of it." This is not unreasonable to ask, right? I'm not crazy, am I?

She steps back like I backhanded her with my hostile words, but she continues to block my escape through the doorway. "I know it's childish, but... Okay, to be honest, I think he's afraid of hurting you. Maybe if you just, I don't know, let him know that you've moved on, then he'll give us a shot again."

I miss the days when this twisting, rolling, sick sensation in my gut didn't feel like a part of who I am and what I live with day after day. And the thought of Natalya and Gabe as a couple—coupling right in front of me—makes it so much worse. It will be like Taylor Swift's "The Outside," one more thing that's pushing me outside the group.

Natalya grabs my hands from where they were clenched by my side and squeezes them. "Kaylee, are you sure you don't still have feelings for Gabe?"

"Yes, I'm sure." I force myself not to growl through clenched teeth. "Those feelings have been burnt to a crisp and ceremoniously sprinkled across the land. It's over. I don't want him."

"Then please tell him that. Please let me have a chance." Tears glisten in her eyes.

And my heart breaks a little because I don't want Natalya to be in pain. "You're right, Natalya. We are friends. But I'm not standing in your way. I never was." Oh, how sad, but how true that is.

She wipes the tears from her eyes and pulls me into a hug. "I can't help it. I see the way he looks at you. I know Gabe says that he doesn't want a relationship and that he doesn't believe in love, but I think it's because of *you*. I don't think he's forgiven himself for whatever happened between the two of you."

Woah! What?

My jaw drops, and I try to say something to refute her, but it seems I've forgotten how to speak. (Or perhaps my ability has been impaired by my flytrap of a mouth and would be resolved if I *shut* my trap.) The memory of how Gabe acted at the *Phantom of the Opera* wedding... Each moment runs through my mind's eye with a fresh interpretation.

Is she right?

And what does that mean for us?

An icy wave of fear crashes over me. There's no "us." There can never be an "us." I can't be an "us" with Gabe ever again. Each moment, each revelation, chisels that law into my stone-protected heart.

I know what you're thinking, but I'm not lying to myself or avoiding how I feel. I don't want a relationship with Gabe.

I'm too afraid, and that's the truth.

"I'll talk to him," I say into Natalya's hair before pulling myself free from her hug. "He may not be in the same place you are, but for your sake, I'll make sure he knows that he doesn't need to punish himself for the past or tiptoe around me."

Natalya pulls me into another hug. "Thank you so much, Kaylee! Thank you!"

"You're welcome." A rogue tear escapes the corner of my eye as I flee.

Gabe paced in the chapel as he waited for Kaylee to arrive. He glanced at his watch. Ten minutes. She wasn't due for another ten minutes. And he'd been pacing for fifteen.

Why was he so nervous? What was wrong with him?

Never mind. That was an easy answer.

Everything.

He glanced out the window, noting the setting sun that cast its golden glow into the dimly lit space. A yawn escaped his lips, and he took the opportunity to stretch his stiff shoulders. His blue t-shirt stretched against the soft middle he couldn't seem to shake. Consistent workouts had toned his arms and chest, but his stomach remained soft and thick. And yet his legs where thin twigs, giving him the body structure of an upside-down triangle. Or better yet, a guitar pick.

Gabe yawned again and glanced at his watch.

Eight minutes.

Okay, enough of this. Gabe marched over to his guitar case and unlocked the latch. His guitar was an extension of him, and sometimes he had an easier time writing a song when he could hear the melody. So he might as well play while he waited for Kaylee, and the distraction should prevent Kaylee from witnessing his nervous pacing.

It worked. He went through his regular warm-up and focused on hitting each chord. Once he finished that, he decided to take a stab at a Jonas Brothers' song he'd heard on the radio. He pulled up the lyrics and sheet music on his iPhone, telling himself it was because the song would be perfect to add to the band's repertoire.

It had nothing to do with a certain emerald-eyed redhead.

Nothing.

But he still saw her face each time he closed his eyes while singing the romantic lyrics.

"Sorry I'm late, but—Wait, are you playing a JoBro song? You are! Stop this!"

Gabe opened his eyes to find Kaylee standing just inside the doorway and pointing an accusing finger at him.

She crossed her arms. "Dude, no. No! I hate the Jonas Brothers."

"This would be a good song for the band to learn." Gabe tried not to smile. Maybe that was the real reason he'd picked this song. Kaylee had never liked the Jonas Brothers, and in the past, he'd thoroughly enjoyed tormenting her with a song—or two—from their catalog.

Old habits died hard.

As did denial.

"I would rather cut out my tongue."

Gabe raised an eyebrow at her ridiculous claim.

"Fine," she growled in defeat. "No, I wouldn't. But I still don't want to sing their songs."

This time he couldn't stop his lips from curling into a smile at her outrage. "This is a good song."

"It's a Jonas Brothers' song, so no. It's not good."

"These guys made a huge comeback in the music industry.

You're kidding yourself if you think we won't be playing their songs—new and old—at some point."

"It's like a nightmare come to life," she said with a huff. She abandoned her position by the door and walked to the nearest pew, setting her bag down and kicking off her shoes.

"Kay." Why did saying her old nickname feel so good? "Set aside your grudge on behalf of Taylor Swift—who publicly apologized to Joe Jonas for her part in their breakup, by the way—and judge the quality of the song." He thoroughly enjoyed the way her nostrils flared while she glared at him.

Three minutes and counting...

"I'll wait for you to admit your defeat," he said after another four minutes of stubborn silence.

"Harrumph!"

"Want me to play the song again?"

Another growl.

Two more minutes...

"So I guess 'Love Her' isn't that bad of a song, but there's no way I can sing their older stuff," Kaylee finally mumbled with just a touch of bitterness before she turned her attention to rummaging through her purse.

And would you look at that...

It appeared someone was more familiar with the Jonas Brothers than she was willing to admit.

Gabe couldn't stop his chortle of victory. Kaylee looked up from where she'd been looking in her purse, presumably for her notebook and a pen, and eyed him warily.

"Mm-hmm, I agree. But at the moment, I'm more interested in how you knew the name of a Jonas Brothers' song. Would you care to explain?" he asked. Man, he enjoyed the way she turned her attention to the floor, the pews, the windows.

She cleared her throat and tucked her notebook under her arm. "Uh, I heard you sing the chorus, so I took a wild guess."

"I'm doubting that," he said with a laugh.

"Then I must have heard it on the radio," Kaylee offered weakly.

"And I think someone might be a closet fan," Gabe suggested with childlike glee.

"No way!" But her tell-tale blush of tomato red told a different story. She covered her face with her hands. "Stop looking at me like that."

"Seems like someone is a 'Sucker' for the Jonas Brothers." Gabe strummed the chords for that song. "Admit it."

"Argh! Fine! I like their new album, but I still hate the older stuff. Now you know my third biggest secret," she bemoaned.

Gabe's mirth vanished, and he turned away from Kaylee, song abandoned.

Would the talk of secrets always remind him of the shame and guilt he continued to carry? Would he ever be free of those chains?

He could feel Kaylee's eyes on him, but he avoided her gaze.

"Gabe, I need to talk to you before we start."

His heartrate tripled, and Gabe worked to keep the panic off his face. "Sure. What's up?" he asked, thankful that his voice sounded normal.

She tilted her head toward the pews to her left. "Can we sit?"

He nodded instead of answering, afraid his voice would betray him if he spoke this time. After slipping his guitar strap over his head while keeping a firm hold on the neck, he placed it in the case and locked it. Gabe took a deep breath as he sat down in the pew in front of her and angled his body so he could look at her.

*God, I don't know what this is about, and I know I don't deserve it, but help me.*

Gabe almost gasped. He prayed! Gabe didn't remember the last time he had prayed—and thought God would actually listen to him. He'd yelled at God (yelling that included taking a page out of Job's wife's playbook) plenty of times over the years, but it had been a long time since Gabe had asked for His help.

But it felt good. His soul felt lighter. Like the prodigal son in him had just taken a step toward his Father's house.

"So I'm just going to say this, and hopefully not screw up every newfound friendship in my life," Kaylee said, drawing him back to the moment at hand. "I want to know why you don't believe in love anymore."

Gabe stifled a groan. He knew this conversation would come back around sooner or later.

"I hope it's not because of me," Kaylee burst, then bit her lower lip—hard, judging by the way she winced—and leaned against the back of the pew.

"Why would it be because of you?" he asked carefully.

"You're not stupid, so I'm just going to level with you." Kaylee rubbed her face with both hands.

"Um, thank you?"

"But I'm sure you've noticed that Natalya likes, uh, is interested in you. Romantically," she said, halting and stuttering every three words before she choked on the last one. And the blush peaking between the fingers that still covered her face had achieved a shade of red that Gabe hadn't thought humanly possible.

Oh, this was awkward. Awkward, uncomfortable, and a smidge painful.

"Wow. Now I finally understand what you've meant when you've said some of the stuff between us is too weird. Like this. This conversation is too weird," Gabe said when he found the ability to speak without sounding like he'd just reached puberty.

Kaylee was right about another thing: Gabe wasn't stupid. Gabe knew Natalya hadn't gotten over him and wanted to rekindled their relationship, but to go to Kaylee like this? That was messed up. So messed up.

"Those other conversations weren't awkward for you?" she asked in a muffled voice, thanks to the hands she hadn't removed from her face.

"This is different."

"How?"

"This is weird for me."

"Then answer the question so we can get past this," she shrieked.

For a moment, Gabe was tempted to let her believe that she was the reason. A brief, cowardly moment, and he hated himself for it. However, Gabe didn't want to lie to her. He wanted to be the man she always thought he was. Maybe he could start here, small and pathetic as it was.

"Kaylee...Kay, please look at me," Gabe said.

She spread her fingers apart on her face, allowing her eyes to meet his. "There."

"Much better," he said sarcastically.

"Is it because of me?" she asked in a small voice.

"Kaylee, I'm not interested in Natalya."

"Because of me." Not a question this time.

He frowned. "Why would it be because of you?"

She dropped her hands into her lap, but she continued to gnaw on her lip as she spoke, causing a slight slur to her words. "Are you punishing yourself because of what happened between us? Are you worried about how I would react if you were to, uh, date Natalya? Or anyone? I would understand if I was the reason because, well, I would be concerned about how you would react in a similar situation, but—"

"I don't like Natalya like that," he said in a firm voice. "I don't. She's a friend. *That's it.*"

"But why? Natalya's great. She's the trifecta—smart, talented, and beautiful. Why wouldn't you like her?"

"Because love is a lie," they said at the same time before falling into silence.

Kaylee stared at him for three minutes and twenty-three seconds, some of the most uncomfortable moments of his life, before speaking. "Gabe, I don't know why you're trying to protect yourself with that lie, but you and I both know that cockamamie excuse *is* a lie."

That hit him where he hurt.

Unfortunately, self-righteous anger was his go-to move.

"I don't understand how *you* can say that after what I did to you." He stood up, too angry at God, his father, and himself to keep sitting. "Because you know full well that love breaks. Love dies. Love doesn't keep its promises. I don't believe in love because no one can love the way God *claims* He intended. People make pretty vows, then they go on lying and hurting each other. And God lets it happen. So love is a joke. A temporary chemical reaction that fizzles into nothing."

"You're right."

"Wh-what?" Gabe wasn't expecting Kaylee's calm answer in response to his resentful tirade. He dropped back into the pew like he'd been slapped.

"Except for the last part," Kaylee said. "Love is more than a chemical reaction. Love is spiritual. A gift from God, a Father whose very essence is pure love. And yeah, love on earth is imperfect, but God's love isn't." She looked into his eyes as she spoke, never blinking, never wavering in the truth Gabe knew she believed with her whole heart.

Gabe turned his back on her and slumped forward, elbows on his knees. He wrapped his hands around the back of his neck. "The answer we've been told our whole lives. I wish it was that simple."

"It's that complicated and that simple at the same time," she said.

He snorted in derision.

Then...a touch. He looked up to see her hand on his shoulder as she slid onto the pew beside him. Her citrus sent surrounded him, dulling his other senses.

"I'm here for you," she whispered. "Let me in. Let me see. Let me help."

"It's complicated." And messy. And shameful. And broken.

And he couldn't let her in to see all of that.

"I'm here for you," she whispered and squeezed his shoulder.

Gabe desperately wanted to believe that. And looking into her eyes, he could delude himself with that wistful hope.

Her emerald eyes pulled him toward her. Gabe reached out and touched a strand of her silky red hair, wrapping it around his finger.

She leaned closer.

Until...

One inch...

One breath...

Separated their lips...

Gabe jerked backward. What was he doing? He couldn't kiss her! Standing up, he grabbed his guitar case from where it sat beside him.

"I've got to go." He didn't even turn around to see her reaction as he stalked across the chapel and disappeared through the front door.

Once a scumbag, always a scumbag.

But he couldn't stay. And he couldn't tell her what she wanted to know.

Gabe climbed into his car and sent a quick text message before getting out of there. He drove for twenty minutes before arriving at his destination. He all but fell out of the car in his hurry. After sprinting across the dirt driveway, Gabe pounded on the front door of the modest Cape Cod style home while attempting to catch his breath.

He couldn't talk to Kaylee.

But he could talk to the one person who knew every sordid detail. His friend. His mentor. His sponsor.

His old youth pastor.

George G. Chiplain—or "Chip" as he preferred to be called—opened his front door.

## Chapter Eleven

I've never been afraid to go home. Never. Even when I was nine and accidently scratched my dad's new BMW with my bike pedal, I wasn't afraid to go home.

I'm afraid to go home now.

Because on the other side of this door, Natalya awaits.

I feel like I'm Gandalf the Gray about to fall into a bottomless chasm with the Balrog. There's no way up. There's no way out without a fight. There's no way to know what's going to happen once we disappear from sight.

But that plummet into darkness has been planned since pen met paper.

Time to face the music.

My internal radio flips to "The End" by Matthew West.

No offense to Matthew West, but I beg to differ.

Turning the doorknob, I peak through the doorway. With the exception of the dim light we leave on in the kitchen, everything is dark and silent. But I know better than to hope that Natalya has any intention of saving my interrogation for tomorrow. When I told her that I would talk to Gabe tonight, she squealed.

Squealed, guys. Squealed. A high-pitch squeal that hurt my ears and caused some dog nearby to start barking like it was an extra in *101 Dalmatians*.

Regardless, I'm still going to embrace the false hope the quiet house gives me and tiptoe toward the sanctuary of my bedroom.

I make it to the stairs.

"Hey! How did it go? What did he say? Do you think I have

a shot?" Natalya asks, jumping up from where she'd been sitting at the top of the stairs.

Smart. I have to hand it to her, that was smart. She knew I couldn't make it to my bedroom without passing through the living room and thus the stairs at the edge of the living room, the stairs right before the blessed hallway that would have been the home stretch to my salvation.

She trots down the stairs and swipes a lock of hair behind her left ear. "Well? How did it go?"

My breath catches.

She searches my face, and disappointment replaces her hopeful expression. "That good, huh?"

"I, uh, no. No. I'm sorry, Natalya," I stutter.

"If he doesn't want a relationship, then I can't force him." She shrugs while she murmurs, but I can see the sorrow in her eyes. She had fallen for Gabe—hard.

"He's a fool," I say for her benefit, even if I'm not really talking about his lack of interest in Natalya at the moment.

She offers me a smile. "Thanks."

I give her a quick hug, mumble something about going to bed, and hightail it to my room. I wipe a bead of sweat off my brow and take the first relaxing breath I've had all day.

There's that false hope again, allowing me to think I've escaped.

But then Natalya walks through the bedroom door that I'd stupidly left open.

"So what did he say?" she asks, leaning against the doorjamb in a prime interrogative position that blocks any hope of escape.

"Hmmm?" I hum and yawn. Take a hint, please.

"What did Gabe say? Please. I'd like to know." There's an aggressiveness to her words that sends a chill down my spine.

Hold onto your hat, friends. It's Balrog time.

I sigh. "I can't tell you that, Natalya," I say in a quiet voice. "Why?"

"Because it was a private conversation. Just like I didn't tell him about our earlier conversation, I can't give you a blow by blow of my conversation with Gabe. I can say that it doesn't seem like he likes you the same way you like him." Goodness, that explanation brought me back to my second-grade playground. Life was way easier when we could pass notes about this stuff.

"Why?"

I frown. Has she been transported back to second grade as well? "What?"

"Why?" she demands through clenched teeth. "Why doesn't he want to be with me?"

I stare at her, too flabbergasted to speak.

"Why?" she demands again.

"Are you serious? How should I know? Sometimes the guy doesn't always like the girl." Lord knows, I've experienced that first-hand with Gabe.

"And sometimes it's complicated. Because it's complicated, right? Your past together is complicated," she accuses.

"You know what?" I round on her, clearly surprising her. "It is complicated, and you knew that. How he may or may not feel about you is not my fault."

"You need to let him go!" she screams at me.

"And you need to stop trying to orchestrate something that's beyond your control!" I yell back.

We both stand there for a moment, heaving with anger at each other. Though to be fair, my stomach is also heaving with anxiety and fear that I'm desperately trying to keep inside.

"Thanks for your help, *friend*," she says with a snarl that tells me "friend" really means "fiend." She turns on her heel and leaves. The *Thud!* of her bedroom door echoes throughout the house, but something tells me that we haven't reached the bottom of that chasm yet.

And if *The Fellowship of the Ring* has taught me anything, only one of us can emerge victorious from the battle that will ensue once we reach the bottom.

"Wow," Chip said as he handed Gabe a bottle of water before sitting at the kitchen table. "That's intense."

"No kidding," Gabe mumbled as he accepted the bottle and proceeded to chug the whole thing.

Chip twisted the cap of his own bottle until it snapped off and took a long sip. He met Gabe's eyes as he replaced the cap. "So why do you keep pushing Kaylee away?"

Gabe startled and nearly dropped his water bottle. That was the last question he expected Chip to ask right now. "You know why. Of all people, *you* know why."

"I know what I think is the reason, but I don't know your reason."

Trust Chip to force an answer out of him. The muscle in Gabe's jaw twitched, and he drank the rest of his water, taking his sweet time. "I've told you this before: love is a lie, and I can't risk hurting her because I will fail her."

"So you say." Ever calm, Chip took another sip of his water.

"So I say?" Gabe repeated in shock, crinkling his now empty water bottle in his death grip. "You make it sound like it's not the truth."

"It's what you believe to be the truth," Chip stated in that matter-of-fact way of his.

"It is the truth, but what do you think is the reason?" Gabe asked, curiosity getting the best of him, as he leaned back. The metal chair squeaked with the shift of weight.

"You don't feel like you're worthy of love because of your past, and you don't feel like you're capable of love because of your father's betrayal."

Gabe held Chip's stare with his own hard gaze. "And your point is?"

"That what you believe *about* love is a lie."

Did Chip and Kaylee plan to tag team this or something? Gabe huffed in derision. "Yeah, you know what, you're right. That is exactly what I think—because it's true."

Chip rubbed the short, gray whiskers on his face while tapping his water bottle against the table. "Do you remember when you first confided in me all those years ago?" he asked slowly.

How could Gabe ever forget? Fresh waves of shame and guilt slammed into his spirit at the vague mention of his past on the Dark Web and the way he'd objectified women in order to feel better about himself, his day, his pain. How did a man come back from using something God had created for marriage and using that twisted, selfish imitation so lustfully?

He didn't. There was no coming back from that. Gabe was tainted and impure.

Which was why the shame and guilt still felt as strong as the day he sat at this very table—only a few days after running out on Kaylee—and he told Chip everything. About his father. About his anger and hatred toward his father. About his own struggles with such a similar sin. About his disgust and hatred toward himself.

Gabe opened his mouth to answer, but the noose of condemnation tightened around his throat, so he nodded in response.

"You told me that you loved Kaylee too much to hurt her like that."

"I remember," Gabe whispered as he studied the tabletop with veracious intensity.

"And then you ran." Chip's statement twisted the knife in his gut.

Gabe hung his head. "I thought that I needed to handle my problem by myself, and I needed to protect Kaylee. Leaving made sense." Recovery had proven him wrong and had taught him there was no shame in needing help to overcome a struggle that could rewire the brain in an addictive way. Realizing that so many others had struggled with exactly this released Gabe from thinking that he needed to get a handle on the problem in his own strength.

"And over the years," Chip continued speaking like Gabe hadn't said anything, "you started clinging to this 'love is a lie' lie."

*Wonderful use of air quotes, man.*

"All to protect yourself."

Gabe opened and closed his mouth a half dozen times in shock because that's exactly what Kaylee had accused him of doing. "What? No. No, I've been trying to protect *her.*"

"Why would you care about protecting her if you thought love was a lie?" Chip asked with a gentle *Gotcha!* look.

"Because," he stuttered, grasping for the logic that had seemed so valid in his head but now felt inadequate. "Because unconditional love is impossible. It's something we tell ourselves so that we can continue to love someone who continues to stab us in the back." *I will not do that to her,* Gabe added silently.

"Unconditional love takes a lot of forgiveness. The kind of forgiveness God gives us."

"Forgiveness for who?" Gabe asked. "My father? Me? No way. That's like saying it's okay."

"No, it's not." Chip leaned forward, tapping the tabletop with his index finger. "Unconditional love is a gift that God offers us and encourages us to give to others. It's not a chain that holds someone in a toxic relationship, and it's not condoning something that is clearly sin. It's freedom in the form of forgiveness, grace, and mercy.

"We were created to love, Gabe. *You* were created to love, but you've closed yourself off from giving or receiving any love. And I'm saying this because I love you like a son and as a brother in Christ, but you're not doing yourself any favors with that mindset."

Gabe's lips quirked into a slight smile. Chip had always been known for his blunt way of presenting the truth.

"I'm not telling you to jump into a new relationship with Kaylee; I'm not even saying that you should pursue a relationship with Kaylee." Chip's hand landed on Gabe's shoulder, causing him to look the older man in the eye. "I'm urging you to stop pushing everyone away and let them have a chance to love you as God loves you—in spite of your past mistakes and brokenness.

"You've repented, Gabe. You've gotten help. You've overcome a sin that shackles so many people for the entirety of life. But your past and your father's lifestyle continues to rob you of all the blessings God wants to give you. Shame. Guilt." Chip held his gaze, and Gabe resisted the overwhelming urge to hang his head again. "His grace is bigger. His love is redemptive. His forgiveness is complete. Live in it."

Gabe's jaw twitched as he mentally wrestled with Chip's words before he sighed in defeat. "I started off blaming God for my father's sins, but then I had to confront the worst in myself. I always knew my sin was my fault. In the end, I screwed up and hurt people just like he did." Gabe shook his head. "There's no coming back from that."

"You're not unforgiveable, Gabe," Chip said in a firm voice.

"Yes...no. It's more than that." Gabe's voice dropped half an octave with every other word. "My father doesn't deserve forgiveness, and I sure don't either."

"It's easier to push God away than accept His forgiveness?" Chip asked.

Gabe didn't answer that. It was a trap. A Biblical trap.

But Chip went for the kill shot. "Or to extend that same forgiveness?"

Gabe snorted in derision at the harsh reality he'd come to know. "There are some things that are too big, too awful to come back from—with God and with society."

"Society isn't the problem," Chip declared.

*Uh, what? Since when?*

"It's your standing before God," Chip stated. "God isn't throwing the sins He's forgiven into your face. That is the work of an accuser, and those are the lies you're claiming as truth. The lies of an accuser instead of the unconditional love and complete forgiveness of God." Chip smiled sadly. "Believing that lie is basically telling Jesus His death wasn't enough to forgive your sins."

Gabe dropped his head into his hands, blatantly ignoring his mother's voice in his head that told him to get his elbows off the table. This was just another brick in the wall of lies that Gabe had allowed to be built around him. Another mark in the *Gabe's an Idiot* column of his life. And more proof that he was a terrible Christian. He couldn't even grasp the basics, could he?

Gabe felt like a war was being fought inside of him. That was the problem with a secret sin. Each failure—no matter how far in the past—said he could never be washed clean. That he could never really, completely approach God or be worthy of God or anyone else's love. And the worst part was discovering just how much other people believed that when they came face-to-face with sin.

People like Gabe. Because he'd never been able to forgive his father. Or himself.

"He loves you, Gabe. His love isn't a lie, and neither is His forgiveness."

"What about Kaylee?" Gabe asked, deflecting the focus from his fragile relationship with God.

Chip smiled in a fatherly way, like the father Gabe wished

he'd had. "First, forgive. Yourself. Your father. Get rid of those chains."

Easier said than done. "Then what?"

"Let her in."

Exactly what Kaylee said. Someone was tag teaming him with this stuff.

God, probably. Breaking the rules of their standoff again.

"Get to know her again. Let her be your friend. Be hers. Let her in. See where God takes you."

Gabe leaned back in his chair again, and his thoughts swirled around him. For the first time in a long time, Gabe wanted to believe in the impossible. That he wouldn't be defined by those failures. That he could live in the same love and forgiveness God extended to others. That he could love someone the way God intended.

And that they could love him the same way.

"I'll try," he told Chip. "I'll try."

# Chapter Twelve

I've done this before.

This would make a total of three times.

Once for each of my besties.

Miss Manners must have a rule about this. For the sake of mental health, there should be a limit to the number of times you're a bridesmaid. It's no wonder Katherine Heigl's character was so bitter in *27 Dresses*.

I'll save you the traditional speech about how happy I've been for each of them, interspersed with lines about how I don't need a man to complete me because God completes me. It's the truth, even if it feels a little lackluster in this moment.

Instead, I'm going to take this washable chalk and finish trashing my friends' getaway car. If I'm lucky, the long, curly eyelashes I'm drawing on the headlights will bake onto the lenses.

I'm emptying my twentieth bag of glitter confetti into the car when someone knocks on the roof of the compact. I jump at the unexpected sound, causing a balloon to pop next to my ear.

"Ow!" I shriek.

"Whoa!" Izze says, grabbing my arm and pulling me out of the car. Balloons, confetti, and half a roll of toilet paper follow me.

Yeah, I went there.

"I see now why you leaped at the chance to 'decorate' the getaway car."

I brush some of the confetti off my leggings and button-up blouse. "I don't know what you're talking about."

She looks at the puddle of confetti at my feet. "Maybe therapists should use this as a way to work out some pent-up aggression."

"I think you're referring to the Carrie Underwood method, which is, sadly, still illegal."

"Not if it's your car."

"Smashing your own car with a baseball bat is just stupid," I say.

Izze inspects my handiwork, leaning as far as she dares into the car. Three balloons squeeze past her, breaking out of their cramped quarters. "Wow! Courtney and Dallas are going to love you."

"I know." I grin wickedly. I can't help it. This was fun. Maybe Izze was on to something with the therapy idea.

"Listen, I wanted you to know that Courtney invited everyone in the band to come to the ceremony."

I sigh and roll my eyes. "That doesn't surprise me."

"And one of Dallas' groomsmen had an unexpected emergency, so he asked Gabe to fill in as a groomsman. You'll be walking with him."

"What?" I shriek. "Please say you're kidding."

"I'm kidding," Izze laughs. "Like I would ever encourage a scenario like that. I just wanted to see how you'd react. We're good."

"We are not good." My limp hand flops over my racing heart. "That is one of the meanest things you've ever done to me. You've gotten sadistic in your old age."

Izze's laugh turns into a snort. "Have I? Interesting. I don't feel like I've changed."

I shove the rogue balloons back into the car and slam the door shut before they escape again. "Then maybe your true nature is coming out more in your old age."

"Once again, I'm going to remind you that you're older than me."

"By two weeks. And you were born two weeks late, so technically—"

"So technically," Izze interrupts, "you're still older."

She tucks my arm through her looped one and we stroll back to the front door of the massive Victorian where Apryl and Courtney run their wedding decorating business. My imaginative mind flitters away, seeing us as ladies of leisure in *Downton Abbey* as we stroll around our very own Highclere Castle.

A car door slams as we walk around the corner of the house, and I see Gabe, Ethan, and Drake climb out of Ethan's tweaked out truck in the temporary parking area. Out of the corner of my eye, I notice Summer's VW van meandering down the long driveway, past Chance's mechanic shop and the carriage house where Apryl and Chance live.

My eyes are drawn back to Gabe, who is decked out in a gray suit that looks like his eyes. He slicked back the slightly longer hair on the top of his head, and he's already loosened the tie around his neck. He turns and shrugs out of the suit jacket, throws it back into the car, and rolls the sleeves of his white shirt up his forearms.

It's not a song in my head this time. Instead, it's Uncle Jesse from Full House delivering his signature line.

All the air is compressed from my lungs as I watch him. Why is this sudden loss of breath a seeming requirement when you see someone you...er, uh, are attracted to?

Were! I mean *were* attracted to.

Ahem.

However, my eyes are still glued to Gabe's every movement, so draw your own conclusions.

I'd rather be crawling with ants or maybe get kicked in the face right now. It would hurt less than having your breath stolen at the sight of someone you can never have.

Izze nudges me with her annoyingly full hips. I can't hip-bump anyone with my green bean build. "You're staring."

"Oh, no. Have I shocked you?" I quip in a pathetic attempt to make light of my awkward faux pas.

"A little actually," she confesses as she grabs my face. "Let me look at your eyes. Do you have a concussion? A sharp blow to the head is the only thing that explains why you're staring at him."

I push her away. "Stop shouting about it for the whole world to hear."

"Who are we staring at?" Courtney asks, bouncing to a stop next to us and throwing her arms around our shoulders. "I'm getting married today!"

"Huzzah!" I say with ten percent less enthusiasm that I should have.

"Courtney!" Apryl bursts through the front door of the house and glares at her twin sister. "I told you that I needed to start curling your hair by now. Where have you been?"

"Um, with them," she looks at Izze and me for help.

I look at Apryl and shake my head while mouthing, *No.*

"Liar," Apryl accuses.

"Thanks a lot," Courtney mumbles.

"Were you talking to Dallas again?" Apryl demands.

Izze feigns shock and gasps. "Courtney! You're not supposed to see the groom before you walk down the aisle."

Courtney holds up her index finger. "I haven't seen him."

"No, she hasn't seen him," Apryl says sarcastically. "However, I think spending the entire morning on the phone with him violates the spirit of the tradition."

"Does anyone else have the overwhelming urge to belt out 'Tradition' from *Fiddler on the Roof*?" I look at each of my friends. "Just me?"

"I know I spend ninety percent of my day imagining myself as an extra in a musical," Apryl says sarcastically before blowing a lock of the blue-black hair that's become her signature color out of her eyes.

"You can mock, but we all know you'd jump at the chance."

"Only if I can dance with my hunky Chance." Apryl grins and wiggles her eyebrows.

Barf. "Can someone hold back my hair for me? I'm going to be sick."

Izze smirks. "Someone is enjoying married life."

"Oh, yes. I am," Apryl replies with a radiant smile.

That's it. I need some single friends.

Summer parks next to Ethan's truck, and she and Natalya join the guys. Somehow, I've continued to watch Gabe while conversing with my friends. I'm hoping Izze hasn't noticed the gawking I should have outgrown a long time ago, but I'm sure a quick glance at her will nuke that theory like an exploding star.

Look. Away.

And yup, Izze is watching me. I can't tell what she's thinking. Without tipping her hand, she nods toward the band members, the other world where I don't quite belong. "Do they know where to set up and everything like that?"

"I had talked to Gabe or Ethan about it earlier this week, but Kaylee," Courtney waits for me to look at her before continuing, "would you mind going over it with them again?"

I would rather star in a YouTube video where I'm singing "Endless Love" in a helium voice while wearing a dinosaur costume. But there's a rule somewhere about how you don't mess with any reasonable request made by the bride on her wedding day, so it seems I have no choice.

I nod and offer my customary smile, the one that says, *No problem! I'm happy to help!*

Apryl grabs Izze and Courtney's arms. "While she's helping them, I need to get started on hair and makeup for you guys. Come on!"

I turn away from my friends who've abandoned me yet again, close my eyes, and take a deep breath.

Breathe in. Breathe out.

Mental karate chop here.

I open my eyes and walk toward my fellow band members. Gabe sees me coming and shifts his weight from one foot to the other. I offer another weird and awkward smile as I greet them. "Hey, guys."

Everyone but Gabe returns my verbal greeting. He meets my eyes and dips his head.

Love the effort, buddy.

"So I thought I'd help you guys start to set up before I have to go get ready for the ceremony," I say.

"Where are we setting up?" Natalya asks.

"Cool," Summer says at the same time while looking around the property. "This place is beautiful."

"It is. Courtney's twin sister also got married out here, but her wedding was in the middle of the willow grove." I point to the willow grove whose golden leaves are on fire with the changing of the seasons. "We'll be setting up so that our backs are to the willow grove. Let's grab some of the stuff, and I'll show you."

We all grab a load of equipment and instruments, and they follow me to the area Apryl marked with four purple bandanas.

I set the amp and music stand I'd been carrying in the middle of the grassy rectangle.

"There isn't a platform or something for us to play on?" Natalya asks, looking around the area like she can't believe she has to stand on dirt.

Poor little princess.

Yeah, we're still not on good terms after the other night.

"No. Courtney wanted it to look like we were playing in the middle of a field since we've had an unseasonably warm and long autumn," I say. "And we already made sure an extension cord would make it out here and work properly." We tested this with a coffee maker, lamp, and an old TV with a VHS player built into it.

Man, those TVs were the jackpot back in the day. And in case you were wondering, we watched a VHS of Cinderella while sitting in a lamp-lit grassy field and sipping coffee. Talk about whimsically surreal, but now "Bibbidi Bobbidi Boo" has been playing almost exclusively on my internal radio for the last forty-one hours.

"Sounds like the setting for a music video," Summer says.

"It does." Drake nods with enthusiastic agreement and looks at Ethan. "Maybe Ethan could get some footage of us playing. After all, Jane Austen said, 'Without music, life would be a blank to me.' That's right. I know Jane Austen." Drake wiggles his eyebrows.

Summer rolls her eyes. "Looking up a quote online only makes you a poser. Read *Pride and Prejudice*, and then we'll talk."

"What are you suggesting we do with this video footage, Drake?" Natalya asks, redirecting the conversation.

"Use it to highlight those embarrassing, squinty, fish mouth kind of pictures that really flatter Gabe?" Ethan delivers his suggestion the same way Tony Stark would deliver a good-natured dig to Thor.

"We could splice it together for our own music video," Drake says. A light breeze flutters through the ends of his shaggy, Season One of *The Office* Jim Halpert blond hair.

"Doesn't that seem tacky? Low budget?" Natalya brushes her dark hair away from her glossed lips.

"We are low budget, Natalya," Gabe says. "But I've seen plenty of music videos like what Drake is suggesting from well-known artists."

"Taylor Swift has done several with that home video feel," I add. "If it's good enough for Taylor, then it's good enough for me."

"What's the worst that could happen? We don't use any of the footage?" Summer shrugs. "I can live with that."

"Me too. Plus, it's about time Ethan did more than eat cake while we're playing a gig." Gabe tosses Ethan a pointed look, and Ethan rolls his eyes.

Why do I get the feeling that this is payback for something Ethan did?

I am *not* hijacking lemons from the bizarre number of fruit baskets in my friends' house.

And that will remain the official party slogan.

Which would be a lot easier to prove if Natalya hadn't just walked into the kitchen, literally catching me with my hand in the fruit basket.

"Can we talk?" Natalya asks, blocking my path from where she leans against the wall.

"Um, sure," I try to say in a normal voice—one not affected by fear of how this conversation might go—as I discreetly return the lemon I'd been clutching to its comrades in the fruit basket and withdraw my hand.

She pushes away from the wall and clasps her hands in front of her black, slinky dress. "I need to apologize to you."

I blink.

She shrugs. "Yeah, I'm sorry. I can't blame you for how Gabe may or may not feel about me."

"Thank you," I say. Got to be honest, I'm kind of shocked. "I forgive you."

A muscle in Natalya's right cheek twitches. "Um, thanks."

I fight the urge to release an exasperated sigh. So far, friendship with Natalya runs hot and cold, back and forth, all or nothing. It's exhausting, like you want someone to throw a cup of hot coffee into your face to revive you, but the scalding heat doesn't register against your weary eyelids.

However, I believe I've seen glimpses of the real Natalya, the one buried under hurts and disappointments. I want to be friends with her, and God loves her, warts and all. So I will grind my teeth, look into purchasing a TMJ nightguard tonight, and persist in being Natalya's friend through the difficult stuff.

"Okay," I say, sliding my foot forward. "I should get back to my bridesmaid duties."

She holds up both hands. "Can I ask a favor?"

Dread zips through my heart. The last favor she asked me didn't go well. "Uh, maybe. I guess. What's the favor?"

"Can I sing the duet with Gabe?" She steps toward me, and I resist the urge to step back.

"I don't know if—"

"It's just," she rushes to continue, "I thought it might be weird for you. After all, you said that you don't want to be in a relationship with Gabe again. Seems like a romantic song would be really uncomfortable." Natalya eyes me, studying me for a reaction.

I almost give her one. The memory of Gabe's nearness the other night warms my entire being, and then being mentally smacked with attraction at the sight of him today...I might need to stomp on my foot again to prevent a full swoon.

Instead, I settle for a deep breath. "That's true—about me, I mean."

"And I would really love the opportunity. I've always wanted the chance." She threads her fingers together and tilts her head down.

I frown. "You don't get to sing? Ever?"

"Mostly backup. Solos, sometimes, but Aria was better than me. Just like you're better than me. I'm usually overlooked, and I'd really like a chance to grow and...shine. I know that sounds dumb, but..." The genuine Natalya I'd been getting to know, the one I had started to call friend, reemerges, and I can't help it. My heart wants to help her.

And I want to protect myself. I can't deny that it's best if I don't confuse my heart with romantic lyrics and Gabe's deep voice. I can't go there again, so I need to fight the attraction and connection and history between us.

Period.

I sigh. "I get it." And I do. It hurts to be passed over, ignored, forgotten. "I guess it would be okay—"

Natalya squeals and throws her arms around my neck, hugging me. "Thank you! Thank you! Thank you!"

I free myself from her hug. "But we need to clear it with Ethan and Gabe."

She holds up both hands, excitement evident on her face. "Leave that to me." She turns and disappears from the kitchen, presumably to find the guys.

I feel...

Disappointed.

But I don't want to think about why I feel like that.

So I'm going to hope it passes.

Gabe tried not to roll his eyes at Ethan.

"I saw that."

Gabe frowned. "Saw what?"

"The urge to roll your eyes."

"What? Be real, man. You can't tell if someone has the urge to roll their eyes."

Ethan gave him a deadpan stare.

"Fine," he relented, "but what do you expect when you drag me over here under false pretenses?"

"What are you talking about?" Ethan asked before opening the back of Summer's VW van. "We're unloading the rest of the equipment, which is exactly what I said we'd be doing when I asked you for help."

"Right, but every trip over here is five uninterrupted minutes of your know-it-all lectures before you even open the van door."

"Fine, fine. All I'm saying is that this is a recipe for disaster. I like Kaylee; she's a fantastic singer. However, you need to get a handle on this, or the band will be in worse shape than we were last time," Ethan said while carefully sliding Natalya's violin case out of the van.

Gabe sighed in exasperation for the fourteenth time. "I hear you, man."

Ethan leveled him with another piercing look. "Do you? Because I feel like we've been having this exact same conversation for months. Months, Gabe. Months."

Gabe let out a slow breath, attempting to reign in his annoyance.

Ethan sighed, then clapped his hand on Gabe's shoulder. "I'm sorry. I'm not trying to badger you. I'm worried about the band, but most importantly, I'm worried about you and Kaylee."

"I've got it all under control." Maybe. Well, he was trying to get it under control. And he planned to start with Chip's advice and get to know Kaylee again—as a friend.

"Mind if I ask how?"

"I do, but I'll tell you anyway: I'm going to be her friend." Only her friend. He couldn't risk hurting Kaylee with anything more than that.

"Sounds perfect," Ethan said with the kind of measurable sarcasm that would break the scale. "Nothing could possibly go wrong with that. And how, pray tell, do you plan to be her friend?"

"What is this? Twenty questions?"

"I'd prefer it if you thought of it as my own special version of the Spanish Inquisition." Ethan swung the door shut.

"We're going to hang out. Get to know each other again."

Ethan raised an eyebrow. "I realize I'm a few years older than you, so I might be out of touch with the current vernacular. However, isn't that essentially dating?"

Gabe did roll his eyes this time. "No. No. No, no, and no."

Ethan shook his head and shifted the violin to his right hand.

Gabe sighed. "Out with it."

"It's nothing."

"I'm not in denial, Ethan."

"Mm-hmm. Okay."

Gabe opened his mouth, prepared to list every reason why this was *not* dating in *any* sense of the word, when the sound of heavy footsteps on gravel caught his ear. Next thing he knew, Natalya had materialized in front of them.

"Hey, guys!"

She felt awfully close to him. Gabe took a step back from her, but she moved with him, subtly shifting forward. He had a bad feeling about this.

"So I realize this is a little awkward," Natalya said in a rush, "but Kaylee wanted me to take her duet with Gabe."

"Oh, really?" Ethan asked, swinging his annoying, I-told-you-so gaze to Gabe for a second, then turned his attention back to Natalya. "Why is that?"

"She felt a little awkward about singing it with Gabe."

Gabe felt the breath *Whoosh!* out of him like Natalya had just taken her violin case and swung it full force at his kidneys.

"You know, because of everything," Natalya added with a little laugh and shrug that was probably meant to be cute.

Really? She was laughing about this? Like it was no big deal? Disgust turned Gabe's stomach sour.

"I figured it would probably be okay since this is her friend's wedding and all. I'm assuming she would know if they'd be okay with it, but I wanted to check with you guys."

Gabe frowned. Something about this was off.

Natalya swayed from foot to foot and clasped her hands in front of her. "Please, guys. You both know how much I've been wanting to sing more at weddings. It would mean so much to me if you guys gave me this chance."

Ethan sighed and looked at him. Gabe shrugged in a vague, flabbergasted response, unsure of what to do.

"Okay. We'll give it a try," Ethan said in a slow way that said he was rethinking his consent even as he gave it.

"Thank you!" Natalya squealed and threw her arms around Ethan's neck. She turned to do the same to Gabe, but he'd had the foresight to grab her violin from where it dangled in Ethan's right hand while she hugged him. He handed it to her in place of a hug. Gabe couldn't determine what her dark expression meant, but then she offered him a big smile. "Thank you both so much."

She trotted back inside with her violin, skipping and humming the lyrics to their—that felt wrong to say—duet.

Gabe's gut churned and perspiration beaded across his forehead. "In retrospect, stopping for tacos from that food truck on the way here might have been a bad idea."

"A portable grill in the back of some dude's pickup is not a food truck. But I think the switch in co-singer is the cause of your internal distress." Ethan's nose wrinkled. "I hope."

"I'll fix it," Gabe promised.

"I hope so, Gabe. For both your sakes."

*If it's the last thing I do, I will fix this,* he promised to himself.

"Don't trip. Don't trip. Don't trip," I mutter underneath my breath while keeping my lips still.

You'd think I would be used to this trek by now.

Walk up the aisle without falling on your face or inappropriately flashing someone with an ill-timed cheerleader kick. Stand there looking deliriously happy for your friends as you count the seconds until you can dump the high-heeled monstrosities you were forced to wear into a gasoline-soaked firepit. Walk back down the aisle on the arm of one of your friend's beaus or a stranger you can only pray has a sufficient hygiene regimen. Eat more cake than is appropriate under normal circumstances but in this case is excusable as you pretend to dance those calories off your hips.

It's not rocket science, but it's a science, nonetheless. A science I've perfected over the years. The science that enables me to imbibe in a piece of cake for every "Cha-cha Slide" I do, free of guilt. Mostly.

I step into my place behind Izze and adjust my body to face toward all the lucky people who are sitting in somewhat chipped and shaky (hey, these antiques were well-loved in their day!) chairs. Then I watch Courtney walk down the aisle. The cathedral length train of her gown and matching veil create the perfect "princess in an enchanted meadow" vibe.

But a certain man in gray catches my eye.

And the science that enabled me to stand here like a normal person fails.

I'm sure I look normal to most. I'm sure my always-the-bridesmaid, always-happy-go-lucky, always-willing-to-go-that-extra-mile persona is in place for the guests gathered to witness this marriage covenant.

But Gabe knows. He can see it. And the way his eyes are

locked on me makes my skin crawl in a way that's not entirely unpleasant.

The variable I hadn't factored into my perfectly tailored equation was my ex-boyfriend/secret fiancé sitting in the middle of the fourth row from the back on the bride's side, watching me with an expression I can't read. Maybe it's warm and hopeful? Maybe it's stomach cramps? I can't be sure anymore, and that infuriates me.

So my face probably reads as follows: *I ate some bad clams, but I'm going to stand up here anyway despite the violent lurching in my gut.*

Everyone here should be so lucky to have a friend like me. Insert mental eyeroll here. What? You know that I can't really roll my eyes while Courtney and Dallas recite their vows. Everyone would see.

It's that horrible, horrible naïveté of mine. I hadn't counted on how hard, awkward, and emotionally traumatizing it would be to see Gabe in a setting like this again. I've been so focused on trying to have a civil conversation with the man. But here we are. At a wedding. And once again, I'm standing up front watching the man watch me.

What are the odds he runs again? Five to one?

What? Too harsh?

I should be watching my friends and *only* my friends. I should be watching Courtney cry while Dallas says his vows in a wobbly voice of his own.

But my eyes continue to drift back to Gabe.

He shifts in his seat.

Natalya, seated to Gabe's left, must be leaning toward him because she's in the shot now.

She leans closer.

Closer...

Closer...

And stinking closer still. For crying out loud! From this angle it looks like she's kissing his ear. I mean, I know she's not, but come on. Decorum, people!

Says the morbidly fascinated woman who continues to stare at them.

Gabe nods in response to whatever she's whispering and blatantly leans away from her. The joyous relief that his response gives me makes me want to attempt the electric slide down the aisle.

I won't, but you guys will know that I'm dancing on the inside.

"You may now kiss the bride," the pastor says, jerking my attention back to where it should have been this whole time. I cheer and whistle with everyone else as Dallas dips Courtney like they're the stars of a romantic comedy.

As the pastor introduces the newlyweds, my eyes find Gabe again. Courtney and Dallas walk down the aisle, stopping to hug this person or that relative, and the inevitable pairing of the bridal party begins. Apryl and Chance go. Izze and Miles go. Each couple, the evidence of the changes in the last few years.

As if the strangers living in my house weren't enough evidence.

A friend of Dallas' nudges my shoulder with his elbow (he's a tall fellow) and whispers to me like a professional ventriloquist, "I think it's our turn."

"Oh! Right!" I slip my arm into the crook of his elbow and try not to take a deep breath. We walk down the aisle with tight smiles. Gabe finally breaks eye contact with me, turning to talk to Drake.

Well, I really can't look at him now.

"What number is this?"

"Hmmm?" I keep my eyes straight ahead, and...yes, I did it! Gabe is no longer visible in my peripheral vision.

"This is my fourth," the groomsman says quietly as the pastor proclaims in a booming voice to enjoy the appetizers while the wedding pictures are taken. "What about you?"

I look at him and—without thinking about the possible toxic ramifications—let out the breath I was holding. "What?" I squeak.

"Wedding," he reiterates for the woman with the lack of oxygen reaching her brain cells. He, to his credit, doesn't bat an eye at my squeaky voice. "This is the third time I've been a groomsman in the last four years."

Lungs. Burning. Oxygen necessary. Oh, thank goodness! I can only smell his woodsy aftershave. "Oh. Gotcha."

"What about you?" He steers us toward where the other

members of the bridal party are standing three or so feet away from the cake table. The others watch the photographer position Courtney and Dallas against a backdrop of autumn-colored willows.

I raise an eyebrow at him and reclaim my arm. "What makes you think I've got a competing number?"

He shrugs and tosses me a knowing smile. "I can recognize the look of annoyed—and may I say, rather begrudging?—experience on the face of an individual who's been instructed on the speed they should walk one too many times. I mean," he says, spreading his hands apart, "I practically invented *that* look. It's my resting face."

"I am not begrudging!" Wow, this guy is rude. How dare he go around saying what I'm privately thinking.

"Really? Must just be me." My mouth opens in shock, and he winks at me. "I'm kidding. Sort of."

I stifle a laugh at that. "This is the third wedding where I've been a bridesmaid within two years," I confess.

"And we have a winner," he whisper-shouts.

I snort. "What do I win?"

He flips his hand toward the three-tiered wedding cake. "An extra piece, of course."

I pretend to sniff in derision. "I'm a bridesmaid. I get all the extra cake I want."

"Well, then how about a dance with me?"

Say what? "Uh..." Oh, yes. That's a charming response.

"What do you say?" he asks again. That's when I realize this guy is flirting with me, and I don't even know his name.

"Can we have all the bridesmaids?" the photographer asks.

*Thank you, God!* I grab the hem of my gown and rush to stand beside Izze, heart pounding like I chugged six energy drinks, three black coffees, and washed it down with a quart of sweet tea. My mind spins like it's stuck in a huge mud hole as the photographer positions us in various poses, some of which include the mystery guy.

What do I say?

Man, I could really use a lemon drop right now.

So...

Okay, here's where I'm at: I know there's no logical reason

why I shouldn't dance with him. And Courtney insisted that we only play two half hour sets so that everyone could enjoy the wedding reception. And this guy... He's funny. Seems nice. Definitely handsome. Has a Kaylee-Approved hygiene regimen.

But somewhere in this sea of wedding guests is Gabe.

I would feel horrible if I watched him dance with another woman tonight, so I'm not going to do that to him.

I know, I know. I don't owe him anything. I remember with painful clarity everything he's done and said. But I can't. I won't. I won't be *that* person. He may be one hundred percent over me, but I can't dance with another man tonight in front of him out of spite. I could tell you it's to keep that emotional distance between us, but I think you and I both know that would not be the truth in this circumstance.

I can't do that to him.

"Okay, now I'd like the bride, groom, sister of the bride, and the bride's grandmother," the photographer instructs.

Now's my chance. The groomsman is standing back where I originally left him. He offers me a charming smile as I approach.

"Listen, uh," I falter. Right. I don't know his name.

"Buzz," he supplies.

I blink. "Like Aldrin or Lightyear?"

"Like I haven't heard that one before." He playfully rolls his eyes.

"Right, I'm sorry. You obviously meant the one from *Toy Story*," I shoot back.

He groans. "Speaking of *Toy Story*, have you seen the new one? It ruined my childhood."

"How did it—" I shake my head slightly. I need some camera-like focus, not a runaway conversation with a man obsessed with *Toy Story*. "I can't dance with you, Buzz. I'm sorry."

He shrugs one shoulder. "I can't say I'm not disappointed, but it seems like your dance card might already be full."

"Huh?"

Buzz gestures with his chin with all the subtly of a pointing finger that I should look behind me. Glancing over my shoulder, I spot Gabe. Even if I wasn't wearing my contacts, I would be able to see his thundercloud expression clear as day. I swing my gaze back to Buzz. "Um, right. Well, not exactly. I mean, it's, uh, complicated."

"I figured, so I won't get in the middle." Buzz winks again, turns, and puts some space between us.

Alrighty then. That was interesting.

Bizarre and a little surreal.

I'm watching Courtney and Dallas pose with his grandfather when I feel something bat my right leg.

I freeze.

Glance down...

Two shiny blue eyes flicker to me and then away.

Oh, thank goodness! It's just Miss Jeremiah, the cat who belongs to Courtney and Apryl's grandmother. However, she's staring intently at the skirt of my bridesmaid gown. Maybe there's a cricket stuck in the layers? It wouldn't be the first time. It happened to Izze at her wedding.

I reach down to stroke her silky black hair, but something rustles inside my dress.

Alarmingly close to my flesh.

And a palm-sized lump of white under the layer of lace in my gown starts to crawl up my thigh.

On cue, Flynn Ryder from *Tangled* starts his account of the story of how he died. Only nothing actually happened to him. Okay, Flynn Ryder the thief as we knew him was transformed into the good and loyal Eugene Fitzherbert. He was not mauled by a feline which is what's about to happened to me because:

Miss Jeremiah leaps for me.

The lump continues to migrate north.

And I scream.

I don't have time to apologize to the appalled people who I'm sure have turned to stare at me with their flytrap mouths as I throw my entire body backward to avoid Miss Jeremiah's lunge.

I'm not advocating it, but it's moments like this when declawing an animal makes a lot of sense.

Fortunately, my *Bring It On* worthy jump/kick/shimmy scares Miss Jeremiah enough to give up the pursuit of her game/snack combo, and she runs back to her Victorian home.

Unfortunately, all sense of balance has been woefully lost.

Remember how I said I hated falling?

I flail my arms like twin helicopters. I don't know why I do this. I know from experience that it never helps a person regain their balance. Instead, I'm providing more vivid imagery for all the people who continue to stare as I fall backward into the table.

Directly into the three-tiered wedding cake.

The rickety antique table collapses under my forceful landing. Cake and frosting smush into places where they should not be smushed, including (but certainly not limited to) my ears.

The world around me goes abnormally silent, something I'm a little thankful for as I lay in the raspberry and chocolate wedding cake because I can't hear the gasps, the guffaws, and the grins I'm sure a few people are trying to pretend is really shock.

It's not, but that's beside the point.

Do you know what the point really is?

The mouse I had momentarily forgotten was in my dress, *is still in my dress*! And that little devil has begun to move again.

"Ahhh!" My scream pierces the not-so-tranquil occasion once again, and I start to thrash and smack my leg as hard and as fast as I can.

And I connect with the wiggling lump of muscles and tiny legs.

"Ewwww!" I touched it! I touched it! I slapped the mouse with my hand. Gross, gross, gross! Shivers of disgust race up and down my spine.

I might pass out.

Good thing I'm already on the ground.

Wait, it's still climbing up my leg. That stupid, directionally challenged mouse who is insistent on finding its own way out. Why wouldn't it run *away* from the person who's screaming and hitting it?

The only way that white devil is coming out the way it insists on going is if I've died of cake suffocation or embarrassment. While both are possible right now, I'm not going down (any more than I've already fallen, that is) without a fight.

Bring it, Mousey!

"Grrr!" I howl my war cry and roll onto my side to stop the mouse with a firm squishing.

It doesn't work. Evil Mickey wiggles and squirms, and I can

feel every movement in a way I couldn't before. It's so much worse! So much worse!

I roll all the way over because I'm now a human rolling pin. Cake and frosting cover my face, temporarily blinding me. This must be what it's like to have a pie smashed into your face.

"Get it off me!" I cry-shriek for help.

"There's something in her dress," someone shouts.

"Yes! It's stuck in the lace!"

Oh, look at that! Some of the frosting must have been dislodged from my ears.

A loud silence claims my ears again. Drat!

If I could hear something other than my own frantic screaming, maybe I would have heard the muffled voice(s) of the person(s) trying to help me. But I can't hear them.

Which is why my palm connects with someone's face.

*Slap!*

*Thud!*

I feel the person collapse into the cake beside me, but I didn't hurt him too badly because I can hear him moving after a moment. Then two strong hands grab both of mine as the person shouts, "It's okay! It's okay! Hold still, and Summer will get the mouse out."

I stop thrashing at the sound of his voice. "Gabe?" I squeak.

"I'm here." His grip loosens, and he rubs his thumbs across the backs of my hands.

It's calming. A long sigh of relief escapes my lips. But the mouse starts to inch his way through the fitted lace and up my leg again. My entire body tenses as his little feet press into me.

*Rip!*

My cake-styled earmuffs must have been dislodged again. Summer—I'm guessing since I still can't see—moves both of her hands across my thigh in a quick, cupping motion until they meet.

"Got him!" Summer proclaims in triumph.

Gabe releases both of my hands. Then I feel a silky cloth moving against my face, removing the smush from my eyes.

Light! I have a pinprick of light, people!

Blinking approximately thirty-three times, I finally focus on Gabe's face directly in front of me.

He moves his tie into my limited field of vision. "Hang on. There's a little more." He wipes the corner of my right eye. "Got it."

"Thank you," I whisper. "Where is it?"

"Right here." I turn my head and see Summer holding up her hands where she supposedly holds the minuscule monster. "Don't worry. I only ripped the lace part of your dress."

Right. Like the dress that is clearly already ruined is what I'm worried about at the moment, but at least I'm not exposing myself.

To everyone present at Courtney's wedding.

Hot tears cut through the frosting on my cheeks as mortification comes in for the grand finale. I cover my face with my raspberry-stained hands. If only I could disappear into the frosting forever.

Gabe pulls me to his chest and wraps an arm around me. "It's okay, Kaylee. It's gone. It's over. It's okay."

"It's okay," Courtney echoes from somewhere to my left, but the sound of her voice only makes me cry harder.

"I ru-ruined your wedding," I sob.

"You didn't ruin anything," Gabe says softly and gently squeezes my shoulder.

"He's right," Izze says to my right.

"Did you hear that?" Gabe asks while squeezing my shoulder for the second time. "Izze agreed with me, so it must be true."

I snort, and a small piece of frosting comes out of my left nostril.

Lovely.

Gabe doesn't comment on my frosting snot. "Let me help you stand up. You can go inside and clean up."

I pull away from the rather cozy cocoon of frosting, cake, and Gabe, embarrassed for a whole new reason now. I sit up and avoid looking at anyone. Which is no easy feat considering every person in attendance stands in a clump around my natural disaster.

That whole thing where the earth opened in the Old Testament always terrified me. Until right now. Now I wish it would happen to me.

Gabe stands and reaches for me. I grab his familiar hand. My high heel slips as the frosting attempts to pull me in for another roll, but Gabe's grip remains firm and secure.

"I've got you," he says.

If only. If only...

"Here." Izze passes me a towel once I'm securely standing. "Come with us. We'll help you get cleaned up." She grabs my arm like it's not slick with raspberry puree. I'd tell her not to ruin her dress, but it's already coated with the colors of Courtney's wedding cake.

Apryl, who also looks like she's been in a food fight, does the same with my right arm. She looks at Gabe and points toward her husband waiting in the wings. "Go with Chance. He'll help you."

I limp away with my friends, favoring the leg I beat with crazed aggression. However, every limb and muscle feels like they took a beating as well. But I guess that's what happens when you fall with enough force to flatten a wedding cake and a table.

I can hear Buzz and Miles start to organize the cleanup behind me, but Apryl and Izze remain quiet, allowing me some time to process one of the most humiliating events to have ever happened to me. And to add insult to injury, clumps of cake fall from me as I walk toward the house.

I am going to have so many bruises, but that's okay. Each hand-shaped bruise will be a testament that I lived to tell the story.

Not that I'm ever going to *willingly* tell this story.

But I know that it will make for a funny story one day. Far, far away. And when that day comes, I have a feeling it's a story that will be pulled out for an agonizing reminiscence on special occasions. Anniversaries. Holidays. Birthdays. Mondays. Tax season.

"I officially hate Mickey and Minnie," I say in a hoarse voice, breaking the silence as another chunk of cake falls to my feet. "And wedding cake."

# Chapter Thirteen

“That's not going to fit me. I don't have hips,” I grumble ten minutes later.

“You have hips. You're not a medical marvel, Kaylee.”

I glare at Apryl. “You know what I mean.”

She holds the taupe, tulle skirt against my waist. “It fits. Courtney's waist is actually annoyingly tiny. Much like yours, but it will sit a little lower because you don't have any hips.”

“I thought I wasn't a medical marvel?” I taunt.

She ignores me and pulls out a sleeveless, cream-colored lace top and a matching cardigan. “Wear this with it.” She tosses the top, but it lands approximately three feet to my right.

“I guess all social protocol goes out the window when someone wrestles with a mouse in your wedding cake.” I stand from where I'd been sitting on Courtney's bed and grab the top.

“And loses!” Izze yells from the bathroom.

“Courtney won't care that you're wearing cream. She instructed me to raid her closet for you and Izze. After I've helped you guys, I'll run across the yard and change,” Apryl says.

I grimace. “Sorry.”

“Stop apologizing! Why in all of the DC universe wouldn't we help you?” she demands.

“To prevent the utter destruction of your bridesmaid gowns?”

Apryl shrugs. “Actually, Courtney ran over to help you as well.”

My eyes widen. “She what? Please, oh, please tell me I didn't ruin her wedding gown.”

“Relax. Izze ordered Dallas to hold her back.”

"I knew you'd never forgive yourself if her gown was ruined, but bridesmaid dresses are worthless," Izze says as she walks into Courtney's bedroom dressed in a bathrobe and patting her damp curls with a towel. "Despite what the movies say, hardly anyone shortens them to wear again at another event."

Apryl tilts her head to the side. "With this logic, shouldn't wedding dresses be the worthless item? At least there's the potential for reuse in a bridesmaid dress."

"Don't reduce my line of work to worthless," Izze shoots back. "Wedding dresses are iconic. They have beautiful meaning and sentiment."

"Lower your blood pressure. I'm only teasing," Apryl says with a flick of her wrist.

I fiddle with the belt of my bathrobe. "Did someone help Summer?"

"She told me that she always keeps another outfit stashed in the car," Apryl responds. "I'm guessing there's another entertaining, if not as dramatic, story to go along with that mantra. Now, go put these on while I help Izze find something to wear."

"Right," Izze snorts. "Like you're going to find something that will fit over the hips my Puerto Rican genetics gave me in the midst of all these tiny clothes."

"You're going to eat those words when I find something adorable for you," Apryl says as she rummages through the closet, back to us.

Izze rolls her eyes as I walk by her.

"I heard that eyeroll," Apryl growls as she continues to search Courtney's overflowing closet.

I walk to the bathroom and put the outfit on, grateful that Apryl's ability to create beautiful things is not limited to just wedding receptions and hairstyles. Nope, her gift extends to piecing together a wedding-appropriate outfit at the drop of a hat. Thankfully, all my personal products where already here. After applying a little makeup, I brush my hair then grab a hair tie and some pins so Apryl can style it.

When I walk back into the bedroom, Apryl is demanding that Izze sing her praises.

"I told you," Apryl says.

"Fine! You were right! Now stop gloating and fix Kaylee's air."

Apryl smirks. "I'm a multitasker when it comes to gloating."

"Oh, good grief," Izze mumbles, sweeping out of the bedroom with an outfit draped over her arm.

"Something simple." I sit on the bed and pass Apryl the hair tie and pins.

"Mm-hmm," she murmurs as she starts tugging and twisting my pin straight red tresses into a hairstyle.

"I don't want to go back out there," I confess once Izze comes back into the bedroom sporting a red, fluttery maxi dress and a black lace, kimono-style cardigan.

Apryl stops tugging the sides of my long hair into a braid around the crown of my head and lays a hand on my shoulder. Izze crouches down in front of me.

Emotion clogs my throat, and tears threaten to destroy the makeup I'd just applied. "I made an absolute fool of myself."

Izze grabs my hands and squeezes them. "It's okay, Kaylee. No one is upset with you. Hey, I would have reacted much worse than you did. But it's okay to feel embarrassed. Anyone in your shoes would feel embarrassed."

"Is this supposed to be a pep talk?" I ask in a high voice.

"Yes! Because your feelings are justified," Izze exclaims.

"Thanks for the validation, Dr. Isabel Clayton," I mumble with a touch of sarcasm.

"And that means everyone will understand," she adds.

"And anyone who doesn't had better disappear before I get ahold of them," Apryl says in a menacing voice.

"That would be more convincing if you weren't wearing Batman pajamas and matching slippers," I shoot back.

"The point," Izze continues, "is that while it's completely justified to feel embarrassed, you don't need to let that embarrassment rule your life. You are stronger than the things that have happened to you."

Why does it feel like she's not talking about my roll in the cake anymore?

"'He who is in you is greater than he who is in the world,'" Apryl says, quoting the fourth verse from the fourth chapter of I John, a verse I could whip out for any other person in any other circumstance.

Any person but myself.

And while I appreciate what they're saying, I'm not sure I believe it when it comes to my life experiences. I'm obviously not stronger than the things that have happened to me. And if God is greater than all the things that have happened to me, wouldn't I be different because He's in me? Wouldn't I be stronger? Wouldn't I be more loving or forgiving or braver?

Wouldn't I have moved past the past?

My quiet yet loud doubt casts a gloominess over the room, but Izze and Apryl don't press me about it. They start talking about their respective jobs, and I add comments here and there. "Bad Day" by Daniel Powter plays on my internal radio, and my mind doesn't connect with anything around me.

It's not present as Apryl declares my hair perfect. It's not present as I leave my friends and start the dreaded journey back to the reception. And it's not present as I wordlessly pass the person who'd been waiting for me by the front door, resulting in them running behind me and touching my shoulder.

Which I interpret as someone trying to murder me in my distracted state. Obviously.

"Ahhh!" I scream, jump, and swing my arm back to hit whoever is trying to accost me. Softball Arm, don't fail me now.

I connect with Gabe's chiseled jaw for the second time today. His head snaps back. "Okay...ouch," he moans.

"Oh, Gabe! I'm so sorry! I didn't realize it was you." I reach out like I'm about to cradle his jaw and then snatch my hand back, tucking it behind my back.

He rubs his jaw before answering. "Yeah, I figured that. Unless that's your alibi. In which case, well done. You've managed to hit me twice today."

"I was distracted," I say with just a touch of defensiveness. "I didn't mean to hit you either time. I didn't even know it was you either time."

"I know, Kay. It was a joke."

I blink at the use of his old nickname for me. That's, like, the second time he's used it. Am I not supposed to comment on that?

He opens his mouth and pops his jaw. "There. That's better."

I cringe. Jaws should not pop. The sound is horrid and offends me on a soul level.

He laughs at my disgusted expression. "Sorry. I know you hate that."

"Sorry for smacking you." I rub my arms to warm them from the afternoon autumn chill that's cutting through my thin cardigan. We'll probably get our first snow any day now.

He smirks and winks. "Sure you are."

Argh! Dude, don't wink at me. "I won't be in a minute when I hit you again because you keep taunting me."

"Promises." His eyes crinkle as he smiles. It's cute. Way too cute.

I frown. I don't know how to handle this. It's all sorts of confusing.

His cute smile sobers, and he touches my elbow. It's sweet, gentle, and adds to the confusion. "I wanted to make sure you were okay."

"I'm fine," I say lightly. This is the second time Gabe's stepped in to make sure I'm okay, and it's not helping my stony resolve.

"Liar."

But that might. "Seriously? Don't call me that. You don't get to call me that." I turn my back on him and start speed walking.

He jogs and catches my hand, and I have to resist the urge to punch him on purpose this time. "I'm sorry. I know you're upset, but I won't make you talk about it. I, uh, brought you a present."

My eyes narrow, but my ears catch the present part and relay it to my heart. Unfortunately, I'm a sucker for a thoughtful present. However, I can't let my defenses down completely. "What? A Trojan Horse?"

He produces a lemon in his other hand that I hadn't noticed him carrying. "For you," he says, offering the delicious fruit to me.

Aww!

Curse these stupid tears that fill my eyes, showing exactly what I think of his gesture. "Where did you get this?"

"From a wooden horse in Troy," he quips.

"I doubt the Greeks stuffed it with lemons."

He shrugs. "Then I guess I saw it on the counter in Chance's kitchen."

"You stole food from my friends?"

"That's a very negative way to look at it."

"How should I look at it?"

"That your friends had a piece of fruit they would willingly give you to put a smile on your face after a difficult afternoon, so I did it for them." His sheepish grin reminds me of Aladdin in the marketplace with Abu.

"You put a smile on my face?"

"Well, I did, didn't I?" he asks. He sounds vulnerable. It matters to him if he made me happy.

I look from him to the fruit to him again. "Yes, I suppose you did."

"Good. Catch." He tosses me another lemon that I didn't see him hiding.

I snatch the lemon out of the air between us. I hope he can't see the way my hand shakes. "Thanks."

Maybe he is a Trojan Horse.

If Gabe missed another cord, Drake was going to challenge his honorary title then and there, adding another dramatic turn to Courtney's wedding reception with an impromptu Battle of the Bands.

Kaylee stood to his right, belting out the song they'd finished writing only a few days ago. And she was killing it.

He watched in pride as she nailed each note, inserting a passion into the lyrics that held the audience rapt. All the couples on the dance floor—even the bride and groom—had stopped dancing. In fact, Courtney was wiping tears from her eyes.

Ethan caught Gabe's eye and raised both of his eyebrows in return. His look was clear. *Be careful.*

Gabe flicked his eyes back to Kaylee. He'd been looking at careful in the rearview mirror the minute he offered Kaylee a place in the band. The most he could hope for now was damage control.

And—yup. He'd missed another chord. Great. He could feel Drake's gleeful eyes boring into the back of his head.

"My love, for the rest of my life," Kaylee sang for the third time, drawing the line into a reverent whisper, a promise, a wish.

The guests roared with applause, hoots, and cheers. Courtney surged forward and threw her arms around Kaylee. "That was amazing! I've never heard you sing like that."

Kaylee laughed. "You hear me sing all the time."

"Something about this time was different." Courtney swung her gaze to Gabe for confirmation. "Right, Gabe? Back me up. And remember, I'm the bride, so you can't disagree with me."

"Oh, I wouldn't dream of it," Gabe said to Courtney, but his eyes were fixed on Kaylee. "She's right. You were amazing."

A blush tinged her cheeks. Man, he'd forgotten how much he loved it when she blushed.

Courtney wrapped her arm around Kaylee's shoulder. "You should take your break now. Get some ca—I mean, food. Water. Dance."

Summer snorted at Courtney's blunder, causing Kaylee to flinch.

Gabe nodded in agreement. "Sounds good. Thanks."

"I'll go start the playlist," Kaylee said over her shoulder to him before leaving with Courtney.

Gabe watched her go until Ethan stepped into his line of vision. "You guys sounded great. I think you've worked out *most* of your kinks," Ethan said pointedly.

Gabe ignored Ethan as he slipped his guitar strap around his head and set his guitar on the stand. "Sorry, guys. Finger cramps."

"More like brain cramps," Ethan retorted quietly.

"Thanks, man," Drake said to Ethan. He swung his broad grin to Gabe and pretended to place a crown on his own head. "And thank you for that."

"It's not yours yet, buddy."

"Oh, we'll see about that," Drake called over his shoulder as he started toward the tables filled with food, Natalya and Summer trailing after him.

Gabe held up his hand to Ethan. "Don't."

"I didn't say anything," Ethan said in mock-innocence.

"You were going to."

"And I'm still going to," Ethan shot back and crossed his arms across his broad chest. "You still love her."

"Love is a lie," Gabe growled in a low voice. He turned from Ethan, jammed his hands into his pockets, and scanned the crowd for Kaylee.

"You can tell me *that* lie all you want, but you don't believe it."

"I do."

"Tell it to your face."

Gabe didn't bother responding to Ethan as the sighting of a certain redhead made his pulse increase dramatically, so much so that he was going to make it a priority to see a doctor on Monday.

"Then go dance with her."

Gabe swung his gaze to Ethan. "What?"

"You heard me. If love is such a complete lie that you don't feel anything for her anymore, then go dance with her," Ethan challenged.

"I don't have to prove myself to you." Because he couldn't. There was no way he could dance with her. That would be blurring the lines of the Friends Zone that Gabe was working to establish with Kaylee.

"Because you can't."

Gabe didn't answer him.

"I will revert to my five-year-old baiting tactics if you make me." Upon hearing Gabe's snort of derision, Ethan moved his arms into chicken wings. "You brought this upon yourself."

Gabe should have left with the others. Why did he stay?

"Buk-buk-buk! Buk-buk-buk!" Ethan flapped his arm wings and pretended to peck at him.

Several people turned to stare at them. One woman pulled her teenage daughter behind her. The groomsman who'd been talking to Kaylee before the cake fiasco pulled out his phone, presumably to film Chicken Man.

"Really? People are looking at you like you're three nuggets short of a Happy Meal."

"Buk! Buk-buk-buky-buk!" Ethan shrieked.

"Do you really want to add another disaster to this wedding? Real professional."

"You're—Buk!—the one causing this little display. Buk! Buk!"

Gabe held up his hands. "Fine!" he said before stalking away from his insane friend.

As he approached, Kaylee caught sight of him from where she was leaning against a willow tree talking to an elderly woman he didn't know. "Uh, what sort of attack was Ethan having?"

"It was a bee." *Really, genius?* Sadly, it was the next best thing that popped into his head because he sure wasn't going to say it was a mouse.

Kaylee smirked. "How very *Ever After* of him."

"It's too late in the season for bees," the elderly woman said, eyeing Gabe like he couldn't be trusted.

She probably wasn't far off in her assessment of Gabe.

The woman poked Kaylee in her arm, causing her to jump. "Sorry. Gabe, this is Mrs. Firee, a friend of the family."

Gabe frowned in confusion. He didn't remember this woman. Great. No wonder she was giving Gabe a look that said, *You scum!*

The exact words used may change from generation to generation, but the sentiment of the message would remain the same.

Kaylee, obviously reading his confused panic, rushed to explain. "She's a friend of Courtney and Apryl's grandmother."

"But this girl is as good as family," Mrs. Firee interjected with a fierceness that dared you to deny her and see what happened.

Gabe had had a lot of stupid moments in his life. The self-imposed fauxhawk for the ninth-grade talent show would rank near the top of that list for eternity. But he wasn't stupid enough to test this Mrs. Firee.

Kaylee offered the elderly woman a loving smile and a sideways hug. "Aww! I feel the same about you."

Mrs. Firee continued to bore holes into his head with her disapproving stare.

Was he sweating?

He discreetly tugged at the neck of his dress shirt. Yup. Gabe was going to need a couple sticks of deodorant and to burn these clothes when he got home tonight.

"Gabe?"

He startled. "What?"

"I've said your name three times," Kaylee informed him with an amused grin on her perfect lips.

There he went thinking about her lips again. He was doomed.

"Is he having some sort of mental breakdown?" Mrs. Firee whispered to Kaylee, who bit her lower lip to keep from laughing out loud. "There was a rerun with Oprah or Dr. Phil about this. According to them, we should get him some help."

"I think he's disturbed by the sight of a grown man acting like a free-range chicken," Kaylee whispered back.

"Ah." Mrs. Firee nodded in understanding. "Should we get his friend some help, too?"

That was enough. "He's fine," Gabe interjected with a loud whisper of his own, "but he was wondering if Kaylee would like to dance."

"What?" both women exclaimed at once.

Gabe looked right into those stunning emerald eyes that were wide with shock. "Please?"

"Um, I-I guess that would be okay," she stuttered.

The response every man wanted to hear.

Judging by her taunt facial features and rigid posture, Mrs. Firee disapproved. In fact, her face was frozen into such hardcore disapproval that it would make a good meme.

Gabe ignored the fiery woman (and the new wave of nervous sweat soaking his shirt) and held out his hand to Kaylee. Her gaze flickered to his outstretched hand for a moment, uncertainty etched into her expression.

Then she placed her hand in his.

And Gabe swore that he heard a rock-n-roll version of the "Hallelujah Chorus" ringing in his ears.

They walked toward the dance floor, and Gabe could feel the heat of several pairs of eyes following them.

This might have been a mistake.

At least it wasn't a slow, painfully romantic song. Couples spun and swayed to the moderate tempo. Oh, and there was Izze, peaking around her husband's shoulder and mouthing unintelligible death threats to him. Swell.

Gabe stopped and glanced at Kaylee, his heart continuing to beat at that alarming pace. He'd wanted Ethan to get off his back about Kaylee, so he hadn't thought through the ramifications of dancing with her. But he could also see Ethan—who'd finally ended his *Chicken Run* monologue and was sitting at a table with the others—angled so that he could watch Gabe and Kaylee dance. He couldn't turn back now.

He took Kaylee's right hand in his left and lightly set his right hand on her back—technically her shoulder blade. Okay, this could work, there was plenty of distance between them, even if he did feel like he should be in one of those period dramas his mother liked to watch.

"Are you waltzing?" Kaylee asked with both eyebrows raised.

The left side of Gabe's mouth tilted upwards. "Is that what this is?"

Her eyes danced with amusement. "Yes."

"Then we're waltzing."

Gabe started counting in his head in time with their steps. *One, two, three... One, two, three...*

He should probably get over himself and talk to her, right? Yeah...

Gabe cleared his throat. "You doing okay after, uh, you know, the mouse thing?" *Real smooth*, he mentally chided himself.

She tilted her head back, but not because of necessity. Kaylee was basically at eye level with him because she was only two or so inches shorter than him. The head tilt was a habit born of thoughtful consideration. "That depends. Do you think I'll need a rabies shot?"

"Did the mouse bite you?" he asked.

"I didn't think to check, but I wouldn't be surprised."

"Then I'd go to the doctor."

"Then I'd say I'm not doing too good."

He laughed. "It's just a precaution."

She snorted. "Easy for you to say. You're not the one who will be getting stabbed."

"It's a poke," he said dryly.

"If it penetrates the skin and draws blood, then it's a tiny stab," she shot back.

A smile stretched across his face as something familiar and entirely unforgotten flooded his senses.

"Thank you for the lemons. They helped," she added.

"Good." Definitely good.

"Why did you ask me to dance?" she asked in a quiet voice.

To his ears, her innocent question sounded like a cacophony of chaos that happened when a cannon ball landed on a piano.

"Because." That answered everything, didn't it?

She tilted her head again and looked up at him expectantly. Waiting.

Apparently not.

"We're friends, so it's okay for us to dance."

"Is it? Some things are weird when you have a history." Vulnerability laced her words.

"Well, it doesn't need to be. Yes, we had a history, but our lives are different now. And for the time being, they include each other. I want us to be friends." And he did. In fact, he needed for them to be friends again. Since she'd walked back into his life, he'd just been trying to come through this arrangement intact, but now...now Gabe couldn't return to his world of the last nine years, a world without her.

But the doubt on Kaylee's face was louder than anything she could have said.

"Really," he said to assure her and gently squeezed her shoulder. A tender action that did not help his heart rate. *I'm going to eat a vegetable every day after this. And apples. And exercise so much that I'll give Dwayne "The Rock" Johnson a run for his money.*

Okay, not really. But maybe the vegetable thing.

"I told you before that I would try to coexist with you. I can be your friend, Gabe. I mean it, and I meant it. Doesn't mean that stuff isn't..."

"Weird," he finished.

"Yeah," she huffed in agreement.

Perfect opening. "Well, let's fix that."

"Huh?"

Man, he was getting a lesson in humility tonight. "We should get to know each other again."

"Gabe, that could be really—"

"Weird," he finished for her. "Yeah, probably at first, but if we're actually going to be friends, then maybe we should give it a try." Judging by the amount of sweat that had re-saturated his shirt, Gabe was way more nervous than he'd anticipated being for this.

She bit her lip, then slowly nodded. "All right. What did you have in mind, buddy?"

Buddy? Definitely a Friend Zone word choice. "I have an idea."

She raised an eyebrow. "One you care to share?"

"It's a surprise." The song changed in the background, but it barely registered in the back of Gabe's mind.

She bit her lip again. "Oh-kay. But nothing should be hurtling toward me, and there should be no rodents of any size within a hundred-mile radius."

"Since most of New Hampshire is basically a mountain forest and we're currently in the middle of a field, I'm just going to tell you that we'll be in a domesticated area. And nothing will be hurtling toward you. You'll be the one hurtling."

"That could mean so many things," Kaylee said with a shake of her head. "When are we doing this?"

"Tomorrow."

"Goody."

"Um," he started, then stopped to clear his throat. "So I've also been wanting to apologize for the other night." He more than owed her an apology—he could give her his car or something, and it still wouldn't make up for the mistakes he'd made.

Kaylee stiffened in his arms. "Not necessary."

"It is. I want to...I...there's no excuse for the things I did back then." He swallowed around the lump of guilt lodged in his throat. "And you didn't deserve it. I never wanted to hurt you, and because I was being—"

"A jerk?" she supplied.

"Ha, yeah." Gabe let out a humorless laugh. "Because I was being a jerk, I didn't think about some of the other things, that felt so small to me in comparison, that I never shared with you—like the car incident. It doesn't excuse it, but that's what happened."

Her brow furrowed, and she glanced past him. "Really, this isn't necessary. You owe me nothing."

Gabe abruptly stopped, causing another couple—the grooms- man Kaylee had been talking to earlier and a strawberry blonde— to bump into them. The guy let out an exasperated sigh before steering away from them.

"Dude, what are you doing?" Kaylee asked.

"Kaylee." He moved both of his hands to her upper shoulders and gently squeezed them, drawing her eyes to his. "It is neces- sary. It may be nine years too late, but it is one hundred and ten percent necessary. I am so sorry."

She stared at him with wide eyes that rivaled the Baby Yoda memes he'd been seeing on Facebook. Another couple bumped into the back of Kaylee, pushing her directly into Gabe's chest.

Without thinking, he wrapped his arms around her, holding her close.

And she hugged him back.

"I'm so sorry," he whispered into her hair.

He felt her nod against his chest. After a few more moments, she stepped out of his arms. "Thank you. I appreciate it. I guess it's...it's closure for that chapter."

"Right." So why did it feel like he'd just been hit in the back of the head with something the size of a cello? "I'm glad it helps you."

Surprisingly, Gabe still felt like a weight had been lifted from his shoulders. Apologizing to Kaylee had broken chains Gabe hadn't realized were strangling him.

"Like I said, I didn't need it. How many times in life do we get an apology? I'll never get an apology from the girl who stuck my hand in warm water at the only slumber party I was invited to in first grade, and I didn't need one from you." She blushed in embarrassment. "Sorry, that sounds harsh."

"No, I understand what you mean," he said.

And he did. Between Chip and Kaylee, Gabe felt like he'd finally started to see his foolish decision for what it was: fear. If he hadn't run into her that day in the wedding chapel, he probably never would have apologized like this. And for the first time, Gabe realized just how cowardly he'd been. How had he deluded himself into thinking he was protecting her? He'd done everything but that. If he could do it without drawing attention, he'd throw a punch at himself. Even now, he wanted to disappear. To run. To hide his mistakes. But Gabe was finally starting to see that response for what it was: he was protecting himself at the expense of everyone else.

Well, no more. From this moment forward, things would be different.

Gabe would be different.

He took another step back, holding out his hands for Kaylee to accept or decline once again. "Would you like to dance some more?"

She didn't hesitate this time. "I would."

Now *that's* what a guy wanted to hear.

# Chapter Fourteen

"This is not what I had in mind."

Gabe smiles like he's George Clooney, we're in *Ocean's Eleven*, and this is the heist of his lifetime.

And it might be.

"I'm not going in there," I state from the safety of Gabe's car.

"Why?"

"Because you'll force me to ride a roller coaster."

"I made a promise: only activities where *you* are the one hurtling toward something. I intend to keep this promise, so yes, that means you have to ride a roller coaster," he declares before opening his car door.

We'll see about that.

Reaching over to the driver's door he just shut, I smash the auto lock. Smirking in triumph, I stick my tongue out at Gabe.

He rolls his eyes and holds up the keys. "Nice try," he calls as he clicks the unlock button.

Lock.

Unlock.

Lock.

And unlock.

Yeah, this goes on for a few minutes.

After I relock the car for the twenty-first time, Gabe holds up both hands, keys dangling from his right hand. He reaches up, and I hear the keys click against the roof. He walks to my window and kneels down.

"I'll do the creepy Joey eyes."

"That only works in *Friends*." But to be safe, I avert my eyes and stare straight ahead. A smile tugs at my lips.

"How about a compromise?" he asks.

"I don't negotiate with people who want me to choke on my own vomit while screaming from the terror of a thousand-foot drop."

"Kaylee, it's an amusement park called Christmas Village, not a legal way to commit homicide. It's a kiddie amusement park. Three-year-olds ride on the roller coasters here."

"Monsters! It's like the pilot episode of *The 100* where the parents send their children plummeting toward a post-apocalyptic Earth in a rickety shuttle. And now it's real! What has society come to?" I lament.

"One roller coaster," he says.

"Nope."

"And I'll buy you all the fudge you want," Gabe continues.

Now I swing my head to meet his eyes. "You serious? This place has fudge?"

"Lots," he says slowly. Oh, the seductive powers of fudge. "And it's delicious."

I'm drooling now. "All the fudge I want?" I question while discreetly wiping the drool from the corner of my lips.

"Just leave me gas money."

"Deal. Move out of the way."

He steps back. "Glad to know fudge is still your Achilles' heel," he says as I climb out.

"Please. There may be a zillion calories and a million grams of sugar, but I can't resist a piece of maple fudge. Plus, we'll walk it off." I grab my wallet from my purse and shove it into the deep pocket of my coat.

"How are you not seven hundred pounds?" He shakes his head, and we start walking to the entrance gate.

"I believe *Gilmore Girls* calls it the 'Lorelai Paradox.'" I eat a lot of salad. That's why I'm not seven hundred pounds, but I prefer to claim kinship with Lorelai Gilmore."

"I'm guessing that was groundbreaking in the scientific community."

"It's revolutionized dieting," I say as we walk. "I didn't know this place existed. How did you hear about it?"

"Oh, we had a wedding out this way last summer. The band decided to come back the next day," Gabe informs me.

"Ah." So he's been here with Natalya. I cannot contain my abundant enthusiasm about that particular piece of information. I might as well be gagging with joy. "Wait, you went in the summer?"

"Haven't you heard of Christmas in July?" he teases with a quirked eyebrow as we wait our turn in line.

"I thought that was only a tropical climate thing." I've lost some of the happiness I was feeling from the initial promise of fudge.

"Not in a state where the weekly forecast can go from summer to winter to dragon attacks within forty-eight hours." Gabe pulls out his wallet to pay for our day passes.

"Thank you," I say on the other side of the gate, map of the amusement park in hand. "I'll buy lunch."

"No, I want to—"

"Friends," I say with a quick, meaningful glance, "treat each other. It's my turn."

He nods slowly. "Okay. That's fair."

"Besides, you won't have any money for lunch after you buy all the fudge this establishment has to offer," I joke. That got awkward o'clock, but I won't let him pay for everything. We are not a couple, and even if we were a couple, the girl can pay for stuff too.

"It will be worth it. Until the ride is over, at least," Gabe says, and an evil gleam lights up his gray eyes. "And I think we should do the roller coaster first."

"Are you sure?" I hold up the map. "Why don't we do the train ride, or oh, we could go to the antique cars."

"Nope. Roller coaster first. This way you can't run out the clock with all the tame rides." Gabe looks at me, and the laugh lines around his eyes and mouth are deep and wonderful.

Ahem. Maybe this "hang out as friends" idea wasn't a good idea. In my defense, it seemed like a good idea in Gabe's arms. Time for a mental redirect.

"Let's get this over with," I moan and shove the map toward him.

He takes the map and steps toward me to allow a family of

five to walk past us. The youngest—a little girl in unicorn snow pants—is crying because her mother said the water park is closed in November.

Her poor parents. Reasoning with a toddler is like sneezing into the wind.

"Okay," Gabe says and taps the map. "This is the one that will conquer your fear of roller coasters."

"It doesn't go backward or upside-down, does it? Do your feet hang out so that you feel like you're falling the entire time? Does it spin?"

"No, no, and no. It's very traditional. Let's go," Gabe says, taking off.

I could make a run for it.

"Remember the fudge," Gabe says without looking over his shoulder.

Sighing, I follow him. "This fudge better be as good as you claim it is," I mutter when I catch up with him.

"Only my mama can make better," he drawls.

"Fine." High praise. I'm convinced Gloria Sanders's fudge is straight from the kitchens of Heaven.

I study the amusement park as we walk through. It's obviously geared toward families with younger children, but I see individuals of all ages in line for the rides, taking pictures with giant reindeer statues, and playing the carnival-like games and activities that always take up half the space in an amusement park. Cute, corny puns name everything from the restrooms to the various eateries to the rides themselves. The first snow of the season blankets everything, giving the park the perfect Hallmark Christmas look.

I'm so glad I wore fleece-lined jeans today.

Not that it matters. My thighs are already frozen.

"And we've arrived," Gabe announces. The roller coaster—Dasher's Dash—is red and green with thirty-something adults and children screaming like their toenails are being pulled off. Some of them have been brainwashed into laughing and smiling. A few are holding their hands up, praying for salvation from their imminent demise.

That's how I'm choosing to interpret the situation.

"Remember the fudge," Gabe says while laughing at my horrified expression. In that deluded place in my mind, I'm imagining that I look like Kathleen Kelly discovering the identity of Joe Fox in *You've Got Mail*—a perfect reference for this snowy day in this Christmassy place.

Sorry, but we're in November. That means it's Christmas season. At least for me and the people who have to listen to me.

Like you.

"It won't be that bad," Gabe assures me.

"Famous last words," I mutter.

He laughs again and takes my hand, gently tugging me into line. He lets go as soon as we're wedged into the throng of people, but my hand is burning like I washed it with battery acid.

Between Gabe holding my hand and this roller coaster, I'm probably going into cardiac arrest.

We move forward with the line, and the attendant with the measuring stick measures every child with over-the-top precision. The mom in front of us wears an annoyed look as the attendant squints and gets down on both knees to see if her toddler reaches the minimum requirements.

"She went on this ride all summer. If she was tall enough then, she's tall enough now," the mother says.

"Yes," the young guy finally says and looks at her. "She's tall enough. Are you at least sixteen years of age? If not, is her mother or father available to ride with her?"

Gabe and I exchange a look.

The mom bristles. "*I'm* her mother. And I'm in my late twenties. Do I need to show you my driver's license, or can I get on the ride with my daughter?"

The guy clears his throat. "Sorry, ma'am. Go ahead."

"I could easily see this happening to Izze," I whisper to Gabe as the mother ushers her child past the teenager who's avoiding looking at her.

Gabe snorts as we step forward. "Yeah, and there would be no attendant left by the time she got done chewing him out."

"Maybe the bones," I say after the attendant pretends to measure us and waves us through.

Our footsteps sound like a heavy rain on the metal, damp walkway as a little detail hits me.

Oh.

My.

Goodness.

We're going to sit in the same car together.

I glance at Gabe as we walk to the empty seats in the back. Time for another Kaylee Dolt Moment. I can't believe I didn't think about that before now.

Gabe stops in front of an empty car. "I'll get in first so that I'm not being thrown into you the whole time. Wouldn't want to crush you."

I feign a laugh, but I feel like every part of me is shaking. "Thanks."

Gabe climbs in and sits. I follow suit, trying not to notice how good he smells or the jolt of electricity that runs up my arm when I bump into him while I settle into my seat.

Clearly, I'm doing a wonderful job.

The attendants walk up and down either side of the coaster, checking seat belts and safety bars. They both walk back to the front of the coaster. The older of the two guys goes into the control booth and starts giving all the safety instructions while the younger one who ticked off that mom—who's seated in front of us—awkwardly goes through the hand motions that are supposed to make the instructions clearer.

However, Gawky Teen Attendant just looks like a mime with no clue how to mime.

"Remember to remain seated at all times while the roller coaster is in motion. Standing while the coaster is still in motion could result in injury, decapitation, or death," the older guy says in a dramatic, booming voice from the control booth while the young guy pretends to choke.

A child behind me gasps. "Daddy, is that true?" she shrieks.

I roll my eyes. That was a brilliant pearl of wisdom that traumatized every child on here. Share another gem with us, please.

"Are you ready?" the older guy fake-shouts. He's like the irritating intro guy from *SpongeBob SquarePants*—one of the most annoying voices known to humankind.

Half the coaster cheers. I guess no one is super eager to get this party started after his comforting monologue.

"That was terrible! Are you ready?" he shouts.

Even less people cheer this time, and a kid at the front of the coaster shouts, "Go!"

"Terrible, but we're off," the guy says. He uses his whole body to move a giant lever and there's a subtle click underneath us. Then he pushes a button.

The coaster jerks forward, barreling around the bend before it lurches inch by inch up the hill. The turn throws me into Gabe's shoulder.

He smiles at me. "Break a leg, and I'll catch you when you fall," he murmurs near my ear.

The coaster crests the top of the hill.

"Believe it or not, that's not comforting right now," I scream as we plunge into a twisting and turning maze. The wind tangles my hair around my face, and each sharp turn sends me slamming into Gabe.

And somewhere in the chaos and shrieks, I grab Gabe's hand and hold on with everything within me.

"Admit it," Gabe said. "You liked it."

Kaylee laughed. "It didn't kill me. That's all I'm willing to say." She grinned as she dipped another French fry into her honey mustard sauce.

"Right. I heard you say that it was fun."

They'd enjoyed two hours exploring the amusement park together before Gabe insisted that he needed to eat. Which was how they found themselves sitting in the bustling cafeteria of The Elf Eatery. Freshly cooked fries and sweat stench that had been hidden by the thirty-three-degree windchill and heavy coats now fought for dominance in the warm room. Thankfully, Kaylee had found a table by the front door. The regular gusts of fresh air were saving him from retching from the stench of the group at the table next to him.

As a guy, Gabe had a pretty high tolerance for stench, so it was bad.

She pointed a chicken tender at him. "You heard no such thing."

"Oh, yes I did. I took notice of it because it was shocking." The only thing that shocked him more was the way she grabbed his hand, wrapping her smaller fingers around his as he gripped the safety bar. Her touch electrified him and terrified him.

He shouldn't make a big deal about it. That's what he was telling himself over and over. *Don't make this into something it's not, genius!* She was scared, and it was natural to lean on a friend for support when you were scared. It meant nothing.

Nothing.

Her emerald eyes sparkled with mirth that sent jolts of electricity throughout his body.

It meant nothing.

Gabe cleared his throat and tapped a French fry against his plate. "Fine, don't admit it. I know the truth." He almost winced at his poor choice of words—the "truth" word would always be a dagger of shame and condemnation to his spirit.

*Have you told her the truth?* that horrible voice asked, taunting Gabe with glee and causing his insides to cringe.

Would he ever be able to let go of the guilt?

Another voice popped into Gabe's head and added His opinion to the conversation, *For the Scripture says, "Everyone who believes in him will not be put to shame."*

Gabe popped the fry into his mouth, buying himself a few seconds to think. Where was that verse? Romans? Yes, Romans chapter ten, verse eleven. It was one his mom quoted a lot. And now, the verse was like a dart hitting the bull's-eye of Gabe's question.

Or maybe armor that could block that dagger before it lodged itself into Gabe's gut.

But he wasn't sure he really believed it. How could he not be ashamed? How could others not heap shame on him? Gabe couldn't erase the stupid mistakes and horrible decisions he'd made.

"We're never going to agree on this," Kaylee said, drawing him out of his musing, "so let's change the subject." She popped another honey mustard-covered fry into her mouth.

"Okay?" Gabe looked through the window at the blue sky dotted with the start of snow clouds. "How is...I don't know. How is your family?" he said, asking about the first thing that popped into his head, but it seemed like a good friend-type question to ask.

She frowned at him, iced tea halfway to her lips. "My family?" she asked.

"Yeah." Oh, perhaps he had crossed into territory that was too personal. "Friends ask stuff like that, right?"

She nodded as she sipped her drink and swallowed. "Um, yeah. My family is good. Jake is in business school. Dad moved to Kansas four years ago for work, and I only talk to him a few times a year. My mom is still in the area, but she's a traveling nurse now. It keeps her busy." She shrugged like there should be more, but there wasn't. Unfortunately, Gabe knew that had always been the case with her family when they'd been dating.

The sadness on her face clawed at his gut. Gabe wanted to draw her into his arms and whisper that everything would be all right, that he'd be there for her.

In a purely platonic way.

"I'm sorry, Kay," he said.

Kaylee shrugged. "We were never a close or happy family. I didn't expect that to change after they got divorced, and I didn't expect that to change when I moved away."

"Still..." While there was no lost love for the lack of relationship between Gabe and his father, he couldn't imagine not having his mom in his corner. But Gabe did know what it was like to feel completely alone in life.

"It's fine. To be honest, I have a hard time stomaching the charade, pretending to be happy when I'm still so angry that they gave up," Kaylee confessed as she stared at her half-eaten tray of food.

"What do you mean?" he asked.

"I mean, who just gives up on their...family?" She glanced at him and threw the onion ring in her hand back onto her tray and pushed it away.

Gabe had a feeling she used a little word substitution there.

"I'm sorry, Kaylee. I'm so sorry," he finally said. What else could he say? He knew she wasn't trying to attack him, but it didn't help that he'd basically abandoned her the same way.

"It's not your fault. Honestly, it's just another area that shows just how terrible a Christian I am."

Gabe's brow furrowed. "What? I have never seen anyone love God the way you do."

She shook her head. "Not lately. My world's been turned upside down, and I haven't been handling it well. And I'm seeing just how messed up I am."

Gabe shifted. He was uncomfortable with the direction the conversation had gone. Very uncomfortable. "Aren't we all messed up? Isn't that the point of grace and all that?" he asked, trying to infuse a lightness he didn't feel into his tone because hey, he hadn't embraced this "truth" any more than she had.

"I'm messed up because I'm realizing just how angry I am at my parents for giving up, for not fighting for the love and well-being of this family. I haven't forgiven them. Not really." Kaylee took a deep breath and released it. "And I'm not sure I want to forgive them."

"It's unforgiveable." Gabe felt like he'd been cut by a thousand broken guitar strings.

"Sometimes it feels that way," she whispered in agreement as she stared out the window.

Unforgiveable. That was usually the case. At least in Gabe's experience. And he knew that he would never forgive himself.

"Don't you feel that way about your dad?" she asked suddenly. "He upped and left with no warning. He gave up on your family."

"I...what?" he stuttered. They had never talked about this. Never. Instead of talking about Mitchem Sanders's betrayal, Gabe had proposed to Kaylee. Ran off to elope with her.

Then he ran away when he'd been forced to confront that he had the potential to be just as horrible as Mitchem.

"I...Kaylee, there's something I never told you." His mouth tasted like rotten eggs, but something inside of him screamed, *Now! Tell her now! Stop letting the lies control you!*

And he wanted that freedom. Oh, how he wanted that freedom.

She raised a delicate, reddish-brown eyebrow. "Okay?"

"Mom filed for divorce after discovering that my dad..." Yeah, he couldn't call him that anymore. "That Mitchem had had another affair."

Kaylee inhaled sharply. Her mouth opened in surprise, but no sound followed. Reaching across the table, she grabbed Gabe's hand in hers.

Again.

"Mom reluctantly admitted it wasn't the first time he'd betrayed her. Betrayed us."

"I'm so sorry, Gabe." She squeezed his hand and intertwined her fingers with his.

Gabe had expected her to flip out again. If he was honest, maybe he had been hoping that she *would* freak out, overcome by anger that he'd kept another secret from her. Gabe deserved that. He deserved her anger and unforgiveness. He'd lied and hidden secrets. He deserved so much worse than her anger, but Gabe knew how to handle anger and disgust. Gabe felt that about himself every day when he looked in the mirror.

Her compassion might be worse. He didn't know how to handle that. And he definitely didn't deserve it.

"I'm so sorry," she said again.

So much worse. Like every inch of him was stepping on the corner of a microscopic Lego brick. That's how much worse it felt.

He met Kaylee's eyes, and his secret waited on the edge of his tongue. Her emerald eyes shimmered with unshed tears for him.

Tears he did not deserve.

"That's the reason, isn't it?" Her voice sounded small as she untangled her fingers from his.

"The reason for what?"

"For your whole 'love is a lie' mantra. It's because of your dad." She searched his eyes for confirmation.

Gabe looked at his tray of half-eaten food.

The whole reason? No. A major factor? Definitely. When his father had found out about Gabe's struggle with images that objectified women, his father said to "knock it off" and that Gabe "disgusted God," adding another chain of shame to Gabe that made him feel like he needed to fix the problem himself.

Then the truth about his father was revealed. His father's long history of affairs and his string of relationships since leaving Gabe's mother had hardened the cement of reality that Gabe didn't want to believe as he struggled to overcome his own secret life. If his father, who had looked so good and upright and righteous to the world around them, could be such a hypocrite, then how could Gabe risk hurting Kaylee the same way? Gabe, through God's grace, may have overcome the sin that had held him captive, but the risk was still too great.

Telling the truth would hurt Kaylee the same way.

Gabe cleared his throat and shoved his thoughts aside. "I don't see or talk with my dad—not that he's tried to be part of my life since he left. But I don't want to see him either. You're right." He shoved his own tray of food to the middle of the table. "Some things are unforgiveable."

The past didn't control him. Not anymore. Not ever again.

However, *this* truth wouldn't set him free either.

# Chapter Fifteen

**"S**o the couple has requested a duet for 'Someday We'll Know' for their first dance this weekend," Ethan says at our first practice of the week. He's in full Tony Stark mode with his gelled hair and hipster glasses while he goes through the contract on his iPad.

It's been a week since Gabe and I hung out at the Christmas Village, and I've been avoiding him since then. I got far too vulnerable with him. Friends or not, it scares me too much to let him that close to my heart again. Yeah, he already knew all about my dysfunctional relationship with my family, but I don't have to remind him that they didn't want me. However, I didn't know about the extent of his father's betrayal.

I wish I had. Known then, that is. Maybe things would have been different.

However, things aren't different. And I...can't. I can't keep going back to *What if?* and allowing the possibility of a new future with Gabe to make me vulnerable. So I don't think we can be friends like that, deep and personal. Best to keep it...

Shallow?

That sounds wrong though.

"Who's that by?" Summer asks.

Drake's brow wrinkles. "New Radicals, I think."

Gabe stops strumming. "Really? I thought it was someone else."

I shake my head. "I know it from *A Walk to Remember.*" I used to love the movie, but when the tragic reality of the storyline finally hit me, I couldn't watch it anymore. However, the movie's soundtrack is perfection. I listen to it all the time.

"Kaylee, Gabe?" Ethan swings his gaze from me to Gabe. "Good with that?"

I nod.

Gabe nods.

"Actually," Natalya interjects.

I really need to invest in a record player and some scratched up vinyl. There are too many moments in life where the only thing to express how you're feeling is the shudder-inducing sound that happens when the needle struggles to free itself from the scratch's grasp.

Like this moment. This moment needs that horrible noise to add to the horribleness.

"Guys," Natalya takes a deep breath before jumping into her speech, "you all know I've really wanted to sing more duets and solos. I have for a long time. It was really awesome to get that chance last week. So I was wondering if maybe I could sing this duet with Gabe and possibly be worked into the regular rotation."

Be my sounding board for a moment, won't you? I just want to be sure I've got all the facts. Here's what I've got:

I love this song.

And she's stealing it from me.

To trick Gabe into falling in love with her.

Drake shrugs. "That doesn't seem unfair." He glances at me.

What is he afraid I'll do? Scream, *I object!*

Though that's not a bad idea.

But I remain frozen as this act of the Greek tragedy that is my life plays out before me.

"Seriously?" Gabe glares at Drake.

"I'm not trying to play devil's advocate, but she *has* always wanted to sing more," Drake argues. "It makes sense to divide that up a little more between the singers."

"That's all I'm asking," Natalya pleads.

My internal DJ is feeling Taylor Swift's "Bad Blood" right now. Feeling it to the core.

"Nat," Gabe turns his withering gaze to Natalya now, "I understand what you're saying, but by that logic, it should be Kaylee's turn."

"I'm not saying we take turns," Natalya deadpans.

"What?" Drake blinks in confusion, clearly not expecting that.

Ethan's got that weird V frown again, but this time it's not for fun. "It sounds like you're saying that you should sing everything."

"Well, that's what it's been like." Tears form in her eyes. "Aria got to sing everything; Kaylee's getting to sing everything. I know they were hired to sing, but I'd like a shot too. I want to grow as a musician. I need to grow."

Love the hired help feelings I'm getting now. So warm and fuzzy.

Natalya lets out a deep breath. "Otherwise, it may be time for me to look for new opportunities."

Ethan sighs and shakes his head, iPad tucked snuggly into his crossed arms like a cradled baby. "This is not the way, Natalya. We can't make the person 'hired to sing' irrelevant. And you're the violinist—an *amazing* violinist!—and that's something you know is popular at weddings. Additionally, you sing backup all the time, so you do get to sing."

"I know," she says. "But I need more."

"So what are you saying we should do?" Gabe growls in frustration. "Because this sounds pretty all or nothing."

"Guys," Summer—who's been oddly quiet—interjects, "let's calm down. We all care about each other, and we're all working toward the same goal here."

Are we though?

The muscle in Gabe's jaw twitches as he takes several deep breaths. "What are you suggesting, Natalya?" he manages to say evenly.

Natalya's looking hopeful now. "Maybe I can take the duets, and Kaylee can do the solos—unless there's a specific request, that is."

The room is quiet as we all consider Natalya's demand in the form of a request. And I can hear Natalya's "thoughtful" explanation from Courtney's wedding in my head.

*"I thought it might be weird for you. After all, you said that you don't want to be in a relationship with Gabe again. Seems like a romantic song would be really uncomfortable."*

I know this is a manipulation. I'm not dumb, and I'm not a

doormat. But I'm going to let her do it. To regain some of that emotional distance between Gabe and me, distance my heart has been closing between us. Self-preservation.

I break the silence. "Let's go for it."

There are moments when it's fun to shock a roomful of people. Throwing candy at bystanders with my softball arm. Tap dancing through a crowded mall. Singing nonsensical words and pretending it's opera at a talent show. My only wish is that this was a fun moment.

Unfortunately, it's a moment that's making me wish for another mouse attack: The Revenge of Mickey.

"Really?" Gabe asks, flabbergasted enough to stumble over the word three times before he says it clearly.

"It doesn't have to be this way forever, but let's try it for a few months," I suggest.

Natalya's expression is triumphant, and you can tell she's floating on a cloud a couple hundred feet above cloud nine. Moving through the room, she throws her arms around me in a hug that I shimmy out of immediately.

Not happening, bro.

Hmmm... Lady? Gal? Sister? There's not a feminine word that seems to express this sentiment. Or rather, there's not a feminine word I would consider using to express this.

Natalya stands and waits, looking at me expectantly.

Oh.

She wants my spot.

I want to flick her in the forehead. Kick her in the shin. Squirt lemon juice in her eye—actually, not that one. I wouldn't want to deplete my stash because I'm going to need it today. However, you get the gist. Anything to remind her that she may have won the duets, but she hasn't won the band. I know that's not "turning the other cheek," but I'm human. And I'm having a human moment.

Feeling humiliated, I grab my stuff and relocate to the back of the room. Summer shoots me a sympathetic look that makes an army of tears threaten a full-frontal attack on my makeup.

Kaylee McGrurd, Unwanted Backup Singer.

"Hey!"

My entire body tenses at the sound of her voice, and I look up, pasting a fake smile on my lips. "Natalya. Hey yourself."

She smiles at me—flashing those big pearly whites—before she sits in the seat next to me and grabs my free hand to give it a quick squeeze. "We live in the same house, but it seems like I've hardly seen you this week. It's funny."

Yeah, someone has *not* been going to great lengths to ensure that very thing. "So funny." But is it though?

"And now I'm running into you at a coffee shop instead of in the kitchen." She pushes a strand of silky dark hair behind her ear.

Seems more like a bad twist of Shakespearian fate. "So funny," I say again. Oh, gosh. I feel so fake right now.

She sets her coffee on the table in front of her. "Do you come here a lot?" She looks around Whipped Cream, a coffee shop Izze's cousins own and run. I came here for a jolt of legally addictive strength before I meet Gabe later tonight for some songwriting. I think he figured out I was avoiding him because he said, "Get a doctor's note if you're planning to be sick again."

I might have used that excuse a few too many times in the last two weeks.

So now I'm drinking black coffee because cream and sugar would dilute the needed effects of the caffeine. However, I'm going to need a vat of espresso to return to the status quo. Thanks to Natalya's sudden arrival, I'm feeling depleted.

"I used to come here more. Before I, uh, got let go from the bridal boutique in this same strip mall." I give her a tight smile. "It turned out okay because they helped arrange a job for me in a sewing shop."

"The place that fired you before you came to the band?" Natalya asks.

"The place that had to close due to a family emergency," I say through gritted teeth.

"Right, sorry. Well, this is the first time I've come here, but I figured they must be believers in 'Whipped Cream,'" she jokes.

Says the bean pole of a woman who tracks every gram of sugar that passes her lips. I bet she isn't even drinking coffee.

"But I'm glad I ran into you because I've missed hanging out with you."

"You have?" Okay, so there's a touch more hostility dancing through my question than I should have allowed.

"Of course," she says before she bites her lower lip.

The irrational side of me wants to scream, *That's my move! Are you going to steal that, too?*

"I...I thought we had become friends," Natalya says softly.

So did I. Before it felt like you manipulated all my duets out from under me in your quest to get a man who doesn't feel the same way about you.

But I won't say that.

However, my fake smile does falter. "It's just been a little weird," I finally say.

Natalya nods. "I know, and I realize I'm to blame for that."

I guffaw. "You do?" Well, I guess that gives her a pretty good idea about how I'm feeling.

"Absolutely! I was really insensitive at that first wedding, about the chandelier. I'm so sorry."

Oh.

I shrug, trying to pretend that I didn't see my life flash before my eyes as the chandelier careened toward me. "I'm sure it was pretty funny to watch."

"Maybe so, but I didn't realize how much it freaked you out. If I had..." She trails off. "And I think I was being catty when I shouldn't have been, so I'm really sorry about that."

Oh, catty? You don't say. "Thanks," I say quietly.

"And I also wanted to thank you."

"Oh, that's not necessary." I know what she wants to thank me for.

And I do not want her thanks. Nope!

"It is! I could tell that Ethan and Gabe didn't want me to take over the majority of the duets. Your input made the difference."

I believe you received all of the duets for the time being, per your list of demands.

"It's not a big deal," I try again.

"But it is. That's what I'm saying."

Oh, for crying out loud! Let me fluff this off and move on. Please!

I don't say that.

But I do say this:

"You handled that whole situation the wrong way." The words tumble out of my mouth, jumping at the opportunity. They've been ready, waiting for a moment when I wouldn't be able to prevent their escape.

"I know." Natalya, to her credit, looks remorseful.

Time to go.

She grabs my hand before I can make a move. "I'm not naive enough to think that singing romantic duets will *make* Gabe fall in love with me. Life isn't *The Little Mermaid*, but maybe it will remind Gabe of the good times."

A brick with the consistency of the last batch of brownies I'd attempted lands in my stomach as my intuition tries to tell me something.

What good times?

"But all that aside," she continues, "you're giving me a chance, and they've never been willing to take a chance on me before you said anything. I love playing the violin, but I also love to sing. I'm so excited to be able to do both now."

I frown. "Why have they never let you sing before? I know you said it was because others were better, but I've heard you sing solos and backup. It's obvious you're an amazing vocalist, and that's something they've all said."

She shifts, settling against the bench seat. "I don't know, to be honest. Everything felt like a dream come true when I first joined the band, but then the breakup... Well, the band almost didn't make it. Afterwards, we just sort of settled into these rolls, and now I feel stuck."

I'm missing massive amounts of band history. What breakup?

"I've asked over the years, but it never worked out for one reason or another. I've always felt sort of forgotten. Passed over. It's been something I've struggled with. I've argued, begged, and pleaded with God. Lately, I've been feeling like if He won't help me or give me answers, then maybe that means I need to take some action. Maybe my lack of action, of speaking up, has been the missing piece. I don't know." A storm of emotion rages in her eyes, startling me with its intensity.

I've never heard Natalya talk about her relationship with God before. The whole band has been going to my church since they relocated to the area, but Natalya has never been chatty. It humanizes the annoyingly perfect ideal I'd given her while adding clarity to the selfish and manipulative actions she's taken recently. In a way, it's reassuring to know that I'm not the only one who wears their "Christian" mask and hides their struggles and hurts.

Is that horrible of me? It just helps me to know, *to see*, that the people I view as perfect and/or horrible are so much more. We've all got junk.

"I know what it's like to feel forgotten and left behind." Boy, I know how it feels. I've been feeling it ever since I could feel, thanks to my parents. For crying out loud, it's been five years since I've gotten a *Happy Birthday!* call or message from either of them. They've moved on and started their real lives, lives without me or my brother. Then my brother and I did the same thing to each other.

Natalya stands up and grabs her coffee. "Well, I'll leave you alone. But thank you again for being a good friend. Even when I haven't been."

"You're welcome." But it takes every iota of mental strength that I possess to keep the bitterness from reemerging and saturating the words. I'm trying. Give me some credit for trying.

"And maybe I'll see you tonight? Maybe the three of us could watch a movie," Natalya adds hopefully.

"Sure," I grin at my sudden stroke of brilliance, "I can introduce you and Summer to *The Lord of the Rings* franchise."

"Oh, yay," Natalya says without any enthusiasm.

"That's what friends are for." I chuckle. I don't know if we are forever friends, but I also don't want an enemy in my house. I figure torturing—ahem, I mean *entertaining*—her with eleven plus hours of my favorite trilogy is acceptable in this situation.

Afterward, we can watch the bonus content.

Gabe gasps. "Woah, you didn't come up with an excuse to cancel."

I roll my eyes. "Tone down the sarcasm."

"In a few minutes," he says. "Did you bring a shawl or something, Grandma? Your constitution has been so delicate lately."

"I'll have you know that shawls are back in fashion," I inform him as I drop my purse onto the pew's seat.

"Which means you'll fit right in, Grams."

"Okay, I'm leaving." I turn around and head to the door, slinging my purse over my shoulder as I go.

"If you leave now, you don't get your present," Gabe calls in a taunting, sing-song voice.

"Please, no more fudge." I never expected to even utter those words, but I'm still eating fudge from our afternoon at Christmas Village. And I've got the new muffin top to prove it.

"Better," he calls from behind me.

I turn around, crossing my arms and sporting a suspicious look. "What? What could be better than fudge?"

"Lemons," he declares while reaching down and pulling out a little blue and yellow gift bag.

I raise my eyebrows. "'Oh, Baby!'" I read.

He blinks. "Uh, what?"

"The bag." I point. "It says, 'Oh, Baby!'"

Turning the bag to read for himself, Gabe's face breaks out with splotchy red spots.

I'll confess, it's adorable when he blushes.

"You should really read the bags before you grab them. That way you won't end up with what is obviously a baby shower gift bag," I tease.

"Okay, please just open it. Preferably without further commentary on the bag." He crosses the distance between us and passes me the bag.

"Oh, there will be further commentary. For crying out loud, there's bottles and rattles on it. How did you not notice?" I set my purse on the floor beside me and look inside. "Wow!"

There's two bottles of lemon juice, four whole lemons, and seven bags of lemon drops.

"And this. I didn't want it to get smushed." I look from the goodie bag to Gabe, and he's producing a piece of cake in a plastic takeout container from behind his back. "Lemon cake is a lot harder to procure than you would think, but I did it."

I stare at him, unable to speak.

This is not Friend Zone!

"I, uh. Why did you do this?"

He shakes the container of cake in front of me. "First, can you acknowledge that I tracked down lemon cake for you?"

"Right. Thank you." I flash him a quick smile. "Now why did you do this?"

He shrugs and shuffles his feet. "Because friends do stuff like this." He's looking at me, but he's not looking me in the eyes. Instead, he's looking to the left of my eyes.

I look from him to the bag of lemon goodies to the lemon cake and back to him.

"And because I felt bad about what happened with Natalya. You didn't deserve that. I should have seen it coming." He's still staring to the left of me.

I raise an eyebrow.

"Ethan should have seen it coming?" he tries, finally making eye contact. His smoky gray eyes whisper a dozen more reasons, reasons I know won't leave Gabe's lips.

I look at the cake.

He tracked me down a piece of cake. Who does that?

Knights. Superheroes. Sweet men that you marry.

This is the Gabe I dated. This is the Gabe I fell in love with. This is the Gabe I mourned.

And this is the Gabe that could sweep me off my feet all over again. Terrifying for so many reasons, and—as we've discussed in length—it can't happen.

The problem—I'm realizing in my brilliantly slow way as "Yours to Hold" by Skillet begins to play in my inner ear—is that I think this has been happening since the moment we found each other in this wedding chapel. Maybe the Gabe I loved and love has been there all along, underneath all the mistakes and hurt and fear he's used as armor. The good in him has always been there.

"I think I'd like that cake now," I squeak, knees shaking. Cake will help me think clearly. Cake makes everything better.

Especially once I invest in a treadmill.

He passes me one of those plastic-wrapped fork/knife/napkin combos. I half fall into the nearest pew, remove the fork from the plastic wrap, and pop open the takeout container. The aroma of lemon begs me to take a bite of this sugary treat.

Who am I to argue with begging cake? I shove one, two, three bites into my mouth in rapid motion, just like Miss Manners taught us.

Insert cake and lemon bliss here, my friends. Excuse me while I savor this.

Oh, it's so good!

"I feel the need to mention the cake is a week old."

I spit my current bite of cake back into the container with an inappropriate amount of spittle coating it. "Argh! What? Are you serious?"

He winks. "The first one was. I got this one today."

"Not cool," I say around another forkful of cake (again, just like Miss Manners taught us) until I'm staring at an empty container a few minutes later.

"That was fast," Gabe teases, and his smile causes the corners of his eyes to crinkle.

"That was a small piece of cake," I respond. Sugar coma, take me away to a wonderland of dancing lollipops and cotton candy clouds. If only Shirley Temple would stop singing "On the Good Ship Lollipop," then this place would be perfect.

"I'm surprised you're not licking the container."

"Mm-hmm." I close my eyes as I step into the sugary daydream, but come on, learn a new candy song, Shirley.

"So why did you do it?"

I pull myself from the world of pink frosting and look at Gabe. "I thought I asked you that."

"And now I'm asking you. Why did you let Natalya get her way? I know you know she was playing you, but I don't know why you went along with her." His gray eyes blaze with intensity, searching my eyes for an answer.

So many reasons. "I know what it feels like to be left behind," I say, going with the simplest reason.

"Not me?"

"Uh."

"Right. Okay, got it." Gabe's voice hardens, and he stands up.

"I'll be right back. Don't make out with the lemons while I'm gone."

"Gabe." I jump to my feet. "Don't run away. Talk to me."

He crosses his arms across his broad chest and the muscle in his jaw ticks. Raising both eyebrows, he waits for me to answer his question.

"Yes," I confess, "you were a reason. We're trying so hard to be friends, and I don't want to mess this up because..."

*Because I still love you!* I silently scream.

"Because I haven't changed?" The coldness in his gray eyes tells me that's what he's expecting me to say.

"What? No! Gabe, you've obviously changed. I-I can see how much you've changed, but..."

"There's always a 'but' when it comes to forgiving someone, isn't there?" he mumbles, looking so defeated.

"There's always fear and anger and bitterness," I admit, tears filling my eyes. "But I want to let go of those things. I don't want to be bitter and unable to forgive people. But my heart feels so fragile where you're concerned. I'm afraid—"

I can't breathe.

I can't think.

I need to sing.

Squeezing my eyes shut to hide my tears, "Careful" erupts from my heart. My voice catches and breaks constantly, but Michelle Featherstone's heartfelt song is everything I can't put into words, everything I'm too afraid and conflicted to say. Everything I want to say.

As I reach the screeching end (emotional phlegm isn't conducive to lyrical capabilities, so the smacked-in-the-face-with-a-wombat screeching is entirely my fault), Gabe's hands are on my shoulders. My stomach feels like it's taking a Zumba class, and my knees are still shaking. Opening my eyes, I see Gabe's tender, broken eyes. His expression—dare I say that I see love there?—coerces my stomach's Zumba class into another vigorous jaunt.

"I understand," he murmurs as he wraps both of his strong arms around me and pulls me against his chest, pulling me home. "I'll be careful with your heart. I promise. I don't ever want to break it again."

My tears soak his shirt, which is always attractive. He shifts backward (probably so I stop using him as a snot rag) and tilts my chin up, then he uses his thumb to wipe the tear tracks from my cheeks. Now my knees feel weak for an entirely different reason.

How do guys know to do that? Is it in some legendary *How to Woo a Girl* handbook? Do they have to practice so they don't accidently poke the girl in the eye?

Whatever the case may be, Gabe executed this move perfectly. And I think...

I think he's going to kiss me.

Unless...

Unless I kiss him first.

Grabbing the neck of his flannel shirt, I start to pull his lips to mine, but he's already coming to claim them. We are a breath away.

"Hello, what do we have here?"

I jump, smashing my forehead into Gabe's nose. He groans as I whirl around to face the intruder like I've been caught sneaking lemon drops. Yes, lemon drops. I always went for the real prize and left the cookies alone as a kid.

No one's there.

My heart races as I search the room.

"Hello, what do we have here?'" the awkward, fake-sounding tenor asks again.

From my purse.

I growl and fish my phone from my purse as the voice speaks again.

"It's your ringtone?" Gabe asks behind me.

"Izze," I spit, but without spittle this time. "She likes to change the tone I use for her whenever she spots my phone unattended. Looks like she decided to record her own this time." Tapping the Home button, I see that I've got two missed calls and a text message from her.

"I guess that explains why Lando sounded funny and got his own quote wrong."

I turn to look at him and hold up my phone. "You know who this is?"

"Of course I do." He rubs his nose but stops when he sees my *Huh?* expression. "Wait, you don't? It's Lando. Lando Calrissian."

Each word is more emphatic than the last, but that doesn't clarify anything for me.

"Oh, Lando. Right. Loved his work on...that, um, thing. Really good." Pretend like you know what gibberish they're talking about, and people will be none the wiser about your pop cultural ignorance. That is, unless those people know how ignorant you are. Then you'll get some over-the-top explanation like this:

"*Star Wars*, Kaylee," he exclaims, slack jaw and eyes like perfect gray circles.

"I like *Lord of the Rings*," I shout back.

"So do I, but everyone has basic *Star Wars* knowledge," he insists.

"So Lando Calzone—"

"Calrissian!" he says with a hint of laughter in his voice.

"Said that?"

He shakes his head and sighs. "Something like that, Kay."

"Good to know," I mutter as I change Izze's ringtone back to the *Friends* theme song, "I'll Be There for You."

And...

Now what?

Welcome to the awkward moment after *another* almost-kiss, a moment that could be compared to one of those horrible dreams where your pants split in a room full of people. Except this is not a dream; it's a real-life nightmare. Goodness, I almost don't blame Gabe for bolting after the first Almost Incident.

We look at anything but each other. I pretend to busy myself on my phone, but I'm just opening and closing various apps. And since most of them require Wi-Fi, this plan isn't working too well.

I glance at Gabe for the seventieth time in sixty-three seconds.

He clears his throat. "Um, so, I'm sorry. I shouldn't have..."

"Oh," I say, shushing my inner disappointment while the mortification laughs at me. "I understand. Really."

"I meant what I said. I don't want to hurt you." He leans forward, then steps back like he thought better of it.

"I understand." It's very sweet. And would be sweeter if I wasn't on the verge of a deranged laughing/crying jag.

"So we should, um..."

"Yeah?" Play it cool, not like you're going to liquify.

"Maybe we should call it a night?" he suggests.

"Absolutely," I say, pretending that I'm completely chill about the situation. I drop my phone into my purse. Slinging my purse over my shoulder, I wave my hand in a little half circle. "Will you extinguish the, uh, illuminating orbs?" Goodness, I'd rather lose the ability to speak than sound like a dipsy Maggie Smith.

"Yeah, I'll get the lights," he says with a sweet, crinkly smile.

"Okay!" Too high. Need to take it down a notch. "Thanks. I'll see you later." I force my voice into an unnatural alto. I sound like a bullfrog. Maybe Kaylee the Bullfrog can write a song about this, really embrace the Phoebe Buffay, awkward song style. Make everyone in the audience super uncomfortable. Yeah, I can see the merits to that.

"See you later," he echoes, but he doesn't move.

That's okay. I don't need another hint. Staying would only prolong the awkwardness, and it's threatening to consume me like a swarm of piranhas if I don't get out of here.

I turn around and, without sparing a backward glance, speed walk to the door and then jog to my car. Yanking the car door open, I'm positive about one thing based on tonight's events:

I definitely should have taken Gabe's former strategy for myself and run away.

"Listen, bub, we need to talk."

Gabe jumped up from the pew where he'd sunk after watching Kaylee disappear not ten minutes ago. Whirling to face the door, Gabe studied the shadows to determine the identity of his uninvited guest.

A pair of Toms covered with coffee cups and espresso makers revealed the owner's identity.

"Is this the part where you kill me?" he asked.

Izze stepped forward enough for the light to reveal her face. "That depends on your answers to my questions."

"How very *Blacklist* of you."

"Exactly what I was going for, thank you." Izze dipped her head in acknowledgement.

"Well, you nailed it—with the exception of the shoes, that is."

"Okay, small talk over," Izze said. "What's going on with you and Kaylee?"

Gabe held up his hands. "Nothing."

She snorted, and her left hand flexed around an object still hidden by the shadows. "Sure, I believe that. I'll give you one more chance."

"There's nothing—"

A small, hard-as-rock object hit him in the thigh. "Ouch! What was that?" Gabe exclaimed.

Izze held up an orange toy that looked like a Nerf gun. "Marshmallow gun."

"Then why did it hurt so much?" Gabe rubbed the sore spot on his leg.

"I let the marshmallows get stale before I use them as ammo."

He rolled his eyes. "You are cruel and sadistic."

"And I'm about to pelt you with my entire stash of marshmallows if you don't answer the question—truthfully."

"I answered."

Gabe dropped to the floor, narrowly missing the next marshmallow rock. He army-crawled to the nearest pew, grabbed the forgotten gift bag, and started returning fire with lemon drops. "Stop shooting marshmallows at me." That might be the most bizarre thing Gabe had ever yelled in his adult life.

"I watched the two of you start to get awfully *chummy* in here, and then I saw my best friend run away. Now tell me what's going on!" Izze yelled after she'd taken cover behind a pew.

"You were hiding in the bushes and watching us when you texted?" He could not believe this.

"Of course I was."

Unbelievable! Gabe took aim with another lemon drop, but a marshmallow hit him in the wrist. "Argh! Stop!"

"Gabriel Sanders, if you lead her on and break my best friend's heart again, I promise you that I will hunt you down with a lifetime supply of stale marshmallows."

"I'm not leading her on!"

"Then what are you doing, Gabe?" She jumped up and marched straight to him. Gabe scrambled to his feet, spilling his entire arsenal of lemon drops in the process. The pure fury radiating off of her made her the scariest thing Gabe had ever beheld.

"I still love her," Gabe blurted.

Izze lowered the marshmallow gun a fraction of an inch. "You what?"

Gabe released a deep breath along with that small piece of truth. "I still love her," he said again. He had done ten rounds in the ring in his mind, wrestling with Chip's words. Every time he'd convinced himself that Chip didn't understand, the truth would sucker punch him all over again. God had had to take a jackhammer to the wall of lies Gabe had allowed to form his perspective, but with each slab that fell away, the truth shone all the brighter: his God was a God of love, and his God was not a lie.

With the desperation of man dying of starvation, Gabe wanted to experience more of that all-encompassing love of God in his life.

And after tonight, Gabe couldn't ignore the fact that he still loved Kaylee—loved her as much as a broken, tainted man could love a woman who deserved far more than he would ever be. He loved her. Always had.

Always would.

"You had better not be saying this just to get on my good side." Her nostrils flared.

"I'm not, Izze. It's the truth."

Izze took a threatening step forward, forcing Gabe to take a step back. The back of his calves pressed into the edge of the pew. "What about your 'love is a lie' nonsense?"

Wonderful. *That* detail Kaylee chose to share with her bulldog of a friend. "That was a lie."

Izze raised the marshmallow gun again. "What?" she growled. "You told her that lie to accomplish what exactly?"

"I mean the 'love is a lie' thing," Gabe explained quickly. "It was a lie I had tricked myself into believing, to protect her...and me. But it's not true." His love was imperfect, no doubt about it, but it wasn't a lie.

Izze's eyes narrowed. "So then what are your intentions?"

Gabe had heard other men share about their experience with this line of questioning for years, each story embellished with details that conveyed the thinly veiled threat: *Hurt her and you're dead meat.*

However, none of those stories were as scary as the story he was living: Izze with a marshmallow gun loaded with stale marshmallows and him with what was sure to be a less-than-satisfactory answer.

"I don't know, Izze," Gabe said through the chalk coating his throat. "All I know is that I don't want to hurt her again, and I don't want to rush into anything. I want to follow God's leading. In the meantime, I'm trying to be her friend, praying." The song Kaylee sang earlier sounded in his ears. "And I want to be careful with her heart. I love her, but I *need* to be careful with her heart. If that's not okay, then I'm sorry, but you'll have to pelt me with another marshmallow."

Izze's eyes narrowed still more as she considered him. "Boy in a plastic bubble kind of careful, Gabe. You have no idea how much your betrayal wrecked her."

"I know," he said in a hoarse voice.

"I mean it. Don't lead her on just to bail again."

"I won't," Gabe promised.

"Okay." She nodded sharply. "In the meantime, I'll be watching you." As her parting shot to him, another marshmallow nailed him in the gut.

# Chapter Sixteen

I feel like I'm channeling my school days, but I can't wait for our Christmas break.

We've had one to two bookings every week since the first weekend of November. Apparently, a lot of people wanted holiday weddings this year, and Courtney and Dallas' wedding got us several additional gigs. Our last wedding before our Christmas break (the week of Christmas) is in three days.

I am ready for a week without a show.

On the plus side, all the busyness has kept me from focusing on Gabe, the first Almost Incident, the second Almost Incident, overanalyzing every interaction since then, and the resulting junior high questions that keep ping-ponging in my head. We haven't met for songwriting since the second Almost Incident, and rehearsal has been business as usual. No deep conversations. No presents. No touching. Very professional.

I hate it.

And I hate how conflicted I feel. It's like I'm thirteen all over again. Guys, I'll spare you the details and simply say that was not a pleasant year, so you can see the comparison is not a good one.

"I can't believe we have to work on New Year's Day," Drake complains as he packs up his bass guitar.

"Dude," Ethan says, looking up from his ever-present iPad. "Most people have to work on New Year's Day. Plus, we're getting a lot of money for that gig. The clients are paying the higher rate, and there's a higher travel fee since it's in Massachusetts."

Drake shakes his head. "I know you think you're making it sound more appealing, but you're really not."

"I'm excited!" Summer bounces on her drum stool and clacks her drumsticks together. "It's going to be at a swanky butterfly garden."

"And remember, it's a themed wedding," Ethan reminds us. "*Alice in Wonderland*. Wear red."

"Yippie," Drake says dryly.

"That's an odd theme for a wedding." Natalya glances at Gabe, wistfulness written on her face.

Despite how much I enjoy the whimsy in *Alice in Wonderland*, I'm a little apprehensive about this wedding. The Queen of Hearts has always terrified me, and given how things did not go in my favor at *The Phantom of the Opera* wedding, I'm not optimistic.

And I like my head.

Okay, enough with the morbid White Rabbit trail.

"Is there a dress code for the wedding this weekend?" Summer asks.

"I don't think so, but let me double check." Ethan taps and scrolls through his iPad before answering. "It's a Nutcracker theme, but no dress code."

Drake makes a face at Gabe, who purses his lips and nods in agreement.

Sigh. Boys.

Shaking my head, I head to the kitchen. While grabbing a half empty bottle of water and lemon juice, I feel a presence behind me.

"Sorry that we haven't been able to hang out lately," Gabe says as he leans against the counter. The move doesn't rip my heart out this time, but it does make me yearn to see it more often. Like every day.

"It's not your fault." I twist the cap off my bottle and upend the lemon juice to squeeze into the water bottle. "It's been busy."

"You don't drink the lemon juice straight anymore?" he asks as he watches me squeeze a third of the lemon juice into the half empty bottle.

"Not very often," I inform him with a grin. "I found out that the amount of concentrated citric acid I was imbibing wasn't good for me."

He points at my bottle. "And that isn't concentrated?"

"Believe it or not, this is pretty diluted for me." I replace the cap and shake the bottle.

"Oh, I believe it." He winks. "So I have a remedy for that."

"My lemon addiction?" I ask. "Sorry, but there's no cure. You should know that."

"No, our lack of hangout time."

My heart flutters. What is wrong with me? Ahhh! "Oh?"

"First of all, my mom wants everyone to come to her house for dinner tonight," Gabe says. "It's non-negotiable."

Not an us thing. I'm uncertain as to whether I'm relieved about that or bummed.

"And I also thought that we could go skiing on our Christmas break. And wow, saying 'Christmas break' makes me feel like I'm seventeen, so maybe we should rename that." Gabe makes a face and chuckles.

"Skiing! How fun!" Natalya's voice exclaims behind us. "What a great idea." Before either one of us can say anything, she's back in the living room, inviting the rest of the band to Gabe's mom's house and on our ski day.

Gabe rolls his eyes and sighs. "Apparently, everyone will be skiing that day."

"That's okay." I shrug like it's no big deal, pretending that a part of me doesn't want to march into the other room and loudly tell Natalya exactly what I think of her manipulation.

He nudges my shoulder with his own. "We'll still be able to hang out."

Not if Natalya has anything to say about it.

Gabe watched the gang laugh and move around his mother's apartment from where he stood in the kitchen space of her main room. The open floor plan was nice for something like this, and he couldn't remember the last time his mother had hosted a group of people. Probably before her diabetes had gotten out of control.

And Gloria Sanders hadn't let Kaylee out of her sight all night. She hugged and doted on Kaylee like she was the daughter-in-law that Gloria never knew she'd lost—though if anyone could

figure it out, it would be his mother. They were sitting together on the couch, laughing like the old friends they were as Drake recounted the infamous bunny story.

"So Gabe's singing to this bunny that the little girl had begged him to hold, and the critter decides that Gabe functions as good as any meadow when nature calls." Drake laughed.

Gabe rolled his eyes as the group laughed, but the story didn't bother him. That stinking bunny had also bitten him and left a scar, but he was over it.

Or maybe he would pretend he'd gotten the scar from something more harrowing.

Kaylee glanced at him, and he held her gaze for a moment. He could still get lost in her emerald eyes, and her smile made him feel like he could do anything. Anything...like forgetting the past and forging a new future with her.

Tucking a strand of red hair behind her ear, she shifted her attention to the group again.

Gabe turned his back to them, gathering the empty plates and cups to wash for his mom. She was on a strict medical diet, but they'd been smacked with a wall of garlic as they crossed the threshold to the one-bedroom apartment where Gloria had made lasagna, garlic bread, and salad—which was the only thing she'd eaten.

He'd just turned the faucet on when he realized that he wasn't alone.

"Let me help you with that," Natalya said as she slid up next to him, acting like this was something they'd done hundreds of times before. In reality, that position went to Kaylee.

And in truth, Gabe didn't want anyone else to stand in that space next to him, even if they were just washing dishes.

Glancing over his shoulder, Gabe saw that Ethan, Summer, and Drake were lounging in the living room area. He could hear voices from the bedroom, and he assumed that's where his mother and Kaylee had disappeared.

"Sure, thanks." Gabe slid as far right as he could to put ample room between them.

She ignored it, stepping as close to him as she could without pressing her body into his. They worked together, washing and drying the dishes for ten or so minutes while Natalya chattered about...something. Gabe had done a horrible job listening to her as he wondered what his mother and Kaylee were talking about in the other room.

"Gabe, I need to talk to you." Natalya set the dish she'd finished drying on the towel she'd been using to dry it.

Oh. No.

She started her speech despite his nonverbal protests. "I think you know—"

Not the time.

"That I still have feelings for you. We've always been such a great team. Is there, well, is there any chance you want to try again?" Hopefulness spilled from her eyes as she waited for his answer.

This would be rough. Porcupine loofah on a sunburn kind of rough.

"I, uh." Oh, this was the worst way to have this conversation. He leaned against the side of the sink, trying to figure out what to say. "I think you're wonderful."

Natalya cringed. So apparently wonderful was the wrong thing to say here.

"But..."

She flinched at the *but*, however, there was no way around that word.

"I value your friendship, but—"

"You still love her," Natalya filled in for him.

Gabe looked toward the bedroom again, and Kaylee's laugh danced from behind the closed door, wrapping itself around Gabe like a warm blanket.

Like home.

Looking back at Natalya, he nodded. "It's more complicated and confusing than that. When it comes to a person God's given you to love, you'll realize that there's never a moment where you stop loving them. No matter how much distance or time has separated you. No matter what's happened in the past, you never stop loving them."

More truth. Another moment where Gabe wasn't running. And it felt good. It felt right.

Natalya clamped her lips together and nodded. "Okay then. I, uh...I hope she's worthy of you."

Gabe's bark of laughter pierced the seriousness for a moment. "Believe me when I say it's the other way around."

"Believe me when I say that's not true. You are a good man, Gabe. Kaylee would be a fool not to see that." There was a bitter bite to her compliment. However, there was nothing Gabe could do about Natalya's unrequited feelings.

All Gabe could do was hope that Kaylee felt the same as he did.

I glance over my shoulder as Gloria leads me to the bedroom to see Natalya making a beeline for Gabe.

That chick best stay away from my man!

I blink.

Where did that come from? When did my heart take that tittering step and tumble down that rabbit hole again?

And ugh, another *Alice in Wonderland* reference. I blame Summer, who's been spouting off information about Lewis Carrol—whose real name 'twas Charles Lutwidge (yeah, I feel bad for him too) Dodgson—and his stories all afternoon. I officially don't know which freaks me out more, the Queen of Hearts or the Jabberwocky.

Gloria, as she has always instructed me to call her, motions for me to sit in the recliner by the window while she sits on the edge of the bed. I settle into the cozy corner, wishing I could curl up with *The Hobbit* or scribble some lyrics into my notebook for an hour or two. Bliss!

Gloria takes my hand and bestows another warm smile on me. "I wanted to chat with you for a few minutes in private and see how you're doing, dear."

When Gabe and I started dating, I couldn't help but love how *motherly* Gloria Sanders is. She's everything my distant mother isn't. It wasn't until a few months after our breakup that I could even process the fact that I had also lost the strongest mother relationship in my life.

But things are different now. And as much as I still love her, I don't want to process my reemerging feelings about her son with her.

"I'm doing good," I offer with a shrug.

She chuckles softly. "I'm sure you are, and you don't have to share anything that you don't want to with me. But I want you to know that no matter what happened or will happen between you and my son, you are like a daughter to me."

My view of Gloria has been distorted by a sheen of tears. After blinking several times, I manage to clear them away.

Nope, they're back, and they're sending reinforcements.

"Thank you," I finally manage to whisper. "That means a lot to me."

"I mean it, Kaylee. I'm so sorry for losing touch with you after everything that happened. I love you, and you are family to me." Gloria turned slightly to open the drawer of her nightstand and pulled out a pen and pad of paper. "If you're willing, I'd love to stay in touch with you. Phone. Email. Christmas cards. Whatever you're comfortable with."

Drat! The tears have won. I choke back a sob. "Of course!" I tell her and reach for the pen and paper.

She leans in and hugs me before relinquishing the supplies. I'm scribbling down all my contact info when I notice the floral, vine design on the pen.

The wood, hand carved pen.

"This is a beautiful pen." I hand the items back to her. Did my voice squeak? I feel flushed, and my heart races like it's been hit with the sugar high I get whenever I accidently drink Izze's coffee.

Gloria sets the pad of paper on her nightstand but holds up the pen. "Gabe made it for me," she says proudly. "He took up wood carving a few years ago. This was one of his first projects."

Gotcha!

"It's beautiful," I say again.

"He's gotten so good. I keep telling him he could sell them on Etsy." Gloria snickers. "But he's got it in his thick head that Etsy is some type of craft fair."

I laugh. "I supposed it's the online version of a craft fair."

"At least he's making some money for his work. He's working with an old friend who specializes in unique fine jewelry, and Gabe does a lot of the work for the pieces with wooden inlays."

"That's cool."

"It is," Gloria says quickly. "The jewelry is beautiful, but I think his other pieces are good enough to sell as well."

"Definitely. His pieces are high quality." I think of the hours he must have spent on the pieces he anonymously gave me. Very high quality.

Kind of like the man himself.

Her eyes light up. "Has he shown you any of his recent work? He won't show anything to me until it's finished. Frustrating man-child." She laughs.

"I've seen a couple pieces," I say, thinking of the Smaug figure and the Evenstar coaster. "I'm not positive, but I think they're recent." Really recent.

Gloria starts to point out other items Gabe's made for her over the years. I comment in all the right places, but I'm one hundred percent distracted. A smile that starts in my heart works its way to my lips, and I'm dancing on the inside to "Love You Like the Movies" by Anthem Lights.

Those gifts are (literally) little things, but they tell me big things and cause me to feel big things. Hopeful things. About us.

Time for the jazz hands!

# Chapter Seventeen

I should not be left alone in my head.

Why am I saying this? Because I overanalyze everything. And I do mean *everything*. What starts as good news in my ears can turn into a tornado of devastation in my mind, and my emotional state is lighter than a feather in the wake of the winds of my crazy round-and-round-and-round thought process. Unfortunately, it's just what girls do. Or at least this girl.

I glance at Gabe from where I'm setting up. He notices me staring at him like the creeper I've become, gives me a quick smile and wink, and turns his attention back to tuning his guitar.

Like that! What did that look mean? And the wink? Another wink!

Argh! This is maddening. Please, somebody save me from myself. I beg of you.

I hate being in limbo. And playing limbo. Attempting to duck under that limbo stick is one of the rare times when being tall isn't all it's cracked up to be. But I really hate being in limbo because I have no idea what Gabe's *really* thinking or feeling.

Ugh. I feel wishy-washy just thinking that. Please erase that from your brains. I mean, it's true; that's how I feel.

But I *hate* feeling like this.

Time to break into the emergency stash of lemon drops in my purse. After grabbing my candy, I turn my attention back to setting up for this Nutcracker wedding.

Bright and early, we drove up to the historic Omni Mount Washington Resort in Bretton Woods for this wedding. The towering white walls and iconic red roof of the grand hotel appeared like an enchanted castle in the mountains, stealing my breath. I have lived in New Hampshire my entire life, and I had never beheld this enchanting place until we turned onto the long, meandering road that would take us to the heart of this beauty overlooking the Presidential Range of the White Mountains. I guess the Omni Mount Washington Resort, Bretton Woods Ski Resort, and Bode Miller are some of the state's claims to fame.

You got to claim what you can when even your state emblem is gone.

Incidentally, we (meaning Natalya) decided that we (meaning everyone) should rent some rooms and go skiing at the Bretton Woods Ski Resort this weekend. So that's happening,

Summer taps me on the shoulder with one of her drumsticks while pointing with the other to the ballroom. "This has got to be one of the most adorable weddings I've ever seen."

"Goodness, I completely agree with you." It even beats out all the wedding reality shows that Izze and I used to watch.

We're setting up on a stage that's perpendicular with the main doors of the rectangular ballroom. Two giant Christmas trees decorated with red and gold tinsel, ornaments, and garland flank either side of the stage. All the tables have been decorated with elaborate centerpieces that consist of slim Christmas trees with red ornaments on gold and ivory tablecloths. The beautiful room is framed with sculpted ivory-colored pillars wrapped with thick, green garland. The simple decorations for the Grand Ballroom consist mostly of red, green, and gold items.

And Nutcrackers. There are Nutcrackers of various sizes everywhere. The trees. The tables. In front of the stage. Against the walls. I could probably pull a Nutcracker instead of the traditional quarter out of my ear, that's how everywhere they are.

A crew of people are working at rapid speed to set up the room for the reception, and I watch one woman place a little Nutcracker ornament at each place setting for the guest favor. The silverware and crystal glasses sparkle like a scene from a fairy tale, which I'm sure is the desired effect since "The Nutcracker" is a Christmas fairy tale.

Happy sigh.

"I feel out of place," I confide in Summer as I watch the hotel staff work to make the room look perfect for the upcoming reception.

She nods. "Yeah, well we got here so early."

Since we had to drive more than two hours, we arrived hours earlier than we needed to be here. However, we weren't the only early birds. As we were led to the Grand Ballroom, we could hear the string quartet warming up in the Conservatory where the wedding ceremony will start in a matter of minutes. Based on how gorgeous this hotel is and how beautiful the decorations are, the ceremony is bound to be breathtaking. If I could get there without getting lost—and most importantly, seen! —then I would sneak off to watch the wedding.

"Hey, Kaylee." Gabe approaches Summer and me. "Would you mind helping me look for Drake's lucky pick? He dropped it or something. Thinks it might be outside near the cars, and he insists that he can't play C sharp without it."

I frown. "Drake has a lucky guitar pick?"

Summer hip checks me and makes a noise that reminds me of a hyperventilating mule.

"Girl, what's your damage?" I ask.

She raises and lowers her eyebrows with emphasis. "Gabe is asking you to *go with him* to help him look for the guitar pick." Then she makes a point of looking around the room.

Oh-kay...

Oh! Okay!

I peep over each shoulder, realizing that Natalya must have went to the bathroom or something. Drake's "lucky pick" probably doesn't even exist and is a convenient excuse to get out of here.

"Absolutely," I say to Gabe.

"Good. You might want to grab your coat," he adds in a quiet voice.

"Dude!" Summer chides. "There goes my plausible deniability."

Gabe rolls his eyes. "So we can look outside for the pick."

Summer sighs. "Weak."

Gabe ignores the rest of her heckling as we walk to retrieve our personal items and equipment from where we stored them under the stage. Gabe holds the lavish red brocade skirt up as we pull our coats from the storage bin we brought with us to keep our stuff in one place. We pull our respective coats on as we walk to the door.

Gabe winks as he pauses by the door. "Act natural."

Famous last words. How many times did that course of action go wrong for Chuck Bartowski?

"Should I look at the floor as we walk? 'For the pick?'" I ask as Gabe opens one of the doors and glances left then right.

"Only if you want to walk into someone or trip over an antique chair that costs more than your car." He motions for me to go first.

"Everything costs more than my car. It's a piece of junk," I retort.

Gabe laughs as we meander through the Great Hall.

"Let's stick to the sides of the room," Gabe whispers.

I raise a mocking eyebrow. "Sure. Dodging giant wingback chairs, thin wooden chairs, solid coffee tables, tiny accent tables with plants or lamps, then the additional standing lamps, and finally the people mingling in and out of these sitting spaces is less obvious than walking down the carpeted floorspace between the elaborate pillars. Makes sense."

"I thought so. It's like a grown-up obstacle course." Gabe steps over the stretched legs of an elderly man who's reading in a striped chair.

I shake my head. "Where are we going?"

Gabe glances at me as he dodges a man in a dark blue suit rising from a wingback chair. "It's a surprise." Playfulness glints in his gray eyes.

"Then at least tell me how we get there," I insist.

"Go to the main entrance and turn left toward the South Veranda," Gabe instructs.

"What?" I ask, mouth gaping like a hooked fish. "Did you study the floor plan or something?"

Gabe snickers. "Of course I did. Why else would I know to say veranda? I'm not even sure what it's supposed to mean."

I shake my head again. "There goes the Mr. Darcy illusion."

"I don't even know how to respond to that." Gabe he holds the door open for me. "Turn left."

"A veranda is basically a wraparound porch with a roof," I say before the icy air of a New Hampshire winter smacks me in the face and steals my breath. It doesn't matter if you were born into this cold, you never get used to it. You're only slightly less cold than the people who migrate from the south.

"Seems like a pretentious name."

"We're at a g-grand hotel. Isn't a-a little pretention k-kind of the point?" I say through my involuntary chattering.

"I suppose," Gabe says as we walk the long veranda to the south side of the hotel. Snow-covered mountains surround us on every side, and delicate snow flurries twist and turn as they fall from heaven, obviously not in a hurry to end their ride on the lazy river.

"If you wanted to admire the view, we could have done that inside. Where it's warm. From one of the many windows that line every wall." My fingers are numb, and I forgot my gloves at home because that's just how I roll.

"You can't appreciate a view like this inside. The cold is half the feeling."

"I'd say it's all I'm feeling," I mutter.

I wish it was summer. Or any time of year when reaching thirty-three degrees Fahrenheit for the high of the day isn't considered a "warm" day. The beautiful white veranda, rocking chairs, and wicker furniture look so sweet and romantic. I'd love to sit and stare at the mountains. Read *The Return of the King*. Sing. And for a few moments while we walk, I convince myself I'm the princess of this beautiful snow globe.

At the corner, we turn left from the south veranda onto the east side of the veranda.

"Okay," Gabe says, snapping me from my fantasy world. "See the way the porch curves with the side of the building up there? That room with all the windows is the Conservatory."

I stop and grab Gabe's arm. "Where the wedding is?" I gasp.

"Yup." He shrugs, shuffles his feet, and grins. "I thought you might want to watch a little of the ceremony since we don't go onstage until after cocktail hour. If we get close enough, we can watch everything on the *veranda* through the Conservatory windows," he says, deepening his voice when he says *veranda*.

"Gabe, I...this is..." I can't cry. If I cry, the tears will freeze to my face. Maybe they'll freeze to my eyeballs, and that sounds painful and awkward. So I can't cry. I won't even tear up.

His smile softens into something more—a look that makes my stomach attempt a few cartwheels. "Your smile is all the thanks I need. Besides, it's past time we made a happy memory at a wedding."

And now a glassy sheen has frozen to my eyeballs. Wonderful.

Gabe takes my hand. "Let's go. It should be starting soon."

We creep along the edge of the railing and stop by an older-styled, coin-operated tower viewer, which immediately makes me think of *Sleepless in Seattle* and the Empire State Building.

Ah, Tom Hanks. You're not Cary Grant, but you're up there.

"What's the plan?" I ask.

"Why don't we just sit there?" He points at a wicker loveseat. "It looks like the only place that's been blocked off is the area directly around the outside of the conservatory while the wedding is in progress. Since every wall of the conservatory is lined with these giant windows, it will be easy to watch without pressing our noses against the windows."

"Simple. I like it."

Gabe raises an eyebrow. "Is that supposed to be a compliment?"

"I'll let you be the judge of that."

He chuckles as we sit on the cold cushion of the loveseat. Since the Conservatory juts out from the rest of the hotel almost like an enclosed balcony, it's easy to watch the wedding from here. From where we sit on the veranda, we're even with the last row of guests.

Craning my neck—in the most casual way possible—I can see the bride walking down the small aisle. The groom, minister, and the rest of the bridal party wait with their backs to the windows in the furthermost curve in the room, partially blocking the guests' view of the gorgeous mountains. But one of the best parts of any wedding is the groom's face when he sees his bride, and if this groom's teary expression is anything to go on, the mountain view is the furthest thing from anyone's mind.

Even if the bride makes the horrible stepsister from *Ever After* seem like Shirley Temple, I would still be in awe of her right now.

The long sleeve, red lace dress that I've already worn to several events underneath a coat that's seen better years pales in comparison to the bride's gorgeous gown, an ivory and gold number that looks so magical the probability little mice made it during the night is high. But that's the way it should be for every bride on her wedding day. Big or small, Zelda or Cinderella, simple or elaborate, she should feel like a princess—or in this case, like Clara marrying her Nutcracker prince.

So many emotions war within me. My heart constricts for the wedding I never had, sitting next to the groom who left me. That over-emotional side of me wants to weep at the look on *this* groom's face as his princess-bride approaches him on the arm of her father. And the hopeful part of me, quiet for so many years after being bruised and burned by life, wants to sing of second chances.

A single, forbidden tear escapes the corner of my eye.

And also freezes to my face.

Gabe takes my hand, intertwining my fingers with his as we watch the ceremony, and my internal radio plays Taylor Swift's "Love Story." This moment seems so surreal, but it feels like a symbolic step in the healing process.

For us?

I glance at Gabe, and my heart wants to jump, sing, and faint all at once. When did sitting next to someone equal an electric reaction? Sparks crackle between us, and I swear I can see them. This feeling is nothing like an evil light switch that shocks you with a little jolt of electricity. It's the attraction and history and the rekindled hope for a future between us.

And it might burn the building down.

I have no desire to be an arsonist and destroy a piece of history, so I need to douse the heat with my brilliant conversation skills. Nothing ruins a moment quite like my inane babbling.

"I love the Nutcracker theme," I mutter quietly. "It's so cute. And sweet. A fairy tale come to life. And I love Nutcrackers."

"I'm not sure I could have told you what a Nutcracker was before today," Gabe confesses without looking at me, but a smile tugs at the corners of his lips.

I turn to stare at him (and that's not a hardship, believe me!). "Are you serious?" I ask.

He looks at me and shrugs. "I thought all nutcrackers were like those walnut openers. The kind with the two long handles that you squeeze together in your hand to crush the walnut." He flexes his hand open and closed.

"Oh. My," I say. "How did I never know you were so uncultured before?"

"Says the woman who doesn't know who Lando Calrissian is," Gabe shoots back with a wry grin. "And you never noticed because you were crazy about me."

My heart jumps like it's playing dodgeball.

"And I never noticed because I was crazy about you," he adds in a low voice before he flicks his gaze back to the stunning scene before us.

Of course, I'm more interested in the stunning man before me.

I need answers. I need answers, and I need them now. No more limbo.

"I know talking about us and all our confusing stuff hasn't done us any favors," I start.

Gabe snorts and leans against the back of the loveseat. "There's been some loud discussions regarding that 'confusing stuff.'"

I blush and shift. "Right, but I really think we need to talk about, uh, what almost...the other, um, night. Get on the same page about the incident."

Gabe laughs softly beside me. "The incident?" he questions.

And now I'm blushing some more as we watch the couple say their vows from our hideout. "Well, what would you call it?" I ask after a few minutes.

Gabe looks at me, and the heat in his smoky gray eyes takes my breath away. "I'd call it what it was: we almost kissed." His eyes flicker to my lips. "Would have if it wasn't for fake Lando's intrusion. Does that clarify things for you?"

"Calzone was actually Izze," I say breathlessly and purposely messing up the character's name this time.

"I know you're only trying to goad me." Gabe crosses his arms across his broad chest. "What page are you on?"

"What page are you on?" I shoot back. I don't care how childish it may seem; I'm not going to be the first one to expose my heart. That terror belongs to Gabe.

Gabe turns to face me and takes my hands in his, rising to the unspoken challenge. "I've been thinking about this a lot. You were right: I have been hiding behind a wall of lies. Twisted as it was, I really did think I was protecting you from myself back then. Honestly, I'm not quite sure what to do or where to go from here. I don't want to jump into anything too fast after everything that's happened between us. However..."

Every part of my body tenses in angst, and I inhale sharply, a feeble attempt to brace myself for whatever he says next.

"I can tell you one thing for sure." His voice drops to a whisper. "I never stopped loving you."

"Wow," I murmur as he strokes the back of my hands with his thumbs.

"And you?" he probes.

"I never stopped loving you. I tried. Believe me, I tried. I begged God to help me get over you," I confess. "But you've always been in my heart."

"I think it's safe to say we're on the same page then," Gabe murmurs.

"But where do we go from here?" I'll admit, I'm a little afraid of the answer—of any answer—because the possibility of us feels like a wish my heart was too afraid to voice.

"We move forward. We follow God's leading. When it comes down to it, that's all we can do." Gabe smiles. "Together."

"Together," I whisper as I intwine my other hand with his. "I like the sound of that."

The left corner of Gabe's mouth tilts heavenward. "As do I."

# Chapter Eighteen

You wouldn't think you could sweat so much when the wind-chill is twelve degrees, whipping around you as you zigzag down the side of the mountain. More importantly, you wouldn't think that sweat would smell so. Stinking (pun intended). Much.

But it does. It's the first thing that assaults you when you walk into a ski lodge, any ski lodge. You can pick the most up-scale ski lodge in the world, but it will smell rank because the second those ski jackets—and worse yet, those ski boots—come off, sweat stench abounds. And no matter how large the room is, when hundreds of people are congregating in a single room, there isn't an air freshener strong enough to cover it.

Yeah, it's gross. Repulsive. Disgusting. Let's be real here. However, I've learned that a neck warmer tugged over the nose functions nicely as a modern handkerchief to protect one's nose from the most unsavory scents and/or to allow you to gag with the illusion of privacy. Unfortunately, the only time you might not smell various degrees of body odor at a ski lodge is when you're flying down the slopes—providing you wore a strong de-odorant.

You've been warned, and you may take a moment to gag if you need it.

Really. It's okay. I gagged the moment we crossed the threshold of the ski lodge as my olfactory receptors shriveled in self-protection, allowing me to get through the day without dry heaving.

You might think I have a very negative outlook on skiing after that not-so-little verbal onslaught about the unfortunate realities of sweaty lodges. In truth, I love to ski. It's one of my favorite things to do. I grew up skiing every winter, but I haven't been able to go in—gulp!—eight years. So I am determined to enjoy the day—and go home without any broken bones.

However, enjoying the day might be trickier than it seems due to the fact that Natalya the Ski Bunny has already staked a claim on Gabe.

"Whoops!" She pretends to fall into Gabe as she's putting on her ski boots. He catches her with ease and removes his hands from her upper shoulders once he's tipped her back to a standing position.

I look down and adjust my thick socks, rolling my eyes six times.

"You're so strong," she purrs.

Make that seven.

"That was so fake," Summer grumbles next to me as she pulls on one of her snowboarding boots.

I snort as I tug the second ski boot onto my left foot. After adjusting the buckles, I stand up and lean against the tongue of the inner boot to determine if it's tight enough.

And I do this without falling into the person next to me. Just saying.

"Okay, enough waiting around," Ethan booms. "Drake, Gabe, you guys good to go?"

"Yeah, let's go," Drake says.

Gabe grabs his helmet and nods. He glances at me and winks. "See you up there."

"Nat, you need to lay off," Summer whisper-shouts as soon as the guys disappear in the throng of people milling around on the main floor of the lodge. She glances at me, offers me a smile I can't quite decipher, and moves to sit in the chair next to Natalya. "Seriously. This is hard to watch."

Natalya avoids looking at Summer as she yanks on her ski coat. "What are you talking about?"

"I heard what he said to you the other night," Summer says in a low voice, but my Vulcan hearing translates the words effortlessly. "I know everything went down before my time, but I don't want to watch you get hurt."

What went down? What did Gabe say? My ears burn with the

desire to know more information, but I'm not going to stand here and gawk. I'm out of here as soon as I'm dressed for the frigid temperatures. I zip my coat, adjust my neck warmer, and pull my hat over my twin braids.

"We're just friends." Natalya swings her penetrating gaze my way. "Like they're just friends."

And that's my cue to leave.

"I'll see you guys later." I loop my helmet strap over my right arm and shuffle away—the equivalent of running in ski boots. Walking in ski boots is a lot trickier than you'd think it is. You don't realize how much of a role your ankles play until they're imprisoned in boots whose sole purpose is to prevent your ankles from moving at all.

"I hate seeing you throw yourself at a guy like this," Summer says as I shuffle away.

"I can't just turn off how I feel about him," Natalya insists.

"Nat, you got busted up pretty bad after—" A screaming kid cuts off the rest of Summer's response.

Pushing open the glass door of the base lodge while putting on my helmet, the first icy blast of air kisses my face, sending tingles down my spine. Going to the rack where I'd placed the skis and poles I'd rented for the day, I toss the skis onto the ground and snap my boots into the bindings. After slipping the poles' wristlets over my gloves and adjusting my goggles, I leverage my poles to push off and move my skis like I'm skating to move across the flat terrain to the Bethlehem Express chair lift.

I always feel like a clown in a marshmallow coat when I'm skating in skis. Don't even get me started on the times when you step on the ski that you're trying to lift. Best-case scenario, you'll fall without impaling yourself on one of your poles; worst-case scenario, you'll fall in the middle of a trafficked area and cause a human pileup that brings the entire ski resort to a crashing halt.

It could happen.

I picture the trail map in my mind's eye as I get in line. I've never skied Bretton Woods before, so I took care studying the trail map last night. I'm planning on sticking to the easier trails, all labeled green or blue based on the difficulty for beginning or intermediate skiers. Despite my former chops, there will be no black diamonds for this rusty skier—and definitely no double black diamonds.

Oy, it's busy today. Talk about being lost in a sea of people.

Finally, I'm getting on the lift with a family of three. Looking over my shoulder so the chair literally doesn't sweep me off my feet and disappear without me (and bring the entire lift to a crashing halt because it really does happen!), I time my plop (there's no graceful way to sit in this process) just so. We're flying up, up, up as we wiggle, scoot, and lower the safety bar across our laps.

I glance over at the family as they quietly talk to each other. It's a special kind of awkward when you have to ride the chair lift with a bunch of strangers. I don't like to feel awkward.

I like to cause the awkward.

Relax, I don't do anything *too* weird.

Unless you think singing various Disney and/or cartoon theme songs at the top of your lungs in a self-imposed helium voice on the chair lift is too weird. In which case, I recant my previous statement.

However, I don't like to cause the awkward alone. I need friendly support if I'm going to be extremely weird.

Regardless of the strangers, I'm smiling. The familiar hum and grind of the chair lift, the whistle of the wind as we zip up the mountain, the occasional shriek or peel of laughter that reaches my ears are the sounds of happy memories.

I'm on the mountains, friends. And when I'm on God's majestic creation, I feel like I'm closer to my Father. Songs of praise well up in my soul, singing in time with the mountains' melody. The part from that verse in Luke...uh, chapter nineteen, and I think it's verse forty. Anyway, that part about the rocks crying out floats through my mind.

There are moments when you can feel all of creation praising Him. Moments like this.

"The Sound of Music" bubbles within my chest, and my lungs and throat ache to let it out. My fingers tingle with the desire to unleash my inner Elsa and sing "Let It Go" while doing helicopters spins down the mountain.

Or the tingling sensation could be frostbite.

I flex my fingers. Nah, I'm fine.

For now.

We're nearing the end of our ride, so I shift my skis off the footrests and readjust my poles. The family wiggles, shaking the chair lift. The father starts to raise the safety bar, and for one brief second, I look down.

Mistake! Now all I can picture is being thrown from the chair lift thirtyish feet (and yes, I'm guessing) above the mountainside because the lift came to a sudden, unexpected stop.

Don't look at me like that. I told you it happens. Sigh. I never used to be scared of the chair lift. I've gotten wimpy in my old age.

I can feel some of you glaring at me.

Okay, fine. I'm not that old, but that sense of frailty has been turned up a few notches.

In the next moment, we're unloading. I turn to the left to take the Cascade trail. Confession: I might be taking this trail because it ends in a clearing where several trails of all levels start and end. Like Bode's Run, a black diamond trail I heard Ethan insisting they go on today.

Yeah, it's a little embarrassing, but after yesterday's talk, I want to spend some time with Gabe. I would oh-so-conveniently appear at this ski intersection all day if that will increase the chances of spending some time with him.

Goodness. If you'd told me a few months ago that I'd actually be feeling hopeful about anything regarding Gabe, I'd have laughed. While mentally spitting in your face. After I mentally kicked you in the shins. And, well, enough with the mental violence. You get the point. I didn't have high hopes.

I didn't have *any* hopes.

But now I do.

Bringing my skis perpendicular to the slopes, I angle the edges of the skis into the side of the mountain, slowing to a stop to allow a group to ski by me. Using my poles to help inch me to the outskirts of the Latitude 44 Restaurant, I tug one glove off and unzip my coat slightly. After unzipping an inner pocket, I pull out my phone to turn on some music.

The sun shines like polished gold. The sky is ice blue. The snowy slopes gleam like they've been frosted in diamonds. And the rocky mountains are singing, so I'm starting this day with praise.

Amanda Lindsey Cook from Bethel Music starts to sing "Starlight" from my phone.

Perfect.

After selecting the shuffle feature, I tuck my phone back into its pocket, mentally preparing myself for that first drop. I don't know why, but any slope with a chair lift always seems to be terrifying. It could even be a beginner trail, and it will still feel like you're about to bungee jump from the Golden Gate Bridge.

Pushing off, I keep my skis perpendicular with the slope. I turn left, then right, then left, turning any time I start to slow down too much. I make it past the initial ice patches at the top of the trail. The end is in sight. Aiming for a spot near the edge, I turn right and tilt my skis into the side of the slope.

And hit a patch of ice.

I'm flying, but not the in-control way I like to fly while skiing. Nope, this type will only result in pain when I crash into—

Landing on my right hip, I slide twenty or so feet before I stop. Taking inventory of myself, I realize one of my skies broke away from the bindings about ten feet up the slope.

This is a great start to the day.

"Need some help?" a male voice calls. The skier in a familiar blue jacket slides to a stop five feet to my left, spraying powder everywhere.

Gabe.

Sigh.

But at least I didn't fall on purpose.

Gabe lifted his goggles and glanced around. Looked like Kaylee was alone. His protective instincts where Kaylee was concerned kicked into gear. Yeah, he was relieved that they wouldn't have to deal with Natalya, but what if she'd gotten hurt while skiing alone?

"One of my skis is about ten feet that way." She pointed up the mountain with her thickly gloved finger.

"That sounds like a personal problem," he teased as he carefully started to climb up the side of the slope, step by step. He kept his skis perpendicular and used the edge to slice into the mountain, but the real battle was keeping his body weight even. Lean too far downslope, and he'd take his own tumble down the mountain. Lean too far upslope, and he'd...

*Thud!*

Fall over when he was six inches from the ground like he was a toddler learning to walk.

"Looks like I'm not the only one with a problem," Kaylee yelled.

"I didn't lose my skis," he shot back. Thrusting both poles into the snow, he used them to pull himself upright.

"I only lost one ski."

"The key word here is that you lost it," he taunted as he reached the ski in question. Curling his left arm up and over the top of both of his poles and Kaylee's ski while tucking the other end of them under his right arm, he took a quick, wide turn that put him almost even with Kaylee. He moved his skis into a wedge so that he didn't spray snow everywhere this time.

"I don't normally fall," she said as he inched toward her and set her ski down.

"How about thank you?"

"Thank you." Her eyes sparkled, but Gabe heard the faint whisper of...singing?

"Do you hear something?"

She tapped the neck of her coat. "I have my phone playing music. I'm surprised you can hear it."

"It's faint." He took a couple steps above her and reached for her hand. "I can pull you up."

"Sure you won't fall into the mountain again?"

"Who's the one helping who here?" Never mind the fact that he'd wiped out—and lost both skis and a pole—on the first trail. That information was need-to-know. And he didn't need Kaylee to know.

Her eyes sparkled. "Thank you," she said as she grabbed his hand.

"That's more like it." He pulled her up, thankfully without falling over.

She snapped her ski boot back into the binding. "It's been a while since I went skiing."

"How long?"

"I don't know. Eight years?"

"Kaylee! Why are you out here alone?"

"What? You know that I used to be a black diamond skier. I figured if I stayed on the easier trails then everything would be fine." She gripped her poles.

"You're not supposed to ski without a buddy," he insisted.

She shrugged. "Summer and Natalya were going to take a while. I didn't want to wait."

"I guess it's a good thing I'm here." He grinned. Actually, this was working out perfectly. Now they'd be able to hang out like he'd originally planned.

"I suppose so," she sighed. He could see she was fighting a smile, working to keep her deadpan charade.

"Thanks for that."

She laughed. "I'm teasing."

"I know." He winked before sliding his goggles into place. "This will be fun. Even if all your falling slows us down."

"Seriously? Are you saying you haven't fallen today?"

"I'm not saying anything."

She stuck her hand on her hip, and her pole clicked against the ski. "What would Ethan and Drake say if I asked them?"

"Well, here's hoping we don't see them for you to ask."

"You've fallen, too," she declares. "You should throw down and sizzle like bacon to make up for all your mockery."

He blinked, not that she could see it with his goggles pulled over his eyes. "I have no idea what that means, but it's not going to happen."

"Fall down—"

"We just got up."

"And do an ineffectual version of Michael Jackson's Worm dance on your back to simulate sizzling like bacon."

He groaned. "You do it."

"You fell first."

"How about this," Gabe said. "The next person to fall has to 'sizzle like bacon.'"

"Saying it sarcastically won't get you out of it." Kaylee's lips pursed into a wicked grin. "In fact, I think I'll record it."

"You're forgetting something."

"What?" She lowered her goggles and looked at him through the reddish-orange tint.

"You'll be the next person to fall."

A saucy smile challenged him. "You're on, Sanders. But I'm going to win."

With Kaylee standing next to him and smiling like that, Gabe felt like he'd already won.

He cleared his throat. "Where to?"

"Where'd you go?"

"We did Bode's Run like Ethan wanted, but I prefer your plan." Gabe thought for a minute. "We could take the Rosebrook lift up to the top of the mountain. There's still easy trails up there. We could take them to In Between. That's a good trail."

"Let's do it."

Gabe blinked. He could almost hear the echo of the exact same words with the exact same inflection when Kaylee had accepted Gabe's unconventional proposal to run off and elope.

"Dude?" She waved her gloved hand in front of his face. "Where'd you go?"

"Sorry. Nowhere. Ready?"

She raised an eyebrow, but she didn't say anything as she nodded.

They took off for the lift, and Gabe had to physically bite his tongue to keep from mentally cursing himself.

Maybe this was a bad idea.

Not that Gabe had any clue what "this" was at this point. They still loved each other, but that didn't mean they were walking down the aisle again.

Did it?

Gabe couldn't do that yet. Not when there were still secrets between them.

Yet?

Yet...

Man, Gabe wanted "yet" to be true. He wanted to believe that second chances, grace, and God's forgiveness could free him from the past.

They got in line for the chair lift, and thankfully, they didn't have to share it with anyone else. Gabe lowered the bar and rested his arm across the back of the seat.

Kaylee glanced at his arm and shifted.

Did she just shift closer to him?

"I've got a question for you," she said. "I was going to ignore it, let it go, forget, and all that jazz, but I want to know."

Gabe almost sighed. There were so many unanswered questions between them, and yeah, he knew that was his fault. But he was determined to man up and face it head on. Stop hiding. Stop running.

Didn't mean he wasn't also a little freaked out. "Yeah?" he said.

"Why'd you name the band after the song we were writing?"

Oh, yes. That. Gabe had expected that one to come back around; honestly, he had expected it to come up before now. He'd seen the fire in her eyes when she finally connected the dots.

"Do you want the short answer or the long answer?" he asked.

"Both."

"The short answer is what I told you last night." Gabe raised his goggles. The wind stung his eyes, but he needed Kaylee to see how serious he was. "I still loved you. I never stopped."

He heard her sharp inhale despite their windy ride. "And the long reason?"

The cold wind was going to blind him. Wait, was that actually a thing? Gabe lowered his goggles, just in case. "The long story is that the wedding band thing kind of fell into my lap. I was going through a lot of stuff when we broke...when I left. Anyway, I connected with a church group, and that's how I met Ethan. He was big into the music scene, but he has no musical ability whatsoever. He kind of sounds like a pubescent donkey trying to master the catcall."

"That's so mean," she said while giggling.

Gabe laughed and shrugged. "It's true. Anyway, when he found out I could play, write, and actually carry a tune, Ethan threw stuff together. His connections got us Natalya, Aria—the last singer before you—and another guy, Josh. We did the music for one of Ethan's buddies who was getting married, and that gig got us some business in the wedding community. Summer and Drake joined about a year after that, and then Josh left shortly after that."

Kaylee nodded, and the wind played with a strand of her red hair. "But that doesn't explain the name."

Gabe shrugged. "I was stupid, but I was trying to protect you back then. And then all of a sudden, irony of all ironies, the guy who runs out of his wedding is the lead guitarist and vocalist in a wedding band. In the end, the name was another way to remember you. Remember what was important."

She tilted her head as she studied him. "What were you trying to protect me from?"

"Me," he said, voice gruff. This wasn't the moment, or he'd tell her the full story now.

"What changed?"

Everything, starting with him. "I've changed."

Kaylee nodded, looked away, then looked back to him. "Want to sing 'Hakuna Matata' with me?"

Gabe snorted at the abrupt change in subject. "Uh, no. Today's my day off, but knock yourself out."

"You'll be the one knocking yourself out, but not before you sizzle like bacon."

"Someone's a little self-assured."

She shrugged. "I call it like I see it." Then she threw her arms out wide and started singing in a loud voice.

Badly. So, so badly.

"I know your off-key shrieks are on purpose, but some of these noises will be hard to shake the next time you have a solo," Gabe yelled as she continued squawking the lyrics to the song.

Her voice caught on a potentially glass-shattering squeak, and she started coughing. "The cold isn't helping," she said, voice hoarse.

He poked her in the shoulder. "Imagine that."

Kaylee tossed him a smile before tugging her neck warmer over her mouth. And then she resumed making noises that sounded like an animal's mating call. He shook his head, smiling at the crazy, silly, beautiful woman next to him.

"Be quiet," someone yelled.

Kaylee ignored them. Or she couldn't hear them over her screeching. That was possible.

"Okay," he said loudly, "we're about to unload. You can stop now."

"In a minute," she sang in an opera voice.

"Oy vey," Gabe teased as he lifted the bar and tilted the tips of his skis up. Kaylee stopped her squawking and did the same.

The bottoms of their skis slid across the unloading platform. They unloaded and turned right, careening down High Ridge and then turning onto Upper Swoop. They whizzed past the Bethlehem Express chair lift. He glanced over his shoulder to see her gaining on him.

Grinning, Gabe tucked his poles under his arms and squatted to lower his center of gravity as they turned onto In Between. He took quick, rapid turns that didn't really qualify as turns. It was all about the speed now.

*Scrape!*

Gabe's skis slid across the patch of ice. He managed to keep his balance, but then he hit a snow drift. His left ski caught in the deep powder, throwing off his balance. He flew headfirst toward the powder, but he twisted his body left and into a roll. Both skis tugged at his legs as the unlock mechanism in the bindings released him.

Then he stopped falling. Or sliding? Both? Definitely both.

Gabe lay on his back and blinked against the snow in his eyes. The tumble must have dislodged his goggles.

"Gabe!" Kaylee screamed from somewhere.

He waved his hand, still lying on his back. "I'm alive." He sat up, snow still covering most of his face. "Careful. There's a patch of ice right before the powder. And it's deep."

*Thud!*

Too late.

First rule of skiing: don't try to stop on a patch of ice.

That one's pretty obvious, isn't it?

I land on my rear, and my tailbone screams—or maybe I do—as it connects with the ice. My speed slows somewhat once I hit the powder, but colliding with Gabe is what keeps me from crashing into a tree for the second time in my life.

Yeah, I've crashed into a tree. Trust me, it really does happen.

Oh, and once I tumbled *over* a baby tree, but that's a story for another time. Like never.

My face slams into Gabe's chest, and pain erupts in my head and neck. Gabe wraps his arms around me, holding me as we slide to a stop. For a few painful moments, it's just the rise and fall of his chest as we lay there.

Everything. Hurts.

"You okay?" he asks. His voice sounds deeper from where I lie against his chest.

I moan in response.

"Would sizzling like bacon help?" he rumbles.

I laugh then groan as pain pierces my temple. "Ow! Don't make me laugh."

"Are you hurt? Can you sit up?" His voice sounds frantic.

I sit up, scooching back so he can do the same. "I'm fine. I'll probably have some bruises because of how I landed on the ice, and I'm going to have a screaming headache. Tweaked my neck. Otherwise, I'm fine."

His eyes look wild with panic. "Are you sure? What do you mean that you tweaked your neck?"

"I'm sure. It's stiff. Are you okay?"

Gabe lets out a ragged breath, and his eyes close for a beat. "I'm fine. I'm fine."

I take off my helmet and straighten my ski cap, grimacing as I do it. Gabe's gray eyes narrow in concern as he watches me. His snow-encrusted goggles dangle from the back of his helmet.

"That was an epic wipeout," I say in an attempt to lighten the moment. "You've earned the right to sizzle like bacon." Grr, somehow I dislodged a strand of hair when I was fixing my hat.

Gabe snorts as he removes his helmet and straightens his own hat. "Excuse me, but you fell as well."

"Excuse me," I say with playful attitude, "but the agreement was that the next person to fall had to sizzle like bacon. And *you* were the first to fall." I jab a finger into his chest.

He rolls his eyes, flops back into the snow, and proceeds to jerk around.

"Make the noises," I instruct him.

He stops his pathetic attempt at sizzling. "That was not part of the agreement."

"It's implied."

"Implied sizzling? No way. Who ever heard of that?"

I flick a handful of snow at him. "Take that, buddy."

He wipes the snow from his face and playfully growls as he sits up. "You're going to regret that." He scoops together a basketball-sized lump of snow.

"No!" I shriek, trying to stand and—

I fall over, while also accidently unsnapping one of my skis. Somehow neither of them unlocked in the wipeout. I try to snap my boot back into the binding, but it's almost impossible to do while sitting.

A soft ball of snow lands on the top of my head, crumbling into my own personal avalanche. I squeal as a little clump of snow slips under my neck warmer, and the cold sends icy chills through my entire body.

My teeth chatter. "You, you're a-a fi-iend."

I can't see him through the snow, but his deep laugh is answer enough. I shake my head like a dog, then I pull off one of my gloves to wipe the snow from my eyes.

"You're a fiend," I say again.

Gabe slides toward me and yanks off one of his gloves. Wiping snow from the side of my face, he whispers, "And you're..."

As if on cue, Ed Sheeran's song "Perfect" starts to play on my phone. Ha, for once it's not just in my head.

The soft lyrics cast a net around us. Just us. And Gabe's hand is warm against the side of my face. His calloused fingertips stroke my temple.

Heaving a mighty sigh, Gabe's hand moves around to the back of my head and neck. His fingertips slip under my ski cap. I don't know if he moved, if I moved, or if we both moved, but I'm in his arms now.

And his lips *finally* claim mine for the first time in nine years. Home.

Gabe's beard tickles my face as he kisses me, as I kiss him back. He pulls away suddenly, and his smoky gray eyes search mine as his warm breath heats the pocket of space between us, warming my lips.

I have a better idea. I wrap both of my arms around his neck and pull him back.

And all I can think is...this...this is...

Perfect. This moment is perfect.

They say a perfect moment is fleeting. It disappears in the vortex of time as quick as it begins, but I'd compare this moment to a beat in our composition. Another beat and another beat and then another beat will forever be following it.

But this musical composition wouldn't be perfect without this beat, this moment.

Thanks for the serenade, Ed.

# Chapter Nineteen

It's New Year's Day, and all through my house, my roommates are coughing, disturbing even the house mouse.

*God, please don't let there be a mouse in my house!*

I shudder. *Mouse* might as well be a four-letter word these days.

It's bright and early this New Year's Day. I'm hiding in my room, packing my Worst-Case Scenario travel bag and admiring the present I found when I checked the mail yesterday afternoon—a little, hand-painted Samwise Gamgee figure.

Gabe doesn't know that I know what I know (sorry, I was channeling Monica and Chandler there for a second). He doesn't know (sorry!) that I know (I'm trying!) that he's the one sending me these hand-carved gifts.

In other words, what I know (and I failed).

Maybe I'll bust him about it in Boston.

Oh, yeah. I should fill you in on the coughing and packing. Summer, Natalya, and Drake are sick. Some kind of viral infection that equals lots of coughing and laryngitis. Ethan, Gabe, and I are fine, but only the three of us are going to Boston today. At least for the time being, Gabe officially asked if I would take over the duets again. He's certainly not as put out by this arrangement as Natalya was, but I'm basing this assumption on the cute grin on his face when he asked me.

Ethan and Gabe are driving down separately. And I'm driving down with—

"Yo! Where did all my coffee go?"

I look over my shoulder at Izze. "Do I need to remind you that you don't live here anymore?"

"Ouch. That was hostile."

I shrug. "The truth hurts."

"The truth shouldn't be spoken before I've had my coffee," she grumbles as she plops on my bed while I pack my bag.

I narrow my eyes. "You've had coffee this morning. There's no way you could have driven here without coffee in your system. It's like oxygen to you. How much have you had?"

"The minimum amount one needs to survive—or drive."

"Six cups?" I ask.

"Only two," she says proudly.

"Impressive." I shove a pair of leggings into my travel bag.

"There is no coffee whatsoever in the cupboards," she moans again.

"I'll get some next time I go grocery shopping. I figured that since I, you know, still lived here, that I needed to prioritize my food preferences."

"You like your morning coffee. How are *you* functioning right now?"

I point at the bottle of lemon juice with the cap flipped back that's sitting on my dresser. "That's how. Big gulps. Really quick."

She makes a face. "Gross! We are stopping at the nearest Starbys for real coffee. If I had known you didn't have any coffee, I would have thought twice before I agreed to this road trip."

"Agreed? Girl, you begged to go when I told you that Summer and Natalya were sick." I throw a pair of socks at her head.

Izze doesn't even try to block them from hitting her in the face. "I thought we could make a luxurious weekend of it, but without coffee, how will we survive?" She moans.

"You're always so calm and rational when hiccups are thrown into your perfectly laid plans. I really admire that."

"Hardy-har-har. Grab your doomsday bag, and let's go get some coffee." Izze slides off my bed and marches through the doorway, a woman on a mission for her coffee.

For the record, the disaster bag is in case the car breaks down, or a sharknado hits while we're traveling.

Okay, the last one probably won't happen. However, like I do before every road trip, I'm packing a change of clothes. An extra pair of socks is vital when traveling in the winter. I mean, it's just good sense.

Okay, that time I did feel old.

I stuff a sweatshirt into my bag as my mind wanders to Gabe. We've only seen each other at rehearsal since that wonderful ski trip. He spent Christmas with his mom, and I spent it with Izze and her family, enjoying a wonderful day at her parent's house.

However, he's texted me.

He's texted me a lot.

Insert giggling here.

And now I feel all silly and young again. But I'm happy. I'm really happy.

*Buzz!*

Speaking of which, I glance at my phone as it buzzes again on my dresser. I had it on silent since it's so early—a quarter after seven! In the morning! Well, it feels like an ungodly hour to me.

I unlock my screen so I can look at Gabe's message:

*Looking forward to seeing you! Soon!*

And here's some more giggling.

Ugh. I'd tell you to slap the giggles out of me, but I'm too giggly and happy to even suggest it.

Hehe.

Stuffing the rest of my stuff into my disaster bag and grabbing the garment bag with my trusty red gown in it, I follow the trail Izze blazed moments ago.

And I find Natalya in the living room. No wonder the coughing was so loud.

Is this Round Two: The Return of the Balrog? Just a working title, guys.

Natalya hasn't seen me yet, so I shoot Izze a quick text before slipping my phone back into my pocket. Taking a deep breath, I fortify myself for the conversation I need to have with my friend.

"Hey," I say as I step into the living room. "How are you doing? Feeling any better?"

"A little," she coughs.

I move to sit on the opposite side of the couch, and we speak at the same time.

"I need to ask your forgiveness," I start.

"I'm sorry," Natalya rasps.

We offer each other small smiles.

I tap my chest. "I'll go first." Deep breath. "I'm sorry. I certainly wasn't trying to lie to you about my feelings for Gabe. Honestly, I didn't want there to be any feelings there after our past, but there is—feelings that is. I...I love him."

Natalya bites her lip and nods. "I know. I'm sorry. I-I loved Gabe for a long time, and I thought maybe we could have another chance."

A whooshing sound fills my ears as Marshal Erikson starts to croon "You Just Got Slapped."

Gabe's strangled words as he confessed the *one* relationship he had after we broke up replays in my ears with a quiet yet loud clarity: *"I...we...It was a mistake, and I regret it."*

"I need to let go of him, the past." She releases a long sigh. "All this time, I really thought the mistake we made was the reason he'd burrowed into that whole 'love is a lie' belief."

*"It was a mistake," he finally choked out. "It was a relationship I never should have been in, and I regret it every single day."*

Natalya looks at me, sadness tinging her eyes, the sadness of a woman who had given away a piece of her soul prematurely. "When really you were the reason. He had never gotten over you."

Then past Natalya's voice booms inside my head like she's holding a megaphone to my ear, *"Because I still have feelings for him, but I will back off if it's too weird for you."*

And then, *"Maybe it will remind Gabe of the good times..."*

Gabe and Natalya.

I clamp my mouth closed to ensure the rolling contents of my stomach stay put.

All this time...and it was *her!*

Numbly, I hug Natalya, wish her well, and watch her pad up the stairs in her thick, wool socks.

How could he not tell me that it was Natalya? Him and Natalya!

What else is he not telling me?

My phone buzzes in my pocket, and I pull it out.

*SOS? Do I need to save you? What's going on?*

Grabbing my stuff, I walk out to join Izze, who's sitting in her car, gloves on, blasting the heat, and the hood of her coat is pulled over her dark curls. Izze doesn't believe that curls mix with hats of any type, so this says how cold she is.

Oh, and she's sipping from a thermos.

I raise my eyebrows and look pointedly at her thermos, forcing a smile to my lips.

"It's one of the two cups I've had this morning," she says.

"That thing is huge. Three cups of coffee could fit in that."

She raises an eyebrow at my wooden voice. "Well, that's not how I choose to count them."

"You need a cardiologist, not more coffee," I mumble as I buckle my seat belt.

"Sure thing, but let's get coffee first." She throws her car into reverse and takes off. "So it went that good, huh?"

I startle from my stupor. "Huh?"

"Telling Natalya that you and Gabe are back together. Judging by your face, she took the news splendidly."

"What are you talking about?"

She smirks. "I know."

"But...but...how?" I stutter.

"I have my ways."

I eye her. "And you would be okay with that? You wouldn't put a price on his head?"

"As long as he doesn't hurt you again, then his name will not appear on some black-market hit list." Izze tosses me a grin, studies my pinched expression, and flicks me in the shoulder. "I'm kidding. Mostly. If this is where God's leading you, then I'm happy for you."

I raise an eyebrow.

"Really!" she says.

"Thanks." The weight of my most recent discovery rolls in my stomach. I can't talk this through with her now, not when she's finally warmed up to Gabe.

"Time for some coffee," Izze declares as she swings into a Starbucks parking lot.

What else is he not telling me?

We roll into the parking lot of the venue around eleven thirty in the morning. Between some traffic and stopping for breakfast, we got here later than anticipated. However, the wedding ceremony doesn't start until one thirty this afternoon, so we've got plenty of time to get the lay of the land, set up, and have a couple run throughs before the reception. Thankfully, the couple opted for a more traditional approach for the ceremony, so all Gabe has to do is strum "The Wedding March" for the processional and recessional.

I text Gabe that we're here, and Izze and I climb out of her car. I sling my bag over my shoulder and drape my garment bag over my forearm. Izze pulls out the rest of my equipment.

"Hey!" Gabe calls from behind me, and I turn to look at him. My heart speeds up at the sight of him.

Goodness, he's so stinking cute.

"Hey," I say, trying to keep my tone casual.

"Hello." Izze's tone is civil even if it's a little cool, but she's not threatening to hurt him anymore. Growth!

"I can take that from you," Gabe says to Izze.

"Thanks." She swings her gaze between us. "Well, I need to go check in at the hotel and get ready."

"See you later," I say.

"I'll be back in a couple hours." She glares at Gabe in a not-so-subtle way. "I will be back. Be careful," she adds as she hands him my equipment, but I know that's only a cover to add deniability to her threat.

Gabe looks Izze in the eye. "I will be," he says seriously.

Find a guy who understands that your best friend's death threats not only come with the territory but also takes those threats seriously.

Izze nods, and—shockingly—I see begrudging respect flash in her eyes.

She gives me a quick hug. "See you later."

We watch Izze go, making sure she completely leaves the parking lot and disappears in the sea of traffic before we look at each other. The smoke in his gray eyes starts today's Zumba class in my stomach, and the little swish of his black hair makes me want to throw my disaster bag to the wind and kiss him right now.

Be. Still. My. Heart.

Gabe smiles at me like he knows exactly what I'm thinking. "Hey," he says in a husky voice.

"Hey." Love how my voice comes out all squeaky. Thanks for that, God.

If ever there was a moment where you could hear God snorting in response to my smart mouth, it would be now.

"So, um, where's, you know. That person-friend." God is howling in laughter right now. I can feel it. "Ethan! I mean Ethan. Um, where is he?" I ask.

Gabe laughs along with God. "He went for a coffee run."

"Coffee. That's good." Maybe I shouldn't have let Izze order coffee for me. In fact, I know better than that. A double shot of expresso always makes me ridiculously awkward. That's what happens when your hands won't stop shaking. It's the coffee.

Gabe looks at the stuff in his arms and sighs. "I guess we should get this stuff inside."

"Sounds like a plan." I wince. Lord, strike me mute.

Gabe and I follow the instructions Ethan gave us to get into the New England Butterfly Garden Conservatory and Event Hall. We walk through the vendor door to find a little boxed room with prints of butterflies covering the azure walls. Twin desks sit away from the right wall, positioned so that whoever is sitting in them can see whoever's coming or going.

A tall blonde stands up from behind the furthest desk. "Are you the entertainment for the Timmons/Avery Wedding?"

"We are, but I was here earlier," Gabe answers.

"Wonderful!" She flutters her long, dark eyelashes at him. "I'm Olivia."

Come on, honey. We both know those lashes (among other things) are fake.

"I'd be happy to escort you back to the conservatory and event room," Olivia the Fake says, following her breathy words with more batting of her eyelashes.

I hope the glue doesn't wear out from all that action.

"Well, I actually know the way already," Gabe says again.

"We're required to escort the vendors. Company policy," she insists. "If you and your assistant will follow me."

"Actually," Gabe interrupts without budging, "she's my partner." He slides his arm around my waist.

I bite my lip to keep the smug look off my face. Though I'm not biting it hard, I'll grant you that.

"How nice." Her voice sounds flat now. "If you'll follow me."

We follow her, and Gabe drops his arm and grabs my hand.

"You can be kind of charming," I whisper. "But don't think for a second that I didn't notice the western accent. We had an agreement, bub."

"I can't help it. 'Partner' has a natural twang to it." Gabe's low voice flutters the loose strands of hair around my ear.

Olivia leads us down several azure hallways, all decorated with butterfly closeups and/or different events in the butterfly garden. I want to stop and study the snapshots of memories, but Olivia moves at a brisk pace.

She opens another door, and at the end of a tiny hallway is one of those clear, panel doorways. Gabe holds three of the panels to the side, allowing me to go through before him.

I stop, causing Gabe to bump into me. Now I know what it felt like when I lanced Ethan with my music stand, but I don't care.

This place. This place is...

Let me put it this way: If I thought I wanted to stop and stare at the photos, then I want to live in this butterfly garden. Plants and flowers fill the domed room. Cobblestone walkways weave around and through the gardens. In the center of the room, painted cobblestones form a butterfly. Chairs have been set up for the wedding ceremony there, and there's a white, wooden arch covered in flowers and vines.

And butterflies! Butterflies flutter everywhere. Everywhere!

Seriously, I'm moving in. It's decided. Once I sprinkle some hobbit gnomes throughout the garden, it will be perfect. I'll build a hobbit hole among the flowers and skip through the garden with my flower crown. This is the dream, people.

"Okay," Olivia says impatiently, "since you know the way to the event room, I'll leave you here." She disappears back through the plastic panels.

Gabe jerks his head toward the right. "The reception space is this way."

I twist my head every way, taking in everything around me. Everything about this space feels like a beautiful daydream. Based on the chairs set up, it's a smaller wedding, only forty or so people. But the space is enchanting. To my right, I catch sight of giant, black and white chess pieces, and it looks like the chessboard is painted onto the cobblestones. To my left, settees and chaise lounges (basically the same thing) have been set up in front of antique mirrors. Giant flowers in pottery made to look like giant teacups decorate the area around them.

"Kay, this way. We can explore Wonderland when we've put everything down," Gabe says with an amused grin.

Turning, I follow him through an arched doorway designed to look like the arch the bride and groom will stand under. Twinkle lights hang in front of more plastic panels. Once again, Gabe holds them aside for me to enter.

This room (the event hall, I presume) has all the greenhouse vibes. Floor-to-ceiling windows make up the room, and rose bushes line the edges of the room with top hats randomly dotting the tops of them. Even the guest's tables follow a more random pattern instead of the formal setup you'd see at most wedding venues. A little platform has been set up for us on the opposite side of the room, the sweetheart table is in front of that, and the dance floor takes up the middle of the room.

And it's warm in here. Like I need to discard my tundra coat or it'll look like I just came in from the ski slopes. The temperature must be very well-maintained in here.

I follow Gabe past a little table with mini cupcakes and tiny little vials filled with blue liquid. Each vial has a tag that says, *Drink Me!* And these tables! Oh, my! It looks like the table runners are made from pages of *Alice in Wonderland*. Mini, heart-shaped topiaries are the centerpieces.

Taking the three steps up the platform where we'll perform, I notice red-colored twinkle lights hanging on the black partition behind the stage. I bet there's more of these twinkle lights on the rose bushes.

When I finally feel like I've seen every detail to this beautifully lavish wedding, I sit on the edge of the platform and dangle my legs off the edge. "Wow," I breathe. "This is stunning."

Gabe looks up from untangling cords and looks around the room. "Yeah, it looks nice." And he's turned his attention back to the cords.

I roll my eyes. "Did you even notice the White Rabbit in the corner?"

"Yeah. Very cool," Gabe mumbles.

"I thought so. He talks and walks on his hind legs."

"Mmhmm. Very cool." He looks up, brow furrowed. "Wait, what?"

I shake my head and let out a pretend, exasperated sigh.

He gives me a sheepish grin and sets the cords down. He squats, plops, and swings his legs over the edge of the platform. Once he's sitting beside me, he leans over and bumps me in the shoulder with his.

I raise an eyebrow at him. I'm not going to make this easy.

"I missed you," Gabe says softly.

"I'm very miss-able," I say with all the smug confidence I don't have. I've got years of nothing from my parents to prove just how unmissable I am.

He bumps my shoulder again. "You are."

"I might have missed you, too." I lean into my hand which rests in the space between us.

His eyes light up with a twinkle. "Yeah?"

"Maybe," I say with a grin.

His smile grows, and he moves his hand to partially cover mine. "How was your Christmas?"

"You know how my Christmas was."

"I know what you said in your text message." He strokes the back of my hand with his thumb.

I feel the start of a blush blooming, but I see an opening in this conversation that I'm going to take. "I had a good Christmas. Thank you, by the way."

He looks confused by that. "For what?"

"Your present. I loved it."

The muscle in his jaw twitches. "I only shopped for Mom this year, Kaylee. I'm sorry."

"Oh, so the same wood? What did you make her?" I ask.

There's that bearded ripple again. Then he sighs. "When did you figure it out?"

"When we were all at your mom's house for dinner," I tell him. "She showed me a bunch of the pieces you've made her over the years."

"Of course." He rubs his neck, just under the place where that muscle twitches when he's anxious.

I flick him on his upper shoulder, right in the bone.

"Ow!" He scowls. "Seriously, where did you learn to flick someone like that?"

"The C.I.A.—Crippling Arm Injuries."

"That acronym would be C.A.I.," Gabe says slowly.

"Crippling Arm Injuries...Association. Let's say the first A is irrelevant to the acronym, and stop trying to distract me from the question." I angle my body and hold my right index finger back with my thumb, prepared to flick him again if necessary. "Why the secrecy, Gabe?"

He meets my eyes and shrugs. That flop of hair falls across his forehead, and I almost forget that I'm supposed to be in interrogator mode. "We were barely on speaking terms when I gave you the Smaug piece. What would you have done if I told you it was from me?"

"I don't know." If I'm honest, I don't know...

What method I would have used to destroy it at the time.

"Yeah, right. You would have set it on fire," Gabe says with a humorless laugh. "Not that I could have blamed you."

"It would have been an option," I confess. "But why not tell me when things started to change?" Shifting my position, I watch Gabe open and close his mouth for the next few moments. It's like someone's pressing rewind over and over.

"Kaylee." A sigh escapes his lips. "There's still some stuff I need to tell you."

A hot ball of lead forms in the pit of my stomach, and a chill of terror shoots through me. Is it about Natalya and what happened between them? Or is there more, something worse? "Okay." I gulp. "What?"

He shakes his head, glances at the door, and then back to me. "We'll talk. I promise. I don't want the past between us anymore, but now isn't the right time."

Dread. Dread. Dread.

Short little breaths start to burst from my lips and mouth. I can't help it. All I can think of is what happened before. The past.

How can the past *not* be between us? Like, dude, it's there. With a big neon sign that proclaims to the world that I'd done something wrong because I wasn't good enough then, that I wasn't wanted then, that I wasn't loved then.

What's changed from the secrets of today to the secrets of The Day That Shall Not Be Named when he left me heartbroken and confused in New Jersey?

Gabe grabs my hand and squeezes it. "I promise, Kaylee. I don't want to mess this up again. We'll talk."

Deep breath.

Everything's fine.

Ignore the mental alarm that's blaring.

Just like last time.

Well, that could have gone better.

*No kidding, you moron,* Gabe thought to himself as he tuned his guitar for the seventh time since they'd finished their run-through.

He could tell he'd freaked her out. Kaylee had been quiet and cagey ever since Gabe had said there was more he needed to tell her. He could only imagine the horrible scenarios that were running through her mind.

And then there was the truth itself. Equally horrible.

However, it was time. If they had any hope of a future together, Gabe needed to tell her the full story. But he was scared. Grown man whimpering in the corner scared. Gideon hiding in the winepress scared. There was no mighty man of valor here, only a flawed coward with more than a lifetime of regrets. He couldn't bear the thought of hurting her again.

But according to the old adage, the truth hurts.

His only hope was that she could see he'd changed.

And he would fight for her.

He wouldn't run this time.

"I've double checked all the fine details." Ethan's appeared at his side, interrupting Gabe's thoughts. "It looks like everything's in order."

"Great," Gabe snarled.

Ethan raised his eyebrows. "Woah, what's up with the attitude?"

"Nothing." Gabe slipped out of his guitar strap and placed the guitar in its stand. "Do you know where Kaylee is?"

"She's changing, dude. Like she told us she was going to do. Where is your brain?"

"I need to go for a walk." Gabe walked away before Ethan could say anything else. He had no idea where that meant Kaylee was, but he'd walk around this floral insect zoo until he could talk to her.

He'd start with the outskirts of the garden. Turning left, Gabe walked the stone path that circled the perimeter. Past plywood cutouts that had been painted to look like characters from the animated *Alice in Wonderland* movie. Past signs with quippy sayings from the novel. Past an absurd number of giant, brightly painted teacups.

Seriously, where did all the teacups come from? No one needed that many teacups. Or the plants that were in them.

Gabe skidded to a halt.

Kaylee stood with her back to him, reading one of the signs. He knew he'd seen her in this red dress before, but the sight still took his breath away like it was the first time.

She was stunning.

Kaylee pushed her long, red tresses over her shoulder with a sigh and turned around. Her eyes immediately found his, and she froze.

Gabe walked to her. "Can we talk for a second?"

She bit her lower lip, glanced at him, then looked away. "I thought this wasn't the time to talk." She studied a blue butterfly to her right. Quiet, but her words packed a punch.

He smarted from the verbal jab. "I know you're freaked out, Kaylee—"

"Of course I'm freaked out," she interrupted him. "Given our history, why wouldn't I be panicking right now?"

He swallowed around the lump in his throat. "Because I'm different. I've changed. I know I screwed up. I will never be able to show you or tell you how sorry I am, but I'm not that guy anymore. I need you to know that, to believe that, before I tell you..."

"Tell me what?" she whispered. Her pale face mirrored a colorful butterfly as it flew past her.

It wasn't the time to have this conversation. Not here. Not when they needed to get on stage together and sing, work.

But there it was. The truth on the tip of his tongue.

"Hello, Gabe. Wow, um. It's good to see you."

Gabe froze. That voice. That voice could belong to only one person. The one and only person he didn't want to see—especially not now.

Mitchem Sanders.

His father.

# Chapter Twenty

Gabe mentally cursed. A lot.

This could *not* be happening. Not here. Not now. It was a twisted joke. A blast from the past triggered by a subconscious memory. A glitch in the matrix. Anything but what Gabe feared was true.

He turned around slowly.

The truth seared into his eyes with blazing intensity.

"What are you doing here?" Gabe asked his father in a flat voice.

"Well...I was invited. I'm a guest." Mitchem looked left and right like he was considering making a break for it.

Ah, so that's where Gabe had gotten it from.

Mitchem looked past Gabe. "Hello, Kaylee. Nice to see you again."

Kaylee! Oh, no! Gabe needed Kaylee to see how much he'd changed, not how much he wanted to let out a string of words that were not suitable for anyone's ears. Gabe swung around to look at Kaylee.

Kaylee dipped her head in greeting to his father. "Nice to see you as well. Gabe, I'll see you later." She whirled and made a beeline to Izze, who waited in the wings with a threat written on her face.

Gabe sighed as he stared after them. Their conversation would have to wait. Again.

"So, how are you?" Mitchem asked hesitantly.

"What does it matter to you?" he snarled as he turned to face his father again. "It's not like you care."

Mitchem frowned. "You're my son. Of course I care."

"I guess I just missed all those cards and phone calls. The smoke signals. That lovely fruit basket," Gabe retorted.

"Hold on." Mitchem took a tentative step toward Gabe and held his hands with his palms toward the ground. "You made it clear that you didn't want to see me. 'Ever again,' you said. You were an adult at that point, and I felt like I needed to respect your wishes."

"A father who cares doesn't cheat on his wife. He doesn't betray his family," Gabe exploded.

What a hypocrite he was.

"You're right," Mitchem said quietly.

Gabe had been prepared to let him have it, unloading years of anger toward Mitchem (and himself) as butterflies flew around their heads in their very own *Twilight Zone*. However, at that comment, he slammed his mouth shut.

"You're right. What I did was horrible. I am so sorry, son." His father's voice broke on the last word. "I know I don't deserve your forgiveness. I shouldn't even ask for it, but I hope one day you can forgive me."

Gabe closed his eyes and tried to calm his rapid breathing as he processed what his father just said.

Forgive him?

No way!

But...didn't Gabe crave that same forgiveness? Wasn't he about to beg Kaylee to forgive him before Mitchem appeared? How could he deny the same forgiveness?

"There you are," a young voice said.

Gabe opened his eyes as a *new* new woman—different from the Facebook fiancée—grabbed Mitchem's arm. Disgust filled Gabe as he appraised his father's guilty expression.

He'd been played.

"I've been looking everywhere for you, sweetie," she said to Mitchem before turning her attention to Gabe. "Hi! I'm Jillian, Mitchem's fiancée."

"Another one, huh?" Gabe said. While Gabe hadn't communicated with Mitchem in the last nine years, he'd kept tabs on him. And he'd become acquainted with his father's ways at this point.

Woman after woman. Relationship after relationship. Scandal after scandal. Oh, the bitter wonders of social media.

It would never change. He would never change.

Jillian frowned and glanced at Mitchem.

"Yeah, I'm Gabe. Mitchem's son." He stuck out his hand to shake hers.

Her eyes widened as she looked at Mitchem. Her hand hung limp at her side. Probably from the realization that she was closer in age to her almost-stepson than her fiancé.

"Honey," Mitchem rushed to explain, "this is my son from my first marriage. I told you I had a son."

"Right." She blinked. "Yes, you did. I'm sorry. I'm just shocked." She gave Gabe a sheepish, half-hearted smile. "I guess I expected you to be younger."

Right, so she could be his new mommy? Barf. What a cliché.

"Well, this has been fun." Not! "However, I need to get back to work."

"Gabe, wait." Mitchem untangled himself from Jillian and moved closer to Gabe. "Can we finish talking?"

"I have work to do." With that, Gabe fled.

His gut churned as he walked away from his father and *Jillian*, and Gabe couldn't blame it on any tacos this time. He wanted to let out a roar, a roar so fierce that it could have single-handedly brought down the walls of Jericho.

He ducked through the plastic panel doorway, bolting down the corridor toward the vendor parking lot.

Forgiveness? Seriously? After what he did? After what he continued to do?

He stalked past Olivia and her boss, ignoring both of them as they asked if he needed anything. He slammed into the release bar of the door with his elbow and stepped into the chill of twenty-four-degree air. His hands curled into fists as he stalked toward his car. Oh, how he wanted to let his anger fly through his fists, but Gabe knew he'd regret it if he took a swing at the car door.

Mitchem had *almost* fooled him. He'd almost done it. If only he'd left his fiancée—a new fiancée for a new year—at home, then he might have tricked Gabe into thinking he'd changed. How had he done it, sounded so sincere? Looked so sincere, so remorseful?

Was it possible it wasn't an act? That Mitchem really was sorry?

How? How was that possible when he continued to choose the same path over and over? Mitchem always said the same thing with each relationship that "deepened" to this point. *"I found the one!"* The next one to betray. It always ended the same way. It never changed.

And that's when the familiar took hold of Gabe. Fear. Guilt. Shame.

Seeing Mitchem with Jillian was like looking into the future.

Gabe thought he'd changed, but what made him so sure? His father seemed to think he'd changed with each relationship. What if Gabe was only kidding himself? What if he was the problem? What if he was destined to follow in his father's footsteps?

What if Kaylee couldn't forgive him—or worse, continued to forgive him when he was toxic and unchanging?

His fiery roar finally pierced the icy air as Gabe realized he only had one choice. Mitchem's appearance had only proven that all of Gabe's fears were true, but it had possibly saved him from devastating the woman he loved.

Again.

He needed to end things with Kaylee.

Again.

I can't seem to hit a single note tonight. Honestly, I sound like I'm using one of those singing apps. It's infinitely harder to hit a note on one of those apps than it is in real life. And that has been my entire performance tonight.

Awful! Truly awful!

All because of the man beside me. That handsome, heartbreaking man beside me. All six feet of him.

Because I've been here before. Nine years ago, in fact.

All right, it might be a little unfair to blame all my off-key caterwauling on Gabe. A great singer should be able to compartmentalize in order to achieve the mantra "The show must go on."

I am not a great singer. I've got some redeeming qualities. Decent voice? Sure, I guess. I would have been kicked off the worship team long ago if I didn't at least have that. Ability to get lost in the music? I might as well be a magician. But I've got strikes against me. Music theory? Virtually no education. Ability to play a "real" musical instrument? See the previous answer because I'm thinking the two weeks I attempted to learn the recorder in second grade don't count. Ability to compartmentalize my emotional angst for the good of the performance? Nada, apparently.

I am not a great singer, which is why I'm out of breath and my throat is sore thanks to improper breathing. And I'm about to break down on this very stage for a million different reasons.

Izze helped me pull myself together in an "Employees Only" bathroom that she steered me into before Gabe and I took the stage. After making the obligatory we-can-bail comment, she helped me fix my tear-streaked makeup while praying for me the entire time.

But then it was time for the show to go on.

Have you heard of lingchi? It's a horrible form of torture that originated in China where the person is subjected to many, many small cuts until they die. While there are certainly more gruesome forms of torture, this one is slow, painful, and methodical.

That's what it felt like the moment our eyes first met on stage.

A smart person, a sane person, would walk away now. They'd have walked away two or three lies ago. They'd wash their hands and thank God for helping them escape the clutches of that sinner.

Clearly, I'm also not a smart person because something in me wants to continue to fight, to fight for Gabe, to fight for the chance to be the couple I know God created us to be. I want to pull on my spiritual boxing gloves and become Rocky Balboa. I want Gabe to see the truth that I see and believe.

That his past doesn't define him.

Maybe this urge to fight can be laid at the feet of my parents. Maybe I don't know when to call it quits simply because I don't want to see someone else give up on love—on me. Maybe if my parents would give me one iota of true affection, then I wouldn't be so confused right now, bleeding from another cut disguised as love.

Maybe I need someone to fight for me.

I chance a look at Gabe as he transitions from the song we

just played to the instrumental interlude the groom requested. For the next five minutes, I get to stand here and smile as the groom makes some surprise speech to his bride.

Talk about another *Slash!* to the heart. Plus, I will never understand these public speaking types. Is their life source sustained by this self-inflicted punishment? I'd rather have my toes eaten by a turtle.

Gabe nods to the best man, who in turn, grabs the wireless microphone that was stashed under his seat.

"And now a word from Derek to Jules," the best man says into the microphone.

While her back is to us, the bride gasps as Derek offers her a nervous grin and grabs the microphone. He turns his back to the guests watching with expressions of various shades of *Aww!* and focuses solely on his bride.

"So early in our engagement, this song came on the radio," Derek starts to recount, "and you said that this would be the perfect song for a first dance."

Jules laughs, and her head bobs up and down.

"Which I thought was crazy because why would a song about a guy who's screwed up so much and is begging his girl not to give up on him be good for a wedding?"

The guests chuckle like someone held up a cue card.

"But you said it was real and raw. That you'd mess up and I would mess up. That we may hurt each other at times," Derek continues.

Out of the corner of my eye, I notice Gabe flinch.

"But no matter what, we were still on the same side. We were still one. We still loved each other," Derek says as he concludes his wife's observations, "and that if you and I remained committed to helping each other navigate those broken places, then nothing would tear us apart."

Jules raises her cloth napkin, presumably to keep her eye makeup from streaking down her face. However, she's not the only one. Through my own blurry vision, I notice many of the guests dabbing their eyes.

"Thankfully, you moved past the idea when I started advocating for the 'The Imperial March' for the recessional." Sniffly laughter bounces around the room, and Derek waits for the mirth to quiet before speaking again. "But I wanted this to be our last dance, an additional seal on our promise in front of all of our friends and family before we embarked on life together. I promise to do whatever it takes. Forever."

After Derek nods to Gabe, Gabe starts to play "Whatever It Takes" by Lifehouse. My heart crumbles in the most beautiful way as Derek gets down on one knee and starts to sing along with Gabe while looking only at his bride.

Only Jason Wade sings the lyrics in Lifehouse's version of their song, but we thought it would be more impactful if I sang the part of the Unknown Girl (a pretty name, French, I think) instead of the recounting-a-story vibe the original song has. So I don't come in until the second verse.

Something I'm infinitely thankful for because my throat is clogged with unshed tears. In my millennial world, it's getting rarer and rarer to see this level of Westley-and-Buttercup commitment. It's beautiful to behold, like glorious rays of heavenly light. As magical and mystical as a baby unicorn. A modern-day fairy tale.

My heart and my eyes turn toward Gabe.

Can I love like that? Can I flood those broken places Gabe's been hiding with forgiveness and more unconditional love? Can I love *anyone* like that, with a love that's so sacrificial, so filled with grace, so...

So much like the way God loves me.

Gabe said he wanted to talk, which would mean he wants to let me into those broken places.

His eyes pop open, as if sensing mine. Right now, it feels like he's singing this song to me—begging, pleading, and desperately hoping that I'll give him another chance. His smoky gray eyes bore into mine with a startling intensity, asking me for an answer he's scared to know.

What do I say?

And then I'm answering via the song.

Clutching the microphone in my left hand with a toddler-like super strength, I sing my answer to him with every ounce of my soul. Our eyes never waver as we sing the remainder of the song together, promising each other that we'll do whatever it takes.

My heart threatens to burst from a magnitude of love I had never given before now.

Unconditional love.

Not to say I've never loved unconditionally. Izze, Apryl, and Courtney would be the obvious refutes to that claim. No, I've never loved someone who's wounded me with an unconditional love, a love soaked in forgiveness. There's always been a price that offenders of my heart had to pay to get back into my good graces, and no one has ever paid it.

Except Jesus.

And the beauty of getting to go and love others like He's loved me is just as overwhelming and humbling as my love for Gabe.

As we sing the chorus for the final time, the skin-cracking smile on my face mirrors Gabe's own smile. He glances down, like he needs to make sure his fingers are actually doing what he's telling them to do, then his gaze flickers to the audience, to the far-right corner, to his father.

And his countenance crumbles.

Three notes before the song should end, Gabe stops playing his guitar. Dropping his pick and ripping the amplifier cord from his guitar, Gabe turns and flees with his guitar still hanging across his chest like a protesting infant with each twangy bounce.

My hand drops to my side as I watch him run away.

And, once again, disappear.

The room is loud with silence as everyone present stares at me as I stare at the exit. Silently, I beg the paneled doorway that swallowed Gabe to spit him out like Jonah. Please, oh, please! Please, I can't bear this again.

The truth pummels me like a thousand stampeding bulls, each one cutting me with their horns until all I can see is red.

He was faking it for the song. He's really and truly given up on love.

On me.

The microphone drops from my hand, and the *Thud!* that follows is swallowed by the heartbreaking silence.

# Chapter Twenty-One

Twenty seconds...
Fifteen...
Ten...
Five...
One...
And...one...
The door creaked open, and the setting sun illuminated Kaylee's silhouette in the doorway.

Along with Izze's.

Gabe bit his tongue to keep his initial reaction from slipping out and scanned them for any marshmallow guns. None, thankfully.

Izze had an arm around Kaylee's shoulder. "Are you sure about this?" she asked.

Kaylee nodded without removing her stony gaze from Gabe.

Izze released Kaylee and stepped backward to the chapel door. She paused at the door and sent Gabe one last nonverbal message that was froth with meaning.

A shiver ran through Kaylee as she stood there, venom and devastation dancing across her paler than normal face.

"You're freezing. Here." Gabe shrugged out of his flannel jacket and offered it to Kaylee.

Instead, she gave him a glare that could set him and the jacket on fire. Not that he blamed her. He more than deserved it. In fact, he welcomed her wrath.

"Don't. Bother," she said through gritted teeth.

Gabe nodded and laid the jacket across the back of the pew.

"Thank you for coming," he said, referring to the text he'd finally sent her this morning, asking to meet here. "I know you had no reason to show up after the way I left yesterday."

Her expression remained unchanged.

Gabe rubbed the back of his neck, feeling like the weight of the world was on his shoulders.

"Izze won't wait for long, so you should probably start talking."

Gabe's eyes slid closed in agony.

"You're not going to talk. Fine. Walk out that door and disappear—again!" She flung her arm to the door behind her.

Oh, that he could...

Gabe opened his eyes. "I'm so sorry, Kaylee, but I can't be with you," Gabe said as his own voice broke. "I shouldn't have led you to believe that we could make this work. We can't—I can't."

Her nostrils flared in rage. "Why, Gabe? After everything that's happened and after everything you said, why? What is stopping you from manning up? You own me that much."

The harsh words that were intended to slice felt dull and battered, maybe because Gabe felt dull and battered. Worthless. Tainted.

"Why?" she screamed before sobs choked her into silence. She doubled over, clutching her stomach for comfort as her shoulders shook in violent anguish.

Now. It was time. She needed to know why. She needed to know just how horrible he was. She needed to know beyond a shadow of a doubt that Gabe would never be anything but tainted.

Gabe let out an uneven breath and gripped the back of the pew to brace himself. "I have a past, Kaylee," he whispered.

The start of his confession broke through her sobs after a few seconds, causing her to look at him. If possible, her complexion paled even more.

"I know about Natalya."

Gabe felt the blood drain from his face. "What?"

"I know you and Natalya...had...I know you have a past with Natalya." Kaylee looked like she wanted to choke on each word. "But that was a long time ago, and it's not like you're still...or that you were cheating on me when it happened. We were broken up."

"It's not that simple." His throat felt like it was coated in tar or wax.

"Yes, it is! You don't have to let the past define you, Gabe."

"Kaylee, I had a problem, one that existed long before Natalya," Gabe burst before she could continue.

Whatever she'd been planning to say died on the tip of her tongue as she stared at him, and Gabe could physically feel the icy doom snuff her last flame of hope.

"I had an...a...problem. One that made me realize I was not dissimilar from my father," Gabe said as he memorized the dry cracks of skin on his hand because he couldn't bear to look into her eyes. "Looking at images." Even after all this time, he still couldn't say the word.

Her sharp inhale told him the exact moment his secret sins became painfully clear to her.

"While we were dating?" she whispered.

Gabe wished for death, swift and painful. "It started long before we got together, but that's why I couldn't marry you. I couldn't marry you with that...problem and all that betrayal between us. That's why I abandoned you."

Silent tears snaked their way down Kaylee's face. "Where does Natalya fit into all of this?"

Gabe's eyes closed in anguish. "After leaving you, I went to Chip and told him everything, but I thought I needed to handle the problem by myself. I ran away to Boston. I found an addiction recovery group at a local church, but I didn't put the work into my recovery that was needed. However, I met Ethan in that group."

"Ethan? He's—"

"Alcoholic," Gabe answered. "He's in recovery, and every day, he works to stay on guard against the temptation." Gabe swallowed against the lump that formed in his throat. "We became friends, started the band, all of that happened like I told you. After a little while, Natalya told me she liked me...and I liked that. I'd been hating myself for so long that the thought of a girlfriend made me feel good again.

"But then we went too far, and that—that horrible mistake—

woke me up. Suddenly, I was my father." Disgust and self-hatred for the man he had been washed over him. "I'd started behaving exactly like him because it was never about love with Natalya, it was only about making myself feel better. That's when I realized I hadn't taken care of the problem. I had only slapped an emotional Band-Aid on it, and it'd only come back stronger—with bigger consequences.

"I broke it off with Natalya and begged her forgiveness. Then I reached out to Chip again, and he's been my sponsor and mentor ever since. Ethan's been one of my accountability people. I attend meetings regularly, listen to teachings, and practice mindfulness," Gabe said in a rush, needing her to understand that he was not the same man.

"And the...problem?" Kaylee asked in a hoarse voice.

Gabe finally looked into her blank, emerald eyes. "Free. God has renewed my mind, but I also stay on the offensive, to guard against *that*," he spat the word in disgust, "from ever gaining a foothold in me again. Those chains won't hold me ever again." Crazy as it seemed, he felt freer than he'd ever felt before. The final chain had fallen from his wrists.

Perhaps that freedom came from setting the truth free. From setting Kaylee free.

"Why didn't you tell me?" she whispered without looking at him.

"Because I'm broken, Kaylee. I'm tainted. Ruined. Impure," he said bitterly. "I could never be good enough for you after those things."

"But if it's in the past," she cried out before biting her lip.

Tears stung Gabe's eyes as he hung his head again. "When I saw Mitchem yesterday, it was like looking into my future. He's tried to change, but he always falls into the same cycle. I will not risk doing that to you."

"That's fear, Gabe."

"It's foresight."

Kaylee gave a bitter laugh. "You are not your father. Has he ever really tried to change? Gotten help? Repented? No! But you did."

"Kaylee, what I did...I am not good enough for you." His weary body threatened to collapse, but he willed his knees to hold him upright a little longer. "You deserve someone who's—"

"Who's what? Perfect? None of us are perfect, Gabe." She took a step toward him. "Why won't you see that, believe that? I love you, and I can—"

"No." His smile was humorless and laced with bitter acceptance. "The truth is that not even your love can redeem a man like me."

And with that, Gabe left.

For the last time.

# Chapter Twenty-Two

Izze has never been known for her patience.

Once she got it in her head that she was going to do this one-thousand-piece jigsaw puzzle, glue it together, and frame it for her boss' birthday. She proceeded to work on this puzzle for two hours (during which she'd somehow managed to piece together all four corners of the puzzle *within* the lovely gown the Victorian woman wore in the image) and declared it impossible. The pieces of this puzzle sat on our kitchen table for a month, and every day she'd attempt to match a few pieces for seven minutes before she gave up again. Izze ended up giving her boss some "brilliant abstract art that depicts the jumbled pieces of the human experience" for her birthday.

In reality, she covered the pieces in glitter glue and shoved them into a shadow box once they were dry.

And that, my friends, is the current record for Izze's patience.

I should note that it's not the length of time that determines Izze's patience. Nope, it's the event. Everyone knows a puzzle is going to take some time. It's the unwritten definition of a puzzle, the mind-numbing killer of time that your grandparents threatened you with if you breathed too loudly. However, Izze sat down at our rickety kitchen table determined to be the Michelangelo of puzzles in a matter of minutes.

During the first edition of the Gabe and Kaylee Heartbreak Saga, she waited two days for me to speak, two days that I spent crying on her bed. Izze is a smart woman, and she knows there's more to this than whatever she overheard yesterday (come on, we all know she was eavesdropping). That dramatically cuts my time down.

I have a matter of minutes.

Because once I open the bathroom door to the adjoining guest room located within her house, she will pounce.

After all, it is her house. I know that's what she's going to say.

The events of the last seventy-two hours play through my mind for the trillionth time. Goodness, I wish that number was an exaggeration.

Since leaving the chapel, we've been holed up in Izze's guest room to process and grieve and cry while she ordered an amount of salty/sweet food that would have stumped Lorelai and Rory. Afterall, emotional turmoil means junk food and sleep.

But the night has passed, and since I'm pushing four hours in the bathroom—I ducked in here as soon as I woke up—it's probably time to face the music.

Turning the doorknob, I slowly push the door open to look for Izze. In the dim haze of light that manages to penetrate the blackout curtains, I can make out her still-sleeping form under the furry blanket.

The doorknob is yanked from my grasp. "Gotcha!" Izze yells.

Facepalm. Rookie mistake, McGrurd. Always check to make sure the door hasn't been compromised before you assume the decoy in the bed is real.

"You thought you could hide from me? I'm the master at hiding," she declares.

"That's only because you're slightly taller than Thumbelina," I mumble as I scoot past her and flop onto the queen-sized bed.

"That's right," Izze says proudly. "To all you vertical over-achievers, the benefits to being short are vastly superior."

I pull my pillow over my face like I'm smothering myself.

Oh, gross! It's still wet from my tears. Gag!

Using both of my hands, I launch the pillow in a steep arch. Izze catches it midair and throws it back at me. I catch it and hug it against my stomach.

"Ready to talk?" she asks.

I roll over. "I on't memver you wantin to talk," I mumble into the mattress.

"First of all, roll over so that I can understand what you're saying before I say tough luck."

I tilt my head to the left so that I'm not speaking into the mattress. "You're so compassionate."

"Precisely why I'm forcing—no, that sounds wrong." I can just see her stroking her beardless chin while she thinks. "Urging. Yes, that's better. That's why I'm urging you to talk. Compassion."

Another pillow lands on my head.

"Once upon a time, you did this for me." Her words are muffled thanks to the pillow that obstructs my hearing.

I roll over all the way and swing my feet over the edge of the bed as I sit up. The pillow topples to the floor beside me. "How much did you hear?"

She shrugs from where she leans against the dresser, nonchalantly picking at the fuzz on her pajamas. "Oh, just a tidbit."

"Mm-hmm. How much?"

"Just something about how he couldn't marry you then or ever because of his past...*problem*." The way she whispers the final word would be comical if not for the subject matter at hand.

I sigh as the conversation slams into me for the nine trillionth time. "Sounds to me like you heard more than a tidbit."

"It's all contextless pieces of a conversation until I've heard the full story from you."

Here it goes. "We ran off to elope."

Her jaw drops and hangs open for ten seconds before she physically shuts it with the back of her right hand. "What? When? No, wait." Her eyes widen. "Are you married? Are you legally married right now?"

"No! For crying out loud, no." I take a deep breath before releasing my own confession. "It was the day after graduation. We got all the way to a justice of the peace's house in New Jersey. Had already started the wedding when he stopped and said he couldn't do this, that he couldn't marry me. Then he left me there. Disappeared until the day I ran into him in the old wedding chapel he proposed in all those years ago."

"Oh, Kaylee." Izze's anguish on my behalf is evident as she crosses the narrow space between us. She sits beside me and wraps me in a hug only besties can give. "I'm so sorry. I am so sorry," she says over and over.

Tears stream down my cheeks as I tell her every sordid detail of my failed elopement, the months since Gabe's reentered my life, and the confession that makes me want to crawl under a shady tree and die. When I've laid every ugly piece out there for her to examine, I am empty. Empty of thought. Empty of action. Empty of feeling. It's a void of nothingness inside of me, one where I could see my heart setting up a home. A cozy, empty home.

I don't know how long we've been sitting there when Izze leans back from her embrace.

"I wish I had known what you were really going through," she murmurs softly as she shakes her head, sending her dark curls dancing.

"I know. I'm so sorry, Izze. I'm so sorry that I never told you." I am a terrible person.

Izze shakes her head. "No, that's not what I mean. I'm not upset with you. Honestly, I understand why you didn't tell me about almost eloping. First of all, I probably would have hired a hit man to take Gabe out—or done it myself. I mean, let's face it. I would have destroyed him."

I choke on a laugh at the smug look on Izze's face—like her potential Black Widow career is something to be proud of—and nod. "Yeah, probably," I agree.

"Exactly, and that would have been if I was feeling generous. But I meant that I wish I had known so that I knew how to help you." She shakes her head. "All those years, you had to carry that heartache alone when you've always been there for me."

I shrug, uncomfortable with the praise. "You were going through your own painful breakup at the time, and then I just wanted to forget it. Move on."

She tilts her head as she studies me. "Did you?"

"I don't know." I sigh. "At times, yes. I couldn't live life waiting for him to reappear and apologize, right? How often does that really happen? I couldn't suspend disbelief and count on that to happen."

"No, you couldn't," she agrees. "But what about now? After everything you've learned, after the way he walked out last night, can you forgive him now?"

"He didn't really give me the chance, did he?" I say bitterly.

"No, but can you forgive him now? Despite that?"

I just had my own moves used against me.

I don't like this feeling.

"Like you said," Izze says gently, "you can't hinge your own emotional health and healing on Gabe. What happened in the past...well, it was bad. Walking out last night, also bad, but can you forgive him for it?"

"Why should I?" The words pop out before I can stop them, and honestly, I don't feel bad about it. I want to carry this hate in my heart forever. Forget moving past it again. I know it's not right; I know it's not what God wants. However, it's what I want.

Ah, good ol' Root of Bitterness. We meet again.

"Because that's the only way you'll be free to move on."

Why is forgiveness synonymous with moving on?

"Forgive and forget, and all that—" I stop myself before I say "garbage."

"Forgive, yeah, but nowhere in the Bible does it say we have to forget. God forgets because He's awesome like that thanks to Jesus, but He doesn't tell us to subject ourselves to the same hurt over and over. He made allowances for the kind of sin that results when people refuse to let God's love change them." She wraps an arm around my shoulder. "But I do know He tells us to forgive."

"At the moment, all I want is to forget Gabe's face." But every time I close my eyes, I see him—along with a new facet of his betrayal.

"I will help with that however I can." She pulls her arm back and rubs her hands together. "But I also need you to know that if you guys can work through this—"

I scoff.

She holds up one hand. "I know I've voiced a lot of negative opinions about Gabe—and goodness, my limerick is downright unflattering—but I saw the way you guys were connecting. I could tell you still loved him. And if, by the grace of God, you guys are able to work things out, I want you to know that I will forgive him as well."

"After everything I just told you, how can you possibly think there's a possibility we can work through this? All the lies and betrayal, never mind the fact that Gabe isn't willing to even try." Bitterness continues to soothe me with her cold embrace and whispers in my ear. "He probably did me a favor."

"Because." She shifts to look me in the eye. "Because I know God's love can redeem anything."

Tears sting my eyes, and I squirm. I'm not in a place to accept this right now. "I appreciate that, Izze," I take a deep breath, "but this is the end. Forever."

She loops her arm around my shoulder again. "Even if it is, I will still forgive him."

I rub my eyes that are still puffy from the night of crying. "That's very mature and wise of you."

"As someone much older than I has said, I've gotten wise in my old age."

Home never looked so awful.

I hesitate on my porch, knowing that all I need to do is turn around and run for Izze's car. She will respond by whisking me back to the haven of her guest bedroom. I can hide for a little longer under a thick, furry blanket while eating a pan of brownies.

Instead, I slide my house key into the lock.

Questions run through my mind, each one gripping the heel of the previous question. How awful will it be to see Gabe at practice this week? Will he just disappear again? Do the others know what happened? How are we supposed to continue working together now? Should I quit?

What's going to happen next?

I unlock the door, put my keys back into my purse, and haul my bag through the doorway. Behind me, I can hear Izze putting her car into reverse, heading home to her happy married life.

Moving through the weird little foyer area—that I refer to as "Roy"—I step into the living room and stop, new questions forming in my mind.

Who brought my stuff back? Ethan...or Gabe? Is he here?

And then Natalya steps into the living room.

This keeps getting better and better. Does she know?

"Hey," she squawks. She sounds better than she did the day of the wedding. However, it feels like that day was a million years ago. "How are you? I heard what happened."

Well, I guess that's one question answered. "From whom?" I ask, voicing my next question. And props to me for using "whom" not "who." After all, it's not like I have Spellcheck or Grammarly in my head.

Nope, all I have is a dumb radio that's switched from Taylor Swift's "White Horse" to her "The Other Side of the Door" as a twinge of hope continues to implore me that maybe he's near, that he came to his senses, that maybe Izze was right and we can work this out. That maybe we can ride off into that sunset while the world around us fades to black.

"Gabe. He dropped off your stuff, but he's gone now."

Another *Slash!* I deflate, not bothering to hide my disappointment.

Natalya's eyes hold sympathy. "I'm so sorry, Kaylee."

I shrug, trying to pretend that I'm not trying to stop this new emotional wound from physically bleeding onto a rug I still can't afford to replace. "I didn't really expect him to be here."

"Yeah, he thought it would be too awkward."

My hands shake. I want to ask her what he said, but I know she'll only use my words against me. "He's probably right."

"Kaylee, I know my feelings haven't helped to bring clarity to your situation with Gabe, but from friend to friend, I hate seeing you do this to yourself. What Summer said to me the day we went skiing gave me a lot of clarity, and I think you need that clarity, too."

My defensive walls rise with force. "This is not the same situation, Natalya."

"The backstory is different, but you are throwing yourself at a man who doesn't love you." She slashes my broken heart with each word.

*Slash! Slash!*

I open my mouth to argue, but with what? "He said he loved me. He just doesn't believe he's capable of love. He can't forgive himself for the past," I finally say, but it sounds weak and contradictive even to my own ears.

"I agree," she says, "but I think being around you again made him want to believe there could be a second chance for you guys."

"Maybe there could be if he'd stop running away." Our roles have reversed, and I got to tell you guys, I do not like it. Not one bit.

Natalya looks at the floor and takes a deep breath before looking at me again. "I think that's what you both wanted to believe, but I think it's all because of your history. I-I'm sorry, Kaylee, but I don't think he loves you anymore."

My nostrils flare in rage. "Did he say that to you?"

"No!" she insists. "No, but everyone has been watching this drama unfold for months. Months. I know Gabe really well." I bristle at the insinuation that she knows him better than I do. "And I think that old chemistry and the idea of a second chance just seemed too good to pass up."

*Slash-ity, slash! Slashy, slash!*

"But I don't think it was real," she adds in a low, sympathetic voice.

"You are not exactly an impartial third party," I say bitterly, attempting to grasp at anything to refute her.

"No," she holds my angry gaze with her calm one, "but the rest of the band is."

And that's the fatal stab to my heart.

My feet fail me, and I stumble for the couch. "What?" I ask as I sink to the couch cushions, barely aware that I've managed to land on them.

"I can't tell you what's been said," she says, finally getting the opportunity to throw my words back into my face, "but everyone is really uncomfortable."

I want to crawl into a hobbit hole and disappear forever as the weight of everything settles on me. I can't help but wonder what's been said, and it breaks my heart to imagine all these people I had called friends collectively wishing I'd get a clue and move on.

I'm a fool.

Natalya sits beside me. "I hate to say this, Kaylee, but no one else will because everyone likes you so much, but—"

"I'm out," I finish for her, devoid of all feeling at this point.

She nods and slips her arm around my shoulder, but it feels like a placating gesture for the clueless girl.

I set my jaw as Lady Bitterness comes out to play. "Then you and Summer are out. Tomorrow."

Natalya nods again like she was expecting that. "We will be."

Shrugging out of her empty embrace, I stand while grabbing the overnight bag I'd dropped somewhere in the middle of this horrible conversation. "I'll be at Izze's house. Be gone by this time tomorrow."

Gabe dusted the wood shavings from his work space into the trash bin. The newly-finished guitar pick sat on the table in front of him. The feeling Gabe had been seeking, pride at another completed project, didn't come. Nothing came as he flipped the smooth pick between his fingers.

He was numb.

It was probably for the best. If he reopened that vault, then the only things he would feel would be familiar companions he didn't want to face again.

Shame. Guilt. Failure.

Going numb had been a survival tactic.

"Hey, man," Drake said from the doorway of Gabe's bedroom. "Natalya's here. Says she needs to speak to all of us."

"Coming," Gabe said. Wow, even his voice sounded numb.

Gabe followed Drake to the small living room of their three-bedroom apartment. Natalya wrung her hands from her spot by the still-open front door as she talked to Ethan. "I already told Summer, and she's at Kaylee's house packing."

"What? What's going on?" Gabe asked, and something in his gut twisted at the mention of Kaylee's name.

Shame. Guilt. Failure. Looked like the vault had cracked.

Natalya let out a long sigh that granted on him. "Kaylee kicked us out."

"You're kidding!" Drake exclaimed. "How can she do that?"

Ethan sighed as he crossed his arms across his torso. "It was part of the deal when they moved in. It was even written into the rental agreement if she left the—"

"She quit!" Gabe exploded in shock.

Ethan leveled him with a look. "What did you expect, man?"

Natalya nodded sadly. "Ethan warned me this could happen when he dropped off her equipment, but I don't think any of us expected her to follow through with it."

Gabe gripped the back of his neck as the muscle in his jaw started to jump up and down, left and right. "I can't believe this."

"I'm so sorry, Gabe." She touched his arm for a brief moment. "I think she realized that the situation couldn't continue like this after some soul-searching."

"What did she say, Natalya?" Ethan asked.

She bit her lip and dragged her heel against the welcome mat she'd gotten them as a housewarming present. "I don't want to betray her confidence, but..."

"But what?" Gabe pressed. Out of the corner of his eye, Drake and Ethan exchanged a look.

She looked over her shoulder at the closed door, like she was expecting Kaylee to walk through it. "I think she realized that her feelings weren't real," Natalya said slowly.

Gabe felt like Natalya had just jabbed him in the throat with her violin bow. "What do you mean?" he asked in a hoarse voice.

"I think she realized you were right, that you couldn't make a future together and..."

"And what!" Gabe yelled.

She looked startled and stared at the floor as she spoke. "That maybe it was your history together that she was in love with, not...you."

Gabe turned around and stalked to his bedroom. He grabbed the door and whipped it behind him, expecting to hear it slam shut.

"Ow, man." Drake rubbed the spot on his forehead where the door had hit him.

"Sorry," Gabe mumbled. "I know you're here to help, but I'd rather be alone for a few minutes to calm down." *After I break something.*

"Man, I know it's bad now..."

Gabe rolled his eyes. "Don't tell me it's going to be okay or serve a purpose."

Drake shook his head. "Not what I was going to say."

Gabe raised an eyebrow. He could feel what remained of his composed patience start to drain from his weary body.

"You're still standing, man. This stings, but you're still standing." Drake turned to leave. "And we are standing with you."

Gabe blinked as he processed Drake's message—devoid of any musical pun. Must mean he was serious. Pity that standing wasn't even on Gabe's radar anymore. Nope. He felt like he'd sunk to the bottom of an ocean with a weight chained to his feet, so he'd settle for not drowning.

Through the thin walls, Gabe could hear Drake and Ethan preparing to leave and help Natalya and Summer start the process of moving out. Gabe should go with them, and he would go at some point.

But he needed to reseal the vault first.

He had no right to be upset. He honestly hadn't figured out what they were going to do going forward. It had barely been twenty-four hours since The Disclosure. However, he hadn't expected Kaylee to react like this. That bitter retaliation wasn't the Kaylee he knew.

But it was probably a decision that could be laid at Gabe's feet.

However, the change of heart toward him stung.

No—that actually *devastated* him. That news threatened to destroy him once and for all. To have her say that she loved him yesterday only to hear secondhand today that she wasn't in love with him felt brutal.

The red monster within roared, and Gabe angrily swiped everything on his work desk onto the floor. The little pick disappeared somewhere under his bed as his lamp cracked and broke into a heap of jagged pieces beside him.

But what could he do?

Gabe gripped the edge of his desk as he tried to think.

Nothing. There wasn't anything he could do. This entire mess was his fault. He'd dragged the band up here. He'd given Kaylee a job. He was the idiot that had started to believe he could outrun the past.

And just like Jason Borne, the past had found him.

And the woman he loved had suffered for it.

The groom's stupid speech hadn't helped. That song had almost pushed him over the edge. In another classic moment of weakness that epitomized Gabe, he'd allowed himself to believe again while he sang to Kaylee, while she sang to him. As he tried to say goodbye, he found himself wishing for a different conclusion to the story they were writing.

But seeing his father kiss *Jillian* had brought Gabe back to his senses.

Nothing had changed.

Gabe stared at the broken lamp, noting the sharp piece of ceramic three inches from his bare feet.

Five more minutes of pity—he didn't even deserve that much—and then it would be time to move on from Kaylee.

For good.

# Chapter Twenty-Three

Precious stomps across the floor of her room, which is the room above mine. She's like a T-Rex hunting some unsuspecting herbivore when it comes to looking for her shoes.

Little flakes of dust (I hope its only dust) release their grip on the ceiling and fall to me instead.

Sigh. Thanks a lot, Precious. I hear ceiling dust mixed with drywall is all the rage for facials this year. Add a little avocado and this mixture really brings out the zits and blackheads in your pores.

"Penny," I yell, "you're stomping again."

Her name isn't really "Precious." It may be funny in *Friends*, but no one is insensitive enough to name their child a passive aggressive endearment. No, as a culture, we've progressed, preferring to name today's youth after compass directions, fruits, and the apparatus we lay our heads on each night.

Seems like a lateral move to me.

"Sorry," she yells back.

"No problem," I shout. *But I'm never doing Sue and Jack a favor ever again,* I silently add.

I can't believe I let them talk me into taking on three new roommates last month. They're all twenty and in college, so I feel like the weird, old dorm mother to all of them. But when Jack (the worship leader at church) found out that I was not only no longer part of the band but also alone and surviving on stale cereal mixed with rainwater (a slight exaggeration, but not by much), he talked to Sue (the leader of the young adult ministry).

They ganged up on me, using Christianese to urge me to take in these "desolate" college students.

I'm sorry, but even if you're paying for it course by course, you're not desolate if you're getting a college education.

Anyway, that's how I've ended up with Penny (Precious), Mackenzie (Apple Jr.), and Jackie (who can only be described as the more eccentric version of Paris Geller). They moved in mid-January and have been here three weeks.

I'm just going to say it and then we can all move on: I miss Summer and even Natalya (before she revealed her angle in the love triangle). I miss having friends and being one of the girls. Instead I've become the "older lady," an endearment Precious so sweetly bestowed to me in a conversation with her parents that I had the privilege of overhearing last week. Last, but not least, I really, really, really miss Izze, Apryl, and Courtney.

Plus, Apple Jr. keeps eating my lemons, which explains why I have a mini fridge stocked with lemons and lemon juice wedged into my room now.

Maybe if I sat her down and explained to her that life will not be what she's imagining it to be eight-ish years from now, that all her dreams will fall apart, and that any semblance of love will be ripped from her grasp, maybe then she'll start to respect her loveless elders and leave the lemons alone.

After backhanding the dust from my eyelashes, I roll onto my side and sit up. I swing my feet over the edge of the bed and reach for a lemon drop from my trusty Aragorn cookie jar, the only man who's ever stuck around for me.

Too bad he's not real.

I pop the sour candy into my mouth and toss the wrapper into my little waste basket. Sighing, I slip my feet into my slippers.

It's time to get ready for work.

The primary reason I let Sue and Jack talk me into becoming a den mother is that they also found me a job.

At a shoe store.

Which I'm totally qualified for because I have feet.

It's a job. It pays the bills. And I get a discount on cute and ugly shoes alike.

But I am dissatisfied with everything in my life right now, just like a true millennial.

I can hear Donna Meagle from *Parks and Recreation* in the corner of my head saying something like it's because of Saturn's orbit around the sun or some other weird reason that I don't believe in the foggiest.

I know the cause of this melancholy.

I glance into the mirror of my dresser, deciding that I'll tug my long, red hair into a messy bun. Hey, I *was* ('cause I'm not anymore) a creative type, so I might as well embrace the bohemian look. At least that's what I'll tell myself. It's better than the truth.

I don't care.

I grab the decorative box where I keep my hair accessories and grab a thick elastic and two bobby pins. Sticking the bobby pins between my lips, I set the box back onto my dresser. Glancing down, my eyes lock onto an object that had escaped my purge the week after New Year's Day. Looks like it had been hiding underneath the box I just moved. My fingers still and the topknot flops awkwardly across my forehead.

The Evenstar coaster.

I pick the coaster up and rub my thumb across the beautiful design Gabe had carved into the smooth surface.

And I throw it across the room with my eight-year, state championship winning, softball pitcher's arm.

It hits the wall with a loud *Crack!* and falls to the floor.

I step backward and plop onto my bed. I wish I would cry. I wish I *could* cry. Crying would be preferable to what I feel whenever I think of Gabe, the only thing I've been feeling for weeks.

Bitterness.

We were so close to a Happily Ever After conclusion. So stinking close.

The electric guitar and rapid drumbeats start to play in my head. Disciple's "Backstabber" has been a fan favorite for the last few weeks, and my soul screams the familiar lyrics to my favorite angry song.

Until the bridge.

Then *Click!*

Silence.

Because I don't want to get to the part about forgiveness, the part about realizing sin makes all of us backstabbers, the part where I have to shed bitterness that's become a stunning ensemble to my scale-covered eyes.

Because I am so angry and bitter at Gabe, and—if I'm honest with myself—God. Because I don't understand. I don't understand why He would bring Gabe back into my life only to allow the same thing to happen with fresh, new wounds. Wounds that make me wish I never knew the whole story. If I could transport myself to the ignorant bliss that came with not knowing, I'd be content to die in that place.

I want to forget, but I don't want to forgive.

And I can't seem to let go.

I bite my lip and sigh.

But God is bigger than my anger at the situation or even at Him. He's not going anywhere, and frankly, He's all I've got at the moment.

Can you hear the begrudging sentiment over there?

But ultimately, if I can't choose to believe my God is still good in what can only be described as one of the worst times of my life, then why bother with Him at all?

"Help me, Daddy," I whisper to the room, where it's just Him and me. "Help me to let go. To move on. To forgive. I can't do it by myself."

A tear burns a trail down the left side of my face.

"And to not love him anymore."

The chances that the earth (or an ice-covered lake in this case) would open (crack) and swallow him whole had dramatically decreased.

Or so the white-haired man in the orange ski cap claimed as Gabe clumsily set up the pop-up shelter he'd purchased for his ice fishing excursion. However, Joe—as he'd instructed Gabe to call him—also suggested that Gabe get some brighter gear should the unthinkable ever happen and the ice break. "Makes it easier to spot you through the ice if it's clear enough," Joe had advised before tossing Gabe an extra orange lifejacket that he claimed he kept on hand.

Now, hours later, Gabe checked for the twenty-seventh time

that the vest was secure from where he sat in the camping chair. And attempted not to dwell on his unasked question, *What happens if the ice isn't clear enough?*

He had a feeling he already knew the answer.

Gabe should be writing, strumming, something. That was the whole point of this sabbatical. Write some original songs.

Without Kaylee.

His old acoustic guitar lay across his lap, and his forearms burned from drilling a hole big enough for fishing. It'd taken Gabe much longer than he'd like to admit to drill through the ice with the hand auger.

Also, the only lyrics he could come up with at the moment consisted of endless screaming at the top of his lungs. Maybe All Yours could become the first heavy metal wedding band in history. It would be groundbreaking.

Or in this case, icebreaking.

Unless there was already another heavy metal wedding band, in which case, Gabe still needed to string together some lyrics.

Sighing, he moved his guitar into position.

And plucked D minor thirty-seven times.

True music in the making.

He released the strangled moan he'd been holding inside before he started to sing Taylor Swift's "Back to December," but he sang "January" instead of "December" as he sang through the song. That's where Gabe found his groove, and he started to sing his own lyrics:

*I know it's my fault.*
*I know there's nothing I can do.*
*Hearing you say "I forgive you" is the hope of a fool.*
*But there's nothing I wouldn't try,*
*To see the light in your eyes.*
*To hear a laugh from your lips.*
*As I remember that snowy kiss,*
*But there's nothing I can do,*
*So I'm staying,*
*So far away from you.*

"Excuse me," a feminine voice called from outside his shelter, "I couldn't help but overhear your awful song."

Wow. This lady had class.

The top corner of the tent door was unzipped, and an older woman stuck her face into the opening. "Throw in some other minor chords, I'm begging you. How about E minor?"

Gabe blinked. Why was this woman talking to him?

"I can tell by your confused expression that you're trying to figure out why I'm sticking my nose into your business," she said as she continued to unzip the door flap, step inside, and reseal *their*—because apparently Gabe was being forced to share?—enclosure. "Do you want the long reason or the short reason?"

"Uh."

"Okay, we'll go with the short reason," she decided as she sat right in front of the door (and it didn't escape Gabe's notice that she had blocked any potential flight with this seating arrangement). Her black snow pants crinkled as she sat on the snow-covered ice, and she grunted as she drew her legs into a crisscross position.

Spry and nosy. A dangerous combination in older women.

"I can tell from your horribly depressing song—didn't you realize that you're also out of tune?—that you're not okay, and there's no bigger ministry than seeing the needs of the people right in front of you in this noisy, broken world. That's why I'm here." She widened her light eyes at him, and her wiry brown-and-silver eyebrows disappeared into the similarly colored strands of hair sticking out from her ski cap. "And I'm seeing you in the midst of that."

What was Gabe supposed to say to that?

*Uh, thanks, Unnamed Lady, but if you knew about the things I've done and the people I've hurt, you'd be shoving me through that hole in the ice with your bare hands. Then you'd pray for a barracuda to come forth from the depths of the lake and—*

"Who's the girl?" she asked as her eyebrows returned to their rightful place on her face.

Gabe opened his mouth, but she cut off his questions with the wave of her gloved hand.

"It's the question you ask in a romantic comedy, and granted, real life isn't a romantic comedy. However, your lyrics were a pretty obvious giveaway that you're experiencing some romantic angst," she concluded.

This woman was seriously creeping Gabe out.

"So if you'd like to talk, my name is Lou, and I will listen without judgment."

Gabe snorted in derision. If only she knew...

She raised a single eyebrow. "Ah. That hit a nerve."

"No offense," Gabe paused and searched his memory for the name she'd just given him.

"Lou Who," she supplied.

His eyebrows took a lift at that. "Seriously?"

Lou's smile stretched across her nearly wrinkle-less face. "No, that's just my sense of humor. As Ken Davis likes to say, 'I'm not right.'"

"Okay, Lou," Gabe said as he worked to keep his voice even as he watched the unmoving line. *Come on, fish! Bite!* "No offense, but I've learned that people don't listen without judgment."

"Try me." Her challenge forced him to meet her determined eyes.

The competitive side of Gabe had a hard time turning down a challenge, but he was going to do just that. However, her unyielding expression said she wasn't going to back down.

He sighed in defeat. "I have a past, and the truth would only disgust you," he confessed.

"Doesn't every human have a past? Sin is sin, Gabe."

Gabe's brow furrowed.

"I won't judge you," she said again. "My job is to point you to God's love and truth."

Gabe still wasn't sure how, but the clamp inside of him released, and he ended up telling Lou everything as the wind whipped against the side of their tent on the middle of the frozen Ossipee Lake. "That's why there's no going back," he concluded thirty minutes later.

Lou shook her head and tapped the ice in front of her. "David was a man after God's own heart, and he was called that after he'd added job descriptions like murderer and adulterer to his résumé. But those mistakes didn't stop God from looking at the heart of the man, a man after His own heart."

Gabe resisted rolling his eyes, but his bitter anger still found a way out. "That's what everyone says. 'Look at David's life.' But that's not how they act. To them, you are forever tainted by the sins of your past. Do you know how many Christians would accept a man like David in their churches today, a man who grew up knowing God and knowing that his sins went against everything God said? They wouldn't. Trust me; I know."

"And for some people, that's true. Doesn't make it right, and it's certainly not God's heart for you—or even your father," Lou added, and a knife twisted in Gabe's gut. "However, so many believers understand that they themselves are forgiven and that they have no right to spit on someone God has redeemed."

"And how many of those people support the people they don't 'condemn,'" Gabe said, adding some air quotes, "for their pasts?"

"Far less than God would like, I have no doubt. Ultimately, their thoughts and opinions are not the ones that matter." Lou cleared her throat with a dramatic flair that demanded Gabe look into her eyes. "Yours are."

Gabe sighed again as he shifted his little chair. He felt like a melodramatic teenage girl, but she wasn't getting it. Lou didn't and couldn't understand.

"I think the problem is you view yourself as condemned," Lou added softly, but no less bluntly.

Gabe wanted to scream. He was so tired of hearing this from people. It wasn't his problem; it was the natural consequences to the stupid choices he'd made long ago.

"You view yourself as tainted, and if that's all you're going to show anyone, then you can't get mad when that's all they see," Lou continued in spite of Gabe's unspoken rant.

"That's all I see," Gabe said adamantly.

"Well, I see a man who's left his past in the past. A man who now stands clean before God, so those chains don't have a right to hold him. I see a man who deserves love, grace, and mercy."

Gabe couldn't even look into Lou's eyes as she spoke. He so didn't see those things in himself.

"You deserve those things, Gabe. Not because you earned them, but because God is good and His grace is bigger. You don't need to keep trying to punish yourself because those things have been completely punished at the cross. That's it. The end."

Gabe shifted in his seat. He knew this—it was like the basics of Jesus—and yet he didn't think he had actually let this truth saturate his spirit the way God had always intended.

"But first, I see a man who needs to forgive himself in order to be free," Lou said. "The problem is not that you can't outrun the past; the problem is that you haven't been freed of the root cause, so the problem transferred over to shame and guilt, continuing to force you to look at your sins again and again."

"Then what's the root cause?" Gabe tensed as he waited for the answer.

"The kind of condemnation that comes from the ultimate accuser, the one who steals, kills, and destroys. The one who's used all these things to lead your spirit to one conclusion: that God's redemption, love, and promises—the very essence of Who He is— is not enough for you."

Gabe's spirit stirred like it had finally awakened from a deathly sleep. The chains of the past tugged at his spirit as they tried to prevent him from rising.

But wait...hadn't those been broken?

They had. He'd broken them. Jesus had broken them. Which meant...

"How can it really be so simple?" he whispered.

She leaned forward while tapping her own heart. "It's not. It's a battle that you will fight again and again. It's a choice that you will make repeatedly, a million and one times a day if necessary. But at the end of the day, you will have continued to choose God's heart for you versus the lies that deny you His grace and love. But you can only fight that battle if you win the war, the war that says you are unworthy of second chances, of grace, of forgiveness. It's a war that's already been won with Jesus' death. So that's good news because Jesus has already won the war for you.

"Today, you have the ability and the opportunity to make better choices than your father. You've already made better choices than your father because you've broken those chains whereas he's still shackled. Continue to make better choices." Lou waggled her eyebrows at him. "You can start by fighting for Kaylee's love."

"You make it sound like a battle to the death," Gabe murmured.

"It is," Lou said, voice one hundred percent serious. "Because pushing love away is just as bad as destroying love."

Gabe frowned. "What's the difference?"

Lou grinned. "Ah, I was hoping you'd catch that. There's no difference. You're essentially killing love one way or another. But there's a loophole: grace. When you push God's love away, it doesn't go anywhere. It's waiting on the other side of your stubbornness to smother you in His love. He is a fan of second chances, our God. Even second chances at love."

"We are way past second chances here," Gabe remarked humorlessly, but still, something hopeful stirred inside of him. It almost felt too dangerous to hope. Hope had gotten him into this mess in the first place.

But was a life without hope worth living? One of the core pieces of God's character was giving hope to the hopeless. *Hopeless*. For crying out loud, that more than described Gabe's life to this point.

"And that's why it's a battle that you have to be willing to fight," Lou continued. "Will you fight for Kaylee's love? Can you commit to fighting for her love forever, no matter how each of you could and will screw up in the future? Can you fight the lies and doubts that tell you otherwise and rest in your position as a redeemed child of the Most High God?"

Could he?

Gabe wanted to, but the fear asked him if he was even capable of those things.

As if reading his inner conflict on his face, Lou said, "There's a lot of grace for those who are willing to fight. But you have to be willing because love is one of the bravest, scariest things you can do. It is sacrificial and vulnerable. Something that will break you until you're whole again, stronger than before."

Gabe tapped his thumb against the body of his guitar that still lay against his lifejacket clad torso as he thought.

This was his crossroads. He could feel it in his soul. He could stay on this course, a life dictated by the man he'd been, not the man he had become in Christ. A life without Kaylee.

Or he could fight, starting with resting in who God said he was.

And slashing any lie that said differently.

And fighting for Kaylee.

Warmth flooded Gabe, burning him from the inside out like a purifying fire. He couldn't sit here. No, the overwhelming urge to get on his knees and release all the guilt and shame to God was too great. So Gabe slid from his little chair onto the ice, still clutching his guitar by the neck. And as his hot tears fell from his face and burned into the ice, Gabe let go for once and for all. He may still have to fight against the attacks from time to time...

But he was no longer chained by the past.

Gabe wasn't aware of when he sat up, though he still sat on the ice. It had been long enough that his backside was numb from the cold. Grunting as he moved to sit in his chair, another urge poked at him, begging him to play.

Later. Right now he needed to figure out how to get Kaylee back.

However, his fingers hand a mind of their own, or maybe they already knew the path Gabe planned to take despite the fact he had yet to voice it. Whatever the reason, he started to play "Always Yours," tweaking chords and adding lyrics as he went. His mind registered Lou getting up and leaving the tent with a broad smile on her face, but Gabe was too focused on their song.

Their song. Their new song.

Because Gabe would fight.

Starting now.

# Chapter Twenty-Four

Gabe had decided to call in reinforcements for a strategy session, so he'd asked the band to meet at the apartment he shared with Drake and Ethan eleven minutes ago, an early start to their regular rehearsal. Yeah, he was late, but forgive-me-and-give-me-another-chance gestures had to be planned in every epic and miniscule detail. And Gabe had planned this down to the last snowflake-covered eyelash.

Unfortunately, he hadn't counted on the wild card: Izze.

She sat on the lumpy futon next to Summer, talking and laughing with Summer like she wouldn't scalp Gabe with a butter knife if given the chance.

The group gradually quieted as they realized Gabe had finally arrived. Gabe, however, glanced around the room for cutlery or other sharp objects while Izze eyed him warily. Her smile faded into a somber expression, and she crossed her arms.

Gabe cleared his throat, hoping Izze hadn't noticed the pen sitting on the coffee table. "I need your help," he said to the group.

And Izze, apparently.

"You said that on the phone," Summer said and glanced at Izze, "but you also said that you needed our help to win back Kaylee. That still the plan?"

Izze raised both of her dark eyebrows in question, her expression challenging him.

"It is," Gabe said loudly for the group's benefit, but his eyes never left Izze.

She nodded once, and begrudging approval flashed through her eyes.

Izze speak for, *I won't kill you—yet.*

Perfectly fine. Gabe could handle the *yet.* After all, he had a plan.

One Izze hopefully wouldn't kill him over.

"That's good." Summer hooked her thumb toward Izze. "I thought Izze's help would be important for our mission, so I invited her."

Gabe noticed Natalya shift from the stool where she was perched. She looked like she would fall over if someone so much as blinked in her direction.

"Thank you, Izze." Gabe hoped she could see his sincerity.

"So tell us your grand plan." Ethan's tapping on his iPad signaled his preparation to record Gabe's plan, step-by-step.

"I'm presuming there's going to be some sort of serenade if we're all involved in this shindig," Drake said dryly.

"Quit whining, Drake," Summer teased.

Drake rolled his eyes and grinned. "I mean, obviously some sort of serenade is involved because—as Henry Wadsworth Longfellow once said—'Music is the universal language of mankind.' So that would also apply to love. Better?"

"I'm ignoring you now." She turned her attention to Gabe. "This is a good plan, right?" Summer asked Gabe. "You need to let us judge and evaluate that because if Kaylee was angry enough to quit—"

"Hold on." Izze leaned forward with her palms to the ground, forcing the conversation to a stop. "What do you mean she quit?" she asked suspiciously.

Gabe exchanged glances with all the others who all wore confused expressions on their faces.

All except Natalya who continued to fidget like ants were crawling up her legs.

"Natalya came here and told us that Kaylee quit," Ethan said in that smooth, diplomatic way of his.

"Really?" Izze said while swinging her fierce gaze to Natalya. "Because Natalya here convinced Kaylee that not only did Gabe realize that he was in love with the *idea* of Kaylee not *in love* with Kaylee herself, she also strongly implied that everyone in the band unanimously agreed that the situation had progressed to the point that Kaylee needed to leave. However, I'm assuming based on your stunned faces, that's not what she told you." Izze's angry breaths continued to rant where her words left off. Wolverine Izze had emerged.

Despite the anger starting to brew within Gabe as everyone in the room came to the same conclusion, Gabe also felt sorry for Natalya. He knew what it felt like to be in a prison of his own making, to be the person to make such a colossally awful decision.

He also felt regret because he had no doubt that their mistake—and Gabe's poor treatment of her heart—had contributed to the lead-up of this moment. Though shame beckoned to him, Gabe silently repeated God's truth: *I am a man redeemed.*

After far too many tense moments had passed, Gabe asked softly, "Nat, why?"

Natalya burst into sobs.

Summer stood up and went to Natalya, enveloping her in a hug while she cried. Izze clamped her mouth shut and leaned back into the couch. Her lips moved like she was counting to ten or praying—or both. Ethan and Drake exchanged awkward looks.

Gabe waited for answers.

And shifted from his right foot to the left because he was the only one standing.

After what felt like hours but was probably only a few minutes, Natalya's tears subsided. She hiccupped three or four times before looking up to face them. "I was jealous. That's what it boils down to. I was jealous that she was getting to sing so much and because you'd fallen back in love with her." She hung her head. "I manipulated the situation. I-I thought that if she left, I'd get to continue singing and maybe you'd finally..."

She didn't finish the thought, but she didn't need to. Gabe knew. They all knew, and frankly, an anvil dropped on a baby grand would hurt less than this right now.

Natalya looked up and swung her gaze from Izze to Gabe. "I'm sorry. I'm so sorry. There's nothing I can say or do to erase what I did, but I am so sorry."

Izze looked at Gabe and raised her eyebrows. *What are you going to do?*

Gabe moved toward Natalya and ignored the way he wanted to crack his stiff neck. Summer scooted to the left while still keeping an arm around Natalya as Gabe kneeled in front of her. Hopefully this image wouldn't be a slap in the face after he said what he needed to say.

"Natalya, I forgive you," Gabe said. "I forgive you."

Natalya's expression said she was expecting Gabe to unleash Wolverine Izze on her. Forgiveness wasn't even on her radar. "Wh-what?" she stuttered.

"I forgive you," he said again.

"But..."

"You messed up. You made some bad decisions that hurt people." Gabe took Natalya's hands in his. "However, if there's one thing God's finally gotten into my thick head, it's that His forgiveness and grace are bigger than our mistakes. Don't let this mistake define you."

"Thank you," she whispered. Her eyes watered as she quickly glanced at her hands in his. "I-I don't think I can stay with the band."

Gabe's gut twisted as he nodded. "Unfortunately, I agree. At least for now. Maybe things will change down the line." Gabe squeezed her hands before he released his friend. "After all, God is a fan of second chances."

"Thank you," she said again. "I think I should go."

Summer helped her stand. "I'll take you home."

Gabe watched them leave. He was feeling a lot of things, and honestly, he'd rather not deal with most of those feelings. Being betrayed by a friend/bandmate. Sadness over losing that friend/bandmate. Hope that maybe the future would bring restoration. Plus, Gabe finally understood how hard it was to watch someone hate themselves for their mistakes.

But the biggest feeling of all?

Hope.

Hope that he'd be able to win Kaylee back.

Gabe turned back to the group. Natalya's betrayal had hit them hard, but Gabe had a plan to roll out. They could fill Summer in later.

It was go time.

Hours later, and then several additional hours once Summer rejoined the group, the plan was in place.

"Operation Fight for Kaylee is officially underway," Izze announced. "Now it's time for me to get some sleep."

"For real," Drake said with a yawn. "My beauty sleep is essential."

Ethan rolled his eyes as Summer picked up the trash from the pizza they'd had delivered around hour four, many hours ago.

Izze shrugged into her coat and grabbed her bag. "See you all later."

"Izze, could you wait a second?" Gabe asked as he rushed to meet her by the front door.

"What's up?" she asked, and for once, animosity didn't ooze from her eyes like she was the victim of a zombie plague.

Unsettling, but in a good way.

"I just wanted to say, well, thank you. Thank you for coming, Izze." Gabe looked at the floor then at her. "You could have told me...well, a lot of things, none of them nice. Your help means a lot."

Izze shrugged. "I told Summer to call me if you ever retrieved your head out of the compact storage unit where you'd decided to keep it when it came to your relationship with Kaylee," she said dryly.

He laughed. "Yeah. My head has been reaffixed to my shoulders, and I got a really good guy—who happens to be a nosy, old lady—to fix that wiring problem in the old noggin."

Izze's eyes sparkled in a knowing way. "Don't worry about it, Gabe. You're forgiven. God knows Miles and I have continued to make our fair share of mistakes. Grace goes a long way."

"It does," he agreed. He was finally walking in that grace.

She paused before stepping through the apartment doorway. "Glad to know that Lou got through to you. Got to love those divine appointments."

It's the "storm of the decade" out there.

Of course, the meteorologists watching New England say that whenever a big storm appears on their radars.

Sure, it's a lot of snow. No one is saying that eighteen inches isn't a lot of snow, but calling it the storm of the decade could be a bit premature. It's almost like saying, *I dare you to top that amount of snow.* Not a wise challenged to issue in New Hampshire, a state where an alarming number of residents can tell you the number of times they—or some animal—climbed onto the roof simply by climbing to the top of the wall of snow surrounding their house. Maybe if they narrowed it down to "snowstorm of the year" instead? Someone should talk to them about that.

I blink.

You know it's been a quiet day when you've started to organize a letter writing campaign to the local meteorologists in your head. However, I am not Leslie Knope, so I need something to do. Right now.

Pushing away from the little checkout counter that stores bins and supplies on the employee side, I glance around the empty store. My appraisal ends with the cash register right in front of me.

I suppose I could clean it.

Again.

Sigh.

You know what this means, right? There's really only one thing left to do.

Build a shoebox fort under the guise of organizing and cleaning.

The door jiggles as I'm making a break for the back-left corner of the store. Ah, man! I wanted to use the light-up kid's shoes in my fort. I will now proceed to pout for a millisecond.

Millisecond over.

I paste a smile to my face and turn to greet the customer. "Hello! Welcome to The New England Shoe Barn. Can I help you find anything today?"

An older woman stomps the snow from her boots on the mat in front of the glass doors. "Goodness, I have never seen this strip mall so empty. Nasty storm out there, though calling it the storm of the decade is a bit premature, if you ask me."

I officially like this lady. "I agree."

She tugs a ski hat off the top of her head, and her brown-sprinkled-with-silver hair stands on end from the static. She shoves the hat into her coat pocket and smooths her frizzy hair. She sighs as another strand of hair sticks to the sleeve of her coat. "I need a haircut, but my favorite hairdresser left the business."

"Ah, that's a shame," I say politely.

She grins. "No, it's a good story, dear. Maybe I'll tell you about it sometime, but right now I'm looking for a pair of snow boots. Does your fine establishment have any of these available?"

"Yes, absolutely," I reply like the yes-man corporate America trains you to be. "If you'll follow me right this way, I can show you what we have in stock."

"Wonderful," the woman says as she follows me to the middle of the store. "By the way, you can call me Lou."

I pause next to a display of last season's sandals that are on sale for fifty percent off. "Have we met before?" I ask her, trying to determine how I know her. Something tells me I know her.

She looks like the average older woman. I realize that might sound a little mean; honestly, I'm not trying to be mean. But she's average. Brown hair with a sprinkle of silver. Average height. Average weight. No distinguishing moles or freckles, birthmarks or piercings. Nothing.

Except a light in her eyes that illuminates the room.

"Nope," Lou says. "Can't say that we've had the pleasure."

I smile awkwardly. "Sorry, you must remind me of someone else." Who that would be, I have no clue. But there's a connection to this little, old woman that I will figure out sooner or later, even if that connection is vaguely resembling the mother of Chris Pratt.

Stopping at the end of the aisle that contains all the snow boots, I smile again. "Here we are."

Lou zips down the aisle. "Oh, wonderful, wonderful. How lovely! Hey, what do you think of these?" She points at a pair of sleek black snow boots that are styled to look like dress boots.

Ah, so she's one of those customers. Likes the constant attention focused on her and/or will send me running to the back room to check for sizes "just in case it's not on the shelf."

There could be worse things. She could be the type of customer that's rude, condescending, and says they will personally make sure I lose my job when the shoe they want isn't on the shelf, then proceed to walk out the door sputtering about how unacceptable the whole situation is. Or she could be the kind of customer that's rude, crass, and makes me wish I could remove the crude things she's said from my ears with a pair of tweezers.

Now me, I'm the kind of customer that would rather find a different pair of shoes than ask someone for help. Ah, the quirks of the introverted.

"They're very classy," I say.

Lou holds a pair of hot pink snow boots with pompoms up for me to see. "What do you think of these?" she asks again.

I think someone is either young at heart or desperately trying to cling to their youth. But I'll stick with saying, "They're so cute."

"I think so, too. I'll add them to the pile."

I gape. Is she the Flash? When did she grab all these boxes? There must be twelve right here.

Make that fourteen!

Seventeen!

I shake my head in wonder. Well, it's not like I had anything better to do today, and I highly doubt any other customers are going to venture out for shoe shopping in this whiteout.

"Okay," Lou says when her pile reaches a total of twenty-seven boxes of different shoes and/or sizes. "I think this is a good place to start."

You think? The woman even grabbed a pair of sandals. Eccentric much?

I grab one of the cushioned stools with the mirror underneath for the individual to admire the shoe on their foot and push it next to the wall of boxes. "Let's make a little hole in the wall right here so you can sit while you try on the shoes."

"Oh, that's wonderful! Thank you," Lou says. "Here. Grab these two boxes. I want to try these on first. Then let's rebuild the wall to the left of the stool."

Huh, will you look at that? Looks like I got to build a fort after all.

"A little to the left. Perfect!" Lou instructs as she adds another box to the Jenga wall in front of her, bringing her total to thirty-one pairs of shoes. "Now the shoes that I don't want can get put to the right, and the shoes that I do want can be put at the end of the aisle."

Oh, dear, I'm going to have to carry all the shoes that she wants to buy to the counter.

"Sounds great. Why don't we start with this pair," I say as I hold up one of the hot pink boots. What I'm really saying is, *Please stop adding more shoes to the pile before it crushes and kills both of us!*

Lou plops into the seat with her back toward me. I pass her the pair of pink shoes. Slipping out of her current shoes, she tugs both of the trendy boots onto her feet. Standing up, she proceeds to walk up and down the three clear feet of the aisle like it's a twenty-foot runway.

Lou places her hand on the hip she's jutted into the unstable wall of boxes. "Yes, I think these are definitely a yes."

I force a tight smile. "Awesome. They look great."

"They do pinch my big toes, though. Maybe I should try the next size up."

I'm beginning to think Lou is the Smaug of shoes. She's established a lair in this store and will sleep on the pile of soft leather shoes for centuries at a time. It's time to take a cue from the dwarves and *get out of here!* This mountain belongs to Lou now.

"Tell me about yourself, dear. For starters, what's your name?"

"Kaylee," I answer her as I kneel to help her tug off a pair of size six boots that are most assuredly not the right size. She's obviously a seven and a half, wide.

"Lovely." She smiles while she grips the stool with both hands to prevent any sort of unexpected takeoff due to the forceful tugging. "Well, I think it's wonderful to see a young woman pursuing her passion."

I drop her booted foot and gape at her before I recover. "Right. Yeah, sure. Thanks."

"To have so much dedication that you come into work during a snowstorm is really impressive," Lou continues.

"Mm-hmm," I murmur. Best not to speak at this point because it won't be pretty if all those emotions are uncorked.

"Really wonderful," Lou says again as I finally get the boot off her foot and set it to the side. "I love seeing someone pursue their God-given passions in life. Blesses my old heart."

"You're a spring chicken," I say, attempting to get the focus off of me.

"Hardly!" Lou laughs and grabs another pair of shoes. These are a size eight. "I'm an old hen, but I find tremendous joy in watching others embrace God's plan for them."

"That's nice," I grumble. Look who's so not getting Employee of the Month.

"How did you decide on this line of work? Are you hoping to pursue a job in the fashion industry? Or maybe become a business owner?" she asks as she sets a pair of leopard print dress boots to the right.

Unfortunately, each question shakes my volatile emotions until the cork pops off doing sixty miles an hour.

"You want to know how I ended up going from my dream job to a job I hate? It's a great story. One filled with heartache, betrayal, and butterflies. I think it could be a *New York Times* Bestseller," I say with a heave of anger before I slap my hands over my mouth in shock.

Yup, I'm getting fired this time.

Oh.

My.

Goodness.

What did I just do?

Doesn't matter. I'm fired. I've never been fired before. Let go, yes. But not fired. I guess it was bound to happen sooner or later.

"I am so, so sorry," I say before I move my hands to cover my eyes. I can't even look Lou in the eye after that horrible outburst.

My cheeks tingle as soft, wrinkly hands pull my hands from my eyes. "Oh, dear. I'm very sorry you've experienced so much heartache. Would you like to talk about it? I've been told I'm an excellent sounding board."

"No, that's okay. I'm so sorry for behaving like that." I hiccup as I try to hold the tears inside, a battle I'm about to lose based on the snot leaking from my left nostril.

"Listen, Kaylee," Lou says as she scoots to the far side of the stool, pats the empty seat, and waits for me to sit next to her. "For me, there's no bigger ministry than seeing the everyday needs of the people right in front of me. Whether that be at a restaurant, a mechanic's shop, a shoe store, or on a frozen lake."

A frozen lake? I was with her right up until that point.

"If you're willing, tell me your story." Lou angles her body to face me better. She takes my hands in hers. "I know it's difficult to be that brave and vulnerable with a person you've just met, but I promise that my heart is only to share God's truth, whatever the situation may be."

I nod and bite my lip as I appraise Lou in new light. Nodding again, I start to share my long, dramatic tale with her.

Ugh! My life has become a stinking soap opera. All I need is for some guy named Lucky to enter from stage left.

Lou pulls me into a hug once I've finished my sob story and holds me for a minute, then she releases me, but her hands have a firm, tender grasp on my upper shoulders. "Thank you for being so vulnerable."

I shrug, unsure what else to do. Vulnerable or not, I'm not used to someone thanking me for sharing my drama with them. It's almost like thanking someone for sneezing on you. *Thanks for the potential germs, dude!*

It just doesn't add up.

"I can't imagine how painful it must have been for you to forgive Gabe, believing that there might actually be a future in store for the two of you after so many years had passed, and then only to have that be crushed. Forgiving someone who's hurt you so deeply is not an easy road to walk."

Insert big, loud mental *Harrumph!* here.

Lou raises a brownish-silver eyebrow at me.

Whoops! Looks like I voiced that harrumph.

"Had you forgiven Gabe?"

"Before or now?" I ask. Is it stuffy in here? Maybe I should open the window, let the snow pile around that display of snow boots. Good advertising.

"Before," Lou says.

"Well, yeah...right?" Very convincing. "I thought I had actually forgiven him. I had hope for the future and stuff, but...I guess I was expecting him to hurt me again," I confess.

She smiles, but the seriousness in her eyes doesn't waver. "There's no sin that's too big for God to forgive, that Jesus didn't take to the cross. He's equipped us with the ability to forgive, and He's ready to help us forgive when we're willing but our emotions haven't caught up."

"But how many times can you forgive the same person before you come to terms that nothing is going to change—and please don't say seventy times seven."

Lou squeezes my upper arms before releasing me. "Sometimes those people change, and they can be part of your life. Sometimes they still freak out after they've changed, and you have to navigate those emotional blows as they come. Sometimes they live in the chains of their past or return to those old ways. Sometimes you have to step away from someone toxic. Regardless of whatever category into which Gabe falls, you still have to forgive him for your own heart's sake."

I bite my lip before I release words for Lou to judge. "I know this is awful, but I'm not sure I can forgive him this time. How do I let all of that go?" I don't say this part out loud, but honestly, I feel like that guy in the parable from Matthew who was forgiven of a huge debt, then freaked out at another guy who owed him a smaller debt. I feel a kinship with him, which is probably not a good thing.

Definitely not a good thing considering how the story ended for this unforgiving man.

"Release it to God."

"Oh, is that all?" I mutter as I roll my eyes. "Maybe I'll write it on a piece of paper and burn it. The Ex-Boyfriend Bonfire worked on *Friends*."

Lou bumps my shoulder with hers. "Resolve in your heart that you've forgiven that person. That their debt against you is paid in full because Jesus paid for it. You're not looking for payment anymore, so bitterness over the past has no root in you.

"In its place is God's love for that person. 'But he who is forgiven little, loves little.' Luke chapter seven, verse forty-seven." Lou pauses, studying me. "Have you been forgiven much, Kaylee?"

I frown and bite my lip as I mentally flip through the pages of the ever-present flipbook of everything I've ever done wrong. "I guess when you compare it to—"

Lou shakes her head. "No, Kaylee. Sin is sin. Society has given labels like 'big' and 'worse' to our sins, but the fact is that any and every sin separates us from God. So have you been forgiven much?"

"I've been forgiven for everything," I whisper.

"That's a lot," Lou says gently.

"So forgive others like He's forgiven me," I finish.

In a way, I'm furious at myself for not understanding this sooner. Yes, I can quote that verse in Luke with the best of them, but I don't think the truth of it sank into my spirit until today. I've "forgiven" people, but that anger is still there, waiting for blood. Payment. I've never forgiven anyone the way God continues to forgive me, in that all-debts-paid way of His. Not Gabe. Not my parents. Not the dude in the truck who cut me off on the highway this morning. Even if Gabe hadn't been the one to break things off again, I still would have been waiting for something to go wrong so I could stand on my pedestal and point my finger.

I am definitely furious at myself.

But there's forgiveness for that, too.

*Oh, God,* I silently cry. *I'm so sorry. Thank you for forgiving me for so much. I want to forgive others the same way, but especially Gabe and my parents. I feel like all of them gave up on loving me, so I have always wanted them to pay for the way they hurt me. But I forgive them. I forgive them! Whether or not anything changes, I forgive them. I'm not waiting around to collect payment anymore. It's paid. You paid it.*

My tears are freeing. I'm no longer bound by unforgiveness and bitterness that's waiting to wrap itself around me the next time a person screws up—because let's face it, there will be a next time. Going forward, my heart's desire is to forgive as freely as God's forgiven me. To love with all of His love. Second chances are worthless without those steps.

Second chances...

The thought deflates my freedom bubble in two beats. There will be no more chances with Gabe.

Lou taps me on the knee with her hot pink fingernail. "Why the long face so soon?"

"I guess I just realized that even if I forgive Gabe completely— and I one hundred percent know that I have this time—there's still not a happy ending in store for us."

"There are certainly times when life doesn't go the way we want it, and it's okay that those disappointments hurt." A grin quirks Lou's smile to the left. "But I'll let you in on a secret: this isn't one of those times."

"With everything that's happened, I can't and won't be the one to put myself out there again, and he's too afraid," I say.

It's fine. I'll be fine. The conclusion to our story isn't one that I'd write. Honestly, it's got that bittersweet ending that makes me feel like one of the Bronte sisters took a stab at it. Sweet, because I finally found freedom in forgiveness. Bitter, because I won't end up with the man I've been in love with for so long because of his own chains.

It hurts, but I'm going to choose to believe that God's writing a different conclusion for me. And there's something exciting knowing that it's in His capable hands.

It's wide open.

Lou's smile grows. "As much as I love it when the woman goes to fight for her man, there's opportunities in every story where the man also needs to make the choice to stand up and fight for his love." She winks at me. "Something tells me this situation is the latter."

# Chapter Twenty-Five

I've always thought that God speaks to each of His children personally because He knows us personally. Like He knows that I am obsessed with lemons and that song lyrics are always running through my head.

Always. Running. Through. My. Head.

I tap the steering wheel as I drive home from work three days after meeting Lou, singing along to The Jackson Five's "I Want You Back." My roommates mentioned a couple days ago that they were all driving home for the weekend, so I have the house to myself.

Michael Jackson and I continue to tear it up on our epic tour via my car as I turn into my driveway and slam the brake.

Then I pull into my usual space, between Izze and Apryl's cars.

Barely remembering to yank my keys from the ignition, I bolt up the snowy walkway to the front door. I can't help it; I'm excited to see my friends. Pretty sure I forgot my purse in the car, too.

"Apryl? Izze? Courtney?" I yell as soon as I cross the threshold of the already unlocked door. "Where are you guys?"

Everything's dark and silent.

What are the odds that a couple of serial killers would have the same cars as my friends?

You know what, never mind. I don't think I actually want the answer to that question. *Any* answer to that question will only ensure that I don't sleep for the next three weeks. The thirty-seventh rule in my nonexistent handbook, *The Handbook for Single Ladies Living Alone*, is to never ask any questions about the odds of serial killers being in your house. Just dial nine-one-one and get out of there.

I turn around to run for my phone which is in my purse that I left in the car, but that's when I hear it.

A song.

Moving through the house, I peep outside the kitchen window.

And gasp.

And then I'm yanking open the kitchen door to step into the magical scene that's been created in my backyard.

It's already dark outside, but soft light from the fairy lights that decorate every tree, bush, and shrub illuminate every corner of the backyard. Mason jars with those battery-operated tea candles sit on the stone benches and line the little snow-covered stone walkways that took me an entire summer to build. Red rose petals have been sprinkled up and down the walkways that somebody took the time to shovel. However, the trail of petals leads to one place.

The wooden arch in the middle of the backyard.

The arch—well, I guess it's not an arch per say because it's been constructed to look like the doorway to a hobbit hole.

Yeah, guys. Yeah. I'm one happy nerd.

Anyway, this hobbit hole/arch stands in a sea of rose petals and is covered with red roses in bloom and even more fairy lights. Summer and Drake play their respective instruments behind the hobbit hole/arch. Ethan stands just behind them and plays a tambourine. Badly. Very, very badly. Oh, and did I mention they're dressed like elves from *The Lord of the Rings* movies? Yup. They've even got the ears.

Seriously. One. Happy. Nerd.

I don't know how I seem to take in all these details (I'm guessing peripheral vision?) because it feels like the handsome man standing in front of the hobbit hole/arch holds all of my attention.

Gabe.

Insert all the happy sighs and squealing and jumping and flailing about right here. I'm doing it on the inside, and I expect you to do it with me.

Gabe plays his old acoustic guitar, and the dark red of his

tie blends nicely with the reddish-brown tint of the mahogany guitar. He's not in elf costume like the others, and while I'm sure Gabe dressed like Legolas would be a heart-stopping sight, I'm not complaining. He's mind-numbingly handsome in his gray suit.

His smoky gray eyes find mine.

Definitely not complaining.

And he's singing...wait for it...The Jackson Five's "I Want You Back." Coincidence? I'm thinking not.

I hiccup as one of those half sob/half laughs burst from my lips. They're already transitioning to another song. I squint, trying to recognize the lyrics. Almost got it... Yes, it's "What a Man Gotta Do" by the Jonas Brothers. Then it's Meghan Trainor's "Like I'm Gonna Lose You." After a few more minutes, they transition again. This time it's that song from the *Alice in Wonderland* wedding on New Year's Day, Lifehouse's "Whatever It Takes."

I shake my head in awe. It's a mashup. A giant, beautiful mashup. For me! Goodness, the boombox scene from *Say Anything* wishes it could be as good as this serenade.

The Lifehouse part of the mashup is slower, a bearing-your-heart kind of song. He sings the original version of the song, but he sings the lyrics with an even greater intensity then he did at the wedding. This time, he means the words he's singing.

But the previous songs couldn't have prepared me for the next transition.

The melody slows again, and the chords are mournful. The evening wind blows my hair to the left as I listen, adding their own backup vocals to the sad melody while sending additional chills up and down my spine.

*I know my faults.*
*I know there's no way to undo.*
*I believed "I forgive you" was the hope of a fool.*
My heart breaks as I recognize Gabe's heart in the lyrics.
*So I said I'd stay, I'd stay away.*
*And Love found me there,*
*And set me straight.*

The melody of the song is vaguely familiar, but I can't place it.

*It feels like a melody,*
*That tangles and consumes me,*
*That breaks me and moves me,*
*And makes me whole again.*
*And it's laid before me,*
*In all of its glory,*
*That I'm always yours.*
*Forever, always, and again.*

And now I'm crying for an entirely different reason. That's our song. The song we started to write together all those years ago, before the ups and downs, before the heartbreak, before any hope of a reconciliation. And now it's been rewritten to reflect every part of our story.

It's beautiful.

*But something inside of me*
*Could only hear the lies speak.*
*So I listened when they said to run away again.*

*And I said I'd stay, I'd stay away.*
*But Love found me there,*
*And set me straight.*

I press my hands to my mouth. They muffle my squeaky cries, but they don't drown them out completely. Romantic comedies are so misleading about this moment and the concept of "happy tears." You may be happy, but there's nothing quiet about those tears. They are loud, obnoxious, and often accompanied by a disgusting amount of nasal fluid. You've been warned.

*It feels like a melody,*
*That tangles and consumes me,*
*That breaks me and moves me,*
*And makes me whole again.*
*And I finally see,*
*In all of its glory,*
*That I'm always yours.*
*Forever, always, and again.*

Gabe sings the last two lines of the chorus we wrote together three more times. His deep baritone gets quieter and quieter with each repeat, and then it's silent.

Except for my squeaky crying. That's far from silent.

Ethan moves forward, and Gabe passes him the guitar without even looking at him. Ethan transfers his tambourine to his other hand and grabs the guitar by the neck.

Gabe strides forward and drops to his knees in front of me. He's eye level now.

Wait? When did I sink to the ground? When did that happen?

"Kaylee, I'm so sorry." Gabe slides forward in the snow until he can touch me. Since my hands are still clasped against my mouth, his hands rest on my upper shoulder. "I'm so sorry. I love you. I love you so much."

Cue the type of crying I refer to as Suffocating Mouse Squeaks.

He slides forward again and wraps his solid arms around me, holding me close as he speaks over my sobs. "I don't deserve another chance. For crying out loud, I didn't deserve the last one. I let fear get the best of me. I failed you again, and the thought of failing you destroys me. I don't deserve you, but I love you, Kaylee. God as my witness, I love you. And I want to make you happy. I want to build a future with you. I want to marry you."

And now I'm honking. Swell. It's like there's a stinking barnyard up my nose.

"I want to love like God does. Without fail. Without fear. And even if there's no hope for us, that will be my mission in life. And I know it would be a life well lived, but it would never be as good as a life with you. Never," he whispers the final word.

*Squeak-sob-honk-sniffle!*

"I know we still have a lot of issues to work through, and we have a lot of trust that needs to be rebuilt. I know shackling your forever to mine would mean that you're signing on to a lot of extra work you never wanted or deserved. I know that—"

Sometimes the rest of the speech needs to wait so you can kiss your man. And after wrapping both of my hands around the back of Gabe's neck, that's exactly what I do.

Though my response momentarily stuns him, Gabe responds quickly. He pulls me against his chest, and his thick arms secure me there as he kisses me back.

Excuse us, would you?

His forehead drops to mine as he draws in a ragged breath. "You didn't let me ask the question."

"I forgive you," I say against his lips, "and I love you, too."

Gabe leans back and searches my soul with his eyes. Finding whatever answer he needed, he squeezes his eyes shut. "Thank you," he says, voice hoarse.

And for a beautiful moment, we rest in that forgiveness and love.

Rest.

Then...

Gabe opens his eyes as I wipe tears from my own. "That actually wasn't the question I was referring to." His eyes twinkle.

I frown. "What?"

Gabe reaches into his pocket.

And pulls out a little box.

I bite my lip.

The box snaps open.

I try to smooth the surprise from my face as I flick my gaze back to Gabe's amused expression.

There's no ring.

Reaching my fingers into the mouth of the velvet box, I grasp the wooden pick with *Pick me?* carved into it. As I do, my fingertips brush against something cool. Lifting the pick from its velvet cushion, I gasp.

A round cut emerald laid in gold winks at me in the twinkling lights. A delicate gold leaf partially covers each of the prongs holding the gem in place, and a beautiful dark wood is inlaid into the golden band.

Abruptly, I jump up and sprint inside the house, still clutching the pick in my hand.

Relax, I'm not running away.

Grabbing a Sharpie from my junk drawer, I scribble my answer onto the back of the pick.

Gabe's standing when I go back outside, clutching the ring box in his hand. The easy smile on his lips as he watches me, completely at peace, makes my heart leap in praise to God.

"Can I quote Galadriel about how much I have desired this 'one ring,'" I tease as I stop three feet from Gabe.

"I would really prefer it if you wouldn't," he says dryly.

So instead, I hold the pick in front of my heart, answer out for him to read. "I still pick you," I say as he skims the same message scribbled in green Sharpie ink.

And then I launch myself into his waiting arms.

This probably doesn't come as a surprise, but we're kissing again.

"She said yes!" Summer screams presumably from her perch on her drum stool.

"Yes!" Izze shouts from above.

The directional detail here catches my attention.

Turning around and looking up, I see Izze, Courtney, Apryl, Chance, Miles, and Dallas watching from the upstairs windows. So that's where they were hiding. Of course. Rookie mistake, Mc-Grurd.

And in the near future, I'll be saying *Sanders* when I chastise myself.

"We're coming down," Apryl yells as each of the other floating heads disappear.

"Finally!" Drake bellows from his spot next to Summer. "I've had to wear a lot of obnoxious getups for this job, but this one takes the cake." He flicks at the elf ear sitting crookedly on his left ear.

Summer smacks his arm. "Be quiet or congratulate them."

"Well, congratulations." Drake offers us a sheepish grin. "I obviously meant to say that."

"Congratulations! I'm really happy for you guys." Ethan sets the tambourine on the rim of Summer's bass drum. "And I'm never playing that thing again."

Summer rushes up to us and grabs me in a fierce hug. "I am so sorry, Kaylee. We never kicked you out of the band."

I suck in a shallow breath—Summer's squeezing me pretty hard—and glance at Gabe in question.

"Natalya lied and manipulated the situation," Gabe says quietly. "She's gone now."

I nod, but I don't ask any other questions. They can fill me in later. My heart hurts for Natalya because I recognize the corner where bitterness has led her, and I don't wish that hardship on her. Not anymore.

The rest of my friends—guys, look at all the friends God gave to lonely ol' me!—squish around each other in their attempt to be the first to hug and congratulate us.

As I turn my attention back to my fiancé, my heart leaps in praise again, dancing to a melody that I could never do justice to, could never put into words. There's no name to this song of praise. I'm not even sure there's words.

But it's there, playing in my head and heart.

It's a beautiful melody, even if it's been revised a time or two. It's the ballad of a couple whose story has been rewritten with a conclusion only God could surmise.

# Epilogue

"This kid had better be really cute," I moan. My unborn daughter must think my kidney is a trampoline or something.

"Just remember to squint until someone washes her up," Izze says as she bends down to pick up four-year-old Madeline, who settles on Izze's right hip. "And don't think about what's coating the top of her forehead when you kiss her."

I gag. "Thanks for that tip. I'd finally stopped throwing up last week."

She laughs as Madeline grabs Izze's face with both hands while chanting, "Mommy, mommy, mommy, mommy."

"What, sweetie?"

"I want baby marshmallow," Madeline says as she sticks out her lower lip. That little move combined with the dark curls she'd inherited from Izze means she has Miles wrapped around her little finger.

Izze growls under her breath. "I'm going to smack Dallas upside the head for bringing ambrosia salad again. She keeps picking the marshmallows out. That's all she'll eat." She sets Madeline down and takes her hand.

"Could you help me up before you go?" I beg from where I've become one with the couch. "I don't want to spend the entire party sitting, but I'm a beached whale."

Izze snickers. "Trust me when I say that you haven't reached the beached whale stage yet."

"I don't know how I could possibly get any bigger." I hold out my arms much like Madeline did moments earlier.

"Arms up!" Madeline chants from behind Izze.

"I can't wait to hear what you say when you finally reach your due date in eight weeks." Izze chuckles as she grabs my hands.

"Fingers crossed she comes early." I grunt as Izze pulls me up.

"She's going to be eight days late." Gabe walks into the living room. "Wasn't Courtney two weeks late with both Conner and Jake?" he asks with a mischievous grin.

I toss him a glare that would send an Orc tripping over backward in its attempt to run away.

"Careful," Izze warns with a laugh as Madeline pulls her to the kitchen for the aforementioned marshmallows.

Despite the Orc-killing glare, Gabe walks right up and wraps his arm around me before kissing me soundly.

I playfully slap my hand against his chest. "Dude, I'm ready to give birth."

"Why? Ready for another one?" he teases.

I roll my eyes before I kiss him, then lay my head against his chest. "I can't believe we're leaving. We've been through so much, and this house has been one of the backdrops to our struggles and triumphs."

And there have been struggles. Izze almost died in childbirth and has been heroically battling anxiety ever since. Summer and Jared (her husband) have been struggling with infertility for three years. Apryl and Courtney's grandmother is dancing with Jesus, no longer inhibited by her broken body. Chance's relationship with his father is still strained, and aside from the occasional Facebook message to Summer or me, Natalya has opted not to remain in contact with us.

But through all the heartache and struggle, we have overcome. We have triumphed. And we are family.

His laugh rumbles against my ear. "Kay, you haven't lived here in four and a half years."

"Four years and four months," I correct, leaning back to see his face. "We've only been married for four years and four months."

After Gabe proposed that snowy day, we opted for an average length engagement. While a part of me wishes we'd just eloped immediately after he proposed, we both knew that forgiveness and love didn't mean that trust had been rebuilt overnight. We did a lot of counseling before and after our wedding, but friends, it's more than possible for trust to be rebuilt.

And for those of you who are wondering, no, there weren't any elves at our wedding.

But there was a hobbit hole/arch.

Anyway, back to the present.

Gabe rolls his eyes. "I was rounding up."

"Oh, so that's what it's like to be married to me, hmmm? It's so tedious that you automatically round up now?"

Gabe cranes his neck to look at the floor around us. "When did the argument start? Did I miss the guy with the checkered flag?"

I sigh. "You know what I mean, Gabe. Summer moved into my old room right after we got married. Then after she bought the house from the previous owners, we continued having rehearsals here. Now she's just decided to up and leave—"

"And by leaving, you mean moving to New York with her husband for the worship ministry they started," Gabe interjects dryly.

"It's the end of an era."

"Yeah," he says, "but that also means it's the start of another era."

"But...it's the end." I whimper.

Gabe raises his eyebrows. "You know, watching *Mulan* every day might not be the best thing for you."

"Just because I keep crying while watching the animated *Mulan*, doesn't mean I'm crying because of it now. Besides, I couldn't help it. She was so brave." I sniffle.

Oh, drat. I'm crying again.

Gabe wipes my tears away with his thumb. "No, but it probably isn't helping when you're already feeling sad."

"Maybe," I admit begrudgingly. "I'm just going to miss her."

"I know, babe. Me too." He holds me close. "But in a few months, we'll be back to work full-time."

"Yeah, Jess is pretty good on the drums," I say of Drake's fiancée who's the official new drummer for All Yours.

He tilts his head toward the kitchen. "Let's go join the others."

We walk into the kitchen as Apryl tosses a mini marshmallow across the table to her three-year-old son. John gets on his knees in his chair and catches it with his mouth as the room erupts in cheers.

Chance tosses an orange marshmallow at Apryl's head. "Hey! Why do I get in trouble when I do that?"

"Because you tossed him a marinara-covered meatball," Apryl exclaims.

"Did he catch it?" Dallas asks from where he also sits at the table with his and Courtney's sons.

"Yup," Chance says proudly as he sways back and forth, rocking the sleeping infant strapped into the pink baby sling on his chest.

"And when are you going to train Addie to do that?" Miles, who sits opposite of Dallas and the boys, asks.

"I figured once she's chewing solid foods, then we're good to go," Chance jokes.

Apryl shakes her head and tucks a strand of her blue-black hair behind her left ear. "You're lucky that you're holding her. Means I can't smack you upside the head."

Chance grins at his wife. "That was the genius logic behind my offer, love."

"How's the transition going?" I ask Apryl as she passes me a bottle of water.

"Good! Miles has been a lot of help figuring out all of the kinks, but we'll be ready to launch as an official wedding venue in June." Apryl and Chance's business as a wedding decorating vendor has done so well that they decided to extend their business and open a space on their property that could also serve as a wedding venue.

"Which is good because we're booked solid," Chance says as Addie coos and stretches her pudgy legs. "Between that and business booming at my shop, I had to hire another mechanic."

"Good, because as the owner of Ever After Bridal Salon and your loyal friend, I am sending every venue-less bride your direction," Izze declares. Two years ago, Izze became the owner of the bridal salon where she's worked for the last fourteen years.

"Nice," Dallas says as he covers a yawn with his hand. "Sorry, guys. I've been working a lot of late nights on a malpractice case that goes to court next week." Poor guy. I know from Courtney that his work as a medical lawyer isn't easy.

Courtney slips over to her husband and squeezes his arm.

"What about you guys?" Chance asks and he swipes his finger back and forth between Courtney and Miles. "How's your merger thing going?"

Courtney and Miles joined forces a couple months ago. With Miles' business and marketing experience and Courtney's degree in small business law, the two merged their respective businesses into one awesome business. Together, they handle the legal and marketing headaches of many local small businesses in addition to Izze's store, Chance's mechanic shop, Apryl's business, and our band.

Courtney rolls her eyes. "Miles likes to start each and every morning playing 'The Imperial March.'"

Miles grins shamelessly as he and Gabe high-five. "Darth Vader. Need I say more?"

"No," Izze moans. "Please don't."

"When do the others get here?" Dallas asks with another yawn. "Sorry."

"They should be here anytime," I answer. "I told them we were absolutely having band practice today."

"And then she gave everyone the crazy eyes," Gabe adds.

I nod. "Like Lane Kim when she was pregnant in the last season of *Gilmore Girls*. And everyone knows that you don't mess with the crazy eyes of a pregnant woman, no matter how impractical the request."

Chance laughs. "Good cover."

Just like the addition of each of our husbands, Summer, Ethan, and Drake (and their respective paramours) have morphed into part of our close-knit group over the years. While I'm devastated that Summer and her husband are moving away, I'm happy for this new chapter in their lives.

It's just...

It's weird, you know? We've all been together for so long. It's hard to know it's ending.

"Auntie Summer is here!" Conner yells from his chair, interrupting the conversation on how to surprise Summer and Jared.

"A little late, bud," Summer says with a laugh before she tickles him.

Taylor Swift's "It's Nice to Have a Friend" plays in my head as the additions to our family of friends pour into the kitchen, laughing and talking. Ethan and his girlfriend Ally (he's going to pop the question next week) chat with Courtney and Apryl. Summer and Jared talk about the move with Izze and Miles. Drake and Jess attempt to sneak some of the cake without any of the kids noticing.

"I want cake!" Madeline shouts.

And the room explodes with demands for cake.

I laugh as Gabe wraps an arm around my swollen middle. Our daughter kicks his hand.

"I think she wants cake too," he murmurs into my ear.

"She'll have to share," I say as I lay my head against his shoulder.

"Or I could bring you two pieces of cake," he teases.

"Not a bad offer, and lemon cake is the only lemon-y thing that's not giving me massive amounts of heartburn. Let me confer with Little Elf," I say as I press my hand to the left side of my belly.

Our daughter proceeds to ram her elbow/foot/knee/head into the palm of my hand.

Message received. "Little Elf likes that plan."

Gabe smiles sweetly at me before his gaze flickers to my bouncing belly. "I'll be right back, Melody."

Okay, yeah, it's the end. The end of an era. The final page of the book. The last note of the song. I'm a big girl (literally, thanks to my prego belly), and I can accept that. It's time to say goodbye.

Insert more whimpers here.

But I'll also sing melody after melody of praise because I see how far God's brought each and every one of us. This perfect moment is a joyful conclusion to this chapter of our lives.

Or as the experts say, Happily Ever After.

# A Note from Me to You

I'm going to be brutally honest about something with you, my dear reader.

This was *NOT* how I planned to write Kaylee and Gabe's story.

Nope.

I plotted the core parts of their story years before I sat down to write it. In so many ways, the heart of this story—music—was my way of honoring the musical part of my soul, and I plotted it as an ode to something I thought (but God planned differently) I had closed the door on for good. Additionally, I knew it would involve forgiveness and struggling with this basic question, *What do you do when you believe love is a lie?*

But I didn't plan to go...there.

Creating a story with God is a great honor. After all, Jesus told stories, and there's a reason so much of the Bible is told in story format. However, creating with God means being vulnerable, taking a leap of faith, and going places you don't want to go.

I've experienced heartache that's made me question if all love is a lie (and admitting that seems scandalous for a Christian romance author). I have struggled to forgive the same person(s) over and over. I've seen different people that I love struggle with the same addiction and its far-reaching chains that Gabe obtained victory over.

And I didn't want to go to such a raw place.

So when God started laying this direction for Kaylee and Gabe's story on my heart, I resisted. I fought it. I wrestled with it.

Even after saying yes, I was still scared. Additionally, as I neared the eleventh hour of my deadline, I panicked and softened Gabe's past. Then my editor nudged me to go even deeper in that area, not knowing at that time how I'd spent countless hours trying to tone down just that.

God asked me to be vulnerable with this story. To be honest, that's still really scary. While I tried to be sensitive and thorough, a journey like the one Gabe and Kaylee took is layered with so many elements—far too many to examine from every angle over the course of a single novel. However, with all my heart, I hope Kaylee and Gabe's story has had an impact on you. I will always hope you laugh (mouse attack, anyone?) and swoon (that snowy kiss equals all the happy sighs!) and delight in the pop culture references (could that *be* any more fun?) sprinkled throughout my stories.

But my heart, dear reader, is always to bless you with a story that proclaims God's deep love for us.

For you.

Hugs,

V. Joy Palmer

P.S. Some of the settings in this story are not real, some are based on real locations, and others are the real deal. Please forgive any mistakes I made in portraying those locations.

# Discussion Questions

1. What scene was the most humorous to you?

2. What was your favorite romantic moment between Kaylee and Gabe?

3. Music plays a huge roll in this story, especially in how Kaylee thinks and navigates her feelings. How did Kaylee's "internal radio" further expand on her thoughts and feelings?

4. Gabe told Lou that many Christians would not accept "a man like David in their churches today, a man who grew up knowing God and knowing that his sins went against everything God said." How should churches be supporting struggling brothers and sisters without condemning them?

5. Romance has gotten a bad reputation for perfect, unrealistic heroes. Are characters like Gabe—characters that represent men who have fought and overcome lusts of the flesh—needed in Christian romance?

6. Gabe told Kaylee that he was free of the addictive lusts of the flesh, but that he also stayed on the offensive to guard against it. Why is this kind of mindfulness important with this—or any—addiction?

7. Izze told Kaylee that God's love can redeem anything. What are the different ways we see this reflected in *Marriage, Melodies, and Rewritten Conclusions*?

8. How did the emotional/spiritual impact of Natalya and Gabe's past contribute to her manipulative decisions later?

9. Kaylee struggled with forgiving people in the "all debts paid" way that God forgives. Why was that difficult for her? How did holding those "debts" affect her heart?

10. Gabe had experienced freedom from the chains of lust, but he had not experienced freedom from the chains of guilt, shame, and condemnation from his past. How was this lie used to torment him? How can the church better support those who are struggling with this lie after repentance?

# Huge Hugs of Thanks

As I type this, I'm sitting on a staircase across from a wall with vivid crayon artwork that I'm thinking of titling *Life in 2020: The Year of the Pandemic, Murder Hornets, and Remote Learning*. As I stare at what I think is a purple tree (maybe?), I know that I'll never be able to thank everyone who poured love, time, prayers, and work into this story—but I'm going to try!

Because guys, this book wouldn't be in your hands without them. It wouldn't have been written.

Abba God. Thank You! Thank You for loving me, for calling me deeper, for giving me the grace I needed to go to those unknown places, and for giving me songs to sing throughout the journey. I love writing with You!

Sam. Thank you for the unwavering support and belief in not only me but also in the belief that this story needed to be written. Thank you for your steadfastness, your warrior spirit, and your nerdy side—all of which make my heart melt! I still pick you. I love you!

Mom. Thank you for being an amazing Mom, Grammie, and friend! I will always look up to you—and not just because I'm shorter than you! Thank you for supporting me in more ways than I'll ever understand. YBB!

Emileigh. Thank you for being an amazing bestie who is always in my corner! You know that not all who wander are lost, the fine print to any True Love's Kiss contract, and the benefits of pixie dust. Love you!

Madeline. Thank you for the joy you bring to my life, sweet child of mine. I love you!

WhiteFire. I can't even begin to cover my gratitude for all you guys have done for me. From the beautiful covers to the powerful insights during edits to the thoughtful ways you help your authors grow to the intentional ways you lift up the WhiteFire family to a myriad of other things I'll never be able to name. It feels entirely inadequate to say in light of all those things, but thank you! With all my heart, thank you!

My church family. Thank you to each and every one of you who poured love, prayer, and encouragement into me as I wrote this story! Thank you!

To everyone at The Inkwell. You guys have no idea what a difference your hearts, your encouragement, and your coffee-making skills make to the writing process. Thank you!

Sam, Mom, Rie, Sarah, Elisabeth, Jess, Angel, Sean, Christine, and sooo many other family members and friends that their names would fill a book in itself. Without your love, help, and prayers, I know this story wouldn't have been written. Thank you!

Heidi Wilson, Kim Ann, Brandy Bruce, Cara Grandle, and all the other authors, bookstagrammers, bloggers, influencers, reviewers, my wonderful friends at JustRead, and the amazing teams of readers who have helped launch my stories into the world. Thank you for all the different ways you have and continue to support me and my books!

My amazing readers. Thank you for picking up my books, for each reread, for each message, for each recommendation, and for sharing that piece of your life with me. You guys help make this dream come true each and every day. Thank you!

*Love, Lace, and Minor Alterations*

Izze Vez, bridal consultant extraordinaire, has been helping brides find The Dress for years. She loves nothing more than helping make wedding dreams come true ... but sometimes the happy endings grate on her. How many times can a girl discover someone else's gown without dreaming of the day it'll be her turn to wear one?

*Weddings, Willows, and Revised Expectations*

Seventeen years after being orphaned, Apryl Burns and her twin sister Courtney have their own expectations for life. While Courtney continues to shine at everything, Apryl holds fast to the mantra that as long as her potato chip stash remains intact, then she'll be fine.